And Fight For Bread

by

Malcolm Seymour

First published in 2004

PUBLISHED BY
PAUL MOULD PUBLISHING

Copyright © Malcolm Seymour 2004

ISBN 1-904959-05-9

Printed in Great Britain by
CLE Print Limited

DEDICATION

I dedicate this book to my wife, Karen.

By the same author

Mansfield Tales

Test Case

Murder In The Eagle's Shadow

CHAPTER 1

Saturday, 10th May, 1817

"Bugger it! Bloody 'osses!"

Tom Stone hurled his spade across the stable floor, scraped the manure from his boots and wiped the stream of sweat from his brow. How many times had he voiced *that* sentiment lately?

Then, instantly regretting that last exclamation, he crossed to the end stall, which housed a large bay gelding, and pressed his face against the soft, velvety muzzle. For several moments, he savoured the comforting caress of the hot breath as it fanned his cheek. All the same, he reflected, he was 16, and all he had to look forward to was a lifetime of mucking out horses. There must be more to life!

"There's nowt wrong wi' bein' an ostler! It wor good enough for yer Dad!" said a large figure, who had just materialized in the doorway.

In the stable's dimness, Tom could just make out the unshaven features of his uncle, Ben Miller, who now leaned across Tom and stroked the smooth neck of the bay gelding.

"There's nowt fits better 'tween a man's legs than a good 'oss — 'cept a good wench!"

Ben laughed, and Tom felt the blast of stale gin. Then the grizzled features grew serious.

"Just remember, lad: yer Dad wor an ostler — an' 'is Dad afore 'im. If *you're* not 'appy wi' this job, there's plenty in Mansfield as'd be glad to tek it."

Tom leaned back against the door of the stall and his mind raced back ten years. He had been playing in the yard just outside the Old Eclipse stables, when his foot had come into contact with something soft, and he had suddenly found himself stretched full length on the cobblestones. He had looked at the thick, brown stains caking his breeches and stockings, and had run into the stable, tears streaming down his grimy cheeks.

His grandfather had been saddling a piebald mare, when Tom's cries had echoed round the bare stone walls of the stables. He had laid aside the saddle, taken one look at the sorry figure of his grandson, and burst out laughing.

Amos Stone had been a giant of a man: well nigh six feet tall. He had bent down from his commanding height, laid an enormous hand on Tom's shoulder and said, in his rich, deep voice: "Stop snivellin', lad! There's no shame in t' smell of 'oss shit!"

Tom's father had taken an equal pride in his work. Like his father Amos before him, Caleb Stone had seemed as large and strong as an ox. It had come as a shock to all at the Old Eclipse when, seven years before, he had succumbed to smallpox at the age of 35. Amos had never recovered from the shock and had died within the year.

Tom blinked away a tear at the memory.

"Good 'uns, t' pair on 'em!" said Ben, as if reading his mind. "Yer Mam, an' all."

Ben's eyes filmed over, and a sound escaped him that was half sigh, half a lecherous chuckle.

Tom suddenly went cold. No, surely not! His uncle's reputation was well known. Indeed, he had often been known to brag in the Old Eclipse that he had never seen a stallion as well-equipped as himself!

For an instant, Ben's mouth twitched in a lascivious grin, exposing yellowing teeth, which then as swiftly vanished, and the grey eyes softened.

"Oh, me an' Caleb coulda bin rivals, once. Mind you, there worn't a man in Mansfield as didn't run after Mary Brown!"

Tom felt his whole body grow tense. How dare Ben say this about his mother?

"Don't worry, Tom," said Ben, with a gruff smile. "She'd eyes for none but Caleb. There were them as tried — not me, mind! — but she soon saw 'em off! An' if *she* didn't, Caleb woulda! 'Andy wi' 'is fists, wor yer Dad."

He looked at Tom, who still stood clenching his fists, and a warm smile suffused his swarthy features.

"Come on, lad. Yer A'nt Margaret'll ay supper ready."

Their route back to the Old Eclipse took them first down a narrow alley between a row of private stables on their left and the True Briton Inn on their right.

From there, they emerged into Spittlehouse Gate. It was drawing towards sunset; although it was practically impossible to tell, since the tall buildings along either side admitted little natural light into the narrow thoroughfare. The odour of manure, which seemed to have followed them from the stables, was at once replaced by the enticing smell of newly-baked bread which emanated from John

Bingley's bakehouse, on the right. Across the lane from the bakery came the sound of hammering from William Leason's nailmaking premises. A few paces further on, this sound was replaced by the scraping of a chisel and the smell of fresh wood shavings, as they passed William Shipstone's carpenter's shop.

Sudden darkness engulfed them as they disappeared beneath the archway between the Old Eclipse and Benjamin Bagshaw's grocery store, before emerging into Market Place.

Tom's mind was so preoccupied with thoughts of bread and ale that, at first, the thudding of hooves and clatter of wheels failed to register.

"Get back!"

His uncle had seized him by the shoulder and pulled him back into the shadow of the archway, as a coach and four thundered down Leeming Street before swinging past them into Church Street.

The air was rent with cries of fear from passengers and bystanders alike, as the coach listed sharply, first to its right, then to its left, before finally grinding to a halt in front of the archway.

"Where's she bound, lad?" asked Ben suddenly.

"Leeds to London," replied Tom promptly, once he had recovered his breath. "Due in at 9 o'clock."

His uncle smiled at him with pride.

"I towd yoh yer wor a born ostler. Yoh'll know all t' schedules better'n me, soon!"

The coachman was now manoeuvring his vehicle towards the far side of Church Street, until it was in front

4

of Dragon Court, opposite the entrance to the Swan Inn, which lay just beyond the Old Eclipse.

"Now, wait for t' fun to start!" cackled Ben. Then, turning to anyone who might be listening, he announced: "I lay any man a sovereign 'e dun't mek it!"

But Tom was not laughing. His mind raced back to a warm June day, three years earlier. A coach had just brought news of the Declaration of Peace and people were running mad with joy at the thought that Bonaparte's tyranny was ended. The horses had been removed, and men had seized the coach and drawn it in triumph out of the Swan Yard. Tom had been too young to help, but his Uncle Ben had been one of the party. So had William Coop. The poor man had slipped and been dragged beneath the iron-rimmed wheels. Whoops of joy had turned to gasps of horror, as all eyes focused on the limp form, which had seemed to Tom like a broken rag doll. But rag dolls don't bleed!

Then, barely six months ago, there had been that stonemason's wife, leaving the yard just as the Nottingham mail coach was swinging in. It had been pitch-black beneath the archway. The coachman would never have seen her: only heard the screams as she was crushed against the wall.

Tom jerked his mind back to the present. The coachman had now swung the carriage round through ninety degrees — no small achievement in such a narrow space — and it was now going beneath the archway and into the Swan Yard. The yard itself was at a lower level than the street, with a sharp fall beneath the archway. The horses were disappearing into its yawning mouth, and the coach would be allowed to run down into the yard under its own weight, the traces swinging loose.

5

"Who's on wi' me?" yelled Ben. "A sovereign!"

There was a loud crunch and a shower of sparks, as the front, offside wheel struck the side of the archway, bringing the coach to an abrupt halt. A loud scream went up from inside the vehicle, as the passengers were violently jostled about, and bystanders rapidly scattered as trunks and bags cascaded into the street from the coach's roof.

"Towd yer!" crowed Ben, but no one paid any attention. "Cost 'em a pretty penny to mend that!"

Suddenly bored with this "sport", Ben slid an arm round his nephew's shoulder, and guided him towards the front entrance of the Old Eclipse.

Tom understood his uncle's bitter resentment. For years, the Swan and the Crown & Anchor had vied for the honour of being Mansfield's premier coaching inn. This had left the Old Eclipse sandwiched between them, having to rely on local carters and hauliers for its business. This was also partly the reason for Tom's own discontent. How long could the Old Eclipse survive in the face of such competition?

Tom pushed open the front door. Some nights, when both the Swan and the Crown & Anchor were fully booked, the Old Eclipse would benefit from the overflow. Perhaps tonight would be one of those nights.

He was wrong. Apart from his uncle and the landlord, George Cadman, there were only two customers. At a table by the door, Tom recognized the broad, swarthy features of Samuel Curtis, one of the dozen of so butchers who occupied shops in Market Place and Stockwell Gate. Tom noticed that the large, muscular hands which gripped the tankard, though newly washed, still reeked of blood and offal; although he seemed blissfully unaware of the even more powerful odour given off by his own boots.

"Evenin', Mr Curtis," said Tom, in an effort to be sociable.

Curtis merely grunted before taking another deep draught from his tankard.

Tom ignored the rebuff and turned his attention to the other customer: a fair-haired young man with spectacles, who was deeply engrossed in a book whilst sipping absentmindedly from a glass of port.

It was this latter fact which caused Tom to observe him more closely: port was not a beverage much in demand in the Old Eclipse. Obviously a gentleman, then, Tom deduced, although the man's clothes were not of the finest cut and quality. Perhaps even the gentry were feeling the pinch, these days.

Tom moved behind the young man so that he had a better view of the book and its title: *Reflections on the Revolution in France* by Edmund Burke. Not a tome he would have cared to tackle himself; though he had enjoyed reading at school. In fact, it had been his best subject — when he had bothered to attend!

In a way, it had been old Amos's fault. "Learnin's no use to yoh, lad. An ostler dun't need readin' an' writin'. I'll teach yer all yer need to know 'ere."

Sometimes, Tom remembered, his father and grandfather had argued over this.

"I want summat better for 'im than I 'ad," Caleb had protested.

"'Ard wokk'll do 'im no 'arm," Amos had countered.

7

"An' where's 'ard wokk gorr *us*?" his father had replied. "There's no future in 'osses."

However, six years at the Faith Clerkson School had been deemed more than sufficient, and, once Caleb had died, Amos had lost no time in removing Tom from the school and starting him as a stable lad at the Old Eclipse.

At the time, Tom had agreed with his grandfather. For one thing, he had always felt such a fool in the uniform: blue coat, waistcoat, breeches and stockings, and that ridiculous blue woollen cap with the yellow top knot. There was the additional stigma that it was a charity school; so its pupils were looked down upon by those from the local Grammar School and the various private academies in the town.

He remembered the hoots of derision from these latter, as he had walked from the Cockpit, down Swan Yard and Spittlehouse Gate, to the Old Eclipse stables. The number of fights he had got into! It was lucky he had been so handy with his fists!

Now, though, he wasn't so sure about the wisdom of his grandfather's decision. And why did his Uncle Ben continue to laud the virtues of being an ostler, when his own son, Richard, had broken free? Oh, yes, dear Cousin Richard no longer soiled his hands mucking out horses: he was articled as a clerk to Mr Robert Hall, attorney-at-law, and now consorted with the local gentry!

Forget Richard! What of his own situation? What other options were there? Well, for a start, he could be a soldier like his elder brother William! How many times had he heard tales of Vitoria, Laon, Toulouse and Waterloo? Later, in moments of boredom in the stables, he would re-enact those same battles in his own imagination. Yes, he'd enlist! After all, the smell of powder could be no worse than that of horse manure!

The young, fair-haired man suddenly seemed to sense Tom's presence behind him. He snapped the book shut and hurriedly concealed it inside his faded brown coat.

Tom ignored the rebuff and crossed to the bar, where George Cadman automatically handed him a tankard of ale from which he took a welcome gulp.

"What's up wi' Mr Curtis?" asked Tom, wiping the froth from his upper lip.

"Business bad, same as t' rest on us," sighed the landlord.

Ben had produced a battered clay pipe from his waistcoat pocket and was drawing contentedly on it. He watched the column of pungent smoke disappear among the shadow of the oak beams and nodded philosophically.

"Folk can't spend what they an't got, George."

"Aye," replied Cadman, dropping his voice to a whisper, as he cast a meaningful glance at the bespectacled young man, "an' some o' them as '*as* gorrit don't part wi' a deal on it!"

The subject of their conversation continued to sip at his drink, his mind absorbed in his own private thoughts.

Cadman stared bleakly at the unoccupied seats and tables.

"Look at it! Nine o'clock on a Sat'day nait, an' only two in! God knows 'ow long I can keep this up!"

"Worr about t' Swainmote? It's allus full, then," said Tom, remembering the occasion, each year, when the agisters and verderers of Sherwood Forest filled the Old

Eclipse to capacity, to feast and conduct their annual business.

"That's not till September," Cadman pointed out. "If things gerr any woss, I'll ay to start thinkin' o' layin' folk off."

He sighed, and looked meaningfully at Ben and Tom.

"I've bin 'ere nigh on forty year," said Ben. "Me Dad an' 'is Dad were ostlers 'ere, afore that. An' 'is, an' all," he added, gesturing towards Tom.

"I know, Ben," replied Cadman. "An' I pray to God it dun't come to that, burr if it does..." He shrugged helplessly.

Tom shivered, as a sudden, inexplicable chill shot through his bones. Things were as bad as he had feared.

Their conversation was interrupted by the sound of the door opening.

"Another customer!" whispered Cadman optimistically.

The figure in the doorway was silhouetted against the setting sun, his face in shadow, but, even without the distinctive uniform, his bearing alone would have marked him out as a soldier.

Cadman was about to say something, when the soldier slowly drew a pistol from its holster, cocked it and levelled it at the trio grouped round the bar.

"In t' name o' King George the Third, I'm arrestin' yoh three fer 'igh treason!"

CHAPTER 2

Saturday, 10th May, 1817

George Cadman was the first to find his voice.

"Will Stone! Pull another trick like that, an' I'll bloody kill yer!"

Samuel Curtis' face had turned a shade of bright puce, and his small, gimlet eyes blazed with a mute fury.

The bespectacled young man watched the drama unfold with an air of almost bored detachment.

The soldier returned the pistol to its holster and crossed over to the bar. Then, indicating the gleaming white chevron on his right sleeve, he chortled: "It's *Lance-Corporal* William Stone to yoh, George Cadman!"

The landlord muttered something under his breath and drew off a pint of ale for the newcomer.

"Lance-corporal?" echoed Tom. "Since when?"

"Yest'dy."

Will Stone grinned, revealing three missing upper teeth, and stretched out a hand to ruffle his brother's tousled brown hair.

Four years older than Tom, Will was slightly shorter, though of equally powerful build. However, whereas, Tom's bulk was solid muscle, that of his elder brother was already running to fat. A casual observer, watching Will voraciously devour the proffered ale, would have quickly deduced the cause.

"Worr're *yoh* doin' back in Mansfield?" asked Ben.

Will's grey eyes darted furtive glances in the direction of the two customers. Now that the tension created by Will's entrance had evaporated, Samuel Curtis had resumed his drinking and the bespectacled young man was once more engrossed in his book.

"Luddites," he whispered.

A puzzled frown creased the landlord's brow.

"I thought we were done wi' all that nonsense, long since?"

"Word is, it'll not be just frame-brekkin', this time."

"Worr're they plannin', then?" asked Tom.

His brother clamped a large, hairy hand over Tom's mouth.

"Norr 'ere! Later!"

Tom pulled a long face.

"'E's bored," cut in Ben. "Gerrin' to be a rait young Lord 'Igh-an'-Mighty. Reckons wokkin' wi' 'osses in't good enough for 'im."

Will shot his younger brother a warning glance, then turned his attention back to Cadman.

"Norr 'eard owt in 'ere, ay yer?" he hissed.

The landlord gestured airily around the near-empty room.

"Aye, there's 'undreds in 'ere, every nait, plottin'! Can't yer see 'em?"

William Stone was a plain, simple soldier, with a plain, simple mind to match. It was only the smirks spreading slowly across the faces of his uncle and brother that alerted him to the fact that he was being made the butt of the landlord's sarcasm.

"Well, keep yer eyes an' ears open," he grunted.

"Are yoh 'ungry, Will?" asked Ben.

"Me belly thinks me throat's cut!"

"Join me, Tom an' yer A'nt Margaret for a bit o' supper, then."

"Norr as we've got much," groaned Tom.

Ben smiled at Will.

"You're welcome to share what there is."

The setting sun had taken on an even more menacing redness by the time the three left the Old Eclipse and made their way along West Gate. Soon, night would come, ushering in a world of footpads and gangs of drunken apprentices, into which not even a seasoned campaigner like Will would dare to venture unarmed. Almost instinctively, his hand reached down to touch the comfortingly familiar shape of his pistol butt.

It was still light enough to see by outside, but already, in many of the cottages they passed, "poor lights", roughly constructed from old rags and grease, had been lit.

They kept well over to the left-hand side of the street, avoiding the open sewer which cut the thoroughfare in two; but, although they succeeded in keeping their feet dry, there was no way they could protect their noses from the all-pervading stench.

West Gate was almost deserted. On the opposite side of the street, a drunk was being ejected from the Bull Inn. Picking himself out of the sewer, and seemingly oblivious to the sodden state of his garments, he exchanged a few incoherent words with the landlord, before staggering off in search of further refreshment; not, Tom noted ruefully, in the direction of the Old Eclipse, but down Stockwell Gate. With over thirty public houses within the vicinity of the town centre, and money in short supply, there would never be enough customers to patronize them all. It wasn't only the Old Eclipse that was in danger of going under.

Crossing the old market place, they turned into Duck Lane. On the right was the large pond, whose feathered occupants gave the thoroughfare its name; on the left was the narrow entrance to their destination: Bark Court.

Tom had often heard people speak of King George and the Royal Court. Did this bear any resemblance to Bark Court? he wondered. If so, he saw no reason why folk should be so envious of the Sovereign living there; for Bark Court was a festering cesspit of cramped stone cottages, which, like drunken roisterers, seemed to lean against each other for support. Stray dogs and cats roamed freely, marking their territories at will, with no respect for property boundaries set by humans. Smoke from the chimneys formed a canopy above the dwellings, blotting out what little light remained.

Pushing open a door on their left, Ben peered into the dim interior and yelled: "We're back!"

The three men squeezed into the narrow living room, where the acrid smell of smoke competed with the more pleasing aroma of cooked vegetables.

"Worr've we got?" demanded Ben.

For a second, the smoke cleared, and a short, thin woman could be seen standing by the fire, stirring the contents of a large pot.

Margaret Miller was 32: ten years younger than her husband. A casual observer, though, might have set her age at anything between 50 and 60. Light brown hair, liberally streaked with grime and sweat, hung down to her shoulders. The features were delicate, and she might have been judged beautiful, were it not for the pockmarked skin and the decayed, discoloured teeth. Somehow, though, her soft brown eyes reflected the kind and generous nature beneath the bedraggled exterior.

"Carrots 'n' taters," she replied, in answer to her husband's query.

"No meat?"

Her thin lips twisted in a sardonic smile.

"At one-an'-eight a pound? There's bread, cheese an' ale, when yer've finished," she added, hoping this would compensate for the disappointment.

Ben peered into the pot.

"Looks more'n usual."

Margaret's already sallow skin seemed to turn even paler beneath the veneer of grime.

"I've invited Ann an' Jonathan fer supper."

A strangled cry came from her husband's throat.

"Yoh've what?"

"Well, they've got nowt much," protested Margaret.

"Neither 'ave we!"

"At least yoh two 'ave got reg'lar money comin' in, thank God!"

For how much longer, though? wondered Tom.

"Anyroad, they're fam'ly," continued Margaret.

"I s'pose so," conceded Ben. Ann was, after all, his niece and Tom's sister.

"An' we an't 'ad to rely on charity 'andouts, neither," persisted Margaret.

That, thought Tom, was true. He remembered how, earlier in the year, the daughters of some of the town's more prosperous citizens had formed a Penny Society, handing out clothes and blankets to those in most need. As ostlers in regular employment, neither he nor his uncle had qualified.

"Y' see," said Ben, rounding on Tom, "yer dun't know when you're well off! Just thank God you're norra framework knitter, like Jonathan. You'd ay summat to bellyache about, then."

Ben took another look round the dark room.

"Our Richard norr in?"

"'E'll not be comin'," replied his wife.

He never does, these days! thought Tom. Too proud!

"'Im an' Mr 'All's bin invited to dinner wi' Samuel Slack an' 'is fam'ly."

"Aye," muttered Ben under his breath, "an' I'll bet *they'll* be ayin' meat!" Aloud, he said: "I reckon t' lad's gorr 'is eye on Slack's daughter."

"Which one?" queried Margaret.

16

"T' youngest, o' course! 'E wun't be after t' eldest, would 'e? Face like an 'oss's arse, that 'un!"

"'E'll do well for 'issen, will our Richard," said Margaret proudly. "Lawyer's clerk! An' 'e'll not be short o' brass, marryin' an 'osier's daughter!"

"'E's got plenty, 'as Samuel Slack," conceded her husband. "Mind yoh, to 'ear 'im talk, yer'd think 'e wor one step away from t' work'ouse!"

"'E's that tight, 'e wouldn't gi' yer t' snot from 'is nose!" added Margaret, with a grunt.

Tom, eager to change the topic of conversation, pointed to his brother.

"Our Will's bin made a lance-corporal."

"That's good," said Margaret, nodding her approval, though it was clear to Tom that the rank meant nothing to her.

For some moments, Tom had been peering at his aunt's left cheek, where an ugly bruise was forming. It wasn't the first time, he recalled.

"Worr 'appened to yer face?"

"I fell — not lookin' where I wor goin'," she replied hastily.

In the half-light, neither Tom nor Will saw the smouldering glance she directed towards her husband; but before anyone could say anything, there was a barely audible knock at the door.

"Tharr'll be them," said Margaret, crossing to the door.

Although his sister and brother-in-law lived only a few yards away, in nearby Mitre Court, it was several days since Tom had seen them. The change in their appearance came as a shock to him.

Ann Parker was 23, but, like her aunt, already appeared twice her age. Her pale features were gaunt and drawn, dark circles were visible beneath the brown eyes, the brown hair hung shoulder-length and unkempt, and her teeth were already blackened with decay, whilst her dress — the one donated by the Penny Society — hung uneasily on her bony frame.

Her husband was five years older. The thick mop of ginger hair seemed merely to accentuate the pallor of his skin, which was relieved only by the patchwork of freckles that covered it.

"Where's young Caleb?" asked Tom.

"Owd Mrs Mason's lookin' after 'im," replied Ann.

"Young Caleb?" asked Will, puzzled.

"We've gorra nephew," announced Tom proudly. "Born last week."

Tom looked at his sister as he spoke, and her brown eyes at once shone with pride and contentment. Despite the other outward signs of grinding poverty, and two stillbirths in as many years, her spirit remained defiantly uncrushed.

"Norra week owd, an' she's left 'im wi' a total stranger?" gasped Will incredulously.

"She's no stranger," broke in Margaret. "She's seen plenty o' kids into this world — includin' yoh! Now, then." She beckoned towards the table. "Sit down."

The visitors did so tentatively, darting glances at Ben, as though fearing that the invitation was yet another act of charity and their presences was unwelcome.

There was an awkward hiatus, until Margaret began to serve the food.

For a while, the meal was conducted in silence, which was finally broken by Tom.

"Worr abaht these Luddites, then, Will?"

There was an uncomfortable pause.

"Shurrup, an' eat yer dinner!" snapped Ben, through a mouthful of bread, but Tom would not be silenced.

"Worn't *yoh* one, Jonathan?"

Ben and Will simultaneously choked on their food.

"'Im?" spluttered Ben. "'E wun't say 'boo' to a goose, would yer?"

Jonathan smiled politely at his host, but hurt and anger simmered behind the green eyes.

"'Is Dad wor one," cut in Ann, with an irate grimace in the direction of Ben. "Jacob wor nearly 'anged for frame-brekkin'," she added, with scarcely-concealed pride.

Tom remembered his sister's father-in-law: a tall, quietly-spoken, stooping man, prematurely bald. But a Luddite? It seemed hardly credible. Nevertheless, Tom craned eagerly forward.

"'Anged? Worr 'appened?"

"Now, Ann," interjected Will. "Don't go fillin' 'is 'ead wi' all *that* nonsense!"

Ann Parker stared back defiantly at her brother.

"No, Will. It's not nonsense."

"Mindless destruction!" snapped Ben.

"Burr it *worn't* mindless!" countered Ann. "Tom's gorra rait to know t' truth." Then, turning to her husband, she added: "Tell 'im, Jonathan."

Jonathan coughed nervously, then took a sip of ale.

"It wor six year back — afore I married Ann. We lived in Nottingham, then — just me, me Mam an' me Dad. I'd served me apprenticeship, so I wor earnin' good money. You could, in them days. Prices were fixed, so yer knew where yer were. They'd bin agreed between t' 'osiers an t' knitters fer years. Then, wi' no warnin', they cut 'em."

"Why?" asked Tom?

Jonathan took another drink of ale and defiantly ignored the menacing stares directed at him by Will and Ben. Tom, though, sensed that every syllable was an effort for him. It was as if his family's history was a source of personal embarrassment.

"Bonaparte, fer one thing. T' whole o' Europe wor at war, so we couldn't sell owt abroad. Then, t' 'osiers brought in unskilled labour — women, kids, even t' paupers in t' work'ouses. O' course, they couldn't mek proper gloves an' stockin's — yer need real skill fer that."

His narrative was cut short by a loud guffaw from Will.

Somehow, the interruption only served to strengthen Jonathan's resolve, and he continued as though Will had not spoken.

"They were usin' wide frames to turn out lengths o' material. Then they made stockin's out o' cut-ups."

"What's a cut-up, when it's at 'om?" sneered Will, who was now on his third pint of ale and becoming increasingly bombastic.

"Worr it sez," replied Jonathan. "They cut rough shapes out o' t' cloth an' sewed 'em together to mek stockin's an' so on. Trouble wor, when they came to do t' seam, they left no selvedge, so t' things fell to bits, five minutes after yer purr 'em on! Cheap labour — cheap goods. All t' stockin'ers got tarred wi' t' same brush an' t' trade folded."

"So, then they smashed up all t' frames!" cried Tom.

Jonathan shook his head.

"Norr *all* on 'em. Honest 'osiers — an' there were still a few — 'ad nowt to fear. It wor only t' ones as practised coltin' — usin' unskilled workers — as 'ad their frames smashed. Me Dad an' some o' t' others organized groups to go round t' cottages."

"Why din't yoh go wi' 'em?" taunted Will.

"There were lots on us thought we could talk to t' 'osiers an' mek 'em see it wor in everyone's int'rest to stop churnin' out shoddy goods," replied Jonathan.

"Violence never solves owt," cut in his wife quietly.

Tom was growing impatient with such ethical distractions.

"Who *did* get their machines smashed, then?"

"Anyone who couldn't prove 'e wor wokkin' fer an 'osier payin' t' agreed rates."

Margaret, who had been listening in wrapt attention, finally spoke.

"Din't anyone try an' stop 'em?"

"They worn't their own machines," butted in Ann. "They rented 'em from t' 'osiers at two bob a week. No one's goin' to risk 'is life defending some else's property."

"An' yer Dad wor goin' to be 'anged, just fer brekkin' frames?"

"That wor t' Law," replied his sister.

"'Angin's too good for 'em!" growled Will.

"I'd've smashed 'em up — 'angin' or no 'angin'!" declared Tom defiantly.

Will leaned across and cuffed Tom sharply across the back of his head.

"We'll ay none o' *that* talk 'ere!"

"Leave 'im be, Will!" cried Ann, her maternal instincts rising to the surface. "'E's only a lad."

"Then it's time 'e wor a man!"

Will leaned forward and broke wind volubly, as if to emphasize the point.

Ben laughed, and even Tom couldn't restrain a snigger, whilst the rest of the company seemed acutely embarrassed by his boorish display.

"We might be poor, Will Stone," reprimanded Margaret, "but we don't ay to be'ave like animals!"

Jonathan got up and crossed to the window. The night sky was pitch black.

"We'd best be goin', Margaret. Mustn't keep Mrs Mason up. Ta."

"Yeah. Ta for ev'rythin'," added Ann.

"It's t' least we can do," replied her aunt. "In't it, Ben?"

Her husband merely grunted, then turned to Tom.

"Time *yoh* wor in bed, an' all. Early start."

Ten minutes later, Tom was sinking gratefully onto his bed. It had been a long, hard, boring day — just like every other day! But, despite the overwhelming physical tiredness, he found it difficult to sleep. His mind was restless with thoughts of adventure. He had decided upon his escape route from the stables: he'd show his brother-in-law an example and become a frame-breaker!

CHAPTER 3

Sunday, 11th May, 1817

"Sun's up, Tom! Time *yoh* wor, an' all!"

Tom slowly forced open his eyes, then yawned. His slumber had been fitful, and the reasons were twofold. Firstly, he had had to endure Will's ear-splitting snores, which would have drowned out an entire artillery battery. Secondly, he had been forced to share his bed, not only with his brother, but also with a small army of bedbugs and cockroaches, which had left reminders of their occupation all over his body.

Within half an hour, he had fortified himself with the remnants of the previous evening's supper and was setting out with his uncle for work, leaving Will to sleep in.

Sunday always seemed an odd day. There was likely to be little activity at the stables: just harness to be inspected and repaired. All the shops were closed, and the only sign of activity was the solemn procession of the faithful to and from the town's seven places of worship.

The most imposing of these was the Anglican parish church of St Peter and St Paul, which had stood proudly on Bridge Street for over eight hundred years.

A hundred yards or so further up, on the opposite side of

the street, stood the Wesleyan Methodist chapel, some of whose older members could remember the movement's founder preaching in West Gate by the Old Market Cross.

The other denominations — ranging from the Anabaptists to the Society of Friends — hid themselves away in narrow alleys, as though they had still not dared to hope that their days of persecution by the Established Church were over.

By midday, having refreshed their souls with the singing of hymns and psalms, those who did not embrace temperance would then proceed to refresh their bodies in one of the local hostelries.

Ann and Jonathan would have made their habitual short journey from Mitre Court, up Union Street, to the Primitive Methodist chapel on South Street. Tom had often wondered what had attracted his sister to this simple framework knitter, who seemed so lacking in ambition. It was only since her marriage that she had ventured anywhere near a place of worship, and she now seemed as infected by religion as he did. All suffering — whether poverty or the stillbirth of a child — was seen by them as part of some Divine Plan, to be endured with humility and patience.

Church and religion had never really been a part of Tom's life. Of course, he had been taught all about the Bible at school, and many of the stories had fired his young imagination: Cain murdering his brother Abel; David slaying the giant Goliath; Jael driving a tent peg through the head of Sisera; and the superhuman exploits of the mighty Samson.

The New Testament had held less appeal, with such doctrines as: "Blessed are the poor." Well, *he* was poor, but he didn't feel particularly blessed! Nor were most of his immediate kindred, although doubtless Ann and Jonathan considered themselves to be so!

Perhaps the exception was Cousin Richard. Yes, it always came back to Cousin Richard, who had spent hours at his books, encouraged by his teachers — and his father.

"T' lad'll go far," Ben was wont to declare, after several glasses of gin. "'E'll mek summat on 'is life, marry well an' become a rich man!"

Such a contrast to his illegitimate half-brother, Jack: a petty thief, transported long ago to Van Diemen's Land, where he had presumably died in obscurity. No one mentioned his name anymore.

Tom, however, always suspected that this paternal pride was also tinged with the hope that Richard would allow his father to share in his newfound prosperity.

After several more drinks, Ben would become increasingly maudlin and sigh: "If only 'is Mam coulda lived to see t' day!"

Mary — Ben's first wife — had died when young Richard was only four, and it was her successor, Tom's Aunt Margaret, who had most encouraged Richard's scholastic endeavours.

Was the pride mutual, though? If so, why did Richard choose to lodge with his employer rather than his family?

If only his own family had offered him the same support! Tom reflected bitterly. But, after the death of his parents, his grandfather had been so set on Tom becoming an ostler that he had almost coerced him into neglecting his schooling. "If *ev'ryone* became a scholar, who'd be left to look after t' 'osses?" he used to say.

Well, it was too late now. Richard was articled to a lawyer, and Tom was destined to spend the rest of his life here. Or was he? If he only had the opportunity...

"Are yoh gonna be all day wi' that?" his uncle's voice cut in upon his reverie. "I've fixed three bridles while yoh've bin on that one!"

Ben sat down, unwrapped a grubby rag bundle and took out some bread and cheese.

Tom crossed to the stable door and looked upwards. The sun was almost directly overhead. Midday, already!

He unwrapped his own bundle, surveyed its rather pathetic contents, and, for several minutes, uncle and nephew chewed in silence, each absorbed in his own thoughts.

At length, Ben picked the last vestiges of food from his clothing, stuffed them greedily in his mouth, wiped it with the rag and stood up.

"Reckon we deserve a drink." He stared disapprovingly at his nephew. "Leastways, *some* on us do! Come on, y' idle young bugger!"

As they made their way towards the Old Eclipse, the midday heat was oppressive, relieved only by a north-easterly breeze, which carried to their nostrils the conflicting smells of Spittlehouse Gate: malt and hops from the Old Eclipse brewhouse; John Bingley's freshly-baked bread; and the rank odours of the privies and pigsties located in the nearby Swan Yard.

When they arrived at their destination, Tom was surprised to find practically every place occupied. Samuel Curtis sat huddled in a corner with Kelham Neale, a fellow-butcher, lamenting the rising price of beef and mutton.

He recognized other traders with shops in the vicinity of Church Street and Market Place: Isaac Worthington, draper; John Thraves, chemist; and George Langley, bookseller. All wore deep frowns, and, from the snatches of dialogue which he picked up, the current depressed state of the economy appeared to be the universal topic of conversation.

The fair-haired, bespectacled young man from the previous evening was also there, occupying the same seat, and still engrossed in his book (and, for all Tom knew, probably consuming the same glass of port!).

Will had by now bestirred himself and was standing at the bar, tankard in hand, deep in conversation with a swarthy, muscular figure, now towered above him at a shade under six feet.

Tom and Ben each ordered a tankard of ale, which constituted part of their wages, and drank in silence for several moments.

"Business seems to be pickin' up," remarked Ben, with an optimistic smile.

"Church is out," smiled George Cadman. "Dun't it say summat in t' Bible about: 'Blessed are those that hunger and thirst'?"

"Aye, after righteousness, George, not your ale!" cut in Will's companion, with a coarse laugh.

"You're goin' t' rait road to be banned, Ned 'Opkins!" boomed Cadman, and then winked jovially at the man.

"An' who'd clear t' tables fer yer *then*, eh?" asked Ned Hopkins. The question was posed good-naturedly, yet there was a hint of bitterness in the voice.

There was an uneasy hiatus. Then Ben turned to the landlord and said: "When're yer gerrin' t' farrier to look at that bay geldin'? If summat's not done quick, 'e'll go lame!"

"Yoh tell me where I can find a decent 'un," sighed Cadman. He suddenly broke off and his face reddened. "Sorry, Ned. I didn't mean to . . ."

There was another embarrassed silence, during which Tom found his gaze fixing itself, as it always did, on Ned's right sleeve, which hung limp and empty at his side.

Noticing Ned return his stare, Tom hastily looked away.

"'S all rait," grunted Ned. "It's nigh on two year now. I'm used to folk starin'."

"It just seems such a waste!" snapped Tom. "T' best farrier in town, an' then that!"

"Waterloo," cut in Will. "French musket ball. I got one 'ere." He pointed to his left shoulder. "T' bugger went rait through. Poor owd Ned worn't so lucky."

"Arm shattered just above t' elbow," added Ned.

Tom had heard the tale a thousand times, but somehow didn't have the heart to interrupt his friend's narrative.

"Took 'em three hours to dig t' ball out. Nowt they could do for t' arm, they said. T' bugger 'ad to come off. For King an' Country!" he added bitterly. "Though much bloody thanks we got from either! Know what Wellington used to call us? 'Scum o' the earth.' In't that rait, Will?"

Will, who was still in uniform, shuffled uneasily.

"It's not for me to say, Ned, what wi' still servin' t' colours."

"'E's a lance-corporal now," interjected Tom proudly, pointing to the chevron on his brother's sleeve.

"So I see," replied Ned, without any great enthusiasm. "Goin' to mek t' Nottinghamshire Militia yer life, then?"

"Why not?" answered Will, with a shrug. "It's as good a life as any. Better'n most."

"Will sez there's goin' to be..." began Tom, but his speech was cut short by his brother's menacing glance.

"Will sez what?" asked Ned, craning forward, his curiosity aroused.

"Nowt," said Will brusquely. "Tek no notice on 'im. Yer know what kids are like."

"I'm sixteen," protested Tom. "I'm a man."

"Well, bloody act like one, then!" growled his brother.

Tom drained his tankard, slammed it down on the bar, and moved away to gaze out of the front window.

Most of the churchgoers had by now dispersed, either to their homes or to one of the surrounding hostelries, but one or two still lingered in groups at the top of Church Street, deep in conversation.

One tall, slender, fair-haired figure he recognized immediately: Cousin Richard, resplendent in a bottle-green coat and breeches, and a lilac silk waistcoat. He was talking animatedly with a short, bald, elderly gentleman in black, whose high collar and neck-cloth gave him the appearance of a tortoise half-submerged in its shell.

The third member of the group was a young woman. Although she took no part in the conversation, her arm was looped through Richard's in a possessive gesture. She was petite — even slightly shorter than the elderly gentleman

30

— but her body was perfectly proportioned: a fact enhanced by the fashionable cut of her dress of dark maroon taffeta. Ringlets of chestnut hair were just visible beneath her matching bonnet. Was this, Tom wondered, one of the girls Ben and Margaret had mentioned, the previous evening?

As Tom watched, his cousin suddenly detached himself from the arm of the young woman and crossed over to a group of fashionably-dressed young men standing nearby in Market Place, leaving her and the elderly gentleman, who continued to make rather halting conversation, until, a few moments later, they were joined by a third party: a tall, angular young man in blue.

It soon became obvious, from the reactions of the young woman and the elderly man, that the newcomer's presence was unwelcome. He took her hand, but, as he bent to kiss it, she drew sharply away.

Her face grew red, and she began to cast nervous glances in the direction of Richard, but he was now preoccupied with his new companions and totally oblivious to her signals for assistance.

At this point, the elderly man laid a hand on the newcomer's sleeve. The latter turned on his with a look of contempt and roughly shook it off.

Quite why Tom decided to intervene, he couldn't have said. The quarrel was nothing to do with him. The woman and old man were total strangers. Nevertheless, he marched out into the street and approached the group.

By the time he reached them, the young woman had backed away and was trying to hide behind her flustered, elderly companion.

"Go away!" she cried. "Richard!"

The cry went unheeded. Richard and the other young bucks continued their talk, which was interrupted, from time to time, with bursts of bawdy laughter.

Tom took a pace towards the man in blue.

"Yoh 'eard what she said. Piss off!"

The hubbub of conversation which filled upper Church Street and Market Place abruptly ceased, and all eyes turned to the scene in front of the Old Eclipse.

The young man slowly turned to face Tom.

"Damn your insolence!"

He raised his silver-topped cane and aimed a vicious blow at Tom's head.

Tom ducked sharply. At the same time, his left hand snaked out, grabbed the cane, and wrenched it from his assailant's hand before hurling it away to his left. In the same movement, he launched himself forward, sinking his right fist into the other's ribcage.

A horrified gasp escaped from the young man's lungs, and this was echoed by the crowd. Then, as his body jack-knifed forward, Tom gripped him by the hair, held his head firm, and brought his knee smartly up into the man's face.

The stranger reeled back, hands to his face, blood pouring down the gleaming white front of his shirt. Then, without a backward glance, he staggered blindly through the crowd, shoving bodies aside, and disappeared down Church Street.

The onlookers remained frozen like statues, until a portly, middle-aged man thrust himself forward. The veins in his temples stood out and his jowls quivered with barely-suppressed fury.

"'Ow dare you?" he roared. "I'll…"

At this point, the young woman ran towards him, threw her arms around his thick neck, and whispered breathlessly into his ear.

The transformation was miraculous. His whole frame relaxed, and a broad smile spread across his rubicund features.

"I, er, me daughter tells me I owe you an apology — an' me thanks," he stammered. "What's yer name?"

"Tom Stone."

The stranger held out a hand, and, after a moment's hesitation, Tom shook it firmly.

"Samuel Slack," said the man, "an' this is Susannah, me younger daughter."

The young woman's eyes were fixed on the ground, but she slowly raised them and favoured Tom with a shy smile.

"Ay y' eaten yet?" enquired Slack.

Tom remembered the meagre portion of bread and cheese he had recently consumed.

"No," he lied.

"Then yer'll dine wi' us, as me guest."

Samuel Slack placed a hand on Tom's shoulder and steered him towards Market Place.

"It's not far," he said. "Just along West Gate."

As Tom and Slack walked through the crowd, most people whispered comments that Tom interpreted as expressions of gratitude and admiration.

The exception was Richard, whose mouth was set in a grim line, whilst his eyes blazed with pure hatred.

CHAPTER 4

Sunday, 11th May, 1817

"Sit 'ere, lad!"

Samuel Slack indicated a chair near the head of the table.

Tom was about to sit, when Richard snatched a linen napkin from the table and ostentatiously spread it out on the seat. He then made great play of sniffing at the air. Even to noses inured against the odours of the street, the smell of horse manure was overpowering.

Richard leaned across to the small, elderly man — who, Tom had discovered, was his cousin's employer, Mr Robert Hall — and mouthed: "My cousin. He's an ostler!"

After all Tom had said recently about the tedium of life in the stables, he should have been the first to agree with Richard's low estimation of his profession. Instead, he found anger seething inside him.

Before he could answer, however, Hall smiled, revealing gleaming ivory dentures, which clicked noisily whenever he spoke, and half-bowed to him.

"Good morning, sir. A pleasure to know you. And may I say what a fine thing it was you did, this morning."

The little lawyer took a small tortoiseshell snuffbox from his waistcoat pocket and inhaled a pinch of the brown powder with relish. He then peered at Tom through thick-lensed spectacles, his pale blue eyes shrewdly scrutinizing the compact, muscular frame.

Tom fidgeted uncomfortably. No one had ever called him "sir" before or paid him such lavish compliments.

"Drink this."

Samuel Slack had materialized at Tom's side and placed a glass of red liquid in his hand.

"Worr is it?" asked Tom.

"Claret. It'll put blood in yer veins — though I fancy yer've plenty o' that a'ready."

A ripple of polite laughter from the assembled company greeted this quip.

Tom was growing increasingly aware that he was the object of universal curiosity, as everyone cast eyes over his grubby shirt and breeches, and the battered shoes liberally encrusted with drying manure.

Only his host seemed oblivious to his sartorial shortcomings. Clapping Tom heartily on the back, he snatched the napkin from the chair and motioned him to sit.

"Susannah," said Slack, with a broad smile, which exposed a set of ivory dentures even more dazzling than Robert Hall's, "come an' sit 'ere by Tom."

Susannah bestowed another shy smile upon her erstwhile saviour, before turning to look at Richard, whose grey eyes were still smouldering with rage and jealousy.

"Susannah!"

The order from Samuel Slack was delivered in a whisper

inaudible to the rest of the assembly, but it carried as much authority as if he had bellowed it across Market Place.

Susannah smiled meekly at her father, then at Tom, and obeyed.

Tom now had leisure to take in his surroundings: simple, but elegant, furnishings; yet everything so neat and clean. There was no sing of the all-pervading odour which permanently hung about Bark Court, although it was less than a quarter of a mile away, being situated at the top end of West Gate, at its junction with Chesterfield Lane and Back Lane West. It was an imposing, half-timbered building, clearly the house of a prosperous man, and Tom now realized why.

During the short walk from Church Street, his host had more formally introduced himself to Tom, who had been wondering why the name "Slack" seemed familiar. Now he knew: Jonathan Parker had often mentioned it. Samuel Slack was one of the wealthiest hosiers in the East Midlands: a man upon whom the livelihoods of thousands of framework knitters depended. It was he — or, rather, his minions, the "putters-out" — who determined who should get any available work.

"Who wor 'e?" Tom asked, feeling he was obliged to say something to the young woman by his side.

"Who?"

"'Im worr I 'it."

Susannah shrugged.

"Jacob Smalley. No one you'd know."

She broke off, realizing how harsh that last remark had sounded. She turned, smiling apologetically, and, as she did so, she leaned against him, so that he felt the warmth of her body against his bare arm. A strange glow passed through his whole frame.

"I meant, you don't go to church, do you?" she said soothingly.

Tom shook his head, and another awkward silence fell. What could he say that would not sound too forward?

He touched her sleeve, feeling the cool, soft taffeta between his thumb and forefinger.

"Pretty dress!" he blurted out, and at once felt foolish.

"Why, thank you, Tom."

She turned to him and smiled again. Her teeth were white and sound, though slightly irregular, but this only added to her charm. She was certainly a beauty — and she knew it!

"It was a present from Richard."

She smiled across the table at the generous donor, but he affected not to notice, and began to engage in conversation with his employer.

"We're cousins, 'im an' me," said Tom, gesturing towards Richard.

Susannah looked from one to the other, and a roguish twinkle appeared in her clear brown eyes.

"Are yoh an' Richard...?"

Tom left the sentence unfinished, but Susannah was sharp enough to understand what remained unsaid.

"There's nothing been announced formally — yet."

With what a wealth of insinuation she invested that final word! She was like an angler trailing bait before an unsuspecting pike. Indeed, Richard was now looking at her, and his wide eyes and gaping mouth put Tom in mind of a helpless fish.

A plump, middle-aged woman, whose cheeks and nose were decorated with a network of purple veins, had now entered the room. She took one look at Tom and shrieked: "What, in God's name, is *that*?"

"It's all rait, Sarah," cooed Slack. "We've an extra guest. This is Tom. 'E's an ostler at… Where is it you're an ostler, Tom?"

"T' Owd Eclipse," replied Tom, his breast swelling with an unexpected sense of pride.

Slack briefly explained to his wife the circumstances which had led to Tom's invitation to dine.

Sarah Slack offered Tom a podgy hand and smiled. Her teeth looked like human teeth, unlike the ivory ones worn by her husband; yet, on closer examination, there was something unnatural about their appearance. Perhaps, Tom surmised, they were "Waterloo" teeth. Ned Hopkins had told him about these. After the battle, healthy teeth had been plundered from the mouths of the dead, and were then sold to dental practitioners in England to fill the mouths of the living.

"Where's Rachel an' Joseph?" enquired Slack, turning to his wife.

As if on cue, the door opened to admit two people.

The first was a small, dumpy woman in her mid-twenties, whose straight, mousy brown hair was severely parted in the centre. Tom guessed that she and Susannah must be sisters, but the resemblance was superficial. Rachel knew that, in terms of beauty, there was no contest between her and her sister, so she had long ago given up trying to compete with her. This must be the one his uncle had described as having "a face like an 'oss's arse".

The second figure was a ten-year-old boy of a similar build to his elder sister, dressed in a dark blue velvet suit in which he looked distinctly uncomfortable. He surveyed the company — and especially Tom — with a haughty air, as though he considered them all his social inferiors.

"Ay yer seen Jessop?" demanded Slack.

Young Joseph tossed back his head disdainfully.

"Forgotten the time, I expect. You know what he's like."

"We'll start wi'out 'im, then," declared Sarah.

"Ah, soup!" announced Samuel Slack, indicating a large porcelain tureen that had just been laid on the table. "Thank you, 'Annah."

The plump servant who had brought in the tureen removed its lid and ladled a generous helping of soup into Tom's bowl.

Tom thrust in his spoon, raised the steaming brown liquid to his lips and sucked it down noisily.

"Shall we say grace?" said Slack quietly, casting a sideways look at Tom.

The latter slowly lowered his spoon, and looked around the table.

Richard greeted his solecism with a withering glare of contempt, whilst the others were more inclined to pardon his ignorance, and smiled tolerantly.

Susannah raised her napkin to her delicate lips, and Tom could have sworn he heard a muffled giggle from behind the folded linen.

Samuel Slack placed the palms of his hands together and closed his eyes.

"For what we are about to receive, may the Lord mek us truly thankful."

"Amen," said a chorus of voices.

"Amen," echoed Tom, a second after everyone else.

Samuel Slack smiled indulgently at his young guest, tucked his napkin into his neckcloth, and began to eat.

The others waited until he had taken his first mouthful before following suit.

"Well, Joseph," said Robert Hall, breaking the silence, "and how's school?"

"'E dun't go to school no more," cut in Slack. "'E used to go to Catlow's place, down West Gate, burr it wor too expensive. It wor costin' me four guineas a year just to keep 'im in tea — not to mention instruction, pens, ink an' books! It wokked out at over ten guineas a term! So I've gorr 'im a tutor now. Eight guineas a term, all found."

The little lawyer nodded approvingly, and then turned back to Joseph.

"Tell me, Joseph, what are seven fours?"

Tom found himself attempting the calculation. He most certainly remembered learning his tables by rote at the Faith Clerkson School, but that was years ago and he had forgotten most of what he had been taught.

Joseph's brow had been knotted in an effort of concentration, whilst his father drummed his fingers impatiently on the table.

"Twenty-four," the boy announced eventually.

Tom was feeling a pang of jealousy at this ten-year-old's display of knowledge, when he noticed the puzzled frowns on the faces of the other diners.

"It's 28!" thundered Samuel Slack, bringing his fist down so hard on the table that several items of crockery and glassware leapt into the air, disgorging their contents onto the neatly-laundered linen tablecloth.

There was an embarrassed silence around the table, and Tom noticed that Susannah had once again raised her napkin to her lips to smother a giggle.

"How are you at Latin?" persisted Hall. Then, turning to Slack, he asked, with scarcely-disguised sarcasm: "He does *do* Latin, I take it?"

"Naturally," replied Slack, grim-faced. "'E'll not get to Oxford or Cambridge wi'out it."

"Decline *mensa* — 'table'," instructed the lawyer.

"This is a dinin' room, norra schoolroom," interjected the boy's mother. "Leave 'im be. 'Is soup's gerrin' cowd."

The boy smiled at his mother with evident relief. Then, seeing that Robert Hall's attention was diverted elsewhere, he thrust out his tongue at the lawyer's back.

The soup was finally cleared away, and the servant returned with a covered serving dish. When she removed the lid, Tom's eyes almost shot from their moorings. Reposing on the dish was the largest leg of mutton he had ever seen, its dark exterior glistening with fat, like a piece of highly-burnished mahogany.

Samuel Slack proceeded to carve it. As the knife sank through the crisp outer layer, the first slice fell back, revealing the meat, pink and succulent.

Tom wiped away a rivulet of saliva on the back of his sleeve, as Slack set two slices on a plate in front of him.

"There's t' vegetables, Tom," said his host, indicating the dishes.

Tom greedily shovelled carrots, cabbage and potatoes onto his plate, as the rest of the company averted their gaze. By now, however, he was oblivious to their stares, being determined to make the most of this stroke of good fortune. After all, he was never likely to enjoy food like *this* on an ostler's wages!

"Fine sermon, this morning, I thought," said Hall, helping himself to a generous portion of vegetables.

"Cursham's a sound man," agreed Slack. "Believes in t' virtues o' thrift an' 'ard wokk."

The hosier then turned to Tom.

"That's t' secret o' success in this life, Tom — thrift an' 'ard wokk. Tek me. Faither wor a framework knitter, mother a seamstress, an' I started off doin' odds 'n' ends for two bob a week. But, unlike me faither, I could see there wor no future in knittin' — that worn't where t' money wor to be made. So, at nineteen, I became a middleman. Wokked for various 'osiers round Nottinghamshire an' Derbyshire, puttin' out wokk, then goin' round, a week later, an' collectin' it in. Did that for seven years, savin' up, till I'd enough to buy me own frames. Then, I could let 'em out to others. 'Course, when I'm talkin' about 'ard wokk, I dun't mean wi' these" — holding up his hands — "I mean this."

He tapped his forehead, and the other guests nodded understandingly. Slack looked at Tom again.

"Tell me, Tom, d'yer want to be an ostler, all yer life?"

43

Tom shrugged. Now he was pressed, he somehow couldn't bring himself to renounce the only life he had known.

"Mr Cadman's allus been good to me," he said.

"'E's a good man, George Cadman," conceded Slack, "but d'yer want to spend all yer life muckin' out 'osses?"

"No!"

There! He'd said it! The vehemence of his reply shocked both himself and the rest of the company.

Cousin Richard tried to control his temper by pouring himself another glass of claret, which he drank in a single gulp, earning himself a silent rebuke from his employer.

Susannah and Joseph both collapsed in fits of giggles, whilst Rachel and her mother tried to pretend that nothing untoward had occurred.

"Ay *yoh* ever bin to school, Tom?" asked Slack, in an effort to dispel the hostile atmosphere which seemed to have filled the dining room.

Tom gave him a brief history of his time at the Faith Clerkson School (though omitting any reference to fighting or playing truant). He also explained Amos' reasons for discontinuing his education.

Slack and Hall exchanged frowns and shook their heads.

"Can you read and write and use numbers?" asked the lawyer.

"A bit."

"It's never too late to learn," said Slack. "It's t' only road to a better life. In fact, I've decided..."

He broke off as the dining room door opened.

"Ah, Jessop! Come in an' meet yer new pupil!"

Tom turned to look at the newcomer, and his jaw fell open.

It was the fair-haired, bespectacled young man from the Old Eclipse.

CHAPTER 5

Sunday, 11th May, 1817

"This is Tom — er — what did yer say yer name wor?"

"Stone."

"Henry Jessop," said the young man, extending a hand to Tom. He smiled pleasantly, but there was no light of recognition in his pale blue eyes. Instead, he turned to Slack and said: "What's this about a new pupil?"

"Young Joseph dun't tek up *all* yer time, does 'e?"

"Well, no, but ..."

"If I'm payin' a man eight guineas a term, I expect eight guineasworth o' wokk out on 'im."

"But," Tom protested, "worr about t' stables an' Mr Cadman?"

Slack dismissed the objections with an airy wave.

"Yer can come an' wokk fer me. I can find plenty fer a strappin' young lad like yoh to do. What d'yer say?"

"Well, I..."

"'Ow much does George Cadman pay yer?" interrupted Slack.

"Eight bob a week."

"I'll pay yer eight-'n'-six, live in. 'Ow about that?"

Tom struggled valiantly to phrase a reply, but any further reservations he may have had, remained stuck firmly in his throat.

"Good, that's settled!" boomed the hosier. "Yer can report 'ere at eight o'clock, tomorrer mornin'. An' dun't worry about George Cadman. I'll square things wi' 'im."

It was not so much George Cadman that Tom was worried about, though. What would Ben have to say about his decision? Or Will?

"What'll I be doin'?" asked Tom, still dazed.

"Owt as needs a bit o' muscle," replied the hosier. Then, gesturing towards Jessop, he quipped: "A good brain in't t' answer to *ev'ry* problem!"

The others tittered, pointing at the tutor, but he merely answered his employer with a faint smile.

Tom reflected that, in Jessop's position, he would most likely have told Slack exactly what he could do with his eight guineas a term. He would rather lose his post than tolerate such public humiliation! The man was a milksop!

"I s'pose yer can ride an 'oss, can yer?" queried Slack. "Drive a carriage 'n' pair?"

Tom bristled with hurt pride. Asking the son of Caleb Stone such questions! He smiled to himself. Perhaps he was more proud of being an ostler than he had dared to admit.

"Good," said Slack. "I'll need someone to drive me around or tek messages. That's t' trouble, when yer knitters're scattered across three counties. Can't be ev'rywhere at once. An' when Jessop's taught yer to add

47

up figures, 'appen yer can go round an' gerr in a few debts for me. They'd norr argue wi' a fine lad like yoh!"

"Debts should be settled through the proper legal channels," said the soft voice of Robert Hall. "You know I don't approve of anyone taking the Law into their own hands!"

"You're too fussy, Robert!" laughed Slack, clapping the lawyer heartily on the shoulder and almost dislocating it in the process. Then, with a wink at Tom, he added: "'E's only thinkin' of all t' fees 'e'd be losin'! So, do we ay a deal, then?"

"Aye," replied Tom. His voice sounded distant and unrecognizable.

"Eight o'clock tomorrer, then. Prompt."

Samuel Slack held out a large, hairy hand, and the bargain was struck.

By the time the meal was concluded, Tom was still in a daze. He said goodbye to his host, then to each member of the family and guest in turn. All, with the exception of Richard and young Joseph, were the epitome of politeness: the former greeting him with an icy stare, the latter with haughty indifference.

"Thank you again," said Susannah. He felt the soft smoothness of her skin and the imperceptible squeeze she gave his hand, even though her face showed nothing beyond the normal expression of civility.

Tom merely shrugged, as though what he had done was the most natural thing in the world; although, in fact, he was simply too tongue-tied to answer. He cheeks seemed to be on fire, and he felt sure his blushes must be visible to all.

"Susannah, will yoh see Tom out?" requested Slack.

Susannah looked first at her father, then at Richard's face, twisted in a scowl, and smiled.

"Of course, father!"

With an ostentatious gesture, she linked her arm through Tom's, guided him out of the dining room, into the spacious hallway, and paused by front door.

She glanced over her shoulder.

They were alone.

Susannah leaned forward and her lips made contact with his.

It wasn't the first time he had been kissed by a woman, but they had been the ordinary kisses exchanged by family members. This one lasted barely a second, but Tom felt as though a raging fire had spread through his whole body.

The clear, brown eyes looked up into his and she mouthed the single word: "Tomorrow."

"Where t' bloody 'ell've *yoh* bin?"

Ben Miller, arms akimbo, glowered at his nephew, whilst Margaret made vain conciliatory gestures in the background.

Tom took a deep breath, looked around at his assembled family, and launched into a detailed narration of the morning's events.

"'Ear that?" said Ben, turning to Jonathan, who sat in a corner, nervously fingering the collar of his best shirt. "Bin dinin' wi' yer master. I 'ope 'e asked 'im to put yer wages up!"

It was at this point that Tom dropped his bombshell.

"'E's gi'd me a job. Eight-'n'-six a week, live in." He thought it prudent not to mention to his uncle the added attraction of Susannah.

Even Ben, normally so voluble, was struck dumb.

"An' what did yer tell 'im?" asked Margaret.

"I said I'd tek it."

"See?" roared Ben, with a sidelong look at Will. "I towd yer 'e wor gerrin' all 'igh an' mighty, din't I?"

"Yer'd best not lerr *'im* 'ear yer talkin' about Luddites an' frame-brekkin'!" warned Will.

Jonathan was smiling.

"What's so funny about that?" demanded Will.

"Slack knows all about frame-brekkin'," replied Jonathan, the smile still playing around the corners of his mouth. "'E took advantage of it — paid t' Luddites to go an' smash up 'is rivals' frames an' purrem out o' business! Burr all that's dead an' done for, now."

Will was shaking his head.

"It's started up again, in Manchester, back in March."

"Frame-brekkin'?" asked Jonathan.

"Not this time. It wor s'posed to be a march to London, petitionin' t' Prince Regent for a Bill o' Rights. They reckon, though, as some o' t' same folk are be'ind it as were be'ind t' Luddites."

"An' did they see 'im?" asked Margaret.

Will uttered a sharp, mirthless laugh.

"Most on 'em got no further than Stockport. There wor a bit o' stone throwin', an' one man wor killed by t' militia — though 'e 'ad nowt to do wi' it. Just standin' by t' front door, watchin' 'em march past. T' rest are locked up."

"Worr'll they do to 'em?" asked Tom, craning eagerly forward.

"'Ang 'em, I expect. They think it'll stop it spreadin'. It won't, though. Word is, there'll be marches an' such in Yorkshire an' down 'ere, afore too long. That's why yoh'll keep yer eyes an' ears open, if yer know what's good fer yer!"

"'Ow d'yer know all this?" asked Tom.

Will made no verbal response, but tapped the side of his broad nose with a stubby forefinger.

Ben, meanwhile, had lit his pipe and was deep in thought.

"What's George Cadman gonna say?" he asked, rounding on Tom. "'E's bin like a faither to yoh."

"Burr 'e only pays eight bob a week," Tom pointed out reasonably. "An' no live in! Besides, 'is lad's tutor's gonna teach me for free!"

Ben removed the pipe from his mouth, hawked loudly and directed a stream of brown phlegm into the fire.

"You're a bloody fool to yersen, lad!"

Still seething with anger and disgust, Ben stormed out into Bark Court, whilst Will deliberately turned away from his brother.

Margaret crossed to Tom and slipped an arm round his shoulder.

"Tek no notice, Tom. It's *your* life. Yer've got to mek yer own decisions — even if they turn out to be t' wrong 'uns."

Tom slowly eased open the door of the Old Eclipse and peered inside. There were several familiar faces, including Henry Jessop, who was still deeply engrossed in his book.

"Go on," prompted Ben, prodding him from behind. "Yoh'd best gerrit over wi'."

Plucking up courage, Tom took a deep breath, walked in and marched up to the bar.

From the warm smile that lit up George Cadman's face on seeing him, it was clear that no one had yet broken the news to him.

Tom proceeded to do so.

The response was not what he had expected: no ranting and cursing, merely a sigh and a slow, sorrowful shake of the head.

"I'll be sorry to lose you," he said, forcing a smile. "Good ostlers don't grow on trees, y' know. I'll go an' see t' work'ouse master, fost thing tomorrer, an' see about gerrin' a pauper lad apprenticed, for Ben to train up."

"At least t' parish'll pay for 'im," remarked Ben bluntly. "Save yoh eight bob a week."

Cadman drew off a tankard of ale and handed it to Tom.

"Mek t' most on it, lad," he smiled. "It's t' last free 'un yer'll gerr in 'ere. I just 'ope yer know what yer've let yersen in for."

Tom halted the tankard halfway to his lips, suddenly

struck by the enormity of what he had done. Perhaps his uncle was right, after all, and he'd just made the worst decision of his life.

CHAPTER 6

Monday, 12th May, 1817

"Eight o'clock precisely!"

Samuel Slack smiled approvingly and returned his watch to his waistcoat pocket. Then, slipping an arm round Tom's shoulder, he shepherded him through the hall and pointed to a room on the right.

"Just wait in there a minute, whilst I ay a word wi' George Hicks. Then, we'll find some decent clothes fer yer!"

Tom looked down at his shirt and breeches, the same ones he had worn the day before, and squirmed with embarrassment.

It was then that Tom realized that there was a third party present. There were two things Tom noticed immediately about him: he had a thick mop of sandy-coloured hair, and a large bruise was forming around his left eye.

At first, Tom thought it might have been the man with whom he had fought outside the Old Eclipse, the previous morning, but a second glance reminded him that Susannah's persecutor had been taller, and his hair brown. His clothes had been of better cut, too.

Tom obediently went into the room indicated, but at once

pressed his ear tight against the door, so as not to miss a single detail of his new master's conversation.

"They wun't ay it, then?" he heard Slack say.

"'Ow d'yer think I got this?" replied the other, in what Tom assumed must be a reference to the black eye. "I towd 'em one-'n'-five a pair, but they demanded two bob."

"They know trade's poor," grumbled Slack. "It's not *my* fault. Yer can't guarantee prices, any more than yer can guarantee t' weather. When demand goes down, so do prices. If I pay 'em any more'n one-'n'-five, I can't sell t' stockin's at a profit."

There was the sound of rustling papers.

"Tek Jonathan Parker," said Hicks. "Nine pairs a week — that's 12/9d."

"So?"

"'E reckons 'im an' 'is wife are starvin'. They've just 'ad their firstborn an' reckon they need at least 16 bob a week for t' three on 'em."

"If 'e wants more money, 'e'll ay to mek more goods," declared Slack bluntly. "If 'e turned out *12* pairs a week, 'e'd mek *17* bob."

"But Parker reckons they wokk 70 hours a week, as it is!" protested Hicks.

Jonathan Parker? wondered Tom. His brother-in-law? Surely not. It wasn't like *him* to complain.

"D'yer think I'm bein' 'ard?" asked Slack, after a pause.

Hicks made no immediate answer, but Tom was certainly beginning to feel the first traces of apprehension.

"T' trouble is," continued Slack, "they 'ad it too easy in

55

t' past. When prices were 'igh, I can remember knitters wokkin' only five or six days a week, an' *still* earnin' enough to feed a family o' four. My faither wor like that. Earned enough for 'is daily bread, an' owt spare 'ud go on beer an' gin — an' other women!"

The last three words were spat out in a torrent of uncontrolled fury. Had Tom been able to glimpse his new master's face, at that moment, he would have seen the jaw tighten and the veins knot — much as they had done, the previous day, when he had first set eyes on Tom and cast *him* in the role of villain. Then, Slack took a deep breath and continued his reminiscences.

"Not me, though. I wokked all t' hours the Good Lord sent, lived frugally, an' saved up t' rest till I'd gorr enough to buy me fost frame. That's where folk like Parker go wrong: can't see further than t' end o' t' week. 'Go to the ant, thou sluggard. Consider her ways, and be wise.' Proverbs: Chapter 6, Verse 6."

"They reckon t' frame rent's too 'igh at two-'n'-six a week," protested Hicks.

"I'll not deny times are 'ard," conceded Slack, "but see it from *my* point o' view. I've wokked damned 'ard to buy them frames. I need to see a return on 'em. Send Parker to me ware'ouses, an' lerrim see 'ow many pairs of unsold stockin's there are! Look 'ow much *I* need, to keep a wife an' fam'ly! This 'ouse dun't run itsen! If trade picks up, I'll pay 'em more. I can't say fairer than that."

"Well, Mr Slack, I 'ope yer know what you're doin', 'cos there's trouble a-plenty brewin'," warned Hicks. "There's a man they call t' Nottingham Captain — I dun't know 'is real name — goin' round stirrin' men up to riot."

"Yoh go an' see Rachel," replied Slack. "Get that eye

seen to."

There was a pause, and the door handle turned.

Tom's reflexes were finely attuned, and, by the time the door opened, he was standing in the middle of the room, gazing at a vase of flowers on the central table.

"Sorry about that, Tom. Business," said Slack. "Now, I said I wor goin' to get yer some new clothes, din't I?"

"Yes, sir," replied Tom eagerly.

"In a short while. Meantime, as you're dressed for it, go round to t' stable an' feed an' groom Hicks' 'oss."

Tom's face fell.

"Dun't worry," said Slack, with a smile, as if reading his mind. "Yoh'll not be spendin' all yer time in t' stables. Jessop's busy wi' young Joseph, all mornin'. Yoh'll get your turn later."

He led Tom out into the back yard, which was cut off from the outside world by a ten-foot high stone wall. At the far end stood the stable, from which a tired, thin piebald surveyed them through rheumy eyes.

"Is tharr 'im?" asked Tom.

Slack nodded.

"'E looks 'aif-starved an' knackered, poor bugger!"

"So would yoh, if yer'd bin ridden over three counties. There's plenty of oats an' water in there."

Tom stepped forward and began to stroke the horse's nose.

It whinnied softly and pressed its muzzle against his cheek.

"It's norr ev'ryone 'e gets on wi'," said Slack, and he smiled, confident that in Tom he had made a shrewd investment.

"An' we'll need some firewood, an' all," he continued, pointing to a pile of logs in the far corner of the yard.

As his new master strolled back into the house, Tom rolled up his sleeves and unbolted the stable door.

"Tom!"

He turned, to see Susannah standing on the steps at the rear of the house.

"Mornin', er, miss," replied Tom, uncertain of the correct mode of address. He set down the axe and wiped his sleeve across his sweating brow. The midday sun was now at its zenith, and he had been working solidly, all morning. He had stripped to the waist, and his whole body glistened with sweat. He could feel her eyes taking in every muscle and sinew.

He pinched his nose with his thumb and forefinger, and noisily cleared his sinuses, before wiping his hand clean on his breeches.

"You've been working hard," smiled Susannah, indicating the pile of firewood.

Tom smiled back.

"There's bread, cheese, cold mutton and beer," Susannah announced, setting down the basket.

"Ta," said Tom, taking the stopper from the stone flagon. He raised it to his lips and took a long, grateful gulp.

Susannah waited until he had slaked his thirst and drew

back the cloth that covered the food.

As he reached for the bread and cheese, his hand brushed against her sleeve. It was not the dress she had worn the day before, but a simple, cotton one, embroidered with tiny flowers. It was soft and cool to the touch, and he found himself involuntarily pressing the fabric between his thumb and forefinger.

He looked up.

She was smiling, but the smile abruptly vanished.

As though he had touched hot metal, he drew his fingers away.

The smile swiftly returned.

"Come on. Eat."

He helped himself to bread and cheese, attacking it like a ravenous animal.

He stopped abruptly, aware of the expression of mild disapproval on Susannah's face, and consumed the rest at a more leisurely pace, washing down each mouthful with another draught of beer.

"Susannah!"

Slack's voice resounded from deep within the massive house.

"I'll have to go," said Susannah, with a sad smile. "When you've finished, take the basket and things back to Hannah in the kitchen."

"Yeah — rait — ta," stammered Tom incoherently.

A roguish light danced in Susannah's brown eyes, and she laughed: not an unkind laugh, but one of genuine amusement. Her eyes lingered on his torso for one brief second. Then, before Tom could do or say anything to remedy his acute embarrassment, she had disappeared back into the house.

"Ten threes are 30; 11 threes are 33; 12 threes are 36."

Tom stopped, his brow aching with the effort of remembering.

"Good," said Jessop, with an encouraging smile. "Now, let's try the four-times table."

"Must we?" groaned Tom.

Jessop removed his spectacles and massaged the bridge of his nose.

"Practice makes perfect, Tom."

Tom sighed.

"All rait. One four's four; two fours are eight..."

"Has he only got *that* far?"

So intense had their concentration been, that neither Tom nor his tutor had heard the door open. Joseph was standing just inside the room, a self-satisfied smirk plastered across his otherwise cherubic features.

"I can do my eight-times table, can't I?" crowed the child.

Jessop replied with a weak, non-committal smile.

"Do you want to hear me recite it?"

"You had *your* lesson, this morning," said Jessop, adding, a trifle irritably: "Have you finished the work I set you?"

"Yes."

"Let me see it."

Joseph handed him a sheet of paper, and he spent several moments glancing through it. From time to time, he winced, as though in some secret pain.

"How do you spell 'receive'?" he asked, lowering the paper.

"R-E-C-I-E-V-E," replied Joseph, enunciating each letter in a weary, singsong voice.

"How many times must I tell you? 'I before E, except after C'!" snarled the tutor, through clenched teeth, before proceeding to reduce the sheet of paper to a pile of shredded fragments before the boy's eyes. "Now, do it again!"

Joseph's face reddened.

"You can't be any good as a teacher, if Father's only paying you eight guineas a term!" he sneered. "They never criticized my work at the Reverend Catlow's Seminary!"

With that, he flounced out of the room, slamming the door.

"They'd hardly *dare* say anything, if his father's paying ten guineas a term in fees!" remarked Jessop, with a chuckle. "Remember, Tom: money can buy you anything — or anyone!"

He injected a hint of bitterness into those final two words, and Tom suspected they were an allusion to his own situation.

"Did yoh go to university?" asked Tom.

"Magdalen College, Oxford. Bachelor of Arts."

"Why dun't yer teach in a school?"

"Money, Tom. There are few schools — especially in Mansfield — that'll pay a schoolmaster eight guineas a term, all found. Men may say they value education — but not those who provide it. It's the same with any craft or trade. Our master values the stockings his workers produce, but he doesn't value the men enough to pay them a wage that'll save them from starvation!"

"Yoh sound like a Luddite!" laughed Tom.

Jessop's eyes glinted behind his spectacles.

"What do *you* know of Luddites?"

"Me brother-in-law's faither wor one."

Jessop removed his spectacles and began to polish them vigorously.

"Let's get on with our four-times table, shall we?"

Tom was full of apprehension as he made his way back to Bark Court. Slack had visitors to dinner and had given him the evening off.

All day, Ben's parting words had been ringing in his ears: "'E's goin' up in t' world, Margaret. 'E'll not want owt to do wi' likes of us, from now on."

Well, he'd show them! He might have a new job — and a fine new black livery to go with it — but he had sworn it wouldn't change him.

"Well, if it in't Lord 'Igh-'n'-Mighty 'issen!"

Ben removed the pipe from his mouth and watched the smoke drift languidly upwards, until it disappeared amongst the shadows and cobwebs that shrouded the ceiling. He ran his eye over Tom's livery, hawked loudly and spat into the dying embers of the fire.

"What's 'appened? 'As 'e chucked yer out already?"

"No!" answered Tom defiantly.

"Worr're yer doin' 'ere, then?" asked Will.

"Leave 'im be, t' pair on yer!" cut in Margaret. Pointing at the pot on the fire, she asked: "D'yer want some stew?"

"Stew?" echoed Ben sarcastically. "Yer can't expect 'Is Lordship to eat stew!"

"I'd love some, A'nt Margaret," replied Tom, ignoring the insult.

"So, worr've yer bin learnin'?" queried Will casually.

Tom gave him a full account of his day's duties and lessons, before suddenly asking: "Who's t' Nottingham Captain?"

Will gripped him by the shoulders, his fingers digging so deep into the flesh that Tom cried out with pain.

"What do *yoh* know about t' Nottingham Captain?"

"Nowt," answered Tom. "I just 'eard 'is name, that's all. Who is 'e?"

"A troublemaker. 'Is real name's Jeremiah Brandreth. What d'yer 'ear about 'im?"

Tom relayed the gist of Slack's conversation with Hicks.

Will finally released his grip on Tom's shoulder.

"Yer've bin wantin' excitement, an't yer?" he said, after a pause.

"Aye," replied Tom eagerly.

"Would yer like to do a bit o' spyin' an' earn yersen some money, an' all?"

"'Ow much?" asked Tom apprehensively.

"That," said his brother, "depends on results."

CHAPTER 7

Friday, 16th May, 1817

"Lord bless us! I've never known such an appetite!"

Hannah Green's ample frame shook with silent laughter.

"Anyone 'ud think yoh'd never seen food afore!"

"Not like this, I an't," replied Tom, through a mouthful of roast chicken.

"D'yer like it 'ere?" asked the cook/housekeeper.

Tom nodded enthusiastically. Sitting in a kitchen, by a roaring fire, in front of a table creaking with food: what more could he ask for?

"Mr Slack's all rait, in't 'e?" he said.

"Not bad, as masters go," agreed Hannah, "an' I've known me fair share!"

She said no more, but edged behind him and continued, with an almost maternal concern, to watch as Tom finished the chicken, then helped himself to bread, cheese and beer.

"I dunno where yoh purrit all!" she giggled, and her hand slid across his shoulders and inside his shirt. "No wonder yoh've got such strong muscles!"

Tom put down his beer and looked more closely at her.

She was 35, small and rather plump, and had never married. She might even have been regarded as attractive, but for a few decayed teeth and a strawberry birthmark that covered most of her left cheek. When out, she wore her dark brown hair long to disguise the blemish, but her tresses were now firmly encased in a mobcap.

"Yoh gorra lass, Tom?" she asked, leaning forward so that her ample breasts rested against the nape of his neck.

"No," he replied truthfully.

"Ever 'ad one?"

Tom shook his head.

"I'm surprised! Good-looking lad like yoh!"

She began to rock backwards and forwards, so that the soft mounds of flesh enfolded his neck like a cushion. The smell of roast meat, vegetables and freshly- baked bread seemed to ooze from every pore of her skin.

Tom started to rise from his chair.

"What's up?" asked Hannah.

"I thought I 'eard Mr Slack callin'."

There was a pause, then Hannah's whole body shook with uncontrollable mirth.

"You're shy, in't you?"

"No!"

The reply was a trifle too quick and too vehement.

Hannah gently pressed him back into his seat.

"Think I'm goin' t' eat yer?"

Tom didn't know what to think. His memories of his

mother were necessarily vague, as she had died when Tom was barely three, but he remembered how she had kissed and caressed him: the close, comforting proximity to her breasts, as she had suckled him.

When Ann, at the tender age of ten, had assumed the maternal role, she had doted on him, in preference to Will, as the "baby" of the family, ever ready with a comforting arm or kiss, if he fell and hurt himself. Later, when she had matured into a young woman, he had often seen her naked.

Nor was he ignorant of the mechanics of reproduction. He had once asked his aunt and uncle. Margaret had frozen in mute shock and embarrassment at such a question; but Ben had duly obliged by explaining the process in graphic detail. Later, he had also witnessed at close quarters the coupling of stallions and mares at the stables.

Nothing, though, had prepared him for the bone-crushing, suffocating embrace of this monstrous she-bear. The more fiercely he resisted, the more tightly she held him.

The stench of her breath was overpowering — worse, even, than that from the stables — as her soft, wet lips greedily smothered his face.

How different from that kiss Susannah had given him, when they had parted, on Sunday morning! That was different, of course: he realized that. A simple mark of gratitude. It hadn't meant anything. Besides, she had an "understanding" with Richard. She wouldn't give a second glance to a mere servant, when she had a lawyer's clerk, would she?

He remembered the Monday morning, how his fingers had lingered over the soft cotton fabric of her dress, and how he had then recoiled in horror, fearful that his actions had offended and alienated her.

Meanwhile, Hannah's hands, large, yet sensitive, were beginning to explore every inch of his strong, firm young body. She felt the involuntary stiffening of his manhood, as her fingers eased themselves inside his breeches.

He was paralyzed.

"Tom!"

Footsteps were coming down the stairs.

Hannah hastily stepped back, and Tom found he could breathe again, as the door swung open.

Never had Tom been so delighted to see his master!

"Tom, d'yer know Mr 'All's 'ouse, on Church Street?"

There was no sign that Samuel Slack had noticed anything amiss in the kitchen.

"Yes, sir."

"Will yer tek this note round there?"

"Yes, sir," replied Tom and almost tore the missive from Slack's hand in his excitement.

Tom followed his new master up the stairs to the hallway. He took care not to look back, not daring to meet Hannah's gaze. Were *all* women such predators?

"Enjoyin' yer lessons?" asked Slack.

"Yes, sir."

"Ay yer learnt owt?"

"Yes, sir. Lots."

"Jessop seems to think you're an apt pupil."

There was pride in Slack's voice, but did Tom also sense

a hint of bitterness, perhaps even envy, that young Joseph's efforts showed up unfavourably by comparison?

Tom paused outside the Old Eclipse, his hand poised over the handle.

No. Chances were, either Will or Ben would be in, and, at the moment, he couldn't face meeting them.

In any case, he was still chewing over what Will had said, on Monday evening, about spying: "Go round diff'rent inns. Keep yer eyes an' ears open, an' yer gob shut!"

On Tuesday, he had been in the Crown & Anchor; on Wednesday, he had visited the White Hart; last night, it had been the Swan. There had been plenty of strangers in each: coach travellers exchanging stories of hard times and current misfortunes; but nothing that could remotely be construed as seditious.

Tonight, he would try the Black's Head.

At the junction of Market Place and Stockwell Gate stood an archway. On one side was a butcher's shop, occupied by Francis Downs; on the other stood the premises of local shoemaker Benjamin Buttery.

Tom went through the archway and into the Black's Head Yard. It was like entering another world. Dusk had fallen, but there was still a trace of red in the sky. Once he passed through the archway, even that little light seemed to vanish.

Next to the inn, in the shadows of the brewhouse, he could just discern two writhing, grunting shapes pressed against the wall. Tom barely blinked: prostitutes plying their sordid trade, their finer senses dulled by copious quantities of cheap gin, were a common sight in these narrow, unlit alleyways.

He had often been propositioned himself, but had never felt any temptation. He always remembered Ben's dire warnings of the foul diseases to be contracted from such liaisons.

Tom pushed open the door and was greeted by the suffocating stench of stale beer, tobacco and sweating humanity, which struck him like a blow in the face.

He peered through the curtain of smoke, in search of a familiar face, and was surprised to see Ned Hopkins at the bar, his eyes darting nervously round the room, as though he was expecting someone. It wasn't like Ned to frequent the Black's Head!

"Ayup, Ned!" said Tom, tapping the former farrier on the shoulder.

Ned spun round like a scalded cat.

"Bloody 'ell, Tom!" he growled, once he had recovered his breath and composure. "Yoh scared me to death!"

Tom ordered himself a tankard of ale.

"Meetin' someone?" he asked casually.

Ned grunted.

"Who is she?" leered Tom, giving his friend a sharp dig in the ribs.

"Nobody *yoh'd* know — an' it's norra 'she', neither!"

Tom shrugged and turned his attention to the ale, which, he decided after a single mouthful, bore no comparison with George Cadman's. Such considerations were not important, though: he was here on business, not pleasure.

"Ned!"

Tom turned his head at the sound of the voice, and saw a man of his own height advancing towards the ex-farrier with outstretched right hand. He was a slim, swarthy figure — possibly a Gypsy, Tom surmised — with a shock of black, curly hair and a thick black beard. The clay pipe which hung, unlit, from the corner of his mouth at a jaunty angle lent him the swaggering air of a brigand. Then, remembering Ned's incapacity, he smiled apologetically, and proffered his left hand, which Ned eagerly embraced.

"T' usual?" asked Ned.

The stranger nodded, and Ned ordered another tankard of ale.

"What's up?" asked Ned noticing the stranger's face had clouded.

"Bad news!"

"What?"

"Norr 'ere!"

Having collected his ale, the stranger took Ned by the elbow and steered him across the room to a table in the corner, where they made themselves comfortable.

Tom followed at a discreet distance, his curiosity aroused. He soon found himself sandwiched between two large farmers, who were standing a few feet from Ned and his companion. He was hidden from their view, but, by straining his ears, he could just make out their conversation.

"What's 'appened?" Ned was urgently demanding.

The stranger wiped a smear of froth from his beard on the back of his sleeve.

71

"Oliver came to see me, last nait. Mitchell's bin arrested."

"When?"

"Twelve days back."

"Where is 'e?"

"London. Cold Baths prison."

"'Ow?"

"'E wor travellin' from Wakefield wi' Oliver. 'E gorr out, near 'Uddersfield, to go for a piss, an' they were waitin' for 'im."

Ned's brow creased in a frown of consternation.

"Waitin'? You reckon it wor a trap?"

His companion shrugged and slowly lit his pipe.

"Who, though?" asked Ned. "Norr Oliver?"

The stranger let out a sharp laugh.

"Oliver? There's no one truer to t' Cause!"

Tom felt his skin prickle. Arrest? Betrayal? Cause? Could this be the Luddite plot about which Will had told him? And Ned Hopkins implicated, too? He must get back and tell what he knew. Then again, what *did* he know? Precious little. Certainly nothing to interest Will. His best plan would be to stay and overhear the rest of the conversation.

"There's bad news from Wakefield, an' all," the stranger was saying. "T' Birmingham delegation's backed out."

"Why?"

"They don't want no violence!"

"'Ow the 'ell do they think we'll tek London wi'out force?" scoffed Ned.

Force! Tom's body tensed. This was something worth reporting!

"So, is it all still on for t' 27th, then?" asked Ned.

The stranger shook his head and drew thoughtfully on his pipe.

"Looks like bein' t' 9th or 10th, now. 'Ow many can we count on from Mansfield?"

"A thousand — maybe more, once we've spread these round," said Ned.

He drew a thick sheaf of papers from his pocket and laid them out on the table for the stranger to examine.

"Good," mused the stranger. "A thousand? An' t' same from Sutton, d'yer reckon?"

"Yeah."

A smile of contentment spread itself across the stranger's face.

"'Ow many d'yer reckon there'll be, all towd?" queried Ned.

"At least 16,000 from Nottinghamshire; probably t' same from Derbyshire. Say 30,000 — an' that's just from round 'ere. Add Leicestershire, Yorkshire, Lancashire. There'll be close on 'aif a million."

The stranger leaned forward, and, in doing so, brushed his elbow against the pile of papers. One of them fluttered gently to the floor.

Tom eased himself out from between the two farmers. There was no time to hear any more. He bent down, picked up the fallen paper, thrust it into his pocket and hastily made for the door.

Pausing outside the Black's Head, he took a deep gulp of cool air to clear the tobacco smoke from his lungs.

"Lookin' fer anyone special, luv?" crooned a low female voice from the shadows. "Only five bob!"

The owner of the voice moved forward until a shaft of moonlight picked out her features. Then she and Tom gazed at each other in mute bewilderment.

It was Aunt Margaret!

CHAPTER 8

Saturday, 17th May, 1817

"Yoh've not said nowt to Ben, ay yer?"

Margaret looked pleadingly at Tom, and he felt the blood rushing to his cheeks and temples. He still could not believe what he had witnessed outside the Black's Head, the previous evening.

"No, I an't," he answered. Then, with a look of disgust, he added: "'Ow *could* yer?"

"D'yer think I *enjoy* doin' it?" replied his aunt, turning away. "D'yer think I'd do it if I din't 'ave to?"

She jerked her head in the direction of the chair where Ben usually sat.

"It's bad enough doin' it wi' 'im, lerr alone wi' men yer've never met afore at five bob a time. All over yer — 'andlin' yer as if yer were a sack o' taters!"

"Why, though?" persisted Tom.

"Ben gi's me ten bob a week. Yoh gi' me two bob. Now Will's billeted 'issen on us. Them two eat enough fer a dozen between 'em. This is t' only way I can mek ends meet."

"An' Ben dun't know?"

Margaret shook her head.

"What would 'e do, if 'e found out?"

Margaret said nothing, but her hand instinctively flew to her left eye, where the bruise Tom had seen the previous Saturday had still not totally faded.

"Did 'e do that?" growled Tom, pointing to the wound.

His aunt nodded.

"Not 'cos o' *that* — though it wor a row about money, as usual. Ten bob a week — an' t' rest 'e pisses up agen t' wall!"

Tom opened his mouth to protest.

"Yoh don't see 'im, Tom," pleaded Margaret, "comin' in 'ere at all hours, reekin' o' gin!"

She straightened a stray strand of hair and busied herself with preparing the midday meal.

"Shun't yoh be at Mr Slack's?"

"'E's gone over to Sutton, this mornin'," said Tom. "Said 'e wun't need me."

Margaret waved her hand over the few meagre vegetables that lay on the table.

"I'd ask yer to stop, but..."

She shrugged helplessly.

"It dun't matter," smiled Tom. "I'm eatin' all rait over there."

His mouth was already watering at the prospect of Hannah's cooking — just so long as he didn't have to endure her amorous attentions as well! Oddly, neither of them had since mentioned the previous evening's incident.

Perhaps Hannah was just as embarrassed about the matter as he was. However, she had been her usual cheerful self at breakfast, and the smile she had given him had borne no hint of lustful desire.

To be honest, though, he had had little appetite, that morning. He had hardly slept, his mind worrying over the encounter with his aunt outside the Black's Head.

It had been a shock at the time, but Margaret's explanation just now had come as no surprise to him: he was familiar with Ben's habits. If it wasn't drink, it was gambling. Tom had known him lose fifteen shillings — a whole week's wages — in an evening, playing dice or cards with anyone who would accept the challenge. When he won, he was the life and soul of the Old Eclipse, buying drinks for friends and strangers alike; but, when he lost, it was as if a demon possessed him. It was not the first time Tom had seen scars and bruises on his aunt's face and body. She invariably put them down to her own clumsiness, but he had long entertained his own suspicions.

"Why d'yer stay wi' 'im?" demanded Tom, a note of anger creeping into his voice.

His aunt looked blankly at him and shrugged.

"'Cos I love 'im."

Tom stared at her in mute incomprehension. What sort of an answer was that?

"Anyroad," she continued, forestalling further questions, "where would I go?"

There was no answer — and Tom knew it.

The hiatus was broken by a faint knock at the door.

"Come in," called Margaret, without looking round.

The door creaked open, and Jonathan's pale, freckled face peered in.

"I — that is, Ann an' me — were just wonderin' — well, that is … could yer spare us a drop o' milk?"

"Well…" faltered Margaret.

"It's not fer us," cut in Jonathan hastily. "We can manage. It's for Caleb."

"In't Ann feedin' 'im 'ersen?" asked Margaret, indicating her breast to emphasize the point.

"She wor, burr 'e's allus cryin', an' she just can't mek enough to keep up wi' 'im — an', wi' milk a tanner a quart, we can't…"

His voice trailed off, and, even in the half-light of the cottage's interior, Tom could see a tear forming in the corner of his eye.

Margaret said nothing, but poured a quantity of milk into the small jug Jonathan had brought with him.

"'E said things were 'ard for yer," remarked Tom.

"Who did?"

"Mr Slack."

Jonathan's thin, pale features tightened.

"What's 'e bin sayin'?" he demanded harshly.

Tom reiterated the gist of Slack's conversation with Hicks. As his narrative proceeded, he noticed his brother-in-law's hand begin to shake, so that the milk spilled over his shoes.

"Steady on!" cried Tom, taking a first grip of Jonathan's

wrist. "What's up?"

"That's it, then," replied Jonathan, letting out a deep, fatalistic sigh, as Tom steered his sagging frame towards the nearest chair and gently lowered him into it. "If I've bin branded a troublemaker, that's it. Hicks'll mek sure I get no more wokk. 'E can be a vindictive bugger!"

"It worn't yoh as thumped 'im, wor it?" asked Tom.

"Of course not! Yer know Ann an' me don't 'owd wi' violence," replied Jonathan.

"Well, *someone's* gi'd 'im a ripe black eye!" chuckled Tom.

Margaret winced, but a wan smile had lit up the corners of Jonathan's mouth.

"I'd like to shake 'ands wi' whoever it wor! That bugger's 'ad it comin' fer a while, now!"

So much, thought Tom, for not holding with violence!

Margaret was looking down into the jug that still nestled in Jonathan's trembling fingers.

"Yer've spilt most on it," she remarked, her voice showing no hint of reproach.

"Oh...I...er..."

"Don't worry," cut in Margaret, with a smile, as she swiftly replenished the vessel.

Jonathan stood up, and, mumbling profuse thanks, made his way out into Bark Court.

"Tell Ann to tek care!" Margaret shouted after him. Then, closing the door, she leaned against it and whispered: "Poor buggers!"

The sound of raucous voices was heard from the street.

Margaret moved away just in time, as the door was rudely kicked open, and Ben and Will lurched over the threshold.

"What wor 'e wantin'?" roared Ben. "On t' cadge agen?"

"Milk," replied his wife placidly.

"An' I s'pose yer've gi'd 'im some?"

"It's not fer 'im an' Ann — it's fer young Caleb. 'E's won t' 'ardest battle — bein' born. At least gi' t' poor little bugger a faitin' chance!"

"'Ow much d'yer gi' 'im?" demanded Ben.

"About a gill, if that."

Ben's brow furrowed as he calculated how many glasses of ale or gin that represented.

"Yoh must think I've more bloody money than sense, woman!" he snarled, taking his filthy pipe from his pocket and lighting it.

"Well, Tom," said Will, "owt to report?"

"Aye. I went in t' Black's 'Ead, last nait."

"Did yer see or 'ear owt?"

"Well," replied Tom, deliberately avoiding Margaret's gaze, "I over'eard Ned 'Opkins an' a stranger talkin'."

"So?" said Will. "Who wor 'e, this stranger?"

Tom shrugged.

"Well, what did 'e look like?"

Tom gave his brother a brief description.

"Shit!" yelped Will, banging his fist on the table.

80

The shock caused Ben to swallow a mouthful of smoke and double up in a fit of violent coughing.

"What's up?" asked Tom.

"It's 'im!" cried Will. "Brandreth!"

"T' Nottingham Captain, yer mean?" gasped Tom.

"What did they talk about?" demanded Will.

Tom recounted as much of the conversation as he could remember, then produced the paper the stranger had knocked to the floor.

Will snatched it from him and read it out:

> For too long now, we have suffered in silence. King George is mad: the Prince Regent debauches himself in Brighton. Meanwhile, thousands of their loyal subjects starve. Now is the time for the British, like the French, to throw off their shackles and establish a republic, which will rule for the benefit of all citizens.
>
> You must play your part. There will be a meeting for all who thirst for Justice in the Black's Head, at 9 o'clock, on Monday, 19th May, 1817.
>
> Long live Freedom! Death to all Tyrants!
>
> BRUTUS

Will screwed up the paper and hurled it forcibly into the fire.

"Poisonous rubbish!"

His face abruptly softened, and he favoured his brother with a smile of genuine warmth.

"Well done, lad!"

He dipped into his pocket and produced a bright silver shilling.

"'Ere, lad! Yer've t' mekin's of a good spy!"

He broke off and shook his head sadly.

"Ned 'Opkins! I'd never 'a' thought it o' Ned!"

"I dunno," said Tom. "T' way 'e wor talkin', last Sunday, about 'is arm..."

"'E wor allus a miserable bugger, afore 'e lost 'is arm!" laughed Will. "I can't see *that* turnin' 'im into a Republican."

He paused and scratched his chin.

"Then agen, 'e wor allus one fer followin' 'are-brained schemes. Come to think on it, it's just t' sort o' thing 'e *would* get mixed up in!"

"Tom!"

Tom halted in his tracks, spun round and looked up towards the top of the stairs, from where the voice had come. Susannah was leaning over the banister.

"Sorry, miss. Didn't realize it wor yoh," said Tom, smiling nervously.

"Can you come up here, for a minute?"

A strange sensation gripped Tom's stomach.

"Just look at your face!" hooted Susannah, tossing back her chestnut tresses. "I'll not eat you!"

Where had he heard *that* before?

"There's a bureau in my bedroom," she said. "I need it moving."

"Oh...er...yeah...rait..." stammered Tom.

It was only when he arrived on the landing that he noticed she was wearing only a pale blue silk bathrobe.

"Oh, er, I din't know ..."

"Come on!" laughed Susannah, taking him by the elbow and guiding him along a short corridor. "In here."

Tom was still taking in the elegant furnishings when Susannah pointed towards a small bureau in the corner by the bed.

"I want that moving over by the window," she said.

"Rait, miss."

"Hannah hasn't swept the room out for two days. There's dust everywhere. You'd better take your coat and shirt off. You don't want to get them dirty."

Tom obeyed, carefully laying the garments over the back of a chair. He then crossed to the far corner of the room, bent his knees, gripped the bureau firmly, took a deep breath and straightened up. The piece was heavier than he had realized, and he felt every muscle in his body stretched to its limit as he lifted it, inch by inch, from the floor.

The distance from the corner of the room was barely ten feet, but it felt like ten miles. It seemed as if his lungs would burst with the effort.

At last, exhaling slowly, he set the bureau down, leaned

heavily against it, and wiped the sweat from his brow. The whole operation could not have taken more than twenty seconds, yet his torso was glistening with perspiration.

"Thanks, Tom."

"That's all rait, miss. I —"

Tom had turned round and now stood frozen like a statue, his mouth agape. Susannah had peeled the bathrobe back from her shoulders and was sitting on the bed, her naked breasts exposed.

Tom continued to open and close his mouth noiselessly like a stranded fish.

Susannah motioned to him to come and sit beside her.

"But wha'…why…?" babbled Tom.

"I wanted to thank you for last Sunday."

"Yoh already 'ave."

"Properly, I meant."

She smiled coquettishly.

"Worr about yer faither?" gasped Tom.

"They're all out. There's just the two of us."

"But worr about Richard?"

"What about him? I've told you: we're alone."

"I thought yoh an' 'im were betrothed."

"We are — informally. It was all arranged with Father, weeks ago," she answered casually. "He's offered Richard a generous dowry, of course. Five hundred pounds, I believe. At any rate, enough to ensure our future."

"'E's just marryin' yer fer yer faither's money?" said

84

Tom, aghast.

"What *other* reason is there to get married?" she replied airily. "Anyway, I don't want to talk about Richard. What about you? Look at you! Come nearer! You're not shy, are you?"

"'Course not!" answered Tom defiantly.

Susannah gently ruffled his hair, for several moments, and then slowly drew his head forward until their lips met.

Again, he experienced the same sensation, as of thousands of small, icy fingers running over his skin.

She opened her lips slightly, forcing his apart, and gently inserted her tongue into his mouth.

Gradually, the kisses became more passionate. The tip of her tongue then probed, and delicately caressed, the contours of his left ear, before her small, sharp teeth nipped the lobe, causing him to let out a loud yelp.

She covered his mouth, then took his right hand and guided it towards her left breast, teaching his strong, callused fingers to explore the firm, smooth mound of flesh.

Meanwhile, the fingers of her other hand were deftly unbuttoning his breeches; reaching inside; running through the thick, tangled undergrowth of rough hair; coaxing; teasing.

To Tom, it suddenly seemed as if a bolt of lightning had struck him in the groin, sending shockwaves through every fibre of his being. His whole body trembled, and, for one brief moment, he feared that Mansfield had been struck by another earthquake, as in March of the previous year.

"Damn!"

Susannah leapt to her feet, pushing Tom away.

"What's up?" he blurted.

"Look!" she cried, pointing to a stream of white, viscous fluid that was trickling down the front of her bathrobe. Then, indicating a washstand in the far corner, she commanded: "Dampen that towel and bring it here!"

Tom hastily obeyed.

"Clumsy fool!" she shrieked, snatching the towel from him.

He made several attempts to apologize, or at least evoke some response from Susannah, but she ignored him, remaining intently absorbed in dabbing furiously at the stain.

Sweeping up his coat and shirt, he backed out of the room, muttering incoherently, and headed for the kitchen at a furious pace.

Would Susannah ever forgive him? If she told her father — or Richard — that would mean immediate dismissal. Not only would he bear the stigma of losing his job, but it was almost certain he would never find another. He could go crawling to George Cadman, asking for his old job back, but then he would have to suffer insults and humiliation from his uncle.

All the rest of the day, and for all of the night, he continued to wrestle with his confused emotions. Women! First, it had been Aunt Margaret, offering herself to any stranger for five shillings. Now, his master's daughter, seemingly prepared to cuckold her own fiancé!

Yet he could not deny that, even though it had ended in disaster and disappointment, he had enjoyed it. He had known that explosion of joy before, stimulated by his own hand; but to have it done by another, and with such a gentle, expert touch, had taken him to a level of pleasure he had never dreamed possible. If only he could have deferred it until that final, ecstatic moment when, as Ben had so crudely described it, "t' man shoves it up 'er"!

In the meantime, his memory retained every graceful curve, every square inch of milk-white flesh he had been privileged to view, and, as he lay in bed, he re-enacted the events of that afternoon, his imagination supplying the ideal climax, which inexperience and impetuosity had denied him.

CHAPTER 9

Sunday, 18th May, 1817

"Mr Jessop, who's Brutus?"

The tutor looked curiously at Tom, and then cleared his throat.

"There were two Brutuses: Marcus Brutus, who assassinated Julius Cæsar, and Junius Brutus, who drove the tyrant Tarquinius from Rome. Why do you ask?"

Before Tom could answer, Samuel Slack appeared, followed by his wife, his two daughters and young Joseph. All were dressed in their most resplendent finery, as was their custom, each Sunday.

"Ready for church, Tom?" asked Slack, who was clad from head to foot in black and carried a Bible and the Book of Common Prayer.

"Church?" echoed Tom, rather foolishly.

"You do go to church, don't yer?" asked Slack, his brow creasing into a frown.

"No, sir."

"Chapel?"

"No, sir. I've allus wokked on a Sunday."

Slack's eyes narrowed.

"Sunday's the Lord's Day. 'Remember the Sabbath day, to keep it holy.' Exodus: Chapter 20, Verse 8. As it goes on to say: 'In it, thou shalt not do any work, thou, nor thy son, nor thy daughter, *nor thy manservant...*'"

He paused to observe the effect that this — especially the last three words — had had on Tom, who was looking towards Jessop for inspiration.

"Oh, *'e'll* not be joinin' us!" scoffed Slack airily. "Dun't believe in God, do yer, Jessop?"

"Man is the master of his own destiny," replied the tutor, with a wan smile.

Slack sniffed loudly, and then shepherded Tom and the rest of the retinue out of the front door. They turned left into West Gate and mingled with the throng making their way towards the parish church of Saints Peter and Paul, whose peal of eight bells could already be heard summoning the faithful to morning worship.

As they neared Market Place and the Old Eclipse, Tom fixed his gaze straight ahead, hoping that nobody be knew would see him. If either Ben or Will spotted him heading for church, they would never let him hear the last of it!

There was the usual collection of idle apprentices and street urchins, many of whom Tom knew well, lounging in groups round the pump in the centre of Market Place, passing loud, often obscene, comments on the gentry and their habits.

"Ayup, it's Tom Stone!" jeered a voice above the rest. "Goin' to church!"

Tom turned at the sound of his name.

The unmistakeable voice belonged to Daniel White, a former workhouse boy of 14, now apprenticed to John Benton, whose shoemaking business in Market Place they had just passed.

Tom, who was walking beside Hannah, took a pace towards White, his clenched fists upraised, his whole frame tensed for action.

"Come 'ere, White, an' I'll punch yer 'ead in!"

White broke away from his companions and squared up to Tom.

"Come on, then!"

The two youths each took a pace forward.

"Tom!"

Heads turned, as the stentorian voice of Samuel Slack echoed along Market Place.

"Tom, come 'ere!" the hosier commanded.

For several moments, Tom continued to glare at White, waiting for him to act.

"Tom!" bellowed Slack, once more.

Reluctantly, Tom lowered his guard and backed away, his eyes never leaving the face of the young apprentice.

"What's up?" scoffed White. "Scared?"

He and the others then set up a mocking chant: "Stone's scared!" which they *ad infinitum* as they followed the Slack entourage in a gaggle down Church Street.

"Tom!" growled Slack, his voice rising above the chime of the bells. "What d'yer mean by faitin' on t' Lord's Day?"

"Burr 'e…"

"'Whosoever shall smite thee on thy right cheek, turn to him the other, also.' Saint Matthew: Chapter 5, Verse 39. Now, let's ay no more nonsense!"

"No, sir."

"Good!"

As Tom fell meekly into line and followed the Slack family down to church, he noticed young Joseph witnessing his humiliation with a studied air of superiority.

The parish church of Saints Peter and Paul was of Norman origin, although subsequent generations had left their individual marks upon it. The most recent of these was a gallery, constructed at the west end of the church, where pews could be rented by the gentry for the annual sum of sixteen guineas. This had the clear advantage for the occupants of establishing their social status: they could, quite literally, look down upon the less fortunate parishioners in their pews in the nave below.

One of these gallery pews was rented by the Slack family, who duly filed into their places: Samuel, Sarah, Susannah and Joseph in the front row, and, behind them, Rachel, Hannah and finally Tom, who managed to squeeze his frame between the plump, comfortable bulk of the cook-housekeeper and the unyielding hardness of the waist-high oak barrier which separated them from the neighbouring pew.

Tom was seated directly behind Susannah. She was wearing the same dark maroon taffeta dress as on the previous Sunday, and he longed to reach forward and touch her. If only she would speak to him! She had said nothing to him since the incident of the previous afternoon. When she had come downstairs, that morning, their eyes had briefly met, but she had quickly turned away again. Would she ever forgive his clumsiness and stupidity?

Then, another thought struck him: what was there to forgive? It was *she* who had invited him into the room to move the bureau: a mere pretext, he now realized. Surely *she* should be apologizing to *him*?

No, that was a foolish expectation! When did the gentry ever apologize for anything?

Still, there was one thing he could be thankful for: clearly, she had mentioned nothing to her father.

Susannah's concentration, meanwhile, was focused on the pew to their right.

Tom immediately recognized the round, shining bald head of Robert Hall. Cousin Richard entered the pew behind his employer and sat down. He caught sight of Tom, but at once turned his attention to the prayer book he was holding.

In the pew to their left sat a figure whom Tom could not immediately place: a tall, pasty, brown-haired youth. It was only when he saw the bruise under the youth's left eye that recognition dawned: it was the young man who had been paying Susannah unwanted attentions, the previous Sunday. She had mentioned his name. What was it? Jacob Smalley! He caught sight of Tom and scowled.

Any further speculations had to be deferred, as the service was about to begin.

Most of the prayers and Bible readings went way over Tom's head: there were none of the bloodthirsty adventures he remembered from school, merely exhortations against the evils of fornication — whatever *that* was!

The hymns were more familiar: he had learnt and sung several at school. However, his own tentative efforts — and those of the choir — were effectively drowned out by his master's powerful, if somewhat tuneless, bass.

At last, the congregation sat down and waited patiently for the Reverend Thomas Cursham to climb into the pulpit. He was in his mid-twenties, fresh-faced, but with piercing grey eyes which scanned the assembled multitude, stilling any murmurs of conversation, until a reverential hush descended. When he spoke, his voice was clear and musical, its resonant tones penetrating every corner of the building.

"The Epistle of Saint Paul the Apostle to the Ephesians: Chapter 5, Verse 3. 'Fornication, and all uncleanliness, or covetousness, let it not once be named amongst you, as becometh saints.'"

This was one of the passages Tom remembered being read out earlier. It was that strange word again: fornication.

"Fornication!" repeated the vicar, as if reading Tom's mind. Again, the flinty, grey eyes swept over the faces in both the lower pews and the upper gallery, as if searching for some guilty reaction. "Uncleanliness!"

Tom noticed the back of Susannah's neck suddenly redden beneath the cascade of chestnut ringlets. For one moment, he thought she was going to turn and look at him. Then, her whole body stiffened, and she remained gazing resolutely ahead, as though, like Lot's wife, she feared the consequences of looking backwards.

Tom then cast a sidelong glance in the direction of

Richard. Was it his imagination, or had Richard edged closer to their own pew?

Joseph, meanwhile, had already lost interest in the sermon and was earnestly picking his nose, to the evident displeasure of his mother, who nudged him sharply in the ribs.

"Marriage, as the Prayer Book tells us, is a holy estate," declared the vicar, "and the physical union of Man and Woman plays an important role within it — but only within it!"

Richard turned to Susannah, as if about to say something, but she swiftly silenced him by raising a delicate finger to her full, soft lips.

"Those who fornicate are little better than the beasts of the field," continued the Reverend Cursham.

Tom felt a large, fleshy hand on his knee.

Hannah smiled down at him, exposing her blackened teeth, and winked lasciviously.

Tom's mind raced back to the scene in the kitchen, on Friday evening. Was *that* what the vicar meant by fornication? Yet there had been no "union" between them — or between him and Susannah, the following day. So, the injunction didn't apply to him.

"But," continued the vicar, "as Our Saviour Himself taught us, in Matthew: Chapter 5, Verse 28, merely for a man to look lustfully at a woman is to have committed adultery with her in his heart! For such as they, whose minds are filled with unclean thoughts, there will be no place in Heaven! The earth shall open and swallow them up. God has reserved for them the very hottest corner of Hell! Their spirits will cry out in eternal torment! For them, every second in Hell will feel like a million years! They will beg for God's mercy, and He will turn His face from them, because they would not heed the words of His Blessed Son!"

Tom froze in horror. He had heard sermons at the Faith Clerkson School, delivered by visiting clergy from the parish church, but it was the first time he had heard the Reverend Cursham, who had arrived four years previously. This man was different: he spoke of Heaven and Hell as though he had visited those places.

Tom remembered, as a boy, seeing pictures of Hell: foul-faced, horned demons roasting the damned on spits over sulphurous flames. He also remembered that, for the past seven days, his mind had been awash with "unclean thoughts" about Susannah Slack! Only his awareness of the social barriers that separated the two of them had pushed such speculation to the back of his mind.

Then, yesterday …

Clearly, she had been harbouring similar thoughts.

He craned forward, trying to get a clearer view of Susannah's face. Had the vicar's words produced any effect upon her?

Richard had now edged even closer to the barrier that separated their pews, and Susannah, her eyes still gazing fixedly to the front, laid of her right hand, almost absently, on top of it, offering no resistance as Richard covered it with his left hand.

Tom felt a sudden spark of jealousy.

Soon, the sermon was over. The organ once more struck up, and Richard and Susannah leapt to their feet, their hands springing apart.

The hymn was not one with which Tom was familiar, and he found his mind wondering again. Supposing he hadn't had that "accident", yesterday. Would Susannah have allowed him to enjoy "physical union", as the vicar had called it? Or had she deliberately caused the accident to frustrate him? Perhaps she suspected his secret "unclean thoughts" towards her, and this was her way of putting him, the humble ostler and factotum, in his place. After all, if her dalliance with Tom had meant anything to her, why would she now be gazing at Richard over the top of her hymnbook like a lovesick faun?

He was jerked from his reverie by a nudge in the ribs from Hannah, and looked down to see a large wooden plate being held beneath his nose.

"What's that for?" asked Tom.

"T' collection," hissed the cook-housekeeper. "Yer put money in t' plate."

"I an't got nowt!" protested Tom.

Samuel Slack spun round and fixed him with a withering glare, before snatching the collection plate from him.

"'God loveth a cheerful giver.' II Corinthians: Chapter 9, Verse 7," he intoned solemnly, above the swell of the hymn singing, as he dropped a handful of coins into the plate with an ostentatious flourish.

Tom wished the earth would open up, as the vicar had described. At that moment, even the hottest flames of Hell would have been preferable to the squirming embarrassment he was enduring. Like the sinners in torment, he prayed for his suffering to end.

CHAPTER 10

Sunday, 18th May, 1817

"Church!"

Ben rocked backwards and forwards in his chair, convulsed with helpless laughter.

"Slack's nowt burra Bible-spoutin' 'ypocrite!" muttered Jonathan, from the far corner of the room. "Why dun't yer ask 'im about Matthew: Chapter 6, Verse 24?"

Tom looked blank.

"'Ye cannot serve God and Mammon.'"

"Mammon!" repeated Will, before belching loudly and subsiding into a corner, a bottle of gin clamped tightly in his fist.

Margaret had just lit the "poor light", whose thick, oily smoke now mingled with that from Ben's pipe, reducing what little illumination the flame offered, and sucking up the meagre supply of air.

"'Ow's young Caleb, Jonathan?" asked Tom.

"Stronger," replied his brother-in-law, though his face showed scant trace of optimism. "'E drank all 'is milk."

"Good," said Margaret. "If you need any more…"

A low grunt from the direction of Ben's chair cut her short.

"When can I see 'im?" asked Tom.

"Now, if yer like," replied Jonathan.

"Good idea!" said Ben. "Y' ought to go round an' see 'im! You're 'is uncle, aren't yer?"

Tom sensed Ben's enthusiasm was more at the thought of getting rid of Jonathan than any encouragement of Tom's avuncular responsibilities.

"Rait," said Tom. "Yoh comin' an' all, Will?"

Will belched, which Tom interpreted as a refusal. It was better, perhaps. The last thing the poor little mite needed, right now, was someone breathing gin fumes over him.

"I might go round to t' Black's 'Ead, later," said Tom.

There was the clash of falling cutlery, and Tom spun round to see Aunt Margaret on her hands and knees, scooping up knives and forks.

"Sorry," she mumbled. "Me bein' clumsy."

Tom was relieved to see that the incident produced no reaction from Ben or Will.

"Try an' gerr in wi' Ned 'Opkins," said Will. "See if yer can find out owt else."

"I found out who Brutus is," Tom suddenly announced.

Will was instantly alert.

"Who?"

"There were two. One killed Julius Cæsar, an' t' other drove some tyrant out o' Rome. Mr Jessop towd me all about 'em."

"What's a bloody schoolmaster know about owt?" snorted Will.

"More'n yoh!" snapped Tom swiftly.

"'E dun't know who wrote them leaflets, though, does 'e?"

"They're all over t' place now," cut in Ben. "Found some in t' Owd Eclipse, this mornin'."

"Tharr'll be Ned, I expect," said Tom.

"'E prob'ly purrem there," agreed Will, "burr 'e din't write 'em. 'E can just about write 'is own name."

"Our Tom 'ere can read 'n' write now," sneered Ben. "'Appen it's 'im be'ind it all!"

Tom considered arguing the point. Instead, he stormed out slamming the door behind him.

Outside, the sun had almost set, leaving a blood-red stain in the sky. A cool breeze was blowing up the alley, bearing with it the sound of the ducks on the pond, yet the air felt heavy and claustrophobic.

Tom followed his brother-in-law down Bark Court to Duck Lane where they turned left. A few yards further on, they turned left again and found themselves in Mitre Court, a cramped, stinking cul-de-sac which even stray animals gave a wide berth. Lines of washing were strung out to dry across the narrow thoroughfare, and they had to fight their way through them.

Somewhere in the court, the loud wail of a baby could be heard.

At the far end, a drunk was urinating up against the front door of one of the cottages. Tom at once recognized it as the Parkers' home. He gripped the man by the scruff of the neck, spun him round and propelled him, unresisting, in the direction of Duck Lane.

Jonathan stared at the puddle of urine on the doorstep, seemingly oblivious to the overpowering stench, sighed, and held the door open for Tom to go through. The screaming of the infant grew louder and more insistent.

"Is that yoh, Jonathan?" shouted Ann, from the back room.

"Aye. I've brung Tom. 'E wants to see Caleb."

"Bring 'im through, then."

Ann had just finished giving Caleb his feed. Her dress was unbuttoned and her breasts lay exposed.

Tom was horrified. They were not full and firmly moulded, like Susannah's, but pendulous and shrivelled, as though every drop of moisture had been sucked out. He could even count his sister's ribs through the taut, dry, palled skin.

"Can I 'owd 'im?" asked Tom.

Ann held Caleb out to him, and Tom gently cradled his nephew in his arms. There seemed something wrong, though. The child was now four weeks old, yet looked no larger than the day he was born. His face was the wizened mask of an old man, and Tom wondered why all babies' faces looked so shapeless. He had witnessed plenty of births in the stables, but at least the foals bore some resemblance to the stallions or mares into which they would one day grow.

He placed his little finger on Caleb's lips, and the infant sucked gratefully at it, as though it were his mother's nipple.

"'E's 'ungry!" remarked Tom.

"Aye," sighed his sister sadly. "Needs more'n *I* can gi' 'im."

"Worr about a wet-nurse?" suggested Tom.

"An' who'd pay?" demanded his brother-in-law. "They'll not do it for nowt — an' most on 'em's got more gin that milk in their tits!"

Tom made a mental note to ask Hannah. Doubtless she'd know all about such matters.

"An' worr've *yoh* 'ad to eat?" persisted Tom.

"Bread," replied his sister. "Jonathan gi's me 'is."

Tom thought of the lunch he had eaten, that day. Even though he was no longer a guest at the Slacks' house, he had still dined well enough: roast beef, vegetables, apples and cheese. The waistband of his breeches was already beginning to stretch.

"So, yoh an't ate owt?"

Jonathan shook his head.

"Din't A'nt Margaret gi' yer owt today?" asked Tom.

"Jonathan went round, but yer uncle an' Will were there," said Ann.

"We don't like to impose," added her husband.

"Bugger what Ben an' Will say!" said Tom. "We can't let yoh an' Caleb starve."

"We could manage," said Jonathan, "if Slack'd only pay fourpence a pair more!"

"'E reckons, if yoh knitted twelve pair a week, instead o' nine, yoh could mek seventeen bob," said Tom.

101

"Twelve!" snorted Jonathan. "On *that* thing?"

He jerked his thumb upwards, in the direction of the attic where he worked.

"What's wrong wi' it?" asked Tom, as he handed Caleb back to his mother.

"What's *rait* wi' it, more like!" exploded Jonathan. "T' shuttle sticks. I need a new 'un, but we couldn't afford t' extra rent on it. I towd George Hicks, burr 'e sez we'll just ay to purrup wi' it. In any case, I made *eleven* pairs on it, last week, but Hicks reckoned only nine on 'em were to standard. Ann an' me 'ad bin through ev'ry pair. Couldn't find a fault in any on 'em. Burr 'e said only nine were fit, so I only got paid for nine!"

"'Ow many ay yer done, this week?" asked Tom.

"Ten — burr I 'ad to spend most o' Friday mendin' t' shuttle. 'Ow many 'e'll pass, this time, God alone knows!"

His gaunt frame began to shake uncontrollably, and his knees suddenly buckled.

Tom caught him and helped him into a chair.

"Stay 'ere," said Tom. "I'll be back in twenty minutes!"

"Where on earth...?"

Ann and Jonathan gazed, open-mouthed, as Tom unwrapped his bundle. Out cascaded bread, cheese, cold roast beef and fruit, as though from some fabled cornucopia.

"Did Margaret gi' yer that?" gasped Jonathan.

Tom shook his head.

"Yoh an't stole it, ay yer?" asked Ann, in a horrified whisper.

"Not really stole," faltered Tom.

"Where d'yer gerrit from, then?" demanded Jonathan.

"Hannah gi'd it me."

"Hannah?"

"T' cook."

"Yoh stole if from Slack's?"

"Not stole," insisted Tom. "I towd Hannah about Caleb, an' she said: 'Poor little mite! Yoh tek it! Owd Rumbleguts can spare it!' That's what she calls 'im. Owd Rumbleguts!"

For all his misgivings, Jonathan could not help but smile.

From a separate bundle, Tom produced a stone flagon.

"Milk," he announced, "for yoh an' Caleb."

Tears welled up in his sister's eyes.

"I don't know what to say."

"Say nowt. Just eat up!"

Setting their qualms aside, Ann and Jonathan complied.

The Black's Head was not as crowded as it had been on Friday.

Tom peered through the smoke.

Yes, Ned Hopkins was there, hunched at a table in the corner, but there was no sign of the stranger, Brandreth.

Tom crossed to the table, peered down and noticed that

Ned's tankard was almost empty.

"Ready for another?" Tom asked.

"I'll not say no," replied Ned, with a wry grin.

Tom crossed to the bar and returned with his order.

"Yer friend norr in tonait?" he queried.

"No."

Tom awaited further information, but none was forthcoming. After a pause, he took from his pocket the leaflet Ned had dropped, the previous Friday, and laid it on the table.

"Where d'yer get that?" Ned demanded.

"They're all over town, I've 'eard," replied Tom, with a non-committal shrug. "Ben found it in t' Owd Eclipse. Who's Brutus?"

"Who 'e is in't important," whispered Ned. "'E's 'elpin' t' Cause; that's all as matters. 'Ave yoh read that?"

"Aye," replied Tom. It wasn't really a lie. Will had read it out, and he was familiar with the gist of it.

"Well, are yer wi' us?"

Tom remembered his brother's advice.

"Rait. Tomorrer nait, 9 o'clock, in 'ere."

"'Ow many's comin'?" asked Tom.

Ned shrugged.

"'Ard to say. Could be a few, could be 'undreds." He broke off suddenly. "'Ow do I know all this in't goin' back to your Will?"

"Bugger 'im!" scoffed Tom. "I've a mind o' my own!"

Tom raised his tankard in a salute. By now, he had begun to warm to his task.

"Death to King George!"

"Ssh!"

Tom looked around. No one had heard. Still, he mustn't get carried away.

A pang of conscience struck him. He remembered how, when he was a mere strip of a boy, Ned Hopkins had picked him up, with as little effort as if he had been a feather, and hoisted him onto those broad, powerful shoulders. Could he do this to an old friend?

Then, he remembered the shilling Will had given him, the previous morning. He had learnt many valuable lessons, just recently. Perhaps the most valuable was that life was hard and unforgiving, and only the selfish survived.

CHAPTER 11

Monday, 19th May, 1817

"'Ow's t' little 'un?"

Hannah looked up from her baking, eager for news.

"Berra," said Tom. "'E drank nearly all that milk 'issen!"

Hannah smiled, basking in the glow of virtue.

"'E dun't know it's gone, does 'e?" queried Tom, pointing in the direction of upstairs.

Hannah smiled, and tapped the side of her bulbous nose in a conspiratorial gesture.

"Yoh should see 'im, Hannah!" enthused Tom. "'E's..."

He felt his eyes suddenly prick, as he described the small, puckered face, its eyes screwed tightly shut, and the rosebud mouth sucking ravenously on his finger, which he had dipped in the milk. Then, with a gurgle, the lips had broken into a happy, toothless grin, which seemed to split the tiny face horizontally.

All the while, Ann and Jonathan had looked on, their faces flushed with pride mixed with apprehension.

"Any chance o' some more, tonait?" Tom's voice instinctively dropped to a whisper, even though there were only the two of them in the smoky kitchen.

"As much as yer want," smiled Hannah.

"You're sure 'e'll not miss it?"

"'Course not!" chuckled the cook-housekeeper. "I can gi' 'im a special treat, tonait. That Mr 'All an' yer cousin are comin' to dinner. There'll be roast duck — an' plenty more milk fer young whatsisname."

"Caleb. Same name as me faither."

Hannah smiled again, and ruffled her fingers through Tom's tousled locks. The gesture was almost maternal and the large brown eyes now radiated genuine compassion and consideration, rather than lust and desire.

"I reckon yoh'll mek a good faither yersen, when t' time comes," she said, but the voice sounded distant and distracted. Perhaps, thought Tom, she was thinking of herself and her own unfulfilled ambitions of motherhood.

"Seen anyone who's took yer fancy, yet?" cooed Hannah, after a pause. Had she uttered the same words on the previous Friday, it might have been with a flirtatious intonation, accompanied by a broad wink. Instead, it was a plain, straightforward question, in the answer to which she had a genuine interest.

Tom said nothing, but the pink flush that rose to his cheeks and ears betrayed his inner conflict.

"I've see 'ow yoh look at Miss Susannah," said Hannah, as if reading his mind. "An' 'er at yoh!"

Tom grew even redder, feeling his palms begin to moisten and his pulse to race.

Hannah gently laid her hand on his shoulder. "She's not fer t' likes o' yoh, lad," she said softly. "She's goin' to marry that cousin o' yourn."

"I know," sighed Tom.

Why couldn't he get her out of his mind? It was two days now since the incident in the bedroom. In the meantime, he had heard the Reverend Cursham's sermon on fornication. He still felt a sense of fear, as he pictured the yawning chasm which, according to the vicar, waited to swallow up sinners. Now, though, the fear was beginning to evaporate and give way to resentment.

Last night, on his way back to the Slacks' house from the Black's Head, he had called on his aunt and uncle once again. Once Ben and Will were in bed, he had confided to Margaret the details of the vicar's sermon — though tactfully omitting the true reason for his guilty conscience.

"Dun't tek no notice," she had said. "Vicars are no diff'rent from t' rest o' t' gentry. They need to keep t' likes of us in us place, so they scare us wi' visions of 'Ell an' damnation. If yer Reverend Cursham wants to see worr 'Ell's like, just send 'im round 'ere — 'specially when Ben's in one of 'is drunken rages!"

"'Ere," said Hannah, suddenly breaking in upon his thoughts, "yoh an' Miss Susannah — yoh an't bin, er, doin' owt, ay yer?"

"'Course not!" thundered Tom, summoning up every ounce of outrage and indignation he could muster.

"Yoh wun't be t' fost 'un," replied Hannah, smiling indulgently. "There wor young Josiah, as wor stable-lad afore yoh. She wor allus smilin' an' winkin' at 'im. A reg'lar gill-flirt, she is! What that cousin o' yourn sees in 'er, I dun't know!"

"'Er faither's money?" suggested Tom, with a wry smile.

"'Er faither thinks she's as sweet an' pure as 'er

108

namesake in t' Bible!" cackled Hannah. "But you're a shrewd 'un, yoh are! She'll not catch *yoh* out!"

Tom smiled back. If only she knew the truth!

"Tom!"

"T' master!" gasped Hannah, at the sound of the voice, and hastily resumed rolling the pastry.

The great bulk of Samuel Slack loomed in the doorway.

"There y'are, lad! 'Ow good are yer at movin' furniture?"

Furniture? Tom's flesh turned to ice. Surely Susannah hadn't told her father everything? He was almost tempted to make a full confession, there and then.

"Yer know Mr 'All, t' lawyer?" asked Slack.

Tom nodded.

"'E wants some things shiftin' in 'is 'ouse an' office. Needs a big, strong lad."

"Worr about Richard?" asked Tom.

His master looked as though he had been pole-axed.

"Richard? 'E's Mr 'All's clerk. Yer can't expect *'im* to shift furniture."

Why not? thought Tom. He'd known his cousin, in his younger days, clean out the stables with Ben and Old Caleb. Still, now he was moving up in the world, he could hardly be expected to get his hands dirty and callused! Not that Susannah was averse to being touched with rough hands, as he very well remembered!

"Yer'd best gerr along down there," said Slack, "'cos I promised 'im yer'd do it."

Tom took a long draught of ale and leaned back against the wall of the back room in the Black's Head. He was exhausted, and every muscle in his body ached.

Robert Hall, like so many bachelors, was very pernickety: everything had to be in exactly the right place. If he had changed his mind once, that day, he had changed it a hundred times!

"Over there. A foot or so to the right. No, a little more to the left. Bring it forward. A little further. Too far."

While his employer had been pre-occupied supervising Tom in the living quarters upstairs, Richard had remained in the office, poring over piles of papers.

There were about twenty people in the back room: more than Tom had expected. Most were known to him: chiefly framework knitters, like his brother-in-law; although Jonathan was conspicuous by his absence.

As he scanned their worn, tired faces, Tom wondered which of them might be the mysterious Brutus.

There was a general air of unease and disaffection, which Ned was doing his best to dispel.

"'As a date bin fixed for t' risin', yet?" demanded a tall, unshaven figure, whom Tom recognized as Simon Wright, a weaver.

"Some time in early June," replied Ned. "Jerry'll tell us, when 'e gets 'ere."

"Why not before?" persisted Wright.

"We need time to get weapons together. Besides, do it

any sooner, an' t' moon'll be full. T' longer we keep it to ussens, t' less chance there is on it bein' leaked to t' Government."

Tom felt sweat forming at the back of his neck.

"Leaked?" repeated another voice. "Who by?"

"There's allus faint-'earts," said Ned. "Some folk'll do owt fer money!"

"Yer really reckon we can do it?" added a third voice.

"We can't fail!" cried Ned triumphantly. "They might as well try stoppin' t' tide!"

Two long knocks sounded on the door. There was a pause, then three more in rapid succession.

"Who's that?" asked Tom.

Ned held up his hand to quell any panic.

"It'll be Jerry."

Ned crossed to the door and opened it. In strode the stranger Tom had seen with Ned, the previous Friday. He was accompanied by a short, fresh-faced man, who smiled continually.

"Evenin', lads!" cried Jeremiah Brandreth. "Any ale goin'?"

"Yes. 'Ere."

Tom poured out two tankards of ale from the large jug on the table in front of him. As he handed one to Brandreth, his hand began to shake, causing some of the ale to spill.

"Careful, lad!" said Brandreth, taking the vessel. "Can't waste good ale — norr at today's prices!"

The room erupted into raucous laughter, all of it directed

111

at Tom, whose embarrassment grew worse.

"Who's this?" asked Brandreth.

"Tom Stone," replied Ned. "'E's a good lad. I'll vouch for 'im."

"I'm sorry, sir," Tom muttered.

"No 'sirs', lad," smiled Brandreth, setting him at ease. "There'll be no ranks or titles in t' new republic — no bowin' an' scrapin' to yer 'betters'. We'll all be equal. We'll create a new world — a new order!"

He clapped Tom heartily on the shoulder. Then, draining his tankard in a single gulp, he turned and indicated his companion.

"This is 'Enry Sampson, t' Bulwell delegate."

The rest mumbled their greetings.

Brandreth's gaze took in the assembled faces.

"Is this all that's comin'?"

"We were expectin' more," said Ned, "but . . ."

"There's plenty next door. Why aren't *they* in 'ere?"

"Most on 'em's got jobs at Stanton Mill an' daren't risk losin' 'em."

Brandreth's brow furrowed.

"Well, so long as we can rely on more, when t' time comes."

"There'll be plenty turn out, Jerry," Ned reassured him. "I know they will."

"Aye," muttered a voice behind Tom, "an' pigs'll fly!"

"It dun't matter," said Brandreth, ignoring the

interruption. "It's best there's only a few in each area as knows t' plans."

"D'yer know when it's gonna be, yet?" asked Ned.

"Aye. June the 9th. Mansfield and Sutton'll rise at 9 o'clock, Bulwell at 10, an' Nottingham at 11. We're all meetin' on t' Forest in Nottingham at 11. When we get there, ev'ry man'll be gi'd 100 guineas, a pound o' bread, a pound o' beef an' a quart of ale."

"An' where's *that* comin' from?" demanded Simon Wright.

"We'll gerrit," insisted Brandreth.

"Steal it, yer mean!"

There was a menacing silence, during which Brandreth took a pace towards the weaver.

"We'll gerrit," he repeated.

"Yer still reckon on 30,000 turnin' up?" asked Ned.

"More."

"An' where's t' Militia, while all this is goin' on?" asked Wright. "Fast asleep?"

"We'll attack t' barracks an' ask 'em to join us."

"An' worr if they don't?"

"We tek a black flag an' go to wokk!"

All laughed, except Wright, who remained unconvinced.

"Worr about t' cavalry? We'll ay *no* chance agen *them*."

Brandreth smiled and produced a small bundle from inside his coat. He laid it on one of the tables and carefully unwrapped it, revealing a strange object consisting of four

113

metal spikes joined together at the base.

"What the 'ell's *that*?" demanded Wright.

"A 'crow's foot'," replied Brandreth. "Yer just chuck 'em on t' ground. Look."

He gave a quick demonstration.

"See? Whichever road it lands, it allus 'as one spike stickin' up. If they use cavalry, it'll cripple t' 'osses!"

Tom felt sick. Laming horses! How could anyone be party to that?

"Supposin' we tek Nottingham," cut in Wright. "Worr 'appens then?"

"We'll tek boats down t' Trent an' seize Newark."

"Worr about t' rest o' t' country?" asked Ned.

"An' worr about weapons?" added Wright. "Where are we s'posed to get *them* from?"

"Weedon army depot. T' Wolverhampton men'll tek that, then go on an' tek Belvoir Castle. There's cannons there."

"An' then we'll march south, pickin' up more men on t' way?" asked Ned.

Brandreth slipped an arm round the ex-farrier's powerful shoulders.

"Aye, Ned," he grinned. "We've even gorr us own battle hymn."

He leapt onto the table and began to sing in a strong, ringing tenor:

> *Ev'ry man his skill must try.*
> *He must turn out and not deny.*
> *No bloody soldier must he dread.*

He must turn out an' fight for
bread.
The time has come, you plainly see,
The Government opposed must be!
"He must turn out an' fight for bread."

As Tom settled down to sleep, that night, those words were still singing through his head.

CHAPTER 12

Thursday, 22nd May, 1817

The following day, Tom had promptly reported to Will, who had duly rewarded him with another shilling. Will had then hired a horse from the Old Eclipse stables, and gone off to present his report to his superiors.

Tom's dreams were troubled, for the next few days, dominated by the handsome, dark features of Jeremiah Brandreth and by the fear that he had betrayed a trust.

By day, though, his thoughts and energies were occupied elsewhere. When not wanted by Samuel Slack for jobs around the house, he was leased out to Robert Hall, who had had a further change of heart, *vis-à-vis* the arrangement of his office furniture.

It had meant the neglecting of his lessons, but Henry Jessop had assured him that, if necessary he would willingly make up the time in the evenings.

There were two rooms on the ground floor of Robert Hall's premises which were used as offices: one as a main reception area, which was occupied by Richard in his capacity as clerk; the other, Hall's inner sanctum.

At about 10 o'clock on the Thursday morning, Hall had gone to visit a client in connection with a will, leaving

Richard to attend to any visitors, whilst Tom was moving furniture in Hall's room.

Tom was hot and dry from his exertions. On a table in a corner stood a small crystal decanter of pale golden sherry. He removed the stopper and took a furtive sip. The decanter was almost full, and Hall was unlikely to notice the absence of such a minuscule quantity.

The liquid tasted very dry and slightly salty, but seemed to cut through the dust in his mouth and throat. All he now needed was a pint of ale to cleanse it thoroughly. If only he could find an excuse for leaving!

Hall himself was out, but Richard was acting as his eyes and ears, and would no doubt relish the opportunity of sneaking to his employer, if he found Tom taking leave from his duties.

Tom suddenly remembered that there was no need to concoct a reason for leaving. There were two doors to Robert Hall's little office: one communicated with the outer office, where Richard sat; the other gave onto the passage leading to the back of the house, where a door opened into Stone Cutter Court. He could then simply slip down the alley to his right into Church Street, and the Ram Inn was almost directly across the road.

He was about to leave, when he heard the outer door of the building open, and someone entered the other office.

"Yoh!" he heard Richard yell. "Worr're *yoh* doin' 'ere?"

In the confusion of the moment, Tom noticed, his cousin had dropped the refined accent he had cultivated for his employer's benefit and lapsed into the local dialect.

"What do *yoh* think?" answered the other. "I've come fer t' money."

117

The door to the outer office was slightly ajar, and Tom manoeuvred himself until he had a perfect view of Richard's desk and the stranger who stood on the other side of it.

In fact, the newcomer was vaguely familiar: about Tom's height, of slim build, with brown hair, wearing a coat in a dazzling shade of green. It was Jacob Smalley, Susannah's unwelcome admirer.

"I haven't got it!" Richard was saying. He seemed to have recovered his composure somewhat and had reverted to the cultured tones befitting a lawyer's clerk.

"Well, yer'd berra gerrit!" retorted Smalley, in a menacing whisper.

"But where can *I* get my hands on twenty guineas?" pleaded Richard. "That's more than a year's salary!"

"Yer shoulda thought o' that, afore yer gorr into playin' cards," replied Smalley, in a voice of almost sweet reasonableness. "Yoh owe George Tully ten, an' all — but that's '*is* affair, not mine."

Richard had turned as pale as his shirt.

"I can't . . ."

"Today's Thursday," cut in Smalley. "Yer've gorr until next Sat'day, or I go straight to 'All an' Slack.'"

"No!"

"An' yer know their views on gamin'," continued Smalley. "Yer could lose yer job. Yer'll certainly lose Susannah — an' then t' way's open fer me!"

"She hates the sight of you!" thundered Richard.

"'Er faither dun't — an' it'll be '*is* view as counts. A

118

druggist's assistant's as good a catch as a lawyer's clerk."

Richard was on his feet. The colour had now returned to his features, and his whole body was tensed, as though he was about to spring across the desk and lock his fingers around Smalley's throat.

"Next Sat'day," repeated Smalley, and, before Richard could react, he had vanished, slamming the outer door behind him.

Tom left by the back exit, as he had planned. Once in Church Street, he looked to right and left, before spotting Smalley's distinctive green coat disappearing in the direction of Market Place.

He set off in pursuit, until his quarry disappeared inside a druggist's shop, just past the White Hart. He noticed the name on the sign outside the door: George Ellis.

Tom smiled to himself, then headed for the Ram. There was much to mull over.

"Miss Susannah!"

Susannah Slack halted on the stairs and peered down into the shadows below in search of the voice's owner.

Tom stepped forward.

"Oh, it's you!" said Susannah, in a voice that would have frozen the River Maun. She had been distant towards him, ever since Sunday morning. Why? Fear of everlasting damnation, inspired by the Reverend Cursham's sermon? Shame, that she had so demonstratively "expressed her gratitude" towards Tom? Or guilt that she had betrayed Richard?

"Miss Susannah, I'm sorry."

Her icy look thawed somewhat, but she said nothing.

"If I've done or said owt to offend yer," continued Tom, "I . . . Well, er, that is, last Sat'day . . . I know 'ow angry yer wor about worr 'appened. What we did wor wrong, an' . . ."

He broke off suddenly. She was smiling at him: a smile with a hint of mockery, certainly, but a warm, gentle mockery such as can only exist between two people who are close.

"It's not *that* I'm angry about," she said softly. "I've no regrets."

"What, then?"

"My robe. It was pure silk — a present from Father. It took Hannah simply *days* to get the stain out. I couldn't tell her what it really was. I had to lie, and say I'd spilt unguent on it!"

She tossed her head back and laughed at the memory.

"You're norr angry wi' *me*, then?"

She laid a hand on his arm and squeezed it gently.

"Of course not."

Panic suddenly seized him.

"Y' an't towd Richard, ay yer?"

"Why should I?"

"Well, yoh an' 'im . . ."

"I told you: it's Father's wish. I have to obey."

Tom swallowed hard before his next question.

"Ay yoh an' Richard ever . . ."

There was a strained pause, as the question sank in; then she tilted her head back and laughed again.

"Of course not. It's only by tempting him with the thought of . . . that — and Father's dowry — that I can keep him interested!"

For one brief moment, Tom felt a twinge of pity for his cousin, dangling from a hook like some angler's prey. He was even tempted to mention Richard's current financial plight and the dire fate which awaited her at the hands of Jacob Smalley.

Above them, a familiar heavy footfall was audible on the landing.

"Father!" whispered Susannah.

Tom made his way hastily towards the cellar, whilst Susannah moved, at a more leisurely pace, in the direction of the drawing room.

"Tom!" cried Slack, as he descended the stairs with unaccustomed rapidity, waving a paper bearing a red wax seal. "D'yoh know John Gresham, t' pawnbroker, corner o' Wass Lane?"

Tom nodded. His father and mother had always been careful with money. Even so, there had been times when they had needed a little extra, and either Tom or Will had been despatched to the little shop with some minor items of household furniture, which had raised the few necessary coppers. He still remembered the shame he had felt, as he had slipped out of the shop, and how he had dreaded meeting anyone he knew.

Since his father had died, and he had moved in with Ben and Margaret, his visits to the pawnshop had become a regular occurrence. Even so, as he had discovered, his aunt still had to sell herself to any stranger to keep body and soul together.

Thinking back to the Reverend Cursham's sermon, Tom suddenly felt cold. If he stood in danger of eternal hellfire merely for harbouring "unclean thoughts" about his master's daughter, how much worse must it be for Margaret?

"Did yoh 'ear worr I just said?" bellowed Slack, jolting Tom's mind back to the present.

"Sorry, sir," he mumbled.

"I thought not," scowled Slack. "Got yer mind on other things, eh?"

Tom nodded. If only he knew!

"John Gresham, pawnbroker, Wass Lane," repeated Slack, thrusting the missive into Tom's hand. "Tek it straight round there."

Good! thought Tom. After that, he'd try and find Ned, and see if there was any more news about Jeremiah Brandreth, before going round to see if young Caleb was improving, thanks to the unwitting contributions to his diet from Slack.

"Then back fer yer lessons."

"Burr I've . . ."

"Yer've missed out t' last two days, wi' wokkin' down at Mr 'All's, an't yer?"

"Well, yeah, but . . ."

"But nowt! Can't neglect yer readin' and writin'," affirmed Slack. "Besides, Jessop 'as too much time on 'is 'ands, these days. As I've said afore: if I pay a man eight guineas a year, I expect eight guineasworth o' wokk out on 'im."

Tom tried to hide his disappointment. Strangely, he was enjoying his lessons; yet he was also eager to find out more about the "Nottingham Captain".

Tucking the letter inside his coat, he set off on his errand.

Passing the rows of shops at the bottom of Stockwell Gate, Tom found Wass Lane about a hundred yards down on his left, where it entered the bottom end of Black's Head Yard, then veered off sharply to the right, running behind tightly-packed cottages and stables, before it finally came out onto Queen Street. Outside the little shop at the right-hand corner hung the three brass balls that marked it out as a pawnbroker's.

Tom had just reached the door, when it unexpectedly opened and a hunched figure emerged.

Tom's jaw shot open in surprise.

"Jonathan!"

The figure straightened, and the dying rays of the sun caught the normally pallid, freckled features, giving them a false appearance of glowing health. He tried to avoid Tom, but the latter shot out an arm and gripped his sleeve.

"There's no shame in it," said Tom gently.

"In't there?" glowered his brother-in-law. "When yoh ay to pop yer wife's weddin' ring to feed yer child? That's not shame? That wor my mother's ring. She gi'd it me, just afore she died. She said to me: 'Jonathan, keep it till yer find yersen a good lass, an' may yer be as 'appy as me an' yer Dad've bin.' I promised I would, an' I kept that promise. Dear God, I never thought it'd come to this!"

"Bad week?"

"It's Hicks. It's as if 'e's punishin' us for ayin' young Caleb — as if 'e *wants* 'im to starve!"

"What's 'appened?"

"'E's purr us on coarse worsteds. Sez there's no demand for fine worsted 'ose, no more. Burr it only pays eightpence a pair. Eightpence!"

He almost spat the word out.

"'Ow much did 'e gi' yer?" asked Tom, pointing towards the pawnbroker's.

"Two bob!"

Tom felt in his pocket. He still had the shilling Will had given him for his latest piece of information. He held the coin out to Jonathan.

"'Ere."

"I can't!"

"Tek it!" insisted Tom, pressing the shilling into his brother-in-law's palm. "If not fer yersen, at least tek it for Ann an' Caleb's sake!"

Jonathan was shaking, tears welling up in his eyes. He threw his arms around Tom's neck and began to sob uncontrollably.

Passers-by stared at the two men locked in an embrace and exchanged lewd comments, but Tom was oblivious to the insults. Perhaps he should miss the lesson, get more food from Hannah and take it round to Mitre Court as soon as possible.

Of course, at heart, he knew that was impossible: Slack would never countenance such an abuse of his trust. It was through him that Tom had been granted this opportunity, and his word was law.

The sobs had subsided, and Jonathan was wiping his eyes on the back of his threadbare sleeve, whilst muttering incoherent expressions of gratitude.

Tom patted him on the back.

"Yer'd best get back. 'Ow're they copin'?"

"Weak — but we'll manage."

Tom remembered how drawn and haggard his sister had looked, when he had called round, the previous day. There had been a vacant look in her eyes, as though they no longer saw this world, but were already focused on the next.

The Stones were not renowned for their longevity. True, he and Will were both strong and healthy, but their parents had both died young, and even "Old" Amos had been a mere 54. Ann, as the eldest child, had taken on huge responsibilities at an early age, and the strain was now proving too much.

Well, he would do what he could, but his lessons beckoned. In the end, it would be education that hauled him out of the rut of poverty that enslaved the others.

CHAPTER 13

Friday, 23rd May, 1817

As his eyes opened on a new day, Tom knew he had made the right choice, the previous evening. The words of the poem Jessop had made him read aloud were still ringing ears:

> *I will not cease from mental fight,*
> *Nor shall my sword sleep in my*
> *hand, Till we have built Jerusalem*
> *In England's green and pleasant*
> *land.*

As he had read, he had noticed Jessop's eyes glinting fiercely behind his polished lenses.

"'Till we have built Jerusalem,'" the tutor had repeated softly. "Inspiring words, eh, Tom?"

"Aye," Tom had agreed. The more he thought about them, the more they reminded him of Jeremiah Brandreth. It was the kind of stirring language *he* had talked.

Having breakfasted heartily, Tom was summoned upstairs to Slack's private room, where his master was sitting at his desk, writing.

"I want yer to go to Mr 'All's office," said Slack.

Tom winced. Not again! The previous day, Hall had

pronounced himself satisfied with the latest re-arrangement of the furniture, both in his office and his living quarters.

Slack smiled.

"Not more furniture removin'," he reassured Tom. "Just summat I want yer to tek down there."

From beneath a mountain of paper, he produced a sealed package, which he handed to Tom.

"Lessons still goin' well?" he enquired, as Tom was about to go out.

Tom nodded enthusiastically.

"I've gorr 'igh 'opes fer yer," smiled the hosier. "So 'as Jessop."

"Aye, 'e said, last nait, 'e wor rait pleased wi' me," confirmed Tom. He did not mention that the tutor had compared his achievements with those of young Joseph, much to the latter's detriment.

As he made his way down West Gate, Tom kept reciting to himself:

> *Till we have built Jerusalem*
> *In England's green and pleasant*
> *land.*

Passing the Old Eclipse, he saw Ned Hopkins leaning against the doorpost, surveying the passing world over the top of a tankard.

The ex-farrier raised his arm, as though about to propose a toast.

"Can't stop!" shouted Tom, waving the sealed package. "See yer in about five minutes!"

Ned acknowledged him with another gesture of the tankard.

As he made his way down Church Street, Tom found his progress impeded for about five minutes by a stagecoach that was attempting to negotiate the archway into Swan Yard. Curious shoppers gathered round, shouting abuse and advice in almost equal measures, to both of which the coachman responded with obscene gestures.

At last, the vehicle disappeared, and Tom was able to resume his journey. Just past the Swan, he passed McLellan's Yard, where actors from the theatre there were practising juggling and acrobatics.

Tom had proceeded barely fifty yards down Church Street, when, to his right, he noticed the door to George Ellis's shop open, and Richard came out, glancing nervously to right and left.

Tom dodged behind a horse and cart, praying he hadn't been seen. When he emerged, there was no sign of his cousin.

He continued his journey, but, as he came abreast of the druggist's shop, he paused. On the outside of the window were pasted advertisements for a wide variety of exotic-sounding remedies: Bostock's Elixir; Belton's British Oil; Stoughton's Stomach Bitters; Brodman's Nervous Cordial; and, most impressive of all, Bateman's Pectoral Drops, "a cure for the stone, gravel, colic, colds and distempers".

Inside, Jacob Smalley stood behind the counter, smiling unctuously at a well-dressed, middle-aged lady, as he weighed a selection of ingredients in his apothecary's scales. Was he merely trying to impress the customer, or was the look of self-satisfaction somehow connected with Richard's recent visit?

From the premises next door came the inviting smell of freshly baked bread and an old crone was engaged in a violent altercation with the proprietor, George Shippam, over the price of his loaves.

Tom was about to follow Richard when a sheet of paper in the road caught his eye. He picked it up and read it. It was in large type, short and to the point:

> The new dawn is about to break!
> Wake up, men of Mansfield! If you
> truly value freedom and justice, be
> at the Black's Head, Market Place,
> at 9 o'clock, on Friday, the 23rd of
> May.
> Long live the Republic!
> Liberty! Equality! Fraternity!
> BRUTUS

Tom hastily folded the sheet and stuffed it in his pocket.

When he arrived at Hall's premises, he rapped sharply on the door of the outer office.

"Come in!"

As Tom entered, Richard shot up from his chair, his face registering surprise and horror. When he saw that the newcomer was Tom, the expression was swiftly replaced by one of relief; so Tom deduced his cousin had not seen him, as he was leaving George Ellis's shop.

"Yes?" enquired Richard, with an air of formal detachment, as though addressing a total stranger.

"I've brung this for Mr 'All," announced Tom, placing the package on the desk. "It's from Mr Slack. Is 'e in?"

"No," replied Richard brusquely. "Leave it here. *I'll* give it him."

"Mr Slack said it wor for Mr 'All, not yoh!" said Tom, snatching up the package.

"I'll see he gets it," replied Richard, his grey eyes blazing.

"What's up wi' yoh?" asked Tom. "Yer look as if yer'd see'd a ghost! Who did yer think I wor — Smalley?"

The colour slowly drained from Richard's cheeks.

"What do *you* know about Smalley?"

"Y' owe 'im twenty guineas — an' 'e wants it by tomorrer."

"How . . ?"

"I over'eard yer, yest'dy, when I wor in there."

Tom gestured towards Robert Hall's inner sanctum.

"Y' an't said owt, ay yer?" begged Richard, again lapsing into the vernacular in his agitation.

"No."

"Good. Well, don't, or . . ."

"Or what?"

Richard stiffened, and became the efficient lawyer's clerk once more.

"Leave the package on the desk, and I'll see Mr Hall gets it."

"Think yer better'n me, 'cos yer can read an' write, don't yer?" snapped Tom. "Well, *I'll* be able to read an' write as good as yoh soon. Then I'll show yer!"

Richard stared for several moments at his cousin in mute astonishment. Then, tossing back his elegantly coiffured mane of fair hair, he howled with laughter, his face growing so red that Tom feared he might succumb to a fir of apoplexy.

"What's so funny?" demanded Tom, leaning across the desk.

"You! Read and write!"

"I allus could, but nobody gi'd me a chance. Jessop sez I'm good."

Richard was no longer laughing.

"You mean old Slack was serious about Jessop giving you lessons?"

"Why not? If *yoh* can do it, so can I! I'm fed up o' t' smell of 'oss shit! *I'm* goin' to be a gentleman, an' all, one day!" Tom added, pointing at his cousin.

"You? A gentleman? When?"

"After . . ."

Tom brought himself up short. He had been about to say: "After the revolution." He must be more careful! Brandreth's oratory was starting to get to him! In any case, there would be no gentlemen after the revolution, if what Brandreth said were true.

"After I can read an' write proper," he finished, rather lamely.

Richard let out an arrogant bray of laughter, as he rocked backwards and forwards in his chair.

Tom spun on his heels and rushed towards the door where he almost collided with the diminutive figure of Robert Hall.

"Steady!" remonstrated the lawyer sternly, before his

expression softened and the pale blue eyes twinkled with a smile of recognition.

"Sorry, sir. Mr Slack just sent me to bring yer that," mumbled Tom, pointing to the sealed package on the table.

The lawyer muttered a brief word of thanks and stood aside to let Tom out.

Tom made no effort to hurry back. His master was a busy man, and would not miss him for a while. Just time for a pint at the Old Eclipse and a word or two with Ned Hopkins.

When he reached the top of Church Street, there was no sign of the ex-farrier, but he could hear the sound of music from within. Pushing open the door, he noticed about a dozen customers, whose attention was focused on the bar, where Ned Hopkins was concluding an old military ballad in his gruff baritone:

> *An' if ever I 'list for a soldier agen,*
> *T' Devil shall be me Sergeant.*

His efforts were greeted by hearty cheers, loud shouts of approbation, requests for encores and the rhythmic banging of tankards on tables, to which Ned responded with a deep bow, as he swept his hat in front of his listeners, inviting financial rewards.

There was a chorus of embarrassed coughs, and a few coins were dropped into the proffered receptacle.

"Gi' us another, Ned!" shouted a voice from the smoke-wreathed shadows.

"'Owd on!" replied the ex-farrier, gesturing towards the bar, where George Cadman was replenishing his tankard.

Ned took a coin from his hat, paid for the drink and took

a deep, refreshing draught.

"Rait," he said, at length, then launched into a bitter rendition of *Over the Hills and Far Away*, the tears visibly welling up in the cornflower blue eyes, as he heard again the cannon's roar and the clash of steel on steel.

Again, the response was vociferous, and Ned held out the hat in anticipation.

A few more coins jingled into it.

As Ned tipped the contents out onto the bar, Tom dipped into his pocket, found two halfpennies, and added them to the collection.

Tom watched him count up the takings and felt tears pricking in his own eyes. One-and-twopence-farthing! That a once-proud artisan should be reduced to singing for a few coppers!

Ned noticed Tom's interest in the pile of coins, and hastily stuffed them back into his hat, as though fearful that Tom might steal them. Surely Ned knew him better than that! No, on second thoughts, perhaps it was not any fear of theft: perhaps it was a sense of shame and embarrassment.

"Are we on fer tonait?" asked Tom. "T' Black's 'Ead?"

Ned looked around. William Dobb and John Benton, two local tradesmen, were at the bar, ordering fresh drinks. Ned manoeuvred Tom out of earshot.

"Can't be too careful."

"No," agreed Tom. "So? Is it on fer tonait?"

"Is *worr* on fer tonait?" asked Ned suspiciously.

Tom showed him the sheet he had found in Church

Street, and Ned cast another furtive look round the bar.

"Yer'd best come early. We're expectin' a good turnout."

The Black's Head was less crowded than he had imagined: perhaps a dozen men, at the most. In particular, he noted that Simon Wright, the outspoken weaver, was conspicuous by his absence.

"It's gone nine," grumbled a voice next to him. He turned, to see a slim figure, with tousled fair hair, whose face was mostly obscured by the upturned collar of his tattered grey coat.

No sign of either Ned or Brandreth, thought Tom. Had the Nottingham Captain suspected he was being spied upon and cried off? Somehow, if that were the case, Tom sensed that his conscience would feel easier.

At that moment, the door swung open, and there he stood, surveying the assembly with that nonchalant, almost arrogant, swagger.

"This is all there is?" he asked, cocking his head back to address Ned who was hovering at his right shoulder.

"There's bin word sent round," replied the ex-farrier, with an apologetic shrug. He showed Brandreth a copy of the latest "Brutus" leaflet.

"Can't be 'elped," said Brandreth, brisk and businesslike. "Yer know who they are, dun't yer, Ned — the faint-'earts?"

"Aye."

"Well, take good note on 'em, 'cos, come t' Republic, they're t' fost 'uns to 'ang!"

He noticed dubious frowns on several faces — including Tom's — and hastily changed the subject.

"Remember 'Enry Sampson, as come wi' me, last time?"

Several heads nodded.

"'E come to see me, this mornin'. 'E reckons there's 100 or more comin' from Bulwell. T' same from 'Ucknall."

An optimistic murmur ran round the tiny room, but Tom noticed that some of the worn, craggy faces wore sceptical expressions.

"There should be another 300 from Sutton," continued Brandreth. Then, with a challenging look at the assembled faces, he asked: "'Ow many from Mansfield?"

"They're just scared to show their faces yet, Jerry," said Ned, trying to sound reassuring. "Yer know 'ow scared they are o' t' masters."

"All t' more reason to get rid o' t' masters!" snapped Brandreth. He was rapidly becoming angered by the surrounding apathy.

"An' what's 'appenin' in t' rest o' t' country?" demanded a voice from the back.

"There's a meetin' in t' Three Salmons, in Nottingham, on Sunday, burr I'll find out more on Monday, when Oliver, t' London delegate, comes."

"Talkin' of Oliver," cut in Ned, "ay we 'eard owt more about Mitchell?"

"Who?" asked a voice from the back.

Ned apprised him of the details of Mitchell's arrest and imprisonment.

"An' this Oliver wor wi' 'im?" pressed the voice.

135

Brandreth nodded.

"So, 'ow do we know Oliver can be trusted?"

There was a deathly silence, as Brandreth located the speaker in the crowd. Then, with a sudden movement, he grabbed the man by the coat and hauled him to his feet.

"If I say 'e can be trusted, 'e can be trusted! Rait!"

The man nodded lamely, and Brandreth released him.

"Anyone else yer don't trust?" demanded Brandreth defiantly of the meeting in general.

"Worr're *yoh* gonna be doin', come June t' 9th?" piped up another voice.

"I've a meetin' over in Pentrich, on t' 8th," replied Brandreth. "I'll be stayin' over an' leadin' 'em to Nottingham, on t' 9th."

The next hour was spent in relaying facts and figures about rebel groups in Derbyshire, Leicestershire, Yorkshire and Lancashire, and signs of boredom soon became evident, as Brandreth's speech was punctuated by loud belches and emissions of wind, all of which he ignored. Either he was a man of steely determination, Tom reflected, or deaf!

At last, the meeting broke up, and only Tom and Ned remained.

"Nobody's found out, ay they, like your Will?" asked Ned.

Tom shook his head.

"'Cos yer know what Jerry'd do to traitors."

Ned slowly drew a finger across his fleshy throat and his eyes hardened.

136

Tom felt his stomach tightening, when the warm, humorous light suddenly returned once more to Ned's eyes and he smiled.

"Good job I can trust yer!" he chortled, slapping Tom heartily across the back.

"Aye," said Tom. He grinned cheerfully at Ned, but his heart was heavy. For how much longer could he keep up this deception?

CHAPTER 14

Wednesday, 28th May, 1817

Almost a week had passed, and nothing had happened. Tom had duly reported to Will, on the Saturday morning, and received his shilling. The information about Pentrich had been particularly welcomed by his brother, and Tom wondered if he should have kept it to himself. In fact, he was beginning to have doubts about *any* involvement in this wretched business. Ned's warning about the fate that awaited traitors had been no joke.

However, Brandreth had made no more appearances in Mansfield, and Ned's face seemed to be growing longer by the day.

"No news?" Tom asked him, that morning, when he had bumped into the ex-farrier by the old market cross.

"Nowt," had come the blunt reply, and Ned continued up West Gate to his home in Alfred Court, one of the warrens of little alleys connecting West Gate with Back Lane West.

Perhaps Ned was growing disillusioned with the Cause. Tom fervently hoped so: his conscience would weigh less heavy, if Ned backed out before 9th June and so avoided arrest with the others.

Tom debated returning at once to Slack's home. There

was no rush, though: his master had gone to Nottingham on business and would not be back before nightfall, and his next lesson with Jessop was not until two o'clock. He decided to head for Bark Court. Ben would be at work, so Aunt Margaret would no doubt welcome the company.

He opened the door and peered round it. There was no sign of his aunt. Perhaps she had gone round to see Ann, Jonathan and Caleb. He decided to call on her, anyway.

"A'nt Margaret!"

There was no reply, and he was about to leave, when he heard a sound from upstairs. He was just able to discern the words: "Who is it?"

"It's Tom. Where are yer?"

"Up 'ere."

Something was not right. Tom swiftly mounted the rickety stairs and entered his aunt's bedroom. The room was in darkness. He opened the shutters, letting the morning sunlight flood into the room, looked down at the bed and gasped in horror at the sight of his aunt's face.

The left eye was completely closed, and an ugly purple bruise was forming around it, whilst the lower lip was split and encrusted in dry blood.

"What the bloody 'ell 'appened?" demanded Tom.

Margaret turned away, recoiling from both the light and Tom's question.

"I fell," she answered, rather lamely.

Tom shook his head.

"It wor 'im again, worn't it?"

His aunt hesitated, and then slowly nodded, though the

139

effort caused her evident pain.

"Worr 'appened?"

She turned her head away, and Tom repeated the question.

"'E caught me."

The swollen lips barely moved as she spoke, and Tom had to strain to hear the words.

"At t' Black's 'Ead?" prompted Tom.

His aunt muttered something that Tom interpreted as assent.

"Wi' another bloke?"

She responded with a painful shake of the head and continued: "'E wor lookin' fer a woman 'issen. 'E come up to me an' sez, "Ow much?' 'E gorr an 'elluva shock when 'e saw it wor me — just like *yoh* did!"

Despite the agony it caused her, she couldn't help a coarse laugh at the memory of the incident, and Tom noticed that two of her upper teeth had been knocked out.

Tom felt his whole body tense, and the blood began to pump furiously in his temples.

"I'll kill the bastard!"

He was about to rush from the room, but his aunt held up her hand.

"No!"

"Why not?"

"It wun't do no good. It'd only get *yoh* into trouble."

"I don't care!"

"Tom! Don't!"

Pain showed in her one visible brown eye, but also a glint of steely determination. Tom knew she meant it. Even if Ben broke every bone in her body, she would not see a single hair of his head harmed. At the same time, he felt there was something she was holding back.

"There's summat else, in't there?" he demanded.

"What?"

"I dunno. Summat."

"There's nowt."

Margaret lapsed into silence.

"D'yer want me to send for Ann?" asked Tom.

"No. Keep 'er out on it."

There was no more to be said, and he left. Yet, however much he wanted to abide by his aunt's wishes, Tom still couldn't stem the tide of anger surging inside him.

Reaching Duck Lane, he contemplated turning right and making for the Old Eclipse. Instead, he forced himself to turn left and return to Slack's house.

As he emerged from Duck Lane into West Passage, he knew that, were he to meet his uncle now he would break his neck without a moment's hesitation.

"Answer, t' door, Tom!"

Tom emerged from the kitchen, in response to his master's bidding and opened the front door.

Richard was standing on the doorstep, hat in hand, and took an involuntary step backwards when he saw Tom.

141

However, within seconds, he had recovered his composure.

"Tell Miss Susannah I'm here," he commanded, in clipped tones.

"I'll enquire if Miss Susannah will see you," replied Tom, affecting his cousin's haughty manner and accent. Then, unable to resist the temptation, he added: "What name shall I say?"

A nerve twitched at the corner of Richard's taut mouth, and twin spots of colour appeared on his cheeks, before he thrust his way unceremoniously past Tom into the hallway.

"They're goin' out to dinner," said Tom.

"I know. I'm going with them, but I need to see Susannah, first — alone!"

"I dun't know," said Tom, feigning stupidity. "Mr Slack said . . ."

Richard was about to argue, when Susannah's clear voice floated down to them: "You'd better come through to the drawing-room, Richard."

Susannah was already halfway down the stairs. She pointed to her right, and followed her fiancé into the room, closing the door behind her.

Tom shut the main door, then glanced swiftly about him. No sign of his master or any other member of the household! He crossed to the drawing-room door and pressed his ear close to it.

"Where's your father?" he heard Richard ask.

"I thought you'd come to see *me*," replied Susannah.

"He won't interrupt us, will he?"

Richard's voice was already rising with tension.

"No. He's getting dressed. Why?"

There was a pause, and Tom could imagine the tortured expression on his cousin's face as he struggled to frame an answer.

"Susannah, I'm in trouble!"

"Trouble? What sort? Another woman?"

"Of course not! I love only you!"

"What then?"

There was another embarrassed silence.

"Debts."

"Who to?"

"Jacob Smalley."

Susannah let out a strangled yelp of horror.

"How do you owe money to *that* odious toad?" she demanded.

"Cards," replied Richard, in a barely audible whisper. "I know your father's abhorrence of gaming. That's why I didn't want him to overhear us."

There was another long, agonising pause.

"How much do you owe him?" asked Susannah.

"Twenty guineas!"

Susannah then uttered a word he had frequently used himself in the stables, especially when he had trodden in the substance in question, but he had never thought to hear it on the lips of his master's daughter! She must have picked it up from that stable-lad, Josiah, whom Hannah had mentioned. Old Amos and his father had always told him that people such as the Slacks were their "betters" because of their refined manners and bearing. Little he had so far seen of Susannah had confirmed that assessment.

"I've got until Saturday to find it," begged Richard, his voice rising to a plaintive whine.

"So, why come to me?"

"Will you lend it me?"

"I don't have twenty guineas."

"You've jewellery," snapped Richard. "Pawn it! Once we're married, I'll buy you new stuff out of the five hundred pounds your father's giving me as a dowry."

"And if I don't?"

"Smalley will tell your father. He'll break off the engagement and the field will be open for Smalley to pay court to you!"

Tom was suddenly aware of a presence behind him. No! His master had caught him spying! He would be dismissed, for certain!

His stomach taut with fear, he slowly turned, then breathed a deep sigh of relief. It was Henry Jessop!

The tutor motioned him to come away from the door.

"Time for your lesson, Tom," he said, once they were out of earshot. "Reading."

Tom's pulse raced. Although he was making fair progress with his arithmetic, it was at reading that he had really begun to excel. Of course, he had been taught the rudiments at Faith Clerkson's School, and he found it was a skill, like riding a horse, which, once learnt, was never forgotten.

"Worr're we readin' tonait?" he asked eagerly.

"Ever seen this book before?" queried Jessop.

The tutor produced from his pocket a small tome, which Tom thought he recognized as the one Jessop had been reading, that first Saturday evening he had seen him in the Old Eclipse.

Tom read the title: *Reflections on the Revolution in France* by Edmund Burke. Yes, the same one, he now remembered.

"There's just one thing," whispered Jessop. "Tell no one in this house you're reading this."

"Why not?"

"If Slack finds out, he'll turn us both out!"

Two hours later, Tom realized the full import of the tutor's warning.

It was gone sunset, but he decided to risk the short journey through the unlit streets to Mitre Court. All the way there, one passage in particular was still ringing through his head:

> Government is a contrivance of
> human wisdom to provide for
> human wants. Men have a right that
> these wants should be provided by
> this wisdom.

"You see what it means, Tom?" Jessop had asked him.

"That t' Government 'as a duty to look after t' people," Tom had answered.

"Ay," replied the tutor. "And woe betide the Government

that neglects that duty!"

He sounded almost like Jeremiah Brandreth! Indeed, Tom marvelled at how strange was Jessop's choice of reading matter. Last week, there had been that poem about building Jerusalem; today, it was the French Revolution!

Reaching the Parker's house in Mitre Court, Tom peered through the grimy window. Inside, all was dark.

He knocked.

At first, there was no answer. Perhaps they were round at Bark Court; though he doubted if Margaret was in either the mood or any fit state to play hostess.

He turned, and had taken about half a dozen steps, when he heard the door creak open. Jonathan stood in the doorway.

"Tom!"

His brother-in-law looked surprised, even though Tom was a regular visitor to the house. Jonathan looked more gaunt and drained than when Tom had seen him emerging from Gresham's pawnshop, the previous Thursday.

"Summat wrong?" asked Tom, his spirits plummeting.

"Yer'd best come in."

Tom followed his brother-in-law through into the back room of the cottage. A few sticks of kindling were burning in the grate, and this constituted the room's sole source of illumination as well as heat. By its dim light, Tom could see his sister hunched in a chair, breathing in short, stertorous gasps. Her dress was unbuttoned, leaving her left breast exposed, and again, Tom could not help but compare that pale, shrivelled appendage with Susannah's full, firm, milk-white globes. Young Caleb clung to it like

146

a drowning man cleaving to a piece of flotsam.

"She just sits there," whispered Jonathan. "Sez nowt. Just sits."

"I've brung yer summat," announced Tom, producing a bundle from beneath his coat and laying its contents on the table: bread, cheese, roast chicken, mutton, milk and ale. "Courtesy o' Mr Slack!"

Jonathan's jaw dropped open several inches.

"Slack — 'e gi'd yer all this?"

"Call it payment in kind."

"Yer've not stole it?"

"I've towd yer: 'e'll not miss it. Anyroad, Hannah gi'd it me. *She* said it wor all rait."

"No!"

"Yoh took that last lot I brung yer, an' yer knew I'd pinched it."

"I know," replied Jonathan, "an' we've not slept a wink since, racked wi' guilt. It wor a moment o' weakness an' we reckon it wor wrong."

Ann half-raised herself in her chair. "Aye, it's wrong; so tek it back!"

"But yoh an' Caleb . . ."

"Tek it back!" repeated his sister. "What did I allus teach yer? 'Thou shalt not steal.' We'll not tek stuff what's bin thieved, no matter *'ow* poor we are!"

"No," affirmed her husband. "We don't need stolen food. The Lord will provide. 'He shall feed his flock like a shepherd.' Isaiah: Chapter 40, Verse 11."

"An' wor if they die?" demanded Tom, pointing at his sister and nephew.

Ann turned her face towards him, but, as before, her brown eyes seemed to be focused elsewhere, as though upon another world.

"It'll be God's will."

Why were they so stubborn? Why this faith in a God who left them to rot in this stinking hovel?

"Now, tek it back," ordered Jonathan, "afore Slack finds it's gone, an' kicks yer out!"

His eyes brimming with burning tears, Tom spun round and dashed from the house, leaving the food on the table.

Perhaps they weren't worth helping!

CHAPTER 15

Thursday, 29th May, 1817

Tom woke, the next morning, with a guilty conscience. He *couldn't* just abandon them — for Caleb's sake!

"Worr am I gonna do, 'Annah?" he pleaded, helping himself to more bread and cheese.

"Yer say yer left t' food on t' table?" replied the cook-housekeeper, pouring him more ale.

"Aye."

"Well, then, yer've done what yer can. Yer can't *mek* 'em eat, if they've a mind not to."

"But worr if Caleb dies?"

Hannah shrugged her broad shoulders.

"Then it'll be on *their* 'eads, not yourn," she replied, in blunt, practical tones.

Tom picked thoughtfully at his bread and cheese.

"I s'pose so, but . . ."

"No 'buts' about it, Tom," cut in Hannah, laying a plump, comforting hand on his shoulder. "There's only so much yer can do to 'elp folk. If they'll norr 'elp theirsens, there's nowt yer can do."

Tom thought back to his last sight of Caleb, so pale and pathetically thin, sucking desperately at his mother's arid, withered nipple and made a decision: he would see his master and apprise him of the situation (without, of course, mentioning the unwitting contribution his master had already made!).

As soon as he had finished his breakfast, he sought out Samuel Slack and found him in the back room he used as a study-cum-office.

"Come in," barked Slack, in response to Tom's knock. When he saw who his visitor was, his face lit up. "Tom! Worr is it, lad?"

His luck was in, thought Tom: his master was in a good mood.

Five minutes later, when he was in full possession of the facts, Slack's expression had grown grave.

"I could ask 'Annah to send 'em some food," he suggested.

"No!" Tom blurted out, adding hastily: "They wun't tek charity. Too proud."

Slack rubbed his chin.

"What, then?"

"More wokk," replied Tom, taking a step forward. "That's all 'e wants – to wokk, so's he can earn, to feed 'is fam'ly."

Slack frowned and shook his head.

"I an't got more wokk to gi' 'im, Tom. Besides, it'd be showin' favours. I'd ay ev'ry knitter in t' East Midlands wantin' t' same. There's norr enough wokk to go round — an' that's t' plain truth."

"It's all '*is* fault!" shouted Tom, pointing towards the door.

Slack looked round, to where George Hicks hovered hesitantly on the threshold.

"What's George done?"

"Nowt, Mr Slack," protested that individual, moving towards the desk. He glowered at Tom. "What's 'e accusin' me of?"

"Jonathan Parker — 'e an't 'ad no wokk for nigh on a fortnait," said Tom. "Why?"

The force of the question struck Hicks like a physical blow between the eyes, and he staggered back

"'E's a troublemaker."

"Why? 'Cos 'e asks fer a decent rate fer t' job?"

"I only mek threepence a pair profit on 'em, as it is!" wailed the middleman, looking to Slack for moral support.

"There's not many 'osiers round these parts pay as much as *I* do," said Slack, "burr if trade gets much woss, I'll ay to drop prices further to compete. Some o' my rivals've gone down already."

Tom remembered what Jonathan had told him of Slack's ruthless and unscrupulous tactics against rival hosiers during the Luddite riots, and wondered if he had employed them to deal with his present problems.

Slack was looking sceptical. "Surely there's summat else Parker could do to support 'is fam'ly?" he said.

Tom shook his head. "It's t' only trade 'e knows."

Slack looked at him thoughtfully, then pulled open the drawer of his desk and took out a small metal box.

151

"If yer could see 'ow sick 'e is!" pleaded Tom.

"Yoh could try prayin', an' all. Now, forget worr 'e said about charity. Gi' 'im this."

From the box he took a gold half-sovereign and handed it to Tom.

"'E'll not tek it," insisted Tom.

"Buy summat wi' it. If things are as bad as yer say, 'e'll tek it — if only for t' child's sake."

Yes, thought Tom. Jonathan and Ann might refuse charity for themselves, but they couldn't deny Caleb the chance of life! Or could they? What had Ann said? That, if Caleb died, it'd be God's will? If there *was* a God, he couldn't be so unfeeling as to allow a helpless infant to die. Could he? Of course, Jonathan and Ann had lost two already, and God had done nothing to save *them*! Well, tonight, he would put God to the test and pray for young Caleb!

The food lay untouched on the table, exactly as he had left it; although a film of green mould was now beginning to cover the bread.

Tom uncorked the stone jar in which he had put the milk and sniffed. It smelled sour.

"Y' an't gi'd 'im none," said Tom.

"I've towd yer: we'll norr eat nowt that's bin stolen."

"Well, at least tek this," insisted Tom, taking out the half-sovereign and putting it on the table.

"Yoh've not bin stealin' *money*, an' all, ay yer?" gasped Ann weakly.

"No, it's from Slack. I *did* steal t' food," admitted Tom, "but not this. Slack gi'd it me."

"Why?"

"For Caleb."

"'Ow does Slack know about Caleb?"

"I towd 'im. An' I towd 'im yer wanted wokk, not charity, burr 'e sez 'e can't treat yoh no diff'rent from t' other knitters, when it comes to puttin'-out. 'E sez 'e wants yer to 'ave this, for Caleb's sake."

Jonathan's pale shaking hand hovered momentarily above the coin.

"No! 'Ow do I know yer din't steal it?"

"Go round to Slack's. Ask 'im."

"Go to Slack's 'ouse!" yelped Jonathan, his frail body trembling with fury. "I'd go to 'Ell fost!"

"Yer'll tek charity from A'nt Margaret," Tom pointed out. "Why not Slack?"

"It's fam'ly. That's diff'rent."

"Diff'rent? 'Ow?"

"Jonathan an' me 'ave got principles about these things, Tom," said Ann, forcing a gentle smile.

"Yer can't feed '*im* on principles!" shouted Tom, pointing at his nephew. The child lay so still in his mother's arms that Tom feared his intervention might already be too late. Only the occasional bubble of saliva rising to his pale lips betokened any sign of lingering life.

"We've still gorra few sticks o' furniture we can sell," said Jonathan, pointing to the table and chair.

Tom struggled to find an answer, but, in the face of such dogged resistance, there was little he could say.

He marched towards the door, paused and turned.

"If yoh lerrim die, I 'ope yer'll both rot in 'Ell!"

Tom put down his tankard. The ale seemed to have cleared his brain, as well as his throat.

He scanned the smoke-filled main room of the Black's Head for Ned or Brandreth. Earlier, he had peered through the window of the Old Eclipse, but there had been no sign of the ex-farrier; so Tom had assumed he must be meeting the Nottingham Captain. It seemed he was wrong.

He was debating whether to have a second drink or leave, when Ned's massive bulk appeared in the doorway.

"Ned! Over 'ere!"

Ned gave him a signal of recognition, then crossed to the bar and ordered a drink, before joining Tom in the far corner.

"'Eard owt more from Jerry?" asked Tom. He was surprised at how easily the familiar reference to Brandreth came to his lips.

"Aye. Oliver — t' London delegate — 'e's bin to see Jerry in Nottingham. Went back up to Sheffield, yest'dy. There's a meetin' at t' Grindin' Wheel, tonait."

"'As 'e 'eard owt?" asked Tom.

"'E's bin back down to London. Went to visit Mitchell at Cold Bath Fields."

"'Ow is 'e?"

"Bearin' up under all t' questionin'. 'E's a tough 'un, though. They'll not gerr owt out on 'im. Still, there's good news from Yorkshire. At t' arms depot in 'Alifax, there's sixty stands of arms — an' only one bloke to guard 'em!"

"Worr about t' Army?" asked Tom.

Ned creased his brow in an effort of concentration.

"About a thousand in t' West Ridin'. None up in Wakefield or 'Alifax. They'll not be able to mobilise fast enough to stop us!"

Tom tightened his grip on the tankard. He must warn Will. Yet doubts were gnawing at the back of his mind. He remembered the passage from Edmund Burke he had read with Jessop. Yes, Governments *did* have a duty to look after their people, particularly the helpless, such as Caleb! There was justice in this Cause!

"Another?" asked Tom.

Ned wiped the froth from his lips and nodded.

Tom emptied his tankard, crossed to the bar, and purchased fresh drinks for Ned and himself.

For a while, the two men sat in silent contemplation.

"'Ow many can we count on?" asked Tom, at length.

Ned took a crumpled paper from his pocket and peered intently at the symbols on it.

"Gi's it 'ere," said Tom, taking the paper from him and reading:

SHEFFIELD	10,000
HUDDERSFIELD	8,000
BARNSLEY	3,000
LEEDS	10,000

Tom made some rapid calculations. (Although he preferred reading and writing, he was beginning to realize that arithmetic had its uses.)

"Phew! That's 36,000 from Yorkshire alone! 'Ow many did Jerry say from round these parts?"

"About 30,000."

Tom saw the colour slowly draining from Ned's cheeks, as the full import of the figures registered.

"My God, Tom! There's no army on earth can stop us!"

Tom downed his ale in a single draught and got up. Ned's oath had reminded him: he had important business to sort out with the Almighty!

CHAPTER 16

Friday, 30th May, 1817

Prayer had been hard: far harder than he had imagined.

On the previous Sunday, the Reverend Cursham had turned his attention from fornication to supplication.

"As Our Saviour said, in the seventh chapter of Saint Matthew's Gospel: 'Ask, and it shall be given you; seek, and ye shall find; knock, and it shall be opened unto you.' God is a loving Father, and will refuse His children nothing. Through prayer, we shall be granted all that we need."

Well, what Tom needed, right now, was to see his nephew strong and well; to see his stubborn sister and her husband unbend and abandon this resistance to all offers of help.

He knelt down and placed his hands together, screwing his eyes tightly shut, whilst tilting his head backwards, so that his face was raised to Heaven. (He had studied his master, during the service, and assumed this to be the correct posture for supplication.)

"Ask, and it shall be given you."

Tom had asked for little, over the last sixteen years. Both Caleb and Amos had instilled into him the maxim that whatever he wanted in this life he would have to earn by hard, physical effort. That night, though, he had asked — pleaded — as never before, repeating over and over: "Dun't lerrim die!"

Finally, he had hurled down a challenge: "Cursham sez you're Almighty — yer can do owt yer like. So, prove it!"

He was halfway through his breakfast of bread, cheese and cold mutton, when he heard Slack descending the stairs.

"Well, Tom, did they tek t' money?"

"I left it on t' table," said Tom. "They'll not touch it, though — I know they'll not."

Slack shrugged his broad shoulders.

"If they'll norr 'elp theirsens, there's nowt yer can do."

Hannah's exact words!

"Look," said Slack gently, "there's nowt urgent needs doin'. Go round agen. See 'ow they are. I'd offer yer more money to gi' em, burr I know they'd not tek it."

Tom shook his head in rueful acknowledgement. He'd already planned to report to Will — though there was little to add — then he would call on his sister and her family, and make one final effort to get them to see sense.

Aunt Margaret answered the door, her face still bruised and disfigured.

"Is Will in?"

"Yoh just caught 'im. 'E wor goin' out."

"Worr about 'im?"

"At t' stables."

Tom was inwardly glad. Although he still planned to avenge the brutal assault on his aunt, the time was not yet ripe. He knew Margaret would do everything in her power to stop him.

"Yer'd best come in," said his aunt.

Will sat at the table, his pipe in one hand and a tankard in the other.

"What's brung *yoh* 'ere?" he demanded, in a slurred voice. He turned his head towards the door, but his eyes were not focused upon Tom.

"I've got more news."

This seemed to rouse Will momentarily from his torpor.

"What?"

Tom passed on the individual figures for each town, which he had committed to memory.

"Thotty-six *thousand*!" cried Will, almost choking on the smoke from his pipe. "They'll norr even get 36!"

"'Ow d'yer know?" replied Tom.

"There'll not be 10,000 from Sheffield, fer a start," stated his brother defiantly.

"'Ow d'yer know?" repeated Tom.

Will made no answer but stood up, and, brushing roughly past Tom, staggered out into the street, muttering: "Thotty-six thousand!"

"What's 'e mean about Sheffield?" asked Tom.

His aunt shrugged.

"'E dun't tell *me* nowt."

In the dimly lit interior, Tom examined his aunt's wounds more closely.

"'As 'e done owt to yer since?" he asked.

His aunt faltered, as though fearful of confiding in him.

"Just this," she said, at length.

She opened the front of her dress, and Tom felt a violent wrenching in his stomach. Her ribs showed through the taut, undernourished flesh, whose habitual pallor was now offset by ugly, purple contusions, and it was clear from their outline that at least two were broken.

"Y' shunta gorrup," protested Tom.

"An' who'da cooked 'is meals?" demanded his aunt plaintively.

"I'da let the bastard starve!" thundered Tom.

Margaret refastened her dress.

"I took 'im fer better or fer woss," she shrugged.

Old Caleb had often opined that a wife was her husband's property, to do with as he wished. His sister eagerly endorsed that view. Tom knew he could argue till the cows came home: she would never change her mind.

He doubted if he would have any better luck with Ann and Jonathan, but at least he ought to try. It would also be an opportunity to find out if prayer accomplished all that the Reverend Cursham claimed for it.

Tom looked at the table, then at his brother-in-law.

"Yer've ate some on it!" he gasped.

"A bit," conceded Jonathan.

"What changed yer mind?"

"T' minister from t' chapel."

"When did 'e come?"

"This mornin'. Said we owed it to Caleb. 'E said it's what the Lord'd want."

"'Ow *is* Caleb?"

"We gi'd 'im some milk," said Ann, "an' 'e drunk it."

She pointed to the infant, who lay on her lap, sound asleep, an almost radiant smile playing around his small, puckered lips.

Perhaps prayer *did* work, reflected Tom. Perhaps the Almighty had sent the minister, in answer to his supplication, to persuade them to accept Slack's food and money. (He had noticed the half-sovereign was no longer on the table.)

At that moment, Caleb woke and began to cry. Tom poured some milk from the stone jar into a cup and handed it to his sister, who held it up to Caleb's mouth.

Tom was relieved to see him gulp it down; yet he was appalled at how painfully thin his nephew still appeared. His sister's initial resistance had been broken down, but there was still a long way to go.

Tom found it difficult to concentrate on his studies: he was too preoccupied with thoughts of Caleb. He still couldn't believe Ann and Jonathan had been prevailed upon to change their minds.

He was working his way, with more difficulty than usual, through another passage by Edmund Burke:

> And having looked to government
> for bread, on the very first scarcity
> they will turn and bite the hand that
> fed them.

Well, that certainly wasn't true of Ann and Jonathan! Rather than take charity from Slack, they had preferred to starve, until persuaded by the minister to do otherwise.

"Tell me, Tom," said Jessop suddenly, "do you think men have a right to rise up against those who govern them?"

"Me faither allus towd me we 'ad a duty to serve an' respect our betters," replied Tom.

"And do you agree with him?"

When the question was put thus bluntly, Tom found himself stumped for an answer. After all, what answer was Jessop expecting? If he said he supported rebellion, would the tutor report his answer back to Slack? Or was the man testing his republican sympathies?

"There's good masters an' bad 'uns," he replied, with a noncommittal shrug.

"You really believe that?"

"Well, Mr Slack's all rait," he answered, after a pause. "'E gi'd me sister food an' money for our Caleb."

"And why d'you think he did that?" asked the tutor.

"'Cos 'e's kind, I s'pose," replied Tom falteringly.

"Because it makes him *appear* kind," smiled Jessop. "Why d'you think he goes to church, every Sunday, and sits on various public bodies? So that people will look at him and say: 'There goes Samuel Slack, the great philanthropist.' How much did he give your sister?"

"'Aif a sovereign."

"A drop in the ocean!" snorted the tutor. "He's worth thousands. And how did he come by it?"

"'Ard wokk," replied Tom, rallying to his master's defence.

"Exploiting his workers!" snapped back Jessop. "Your sister's husband works for Slack, doesn't he?"

"Aye."

"The man mouths pious sentiments, shows himself at the parish church, and generally parades his good works. Yet your sister wouldn't need charity, if Slack paid her husband enough to live on, in the first place."

"'E sez 'e can't afford more," said Tom.

The tutor's eyes glinted behind his polished lenses.

"He and his like'll pay, one day."

The face gradually softened.

"When I said 'masters', I didn't really mean Slack: I meant the Prince Regent and his Government. Have men the right to rise up against *them*?"

Tom again paused. By now, it was clear where the tutor's sympathies lay. It was also obvious that Jessop expected him to answer in the affirmative.

"Yes," he answered boldly.

Why, though, was the man sounding him out?

The tutor removed his spectacles, breathed heavily upon the lenses, and polished them vigorously with his handkerchief. Meanwhile, the pale blue, myopic eyes never left Tom's face.

"Do you remember, the other Sunday, asking me who Brutus was?"

"There were two on 'em, yoh said," replied Tom.

"You never got the chance to tell me why you wanted to know. Some newfound interest in Roman history?"

"Well, er, no. I . . ."

Jessop reached inside his coat and pulled out a piece of paper, which he slowly unfolded and laid out on the table.

"Did it have anything to do with this?"

Tom peered closely at the paper: it was the first of the "Brutus" leaflets.

Tom felt his whole body suddenly freeze. He had been trapped! The man wasn't a Republican, after all! Perhaps the time was ripe to own up to his own spying activities for Will. He was about to open his mouth, when he noticed a broad grin spreading across the tutor's face.

"Ned said you were safe, but I had to be certain."

Tom's jaw dropped.

"Ned 'Opkins?"

The tutor nodded.

"'Ow do *yoh* know Ned?" stammered Tom.

"From the Black's Head meetings — and before. He's known you a long time. He says you can be trusted. It's hard to know who to trust."

"But *yoh* an't bin to t' Black's 'Ead meetings!" protested Tom.

"Oh, but I *have*, Tom. I was sitting right beside you, at the last one. It's amazing what one can achieve by removing one's spectacles and donning a few dirty old clothes. You didn't know I was acknowledged to be quite an accomplished actor, when I was up at Oxford, did you?"

The room suddenly started to spin. Tom tried to rise, but found himself rooted to his chair. At once, everything fell into place.

"Bloody 'ell! *You're* Brutus!"

CHAPTER 17

Friday, 30th May, 1817

As he left the room, some twenty minutes later, his head was still spinning. It couldn't be true, yet he knew it was! What should he do about it? It was his duty to report this intelligence at once to Will — perhaps also to Slack. He thought of another bright, silver shilling nestling in the palm of his hand: money that could buy further nourishment for young Caleb.

During those twenty minutes, Jessop had expounded his own reasons for espousing the Cause, and certain words still resonated obstinately inside Tom's head: poverty, justice, equality. Were not these more important than keeping a corrupt Government in power, through grovelling compliance with evil laws? The tutor had quoted a letter from Edmund Burke to Charles James Fox (whoever *he* was!):

> People crushed by law have no
> hope but from power. If laws are
> their enemies, they will be enemies
> to laws.

"So, if t' law's bad, yer can brek it?" Tom had asked, still puzzled.

"Yes. Through the ages, men have defied evil laws, and

been executed — murdered by the State — because they believed in justice and equality. Good laws can protect citizens: evil laws can crush them. I know. My father was a stockinger, working for Slack. He had the courage to stand up for what he believed in — he was a Luddite — and Slack made sure he never worked again. He and my mother were thrown out of their cottage. There was nothing they could do. The Law was on Slack's side."

Tom looked dumbstruck.

"Now, *I* work for him. The supreme irony! But it makes the perfect cover for my activities as Brutus — the mild, inoffensive tutor!"

"Does Slack know who y' are?"

"No — and swear you'll never tell him!"

"Cross me 'eart!"

"Good!"

Tom had lapsed into deep concentration, before asking: "This revolution — will it wokk?"

"Why not? Think of the French, ground down by the tyranny of the aristocracy. But they rose up and cast off the yoke."

"Are we gonna chop off t' Prince Regent's 'ead?" Tom had asked.

"All will be granted a fair trial," Jessop had replied bluntly.

Tom had found himself swept along by the rhetoric. There were serious injustices to be righted. He had thought again of his sister and nephew. Yet grave doubts now gnawed away at the back of his mind. As Old Amos had once reminded him, the French had ridded themselves of a

Bourbon, only to replace him with a Bonaparte. Were they any better off?

Nevertheless, there was to be another meeting in the Black's Head, that evening; although it was not yet known whether the Nottingham Captain would be present. After all, it must be hazardous for him to travel, and not just because of the habitual dangers from footpads that awaited travellers between Nottingham and Mansfield. He was a marked man — and Tom realized, with a start, that part of the reason lay with him. If Brandreth were caught and hanged, it would have been *his* hand that had placed the noose round his neck!

Church Street was choked with traffic: carts, horses, coaches and pedestrians vying for a right of way through the narrow thoroughfare, much of which was permanently blocked by the shopkeepers' stalls, jutting out in front of their premises.

Tom made his way towards Robert Hall's house-cum-office, jostled on all sides, yet determined to forge a passage through the throng.

Then, he saw them: Richard and Smalley in heated conversation. He pressed closer to listen.

"You've got to give me more time!" Richard was pleading.

"Twenty-four hours," Smalley replied. "Twenty-four, or I go straight to Slack."

Richard raised the elegant, silver-topped cane he was carrying, his whole face and body grown rigid with suppressed anger.

"Don't think yer can scare me!" said Smalley defiantly; though Tom noticed that a greyish pallor had suffused his

168

gaunt features.

For several moments, Richard stood, cane raised. Then, he slowly lowered his arm.

"I'll get it!"

With a sweep of his cane, Richard pushed the slighter man aside, and set off down Church Street at a brisk pace, with which Tom strove to keep up.

Richard was a few yards from Robert Hall's door when Tom caught up with him.

"What do *you* want?" demanded Richard looking down at Tom as though he was one of the numerous lumps of animal excrement that littered Church Street.

"Ay yoh seen yer Mam lately?" asked Tom.

"No!" came the blunt response. "And, in any case, what business is it of yours?"

Tom told him of Ben's recent beating of his aunt, whilst tactfully omitting details of the circumstances surrounding it, and noticed his cousin's face grow taut.

"He always *was* a pig!" said Richard. "Why do you think I moved out, when I took this post? I wanted to get as far away from him as possible!"

"Well, *I* moved out, when Slack offered me t' chance," said Tom, "burr I still go to see 'em, most days. *I'm* norr ashamed on 'em!"

"You'll still be Slack's servant, if you live to be fifty!" said Richard, with an imperious sniff.

"I'm ayin' lessons!" countered Tom defiantly.

"I've told you before: education's wasted on the likes of you! Now, if you've nothing else to tell me, I've other,

169

more important, business to attend to."

Richard entered the office, and was surprised to see Tom dogging his steps.

"What now?"

"It's nowt to do wi' yoh!" said Tom. "It's business wi' Mr 'All."

"And what business could he possibly have with the likes of you?"

"It's Mr Slack's business."

Richard's lip curled back in a supercilious smile, revealing his strong, white teeth.

"Like I said: Slack's perpetual errand boy!"

He disappeared into the office, and Tom followed him.

Robert Hall looked up, as they entered, and his face broke into a broad smile.

"And what can we do for you?"

Tom took a sealed envelope from his pocket and handed it to the little lawyer, who broke the seal and studied its contents carefully. He then consulted a large book on his desk, muttering to himself, as he did so.

"Yes," he said eventually. "Tell your master I can see him at ten o'clock on Monday morning."

Hall entered the appointment in the book, and Tom committed it to memory before turning to leave.

"Before you go," said the lawyer, "there's one small favour I'd like you to do for me."

More furniture moving! thought Tom.

He was not mistaken. Hall led him upstairs and into his private apartments, where he indicated a pile of books by a large tea chest in a corner near the fireplace.

"I have to go out," said the lawyer, "but I'd much appreciate it if you'd finish packing those books into that box. They're mostly out-of-date law books that are taking up valuable shelf space in the bookcase."

He broke off and scrutinized Tom through his thick lenses.

"I understand you're receiving lessons from young Joseph's tutor?"

"Yes, sir."

"Are you making progress?"

"Mr Jessop sez I am."

"Good. Well, you'll find some books of general interest there. If any of them are of any use to you, feel free to help yourself."

"But, sir, I couldn't!" stammered Tom.

"Why ever not? They're of no further use to me. So, if you can make use of them, so much the better! You used to be an ostler, didn't you?"

"Yes, sir."

"Well, there's one on horses you may be interested in — and there's an old Bible in there, somewhere."

"Thank you, sir," muttered Tom.

Tom was aghast, and, as soon as he heard the little lawyer's footsteps retreating down the stairs, he set about his task with enthusiasm. Now, he would have books of his very own — even though horses were the last things he wanted to be involved with again.

Yet Richard's words still rankled. Perhaps he *was* becoming cast in the role of perpetual servant!

Ned Hopkins was not alone. His companion was not Jeremiah Brandreth, but a short, bald, red-faced man, whose small, pig-like eyes darted nervously around the assembled company. Tom, unaccountably and illogically, took an instant dislike to the man.

"Tom, this is John Henderson," said Ned. "'E's just gorr 'ere by coach from Sheffield."

"'Aif an hour late!" grumbled Henderson.

Apart from the three of them, Tom could see about eight or nine others. He glanced round the room, looking for Jessop. Yes, there he was, muffled up in the same tattered grey coat. To judge from the size of it, it was probably one of Ned's that he had borrowed.

Their eyes met briefly, but neither made any sign of recognition.

"'E's brung bad news," said Ned, pointing to Henderson.

"Aye," replied the Yorkshireman. "I wor at t' Grindin' Wheel, last neet. Oliver, t' London delegate, 'ad come to speak to us. 'E starts talkin', an' t' next thing we know, t' place is full o' soldiers."

The room had gone deadly quiet.

"T' sergeant shouts out: 'Nobody move!' I wor near t' door, so, while they're all lookin' at t' sergeant, I slipped out."

"Worn't nobody guardin' t' back, then?" asked a voice

from the far side of the room.

Henderson shook his head.

"There were one or two tried to follow me, but t' soldiers fired off a couple o' rounds. Next thing I 'eard, there wor an almighty crash o' brekkin' glass, an' a figure in a green coat comes flyin' out! It wor Oliver."

"So, 'e gorr away?" said Tom.

Henderson nodded.

"An' where is 'e now?" demanded another voice.

"Gone back to London, I should think," replied the Sheffield man, with a non-committal shrug.

"An' wor yoh an' 'im t' only 'uns as gorr away?"

"As far as I know. I 'id out in an owd farm buildin' fer t' neet. This mornin', word wor all over Sheffield. Four's bin arrested, includin' James Westenholme. 'E's t' delegate fer Sheffield."

"Worr're they goin' to do to 'em?" asked Tom.

"They'll go on trial — burr I reckon it wor Oliver they were really after."

"It seems to me," said Jessop, in a deep, gruff voice, muffled by the upturned collar of his coat, "that Oliver's had a few narrow escapes, of late. First, there was the business with Mitchell, near Huddersfield: now, this."

"Are yoh sayin' Oliver's a traitor?" demanded Ned, the colour rising to his cheeks.

Jessop seemed to hesitate before answering: "I'm saying there are too many coincidences. But it's strange how the authorities knew about the meeting. *Some-body's* leaking information."

Although no one was looking in his direction, Tom suddenly felt a strange churning in his stomach. It was the first time he had known real fear.

CHAPTER 18

Saturday, 31st May, 1817

Will seemed singularly unimpressed.

"I already 'eard," he said, removing his pipe, and noisily expelling a large gobbet of brown phlegm.

Tom stood looking sheepishly at his brother.

"Worr're yer waitin' for?" demanded Will.

"Me shillin'."

"Well, you're wastin' yer time!"

"Yoh promised!" stormed Tom.

"Yer dun't gerr owt fer stale news!"

Tom felt sick. After everything he'd risked to bring his brother news of the Sheffield meeting, this was all the thanks he got! If Ned or Brandreth got to hear what he was doing, God alone knew what punishment they would exact. Tom pointed this out to his brother.

"Yer knew t' risks," replied Will bluntly. "I know Ned's an own friend o' yourn, but dun't forget: *'e's* t' traitor, not yoh!"

"Yeah," conceded Tom; then before he could check himself, he blurted out: "Mr Jessop sez that, sometimes, it's all rait for subjects to rebel."

Will's eyes narrowed.

"Oh, 'e does, does 'e?"

Tom felt his innards turn to ice.

Slowly, Will's facial muscles relaxed and split into a broad grin.

"Bloody teachers!" he roared. "What do *they* bloody know? See what learnin' does fer yer? Fills up yer 'ead wi' daft ideas!"

"Aye," replied Tom, concealing a deep sigh of relief. "'Appen you're rait."

"'Course I am!" blustered Will, pointing to the chevron on his sleeve. "Look at that! In another two years, I could mek full corporal. Sergeant in five. Yer dun't get *that* out o' books!"

He leaned forward, and Tom caught the reek of stale rum.

"Worr about me shillin'?" persisted Tom.

"Bring us summat worthwhile, an' yer'll gerrit."

His uncle was at work; his aunt out shopping. Not that he would get any backing from the former; and the latter was too scared to provide support. Tom stormed off, feeling betrayed.

West Gate was packed, and it took him nearly five minutes to cover the short distance from Duck Lane to Market Place. As he reached the Moot Hall he saw a familiar figure in a green coat striding in his direction across Market Place. Richard!

He was in two minds whether to hail his cousin, when

176

the latter turned into Stockwell Gate.

Tom decided to follow him.

When Richard reached Wass Lane, he paused, glanced furtively round, and darted into the premises of John Gresham, pawnbroker.

What was Richard doing in a pawnbroker's? Then, Tom remembered: today was his cousin's final day for settling his debt with Jacob Smalley. Obviously, since their conversation, that evening, Susannah had relented and given him some of her jewellery to pawn.

Opposite Wass Lane stood a grocery and wine merchant's establishment, belonging to John Cutts. Tom found that, by staring at the reflection in the mullioned window, he had a perfect view of the pawnbroker's.

Affecting to take an interest in spices, teas and bottles of rare port, he remained there for fully three minutes, before Gresham's door opened and his cousin reappeared.

Richard stood on the threshold, patting his coat, as though checking that the contents of his pocket were still safe. He still looked grim-faced. Once again, he peered round, his eyes coming to rest on Cutts' window.

Tom froze, his eyes never leaving the reflection of his cousin's distinguished figure.

However, Richard showed no sign of recognition, and made his way back down Stockwell Gate, towards Market Place, with Tom close at his heels, but shielded behind a wall of citizens going about their everyday business.

As Richard crossed Market Place, it became obvious to Tom that his cousin's destination was, as he had speculated, George Ellis's shop; so he slowed down, to open up a gap between himself and his quarry.

As they passed the Crown & Anchor, a small, shaven-headed man lurched out, bumping into Richard and almost throwing him off balance.

Richard pushed him aside, and continued on his way, but the man began to follow him.

Was *he* trailing Richard, too? Tom wondered.

At last, Tom saw Richard pause outside the druggist's premises, peer through the window and signal.

A few minutes later, Jacob Smalley came out.

Richard reached inside his coat and produced a number of coins that Smalley greedily snatched from his hands.

A sickly grin passed over the pallid features of the druggist's assistant, as he counted the money.

"I knew yer'd see sense."

"Well," snarled Richard, "now you've got your money, just keep away from Slack and his daughter!"

"You're not out o' t' wood yet," smirked Smalley. He was looking past Richard towards a tall, red-faced figure of about twenty, labouring down Church Street with a pig's carcass slung over his broad left shoulder. "There's t' ten guineas y' owe George Tully there."

As he drew abreast of them, Tully favoured both men with a cheerful, yellow-toothed smile.

"I can't pay *that* back!" protested Richard. "I've only just paid Smalley back the twenty guineas I owe *him* — and I had the Devil's own job to do that!"

"Strong language!" said Smalley reprovingly, his lips pursed in an expression of mock horror. "What would Slack say, if 'e 'eard yer?"

Tully craned his massive frame forward until it was within inches of Richard's face.

"I'm a reasonable man, Miller," he said, gesturing towards the White Hart, further down to their left. "I'll gi' yer till next Friday to pay it back!"

As Tom moved away, he noticed the shaven-headed man disappearing into the White Hart. Just another drunkard!

"Tom!"

Tom spun round with a start at the sound of his name.

Susannah stood at the head of the stairs, radiant in a dress of cream satin brocade. The colour complemented her complexion and the tightly fastened bodice showed her well-rounded breasts to their best advantage. Once again, Tom found himself comparing them with those of his sister, so shrunken and drained.

"Yes, Miss Susannah?" said Tom, springing to attention.

"Come up here."

"Why, miss?"

Susannah's mouth tightened.

"Because I tell you to," she replied imperiously.

Tom took an involuntary step backwards.

"But yer faither . . ." he spluttered.

Susannah's expression softened.

"Father's taken Mother, Rachel and Joseph to Pleasley, to visit his sister. Hannah's gone to Blidworth. Jessop's in Sutton. They'll none of them be back until evening. We'll have the house to ourselves for at least three hours."

"Yer mean yer faither's left yer on yer own in t' 'ouse wi' *me*?" said Tom incredulously.

A roguish light danced in Susannah's brown eyes.

"Father trusts you! Now, come up here!"

Like a fly lured towards a spider's web, Tom found his footsteps drawn up the stairs. As he came level with her, his nostrils caught the scent of her perfume.

She ran her tongue slowly across her full, red, sensuous lips.

"We've unfinished business, Tom."

"Unfinished . . ?"

"From two weeks ago."

"But yer robe . . ."

The brown eyes twinkled, as she tossed back her chestnut tresses.

"I told you: the stain came out. No damage done."

She turned and made off down the landing, beckoning him to follow.

Her bedroom overlooked the back yard, so she saw no need to close the curtains. She stood by the window, her back towards him, and indicated that he should begin to undress her.

"Burr I . . ." stammered Tom.

"What's the matter, Tom? Afraid you might have another 'accident'?"

"No."

"What, then?"

"Well, it's what t' Reverend Cursham said about — yer know — that Sunday."

"Fornication?" laughed Susannah, rolling the word round her mouth, savouring it, as though it were a rare vintage wine.

Tom nodded.

"Never mind what the Reverend Cursham says. Do *you* want to?"

A brief vision of Hell, as described by the parish priest, flashed before Tom's eyes; but, with an effort, he forced all thoughts of damnation from his head.

"Aye. I do."

"Well, then," smiled Susannah, and she turned and planted a soft kiss on his lips. "Come, now. Three hours can pass as swiftly as three minutes!"

His nervous fingers fumbled at the buttons down the back of her bodice, lingering over each one, as the milk-white flesh beneath was gradually exposed. He drew aside the curtain of hair and kissed in turn each vertebra of her graceful, swan-like neck.

The final undergarment slid noiselessly to the floor, and she stood before him in all her natural splendour. His eye was drawn to the clump of chestnut hairs between her thighs, concealing untold forbidden delights.

She then performed the same service for him, and they rolled, naked, onto the bed, their lips locked together, tongues fervently exploring each other's mouth.

At last, she rolled Tom onto his back and gently lowered herself onto his rigid, erect member. She then began to rock slowly to and fro, her pendulous breasts swaying rhythmically, tantalizingly above his open mouth. Her eager tongue licked voraciously at the craggy contours of his body, as the tumbling chestnut locks cascaded over his naked flesh.

As he approached his climax, Tom thought again of the Reverend Thomas Cursham. Had *he* ever experienced such heavenly pleasures? Tom thought not, or he would not have railed so venomously against them!

Finally, as on that previous Saturday, shockwaves surged through his loins and he felt his life-juices exploding inside her body. Suddenly, he felt his every sense heightened, before he fell back on the pillow, exhausted.

It was fully five minutes before either of them spoke.

"How does it feel, Tom?" enquired Susannah teasingly.

Tom could only manage a weak smile. He closed his eyes, savouring the sensation, as his loins still glowed with the pride of newfound manhood. There was also the secret satisfaction of having cuckolded Richard.

Susannah suddenly stood up and began to put on her undergarments.

"I'll need you to help me dress, Tom."

He hauled his body into an upright posture, and was surprised at how it ached — as though he had completed several hours of hard manual labour. However, the tide of elation that coursed through his frame amply compensated for any discomfort.

"You learn quickly, Tom," said Susannah, with a coquettish smile.

"Aye," grinned Tom. He could not help reflecting that Jessop had expressed exactly the same sentiments, and, whilst he understood the value of reading, writing and arithmetic, he felt that the lesson his master's daughter had just given him had been of equal importance. So much for the Reverend Cursham and his pompous sermons!

A broad grin spread across Tom's face.

"If our Richard ever found out . . !"

Susannah grew serious.

"Don't tell him, Tom!" she pleaded. "I've heard how you men brag of your 'conquests'."

Tom managed to suppress a smile. He could hardly regard their recent encounter as his "conquest", since it had been she who had instigated it. Perhaps Hannah had been right, warning him that Susannah was dangerous. Then again, Hannah was in Blidworth, and in no position to comment!

"I'll not tell 'im," promised Tom.

A sudden rush of guilt swept over him.

"Dun't it worry yer — yer know — doin' it wi' me, when you're betrothed to Richard?"

Susannah bent forward and kissed him.

"As I told you, Father wills the match," she replied, with a smile. "There's his money, too."

"Money?" said Tom. "'E an't got none."

"He will, when Mr Hall dies."

Tom looked puzzled.

"Richard confided in me, on Wednesday evening. Hall's a bachelor, with no children of his own, so he dotes on Richard as if he were his own son. He's made Richard his heir; so, when Hall dies, Richard stands to inherit his personal wealth, as well as the legal practice."

Tom let out a long, low whistle.

"When the time comes," continued Susannah, "I'll marry him, be a dutiful and faithful wife, and bear his children. Until then . . ."

"But yer must love 'im."

Susannah raised a quizzical eyebrow.

"Why?"

"Well, yer gi'd 'im them jewels to pop."

The frown deepened.

"Jewels?" she echoed.

"To pay off 'is debts," said Tom, already sensing something was amiss.

Her brown eyes were wide with disbelief, and her milk-white skin had turned almost grey with shock.

"But I gave him nothing!"

CHAPTER 19

Sunday, 1st June, 1817

Richard was already in his pew, ramrod-straight and grim-visaged, his head held erect by a high collar and tightly knotted black stock, staring resolutely to the front. As the Slack family filed into their pew, his gaze never wavered, even when Susannah favoured him with her most dazzling smile.

Robert Hall looked up from his prayer book, and flashed his gleaming dentures in friendly acknowledgement.

Tom also noticed that Jacob Smalley was in his place, along with George Ellis, an expression of self-satisfaction fixed across his gaunt features. Tom wished George Tully, too, had been present in church, so that he might have learnt whether Richard had managed to raise sufficient funds to clear all his debts. From Richard's tight-lipped expression, Tom judged he had not.

Most of all, though, Tom was eager to know what Richard had pawned. Certainly not his fiancée's jewellery: Susannah herself had confirmed that.

His speculations were interrupted by the sound of the organ, at which the whole congregation rose. What would be the Reverend Cursham's theme, this week? he wondered. Not fornication again! He looked at Susannah, and his mind went back to the previous afternoon. Was what she had done, in offering her body to him, any worse than what his aunt did with total strangers in the Black's Head Yard? At least Susannah offered her favours freely! Why was it so evil, then? Cursham had said, in his sermon on fornication, that sexual union between men and women was invented by God as a purely functional mechanism for procreating the human species. By implication, therefore, it was not meant to be indulged in as an act of enjoyment. Why, then, was it such an enjoyable experience? The answer was simple, thought Tom: God must have made it so because He wanted His creatures to enjoy it.

Tom's mind then went back to the subject of the previous Sunday's sermon: prayer. "Ask, and it shall be given you." He thought of Caleb. If Cursham had been so wrong about sexual union, might he not also have erred about the efficacy of prayer? Jonathan was convinced that the minister's visit had been in answer to Tom's prayer; but suppose it had been pure coincidence?

Tom felt a sharp dig in his ribs, and looked up to see Hannah frowning down at him. The congregation was now halfway through the first hymn, and Tom was the only member of the Slack entourage who was not singing. His master's thunderous bass growl contrasted with Susannah's sweet, if hesitant, soprano, whilst Mrs Slack and Hannah each attempted to harmonize in a wheezing contralto. George Hicks, who had joined the family for the service, contributed a wavering tenor, whilst young Joseph's squeaking treble and Rachel's mournful mezzo completed the family ensemble. Tom, musically ignorant and unsure of his own vocal range, finally opted for a muffled whisper, somewhere between baritone and tenor.

At last, he was able to sit down, in a state of some

trepidation, as the Reverend Cursham mounted the pulpit.

"My theme today," began the vicar, "is honesty."

Tom breathed a sigh of relief. He was on safe ground there. At the Faith Clerkson School, he had been taught the Ten Commandments and the staff had ensured that they were rigidly enforced. "Thou shalt not steal." He remembered vividly the time — he had been about eight — when he had stolen a ball from a fellow pupil. Mr Benson, the schoolmaster, had had him suspended from a hook on the classroom wall.

"I'm sorry, boy," the master had said, "but it's for your own good!"

Then, in the presence of the whole school, he had been thrashed with the cane at least a dozen times. The pain had been excruciating, but he had forced back the tears, determined not to show any signs of weakness in front of his contemporaries.

As he was taken down, he had looked at Benson. The man was panting heavily, his face glowing red and perspiring with the effort he had just expended. However, the thing Tom still clearly remembered was the expression of sheer enjoyment that suffused the bloated features. It was something he had noticed on previous occasions, when Benson had administered corporal punishment to one of his classmates.

When he had arrived back home, his father had noticed that he was limping and in evident pain.

"What's up?" he had demanded.

Tom had reluctantly explained the caning — and the circumstances which had provoked it.

If he had expected sympathy and understanding from his

father, he was to be sadly disappointed. Caleb had removed his belt, stretched Tom over the back of a chair, and given him a further beating.

"Tharr'll teach yer to pinch stuff!"

Well, it had — at least, up to a point. That day, he had vowed that, in future, if he ever stole anything, it would be under circumstances where he could be assured of avoiding detection!

It had been Ann, once she had found religion, who had finally convinced him that he should never steal.

"Tom, what's yer most treasured possession?" she had asked.

Tom had shrugged: he possessed little.

"Well, there must be *summat* yer care about," she persisted. "Worr about Mr Cadman's 'osses?"

Yes, Tom had admitted, there was a close bond between them.

"Then, 'ow would *yoh* feel, if someone pinched one o' them? Yer'd be upset, wun't yer?"

"'Course."

"So, if yer wun't like it to 'appen to yoh, think 'ow others feel when it 'appens to them. It's not just 'cos o' t' whippin' yer'll get. It's 'cos it's wrong, Tom. That's why yer mustn't ever do it again."

Put like that, Tom had seen the logic of the argument. He had vowed that, in future, he would never steal: not because he feared another caning — though that prospect was daunting enough — but because it hurt other people. (However, he suspected that, if he ever *were* caught stealing, Ann would hand out a whipping as hard as his

188

father's!)

He glanced across at the neighbouring pew. Richard's face had turned as white as his shirt. Had the sermon on honesty had the same effect on him that the one on fornication had had on Tom — and for the same reason?

Tom thought back to Richard's visit to the pawnbroker's. He knew now that it was not Susannah's jewellery that had yielded the money to pay off Jacob Smalley. Tom had not been unduly surprised by the revelation: during the snippet of conversation he had overheard between them, Susannah had shown no inclination to bail her fiancé out. So, just what *had* he pawned?

The worshippers filed out of the south door on the stroke of noon and fragmented into small groups, exchanging pleasantries and gossip.

Hicks was walking arm in arm with Rachel, and Tom overheard Slack introduce him to an acquaintance as his elder daughter's fiancé. Well, thought Tom, as he watched her gazing adoringly at her escort, Hicks could only be doing it for the money — or to insinuate himself with Slack! Tom had learnt that Rachel was Slack's daughter by his first wife, Margaret, who had died in 1797. This probably explained the disparity in looks between her and Susannah.

Richard appeared to be more eager than usual to be off (he and Hall were again dining with the Slacks), but his progress down Church Yard Side was suddenly blocked by George Tully.

A small crowd had gathered behind. In it, Tom spotted several vaguely familiar faces, including the shaven-headed man who had bumped into Richard outside the Crown & Anchor, the previous afternoon, and had

189

followed him down Church Street. He was able to take a closer look at the man. A pauper from the workhouse, maybe? A lunatic? His face was pale and gaunt, and the staring eyes never left Richard. The latter cast a swift glance in his direction, and it seemed to Tom as if his cousin recognized the man; but the moment past, and Richard turned his attention back to Tully.

Tom sensed a fight was imminent. As he approached, he caught Tully's words: "Dun't forget next Friday, Miller!" Should he intervene? No, it was not his quarrel. Saving Susannah from Jacob Smalley's unwanted attentions was a natural, excusable act: bailing out Cousin Richard, though, was not his business.

It was Slack, however, who proved to be the saviour.

"Who are you?" he demanded.

"George Tully."

"Is there some problem, Mr Tully?" he enquired, interposing his considerable bulk between the two men.

"It's private," replied Tully.

"Dinner'll be gerrin' cowd," said Slack, fixing Richard with a basilisk stare.

"Of course, sir," said Richard, his smug smile evidently concealing a deep sense of relief. "I'd not wish to keep Miss Susannah waiting."

He moved to his fiancée's side, and offered her his arm, which she took with a gracious smile.

At the same moment, her eyes met Tom's and communicated an unspoken message: her memories of the previous afternoon were still fresh and warm.

Tom stuffed his hands deep into his breeches pockets to

stifle his incipient erection, and he checked the expressions of Slack and Richard for any sign that either might have witnessed the interchange of looks.

Neither appeared to have done so.

Under the combined gaze of Slack and Richard, Tully backed off and allowed the little entourage to continue its progress up Church Street unhindered. Tom looked again for the shaven-headed man, but he had gone.

As they filed past him, Tom heard the butcher's assistant mutter: "Yoh've bin warned, Miller!"

Richard was clearly in deep trouble; but, as Tom had told himself earlier, it was none of his business.

As they approached the top of Church Street, a familiar figure was tottering rather unsteadily out of the archway leading into Spittlehouse Gate. Uncle Ben!

Now, that *was* his business!

"Oi! Yoh!" he yelled, breaking ranks.

Ben Miller halted on the threshold of the Old Eclipse, looked round and tried to focus on the owner of the voice which had just addressed him.

"Tom!"

His master's voice rose above the general clamour like a clarion call.

Tom recoiled from Slack's scowling visage, looking instead at Richard, who was glaring at his father with undisguised loathing.

"Dinin' wi' Mr Slack?" sneered Ben, directing his question at Richard. "Ain't we good enough fer yer?"

"Who's that foul brute?" demanded Susannah.

"Just some drunken oaf!"

"It's 'is faither!" piped up Tom, earning himself a withering glance from his cousin. "Me uncle," he added, spitting contemptuously at Ben's feet.

"Tom!" interjected a female voice. "No brawling on the Sabbath!"

In the three weeks Tom had been with them, Sarah Slack had addressed barely half a dozen words to him. Tom now understood why. The set of "Waterloo" teeth she wore, although of cosmetic value, were of little practical use. The effort of issuing the reprimand loosened them from their moorings, and it required an athletic display from Hicks to catch them as they described a graceful arc through the air, much to the amusement of the gang of apprentices and street urchins who were watching the little drama unfold.

Slack, his face crimson with anger and embarrassment, gripped his wife firmly by the elbow and steered her in the direction of West Gate, beckoning the rest of the group to follow.

"Tom!" he hissed.

Tom fell into line beside him.

"What wor all *tharr* about?"

"Private," mumbled Tom.

Slack glowered at him.

"If I 'adn't took yoh in an' offered yer a decent education, that'd be *yoh*, in another 30 years! A drunken good-fer-nowt! So, be thankful!"

"Yes, sir. I am."

Slack laid an almost paternal arm around Tom's

shoulders, and his expression softened.

"Come on, then. Dinner'll be ready soon."

As if on cue, Tom felt his stomach rumble. Ben could wait. There was time enough for revenge!

CHAPTER 20

Thursday, 5th June, 1817

"Why t' long face, luv?"

Hannah pressed her well-rounded body against Tom's, as he sat staring listlessly at his untouched breakfast, and ruffled his tousled hair.

"It's Caleb," said Tom softly. "'E worn't lookin' too good, last Sunday. Nor Ann."

Indeed, the sight that had greeted Tom at his sister's house had horrified him. As usual, Jonathan had answered the door, but, when Tom passed through into the cottage, there had been no sign of either Ann or Caleb.

"Where are they?" Tom had asked.

His brother-in-law had motioned him through to the back room.

Ann had lain in a makeshift bed in the far corner, barely visible in the shadows, with Caleb beside her on the pillow. He had been naked, his skin translucent, his little stomach distended with malnutrition. From his twisted face, it had been clear to Tom that he was in agony, yet he lacked the strength to cry out.

"Worr 'appened to that food?" Tom had asked.

194

"We ate it," Jonathan had answered simply.

"An' t' money?"

Jonathan had kept his eyes focused rigidly on the floor, as Tom had continued to press him.

"We gi'd it to t' Chapel," Jonathan had finally blurted out.

"Yoh what?"

"We gi'd it to Mr Marshall, t' minister, as an offerin' to God. T' chapel needs a new roof."

"So do yoh!" Tom had replied bluntly, pointing to the damp seeping down the walls. "An' I dun't s'pose Mr Marshall thought yoh needed t' money more than God?"

A wan smile had flickered across Jonathan's pale lips, and he had looked at Tom as though he had suddenly come into possession of a knowledge of things greater than this world.

"'Cast thy bread upon the waters: for thou shalt find it after many days.' Ecclesiastes: Chapter 11, Verse 1."

Tom had shaken his head despairingly.

"When did yer last eat?"

A vague expression had passed over Jonathan's face, as he had trawled his memory for the answer.

"Yest'dy mornin' — I think."

"Think? Dun't yer know?"

Jonathan had shrugged.

"It's bin that long. Caleb 'ad most o' t' milk, an' Ann 'ad most o' t' food."

195

"An' yoh?"

"Enough," Jonathan had replied simply.

"Good job I brung yer some more, then," Tom had said, unwrapping his bundle. Then, noting his brother-in-law's sceptical expression, he had added: "Slack knows all about it."

After an agonizing hiatus, during which he had glanced anxiously at his wife and son, Jonathan had relented.

"Thanks," he had said, with a weary smile. "I'm sure God 'as guided 'im. It's norr *'im* I blame — it's Hicks!"

"An't y' 'eard?" Tom had said. "'Im an' Rachel's betrothed!"

For all his piety, Jonathan had been unable to suppress a cruel laugh.

"Poor lass! I knew she wor desperate for an 'usband, but, dear God —!"

Even Ann had looked up from her pillow and managed a weak smile.

On the Monday evening, during his lesson, he had confided his fears to Jessop.

"I've prayed," Tom had told him, "burr it dun't seem to 'ave done no good."

"It won't," the tutor had replied brusquely. "Talking to the empty air never does."

"But t' Reverend Cursham sez . . ."

Jessop had looked at him pityingly.

"God is a concept invented by our 'lords and masters' to keep the poor in submissive obedience, by filling their minds with the fear of an imaginary Hell and the hope of an equally fictitious Heaven!"

Tom looked up from the bread and cheese into Hannah's warm, kind face, which seemed somehow enhanced, rather than disfigured, by that strawberry birthmark. From the aching longing visible behind her smiling brown eyes, Tom knew that she would have made a fine wife and mother, had someone only taken the trouble to discover the purity of her soul beneath the blemished surface.

"What should I do, 'Annah?" he pleaded.

"What did I tell yer, last time?"

"If folk'll norr 'elp theirsens, there's nowt yer can do fer 'em."

"Well, then," smiled Hannah. "Yer gi'd 'em that food, din't yer?"

Tom nodded.

"Then, 'appen your Jonathan's come to 'is senses! Does 'e love yer sister?"

"'E married 'er," answered Tom.

"That's not t' same thing," countered Hannah, exposing her decaying teeth in a wry grin. "Miss Susannah's marryin' that cousin o' yourn, but she dun't love 'im."

Tom smiled at the memory of the Saturday afternoon they had spent together, when Susannah had confessed as much. In fact, he doubted if she was capable of love for any creature, but merely enjoyed the thrill of coupling for its own sake. And, Tom reflected, there was certainly much to enjoy! The way Ben had described the mechanics of the act had given him no inkling of the pleasurable nature of the experience. However, that had nothing to do

197

with Ann and Jonathan.

"Aye, 'e loves 'em both. I know 'e does. Burr 'e thinks there's nowt 'e can do about whether they live or die. 'E reckons it's all in God's 'ands — if 'E exists."

"'Course 'E does — an' in a way, Jonathan's rait. It's not fer t' likes of us to question God's ways. 'E'll mek 'em known to us in 'Is own good time. Burr, in t' meantime, 'E dun't expect us just to sit on our arses, doin' nowt. God 'elps them as 'elps theirsens."

Tom sighed impatiently.

"I've gorra do summat!"

Hannah leaned forward and kissed him on the left temple. He did not resist.

As Tom turned into Mitre Court, a familiar figure was leaving Ann and Jonathan's cottage: George Hicks. His sallow face looked paler than usual, and the lower half of it was obscured by a large linen handkerchief. As he passed Tom, he barely acknowledged his presence; such was his keenness to be out of the cul-de-sac.

Tom reached the cottage and knocked.

Jonathan opened the door. His gaunt face was almost radiant.

"Yer'll never guess what, Tom! Hicks 'as bin!"

"I know. I've just seen 'im."

"'E's brung me an order. A dozen pairs o' silk stockings by next Friday! An' 'e's gi'd me an advance o' ten bob!"

Tom feigned surprise, but, in fact, it was not unexpected.

After his talk with Hannah, he had contemplated going to see Slack again, and pleading with him to persuade Hicks to give Jonathan work.

Then, he had had a better idea. He had little chance of changing his master's mind. However, he had lately discovered that Miss Rachel, though a somewhat reticent young woman, had a kindly nature and could perhaps be prevailed upon to exercise some influence over her fiancé.

She had heard Tom's tale patiently, and, from time to time, her brown eyes blinked away a rising tear.

"Of course I'll help," she had said. "Has George left on his rounds yet?"

"No, Miss Rachel."

"Good. Catch him before he goes, and tell him I wish to see him."

Tom's heart soared.

"Yes, miss!"

Hicks had been duly summoned to his fiancée's presence.

Five minutes later, he had emerged from her room, scowling, yet cowed into submission.

Tom had smiled: his little stratagem had worked.

Jonathan now ushered him inside the cottage, still babbling incoherently of his stroke of good fortune.

Tom looked round. There were a few fragments of food left on the table, but the majority had been consumed.

"Where's Ann an' Caleb?" Tom asked apprehensively. "Still in bed?"

"Aye, but stronger. Ann ate a bit o' bread, an' Caleb drank all 'is milk."

He showed Tom through to the back room. The tableau was more or less that of the previous day, except that Ann was now propped up in bed, Caleb's tiny form cradled close to her bosom. As Tom approached the bed on tiptoe, he noticed Caleb's minuscule chest rising and falling in a rather irregular rhythm, as though his breathing was laboured.

"I think 'e's gerrin' stronger," said Ann, in a pained whisper, a pathetic hope shining in her tired eyes.

"'E looks it," lied Tom, as Jonathan led him upstairs into the attic.

The knitting frame stood in the far corner of the room by the tall window, near which was suspended a bowl of water. Jonathan had once explained to him that this magnified the rays of the dying sun and delayed the need for artificial lighting.

Tom ran a finger across the frame: it was caked in dust and cobwebs from long weeks of disuse.

"It'll be good to get back to wokk," smiled Jonathan. "Earn an honest livin', instead o' relyin' on charity. I still can't understand why Hicks changed 'is mind, though."

Tom managed to stifle a smirk.

"'Appen 'e wor guided by God!"

"'Appen so," agreed Jonathan, with a broad smile, clearly oblivious of the irony in his brother-in-law's voice. "God moves in mysterious ways."

And so, thought Tom, does Miss Rachel!

That afternoon, Tom sat in his room and reflected on the week's events so far. At least he felt happier about Ann, Jonathan and Caleb, now that Rachel had persuaded Hicks to put some work Jonathan's way.

Although Jonathan was in many respects a fool, he was a conscientious and industrious worker, and would take full advantage of the opportunity Chance — or God, as he would see it — had offered him. He was a good husband and father, and would welcome the chance to support his family by his own endeavours.

Meanwhile, Tom had been to another meeting at the Black's Head, on the Wednesday evening; but he had learnt nothing of value, and no shilling had been forthcoming from Will.

Like an untended fire, the revolutionary fervour in Mansfield seemed to be dying out.

Jessop closed the book, and looked up at Tom, pride shining in his pale blue eyes.

"Well done, Tom! I've never known a pupil make such progress!"

Tom basked in the warm glow of his tutor's praise. Of course, it was not as if he was new to reading. It was like riding a horse: a skill, once learnt, that you never forgot.

"I s'pose I've got Mr 'All to thank, an' all," he conceded.

"Hall? Why? What's he done?"

Tom told him about the books the lawyer had let him

take.

"I've bin readin' 'em, ev'ry nait. There wor even an owd Bible as 'e let me 'ave."

Jessop's face clouded.

"You don't want to fill your head with *that* nonsense!"

Tom decided to change the subject.

"When's t' next meetin'?"

"Sunday night. I've had more pamphlets printed. They'll be distributed tomorrow."

"'Ow many d'yer reckon'll come?"

Jessop sighed deeply and shrugged.

"Ned, you and I, for a guess! I just don't understand Mansfield. Every other town and city holds meetings that attract disaffected men by the hundred. Things are just as bad here as elsewhere in the country, yet we can barely manage a dozen! Why?"

Tom thought hard.

"Me Dad said there were riots over bread, back in 1800. 'E chucked a stone through George Shippam's window, top o' Church Street. 'Appen folk are scared t' Militia'll be sent in again, same as they were then."

Jessop removed his spectacles and polished them.

"Perhaps so, Tom. We'll see."

There conversation was interrupted by the sound of hammering on the front door.

Tom made his excuses and went down to answer it. However, his master had reached the door first and opened it. Robert Hall stood on the threshold.

"Hall!" boomed Slack. "What can we do fer yer?"

The little lawyer looked past him at the figure of Tom descending the stairs.

"I want him!"

"Tom? Why?"

Hall's plump face had turned a deep puce with rage.

"The boy's a thief!"

CHAPTER 21

Thursday, 5th June, 1817

"Yer'd best come in."

Slack stood aside to let the little lawyer through. He then led the way into the front parlour, motioned to Hall to take a seat, and slammed the door shut behind him.

It was nearly dusk, and the dying sun filled the room with a warm, russet glow; but the atmosphere within was distinctly frosty.

"Brandy?" Slack enquired, crossing to the sideboard.

"Not for me," snapped Hall.

"Well, *I* certainly need one!" said Slack, pouring himself a generous measure. He drank it in a single draught, then turned back to Hall. "Yer'd best explain yersen."

Hall pointed at Tom.

"It's *he* should be explaining himself!" exploded the lawyer.

"Burr I an't done nowt!" protested Tom, looking to his master for support.

"Thief, yer say?" queried Slack incredulously.

Hall nodded.

"An' what's 'e s'posed to 'ave stolen?" demanded Slack, pouring himself a second brandy.

"A valuable gold watch, belonging to my grandfather."

Tom took a pace forward.

"I dun't know nowt about no watch!"

Slack indicated a chair.

"Sit down, Tom. Yer'll ay *your* chance later."

Tom meekly obeyed.

Once Tom was ensconced in his chair, Hall stood up and crossed towards him. With his hands clasped firmly behind his back and his chest thrust forward, the little lawyer presented a faintly pompous figure; but the steely glint behind his thick lenses sent a thrill of terror through Tom's body. Even though he had nothing to hide, he knew that Hall was so practised in the art of cross-examination that he could make a witness swear black was white.

"You were at my office, last Friday morning, were you not?" he demanded.

"'Course 'e wor!" interjected Slack. "It wor me as sent 'im!"

Hall inflated his barrel chest, until Tom feared he would explode, as he slowly rounded on the hosier.

"Let the boy answer the question himself!"

"Aye, I wor there," confirmed Tom. "Mr Slack sent me wi' a sealed package fer yer, if yer remember."

"And what happened after you handed over the package?"

"Yoh asked me to go up to yer room to pack some books

205

up fer yer."

"So, you admit you were in my room, last Friday morning?"

"'Course I wor!" said Tom. "Like I just said, yoh asked me to go in there."

Tom looked to his master for moral support, but Slack's face remained as expressionless as a stone mask.

"Then I left, shortly afterwards, did I not?" continued the lawyer.

Tom nodded in agreement.

"And what did you do, whilst you were in there alone?"

Tom returned his eagle gaze with a blank stare.

"Packed t' books for yer, like yer towd me to."

"Did you take anything from there?"

Tom's face brightened.

"Aye. An owd Bible an' a book on 'osses. Yoh said, if I saw owt I liked, I could ay it."

"True," conceded the lawyer, somewhat rattled by the vehemence of Tom's reply. "But did you take anything else?"

"No!"

Tom sprang from his chair, until he towered above the little lawyer.

"Tom! Sit down!"

His master's voice came like a bucket of cold water thrown in his face, and he slowly lowered himself back into the chair.

"Keep calm," Slack advised him. "Yer've nowt to fear, if yer tell t' truth."

Hall began to pace up and down the room before continuing.

"Did you see a bureau in the corner, by the window?" he persisted.

"Aye."

"Did you look inside any of the drawers?"

"No."

Slack was refilling his glass. He spun round to face Hall.

"When did yer last see t' watch?"

The lawyer was brought up short in his perambulations, unused to being on the receiving end of hostile interrogation.

"That very morning," he stammered, once he had recovered his composure, "about nine o'clock. I took it out to wind it."

Tom waited for his master to pursue his line of questioning. Instead, he sat down, seemingly disappointed by the answer. Perhaps he had expected Hall to say he had not seen it for several weeks.

"Richard tells me you were alone up there for three-quarters of an hour. Ample time to rifle through the bureau, find the watch and pocket it."

By now, Tom had recovered from the initial shock of the accusation and had begun to marshal his wits. How could he prove his innocence? The fact slowly dawned on him that the only way to vindicate himself was to find the real culprit, and his suspicions were already forming in that direction. Richard! It *had* to be Richard! Since Susannah had confirmed that she had not given him any of her jewellery, Hall's watch seemed to be the most likely object he had pawned.

And what of the shaven-headed man he had taken for a drunkard and who had seemed to take such a keen interest in Richard that weekend? What part did *he* play in all this?

"Plenty o' time fer others, an' all!" said Tom.

The colour in Hall's apple-red cheeks intensified, as he clamped his ivory dentures together, and a strange gurgling sound escaped from his throat.

"What d'you mean?" demanded the lawyer, in a hoarse, menacing whisper.

"Richard, fer a start."

Hall's mouth opened and closed, like that of a stranded halibut, and it was Slack who reacted first.

"Be careful, Tom!"

Hall finally found his voice. "Are you daring to suggest that . . ?"

Why not? thought Tom, remembering Richard's half-brother, Jack. If there had been one thief in the family, why not two.

"'E come round 'ere, last Wednesday," said Tom.

"I know," cut in Slack. "We all went out to dinner wi' t' Thompsons, on Leeming Street."

"Aye, burr 'e 'ad a word wi' Miss Susannah, fost."

"Word?" echoed Hall.

Tom summarized the gist of the conversation between

208

Richard and Susannah he had overheard, that evening.

"Ask Miss Susannah, if yer dun't believe me!"

"I will!" declared Slack. He marched over to the door, flung it open and bellowed: "Susannah!"

A few moments later, Susannah, in a high waisted, peach dress, entered and stood just inside the doorway, gazing dutifully at her father.

"Susannah," said Hall, "I want you to think back to last Wednesday evening. Did Richard call round?"

"Yes. We'd been invited to dine with the Thompsons. The invitation was extended to Richard."

"And did you and he have a private conversation together, before you set out?"

Susannah looked at Tom, who was staring back intently, willing her to tell the truth.

"Yes," she conceded.

"An' what did yer talk about?" demanded Slack.

"What did you and Mama talk about, Papa, when you were betrothed?" asked Susannah, with a demure smile.

Slack almost choked on his brandy, but quickly recovered.

"'E din't say owt about bein' in any trouble, did 'e?"

"Trouble?"

"Debts."

Now! thought Tom, staring at her intently. Say that he did, and prove to them I'm telling the truth!

"He mentioned no debts," replied Susannah, staring

fixedly at her father.

"Tom said 'e 'eard 'im say it," said Slack.

Susannah turned on Tom, her eyes blazing with fury.

"You dare to spy on people?"

"Never mind that!" interjected Slack. "Did Richard ask yer to pawn yer jewels to bail 'im out o' gamin' debts?"

"Did he what?" gasped Susannah.

"I warn yer: if I find out there's a single grain o' truth in this, I'll call off t' engagement, an' mek sure 'e never sets foot in this 'ouse agen!"

Susannah's gaze travelled round the room, until it finally came to rest on Tom.

"No."

"'E did!" shrieked Tom. Why was she denying it?

"No!" repeated Susannah, more forcefully.

"The case appears to be proven," cut in Hall.

Slack's face seemed to crumple like a deflated balloon.

"Well, Tom, yoh 'eard what she said."

"Then, she's lyin'!"

A strangled cry arose from the depth of Slack's throat.

"Call my daughter a liar? It's *yoh* that's the liar! God, I rue t' day I ever brung yer into this 'ouse!"

"Ask Jacob Smalley. 'E knows — an' George Tully!"

"Smalley!" snapped Susannah. "You'd take *his* word against mine?"

"I'll gi' yer one last chance to own up, Tom," said Slack.

Tom felt his head spinning, and gripped the back of a chair for support.

"I'm a fair man," cut in Hall, turning to Tom. "Hand back the watch at once, and I'll not press charges."

"I can't, 'cos I an't gorrit!" protested Tom.

"I'll norr 'arbour a thief under me roof," said Slack. "You're out of 'ere tonait!"

"It wor Richard!" insisted Tom vehemently. "I saw 'im, Sat'day mornin', comin' out o' t' pawnshop on t' corner o' Wass Lane."

"You're only making things worse for yourself," said Hall. Then, turning to Slack, he added: "Hold him here overnight, and we'll take him before the magistrate, first thing in the morning."

Slack looked long and hard at the lawyer, then at Tom.

"Rait."

Tom lunged at Susannah and gripped her so firmly by the elbow that she let out a shriek of pain.

"Yer've gorra tell 'em t' truth!" pleaded Tom.

Susannah shook herself free. "He said nothing to me, either about having gambling debts or about pawning my jewellery."

Slack took a step towards Tom, his fists clenched so tightly that his knuckles gleamed white in contrast to the ruddy colouring of the surrounding skin, and Tom braced himself to repel his master's onslaught.

"A thief an' a liar — an' now you're tryin' to drag me daughter's name through t' mud! I swear I'll . . !"

"Slack!"

211

It was the little lawyer who had spoken, and the hosier stopped in his tracks.

"Leave him!" commanded Hall. "This is a matter for the Law to deal with. Do you want to find *yourself* on the gallows, swinging alongside him?"

Tom's throat tightened. Hanging? For a watch? He'd known young men of his age transported to Van Diemen's Land for such offences, but hanging . . .

Slack seemed to relax. He crossed to the door and yelled: "Jessop!"

Within moments, the tutor had descended the stairs, and Slack had apprised him of the situation.

"I'm purrin' yoh in charge on 'im, till we gerrim in front o' t' justice, tomorrer."

Jessop stared at him incredulously.

"Tom? A thief? I can't . . ."

"Are yoh questionin' my orders?" demanded Slack.

"No, but . . ."

"'Cos, if yer do, yoh'll be follerin' 'im out into t' street!"

Jessop placed a hand on Tom's shoulder.

"No point arguing, Tom. We'd better do as he says."

Tom reluctantly followed the tutor upstairs to the study. Within twelve hours, his fate would be sealed. It could be the end of his life in England — even the end of his life altogether!

"And that's the whole story?"

Ten minutes had elapsed, and Tom and Jessop were seated in the latter's room.

"Aye, an' it's true! *Yoh* believe me, dun't yer?"

"Yes, I do."

Tom brightened.

"Well, then, if I tell t' magistrate t' truth, same as I've towd yoh, 'e'll . . ."

Jessop let out a sharp, mirthless laugh.

"Truth! D'you think *that's* going to do you any good?"

"Our Ann allus towd me: 'Tell t' truth, an' shame t' Devil.'"

"Fine sentiments!" scoffed Jessop. "But all these local magistrates are landowners. They'll take the side of Hall and Slack — not the likes of you and me. But, come the Revolution, their kind'll be swept away like chaff at winnowing time."

"Worr'll we do till then?" asked Tom mournfully.

Jessop paced restlessly up and down for several moments.

"There's only one solution, Tom. You'll have to escape."

Tom looked blankly at the tutor.

"Escape? 'Ow?"

"I heard the others go out, about five minutes ago," said Jessop. "We're alone now. I'll let you out; then it's up to you."

"Worr about yoh?" protested Tom. "Yer'll gerr into no end o' trouble."

Jessop smiled.

"That's for *me* to worry about. Now, hurry. I don't know how long they'll be."

Darkness had almost descended, as Tom made his way cautiously down West Gate. Already, a plan was forming in his head.

Before he had left, he had checked the time: 8.20. He still remembered enough of the coach schedules to know that one was due to depart from the Swan Inn for Nottingham at 8.30.

Jessop had provided him with a further useful piece of information: the address, in Barker Gate, Nottingham, of Jeremiah Brandreth.

"S'pose 'e thinks I'm a spy or summat?" Tom had asked.

"If he — or anyone — questions your loyalty to the Cause, tell them Brutus sent you."

As he crossed Market Place, Tom's keen hearing picked up the jingle of harness and whinnying of horses. Moments later, this was followed by the emergence of the coach from the Swan Yard.

It headed towards him, and then stopped at the bottom of Leeming Street to execute a complicated manoeuvre that brought it into line with the archway leading to Spittle-house Gate.

He waited until the horses had disappeared under the archway, then clambered onto the pile of trunks and cases strapped to the back of the coach.

Once in position, Tom braced himself for a rough ride.

CHAPTER 22

Thursday, 5th June, 1817

He could hold on no longer.

"Ayup! What's this?"

With difficulty, Tom turned his head and looked up. A long, gaunt face was gazing down at him.

"Stowaway, eh?" said the face.

The coach ground to an abrupt halt.

"What's up?" boomed a deep voice.

"We've gorran extra passenger," replied the gaunt-featured man. "Abscondin' apprentice?"

"No!" cried Tom.

Now that the coach had stopped, he was able to take in his surroundings. They had left the town behind and were deep into the forest, where the occasional shaft of moonlight found its way through the thick curtain of foliage overhead.

The coachman had dismounted and come round to the back of the vehicle. He ran an appraising eye over Tom's livery.

"Runnin' away from yer master?"

"No!"

"On t' run from t' Law, then?"

"No!"

"Ah!" said the gaunt-featured man, with a jovial laugh. "I reckon yoh've 'it on t' truth."

"I an't done nowt!" protested Tom.

"Worr're yer doin' on there, then?" demanded the coachman.

"Goin' to Nottingham," replied Tom, adding, in a moment of inspiration, "to see me uncle."

The coachman continued gazing intently at Tom.

"I know yoh, dun't I?"

Tom shrugged.

"I've gorra good memory fer faces," said the coachman. "I'll gerrit, in a minute."

Tom had now dismounted from his perch on top on the luggage. For a moment, he contemplated running off. No, that would be stupid: it was virtually pitch-black, and he hadn't the faintest idea where he was.

"T' Owd Eclipse!" said the coachman. "You're an ostler there! See, I towd yer I never forget a face."

"I left there," said Tom.

"To go where?"

There was no point in lying, and, in any case, he had no need to fear telling the truth, whatever Jessop might say.

"Samuel Slack, t' 'osier, t' top end o' West Gate," he answered.

By now, anxious heads were poking out of the carriage windows, enquiring as to the cause of the hold-up.

"Nowt to worry yersen over," the coachman reassured them.

The heads disappeared.

"'Ow much money ay yer gorr on yer?" asked the coachman.

"Nowt," replied Tom.

The coachman removed his hat and scratched his balding head.

"'Ere," said the gaunt-featured man, reaching down from the roof and passing a handful of coins to the coachman. "Tek this fer t' lad's fare."

The coachman mumbled something in reply and hastily pocketed the money.

"Come on!" yelled the gaunt-featured man, reaching down to Tom. "It's more comfortable up 'ere."

Within seconds, Tom was seated beside his saviour, and the coachman was encouraging the horses to resume their labours.

"I dun't know 'ow to thank yer," stammered Tom.

"What's yer name?" asked the stranger.

"Tom Stone. An' yourn?"

"Bradley," replied the other. "Tommy Bradley. Rait, lad, where's this uncle o' yourn live?"

"Barker Gate."

The stranger almost fell off his seat, and only prompt assistance from Tom prevented him from being hurled from the roof into the inky blackness below.

"Barker Gate?" he repeated softly.

Tom nodded.

"What's yer uncle's name?"

"Jerry."

"Jerry what?"

"Brandreth."

Bradley gripped Tom's shoulder hard, until he winced with pain, and stared at him through narrowed eyes.

"Jerry Brandreth an't got no nephews!" he whispered hoarsely. "Who are yer? A spy fer King George?"

Tom shook his head.

"Who, then?"

Tom remembered Jessop's message.

"Brutus sent me."

Bradley's grip relaxed, and a smile spread slowly across his craggy features.

"Well, why the 'ell din't yer say so before?"

"What the 'ell wor that?"

Ann Brandreth slowly raised her head from the pillow, then turned to nudge her husband.

"What's up?" grunted Jeremiah Brandreth, opening one eye.

"Someone at t' door. 'Ark at it!"

There was another rapid series of bangs from downstairs.

At the same moment, the cry of a child sounded from the neighbouring room.

"Damn!" screamed Ann. "They've woke Elizabeth! Who the 'ell'd come knockin' at *this* hour?"

"I'll go an' see," said Brandreth, easing himself out from between the sheets. "Yoh try an' get t' kids off agen."

He lit a "poor light", made his way tentatively downstairs, opened the door and blinked rapidly.

"Tommy! Worr're *yoh* doin' 'ere? It's nigh on two o'clock in t' mornin'!"

"Sorry I woke yer, Jerry," mumbled Bradley, "burr I . . ."

"Who's this?" cut in Brandreth, pointing at Tom.

"Tom Stone, Mr Brandreth."

"No need for formality, lad. Call me Jerry."

"I'm a friend o' Ned 'Opkins' in Mansfield," added Tom. "Brutus sent me."

Tom went cold. By this time, his escape would have been discovered, and Jessop would be faced with the task of explaining it.

"I thought t' face wor familiar," said Jerry, ushering his visitors over the threshold. "I've seen yer at t' meetings."

If only Jerry knew the *true* reason he had been there!

"'Ow come *yoh* know Brutus?" asked Jerry warily.

Tom gave him a résumé of recent events since he had entered the Slack household.

"Yoh go through to t' back, lad," said Jerry, "while me an' Tommy 'ere 'as a word. If you're 'ungry, yer might find a stale crust in there."

Tom suddenly realized he had been so used to eating well, over the last three or four weeks, that he had almost forgotten what it was like to subsist on a few bare scraps. It seemed unfair to impose on people who had so little; yet it was almost seven hours since he had eaten, and the rumblings from his stomach were now quite audible.

He gradually took in his surroundings. The cottage was an almost exact replica of the one where Ann and Jonathan lived — no doubt there was also an idle knitting frame in the attic. There were more domestic touches, though, and an effort had clearly been made — by Jerry's wife, presumably — to make it tidy and respectable.

He found the bread, broke off a piece, and slowly gnawed it, as he concentrated on the conversation from the front room.

"Now," said Jerry, "what's so urgent?"

"I've just got back from Dewsbury," replied Bradley. "Remember that meetin' at Thornhill Lees that Oliver wor goin' to, Wednesday nait?"

"Worr about it?"

"It wor broke up by t' Militia. Three's bin arrested — Smaller, Mann an' Murray."

Tom strained his ears to catch the details. Did Will know about this? How much would it have been worth, if only he could have got the details through to Mansfield?

By mentioning the name of Brutus, he now had the full confidence of these men: the perfect cover for his spying operation!

No! Why should he help Will and his paymasters? Slack, the Law, the Church, the Army, Lord Liverpool: they were all part of the same conspiracy against the working man, as

Jessop had so cogently pointed out. He was an outcast, now, with the shadow of the noose hanging above his head. He could no longer think of going back to Mansfield to clear his name. Neither Slack nor Hall believed him. He might as well throw in his lot with these men!

He heard Jerry mutter a curse.

"Worr about Oliver?"

There was a sharp exhalation of breath.

"'E gorr out through t' back window o' t' Sportsman's Arms — same as at Sheffield! 'E seems to mek an 'abit on it!"

"What's *that* mean?" asked Jerry.

"It means I dun't trust 'im," said Bradley, "an' there's a good many round 'ere agrees wi' me."

"Why not?"

"I wor talkin' wi' John Dickenson — owns a linen draper's in Dewsbury. 'E sez 'im an' a fellow called Willans saw Oliver, yest'dy mornin', ridin' in a gig."

Tom felt his eyelids begin to droop. He shook himself.

"So?" demanded Jerry.

"A gig belongin' to Colonel Byng — t' local magistrate."

There was the sound of nervous pacing.

"Did they say owt to 'im?" asked Jerry, clearly unconvinced by Bradley's argument.

"Aye. They asked 'im why 'e 'adn't bin arrested."

Again, Tom felt himself succumbing to drowsiness. Only a monumental effort of concentration kept him awake.

"An' what did 'e say?" asked Jerry.

"'E said 'e *'ad* bin — but they found nowt on 'im, so they 'ad to lerrim go!"

"Oliver's due in Nottingham, today," said Jerry. "There's a meetin' at t' Punch Bowl, this afternoon. 'E'll ay plenty o' chance to clear 'issen then."

"Yoh still reckon 'e's true to t' Cause?" challenged Bradley.

Tom never heard the reply. His body could resist no longer, and he sank into a deep slumber.

CHAPTER 23

Friday, 6th June, 1817

"Sleep well, lad?"

The sunlight almost burned his eyes. The morning must have been well advanced.

The face above him gradually came into focus. It belonged to a woman of about the same age as his sister — perhaps slightly older — but with the same careworn expression. Although her clothes were poor, there was evidence that she had tried to keep them in a state of good repair. Her body was thin, yet Tom noticed a swelling around the abdomen. She was pregnant. Another child condemned to a harsh existence in an unforgiving world!

From the front room came the sound of two young children engaged in boisterous play. There were cries of: "Death to t' King! Long live t' Republic!"

The woman ran thin, callused fingers through her tangled black hair.

"Timothy, Elizabeth, shurrup!" she screamed, dashing into the front room, with Tom hot on her heels.

A boy of about eight, armed with a stick, which he brandished like a cavalry sabre, was chasing a girl, some two years his junior, round the room.

"Timothy!" yelled Ann Brandreth, causing the child to stop abruptly in his tracks. "'Ow many more times? Them words is treason!"

"Bu' me Dad sez . . ."

"I dun't care worr 'e sez," snapped Ann. "I'll norr ay 'im teachin' yer treason — though it's a wonder 'e teaches yer owt, seein' as 'ow 'e's never 'ere!"

"Where *is* 'e?" cut in Tom.

"T' Three Salmons or t' Duke o' York, at a guess!"

"What's 'e do there, all day?" asked Elizabeth.

"'E's plannin' to kill t' King," said Timothy, "like this!"

He lunged at his sister with the makeshift sword, and Tom's fears that he might cause her serious injury were only allayed when Ann grabbed the boy by the scruff of his neck, like a cat bringing an errant kitten into line.

"Stop yer runnin' round — frightenin' yer poor sister like that!"

"I worn't scared!" responded Elizabeth defiantly, and promptly launched herself at her brother, so that they fell to the floor in a threshing heap of tangled limbs.

"Stop it, t' pair on yer!" screamed Ann. "Yer know me 'ead can't be doin' wi' it!"

The noise subsided, and Ann sat down, one hand clasped to her brow, the other to her swollen belly.

The children stood up, mumbling apologies.

"Yer can mek yersens useful, an' cut t' 'eads off them turnips!" said Ann, pointing to a meagre pile of vegetables by the hearth.

"Dad sez it'll be t' King's 'ead we'll be cuttin' off, soon," said Timothy.

His mother was about to reprimand him further, when the door opened and Jeremiah Brandreth walked in. There was still the same jaunty swagger in his gait that Tom remembered from their first meeting, and the same fire smouldered in his dark eyes.

"What's for dinner?" he demanded, ignoring both Tom and his children.

"Turnips."

"No meat?"

"Norr unless *yoh've* brung some."

Jerry glowered at her.

"We'll ay plenty, after Monday."

"Is that when yer cut t' King's 'ead off?" asked Timothy eagerly.

"It's when we march on London, son," replied Jerry proudly. "It'll not be long after, when we topple t' King."

Jerry bent forward to kiss his wife, who promptly recoiled.

"I thought as much! You're drunk!"

"Drunk?" echoed Jerry. "On a quart o' that rat's piss they serve in t' Duke o' York?"

"A quart?" gasped Ann. "'Ow can yer afford a quart of ale, when yer can't even afford decent food fer yer fam'ly?"

"It wor bought for me!" snapped Jerry. "Anyroad, like I said, yer'll soon be eatin' all t' food yer want — of silver plates!"

"Silver!" cried Timothy, awestruck. "Like a lord?"

Jerry slipped an arm round his son's shoulders.

"Like t' King 'issen, lad!"

"An' that's another thing," said Ann. "I'll norr ay yoh fillin' t' lad's 'ead wi' all this nonsense about a republic."

She was beginning to sound like his own sister, thought Tom. Next thing, she'd be quoting from the Bible, and saying it was all God's will that they lived in squalor!

"We're only tekkin' back what's ourn by rights," said Jerry.

"More treason!" snapped Ann. "Remember Jeremiah: Chapter 17, Verse 11. 'He that getteth riches, and not by right, shall leave them in the midst of his days.'"

Tom groaned, his worst fears confirmed. Still, at least Jerry — unlike Jonathan — was prepared to do something to improve his lot!

The thought of self-improvement sent a shiver through Tom's frame. Where had his efforts to improve himself got him? Branded a thief and a liar! As he listened to Ned, Jerry and Jessop, he was slowly coming round to their way of thinking: that open revolt was the only answer for the likes of him!

"I know what's rait, Ann," said Jerry. "I dun't need yoh quotin' t' bloody Bible at me!"

"I'll norr ay blasphemy, neither!" retorted his wife. "An' yoh a man as goes to Chapel, ev'ry Sunday! Some's born to be poor. Yer can't ay a world where ev'ryone's rich."

How she reminded Tom of his own dear Ann! Yet he

was beginning to feel acutely embarrassed, acting like an eavesdropper upon a domestic squabble.

"You're just like Lord Liverpool an' t' rest," countered Jerry, "spoutin' t' Bible to justify keepin' us in poverty!"

Samuel Slack, too, thought Tom. He was now having reservations about running away. It would only make him seem the more guilty. Jessop was right, though. Who would believe *his* word against those of Richard and Susannah?

"Why dun't yer go out there an' look fer wokk, instead o' moanin'?" shouted Ann, the whole of her tiny frame shaking with rage.

"'Cos there in't none!"

"There must be summat!"

"There's nowt!"

Jerry spun round on his heels and headed for the stairs. He stopped at the foot and turned round.

"Anyroad, I've gorra meetin' at t' Punch Bowl, at three," he said. "Oliver's comin'. We've gorra settle that Thornhill Lees business."

The Punch Bowl was packed to capacity: a sharp contrast to the poor turnouts in Mansfield. The air was so thick with acrid tobacco smoke, it was almost impossible to breathe, and Tom looked round in vain for an open window near to which he could station himself.

"Yer mun't mind Ann," Jerry was saying. "Women dun't understand these things."

Tom was not really listening. The mood of the room was

growing increasingly restless.

"Where is 'e?" demanded a voice from the back.

"Too scared to come!" shouted another.

"'E'll be 'ere," Jerry tried to reassure them. "'Appen t' Sheffield coach is late."

The buzz of discontent gradually subsided, but the expressions of the assembled men remained grim.

At that moment, the door opened, and a tall, imposing figure stood in the doorway. His handsome face was topped with a mane of red hair, and his well-cut green coat was in sharp contrast to the patched, threadbare garments of the labourers and craftsmen he had come to address.

"I'm sorry I'm late," said Oliver, in a quiet, musical voice. "I'm unable to stay long. I have to get back to London, by tomorrow, and . . ."

"D'yer still claim to be a true republican?" demanded a tall, swarthy man near the front.

"And who might *you* be?" enquired Oliver.

The speaker rose from his chair and came forward.

"John Holmes, t' Nottingham delegate."

Tom noticed a muscle at the corner of Oliver's mouth twitch.

"I'm no traitor."

"Then, why are yer in such a rush to get back to London?" demanded Holmes.

"Because the dissenters in London are waiting for me. If I don't go, *they'll* start to doubt me."

Holmes seemed unconvinced.

"Who's payin' yer fares?"

"The London republicans."

"An' where's t' money come from?"

"A secret fund."

"Who controls it?"

"Thomas Wooler. He's a printer."

As he listened to these exchanges, Tom was reminded of being forced to learn his Catechism at school: a set of prepared answers reeled off without a second's pause.

Holmes had now edged closer to Oliver.

"An' what line o' wokk are *yoh* in?" he demanded.

"I'm a carpenter."

Like a snake pouncing upon its prey, Holmes sprang forward, gripped Oliver by the wrists, and turned his hands palm upwards.

"Look at this!" said Holmes, beckoning to his comrades to gather round for a more detailed inspection. "Are *them* a carpenter's 'ands?"

Those who were closest shook their heads sceptically.

"I *was* a carpenter," answered Oliver, by now clearly flustered. "I've been a surveyor, of late."

"Aye," said Holmes, "surveyin' our plans fer King George!"

"No! I swear it!"

Oliver's composure had now returned, and he wriggled free of Holmes' grasp.

Holmes then produced a sheet of paper from inside his

coat and waved it under Oliver's nose.

"Yoh reckon there's 70,000 men waitin' to rise in London?"

Oliver shrugged.

"That's what Mitchell told me."

"You're not sure, then?"

"It's difficult to be exact," replied Oliver, going on the defensive. "So few men in London know the true figure."

Tommy Bradley now stepped forward.

"Worr 'appened at Thornhill Lees?"

"We were surprised by the Militia," replied Oliver.

"Surprised? Someone 'ad towd 'em, more like!"

There were murmurs of agreement.

"An' 'ow come yoh were in Dewsbury, t' day after, ridin' in Colonel Byng's gig?"

"Dewsbury?" echoed Oliver, his eyebrows rising sharply. "Colonel Byng?"

"T' local magistrate."

"What makes you think that?"

"There were witnesses."

"Then, I'm afraid they were mistaken," replied Oliver, with a sad shake of the head.

"Liar!"

"Tommy," said Jerry, intervening, "let's not quarrel among ussens. It's not good fer t' Cause."

This seemed to pacify most people, except for Holmes,

who dug a stubby index finger into Oliver's chest.

"Round 'ere, we're not so fond o' bein' 'anged fer nowt. Stay, an' I might just believe yer."

There followed a tense hiatus, broken by Oliver, who laid a placatory hand on Holmes' shoulder.

"I'll make a bargain with you," he said softly. "I'll stay, if you'll send someone to London with information."

For a moment, his gaze fell on Tom, who looked to Jerry for guidance.

"Sounds a fair offer," said Jerry. "What d'yer say, lads?"

"I believe 'im," said a voice from the back.

"Me, an' all," added another.

There followed a general babble of voices.

"Shurrup!"

Jerry had sprung onto a chair and was glaring round the room in a desperate attempt to restore order.

"I say we lerrim go to London by 'issen," said Jerry, when the noise had finally subsided.

A small, thin-faced man came forward. Tom recognized him at once as Henry Sampson, the man Jerry had brought to the Black's Head.

"Jerry's rait," he said. "If we dun't trust each other, the 'ole thing'll come to nowt."

There were several murmurs of agreement.

"All rait, then," agreed Holmes grudgingly, "burr I say 'e leaves afore we discuss t' final plans."

Oliver smiled condescendingly at him.

"A very prudent and cautious decision!"

Holmes pointed to the door.

"Go, then!"

With a gracious bow, Oliver swept out into the street.

Jerry led Holmes to one side.

"Yer still dun't trust 'im, do yer, John?"

Holmes scratched his jaw.

"There's summat about 'im, Jerry."

"'E gave 'is word."

Holmes was clearly unconvinced, and, truth to tell, so was Tom. There had been something in Oliver's manner and bearing — a certain arrogance — that had reminded him of Cousin Richard.

Tom looked on, a deep frown creasing his brow, as Jerry continued to laugh and joke with his fellow delegates. He had made his decision. Was it one he would come to regret?

CHAPTER 24

Saturday, 7th June, 1817

"'Enry!"

Jerry gaped in astonishment at the figure on the doorstep, and then stood aside to admit Henry Sampson.

"Summat up?" asked Tom, drawing up a chair for their visitor.

"It's Arnold an' Bulwell," said Sampson. "They'll not rise."

"Why?" demanded Jerry.

Sampson shrugged.

"'Cos they're cowards!" cut in Tom. He paused, conscious of the vehemence of his response. Why, only a few days ago, he would have betrayed these two to his brother for a shilling and not turned a hair! Now, he was beginning to sound like a true republican! But with Tom, it had always been all or nothing: never the middle path.

"'Ave they said owt?" asked Jerry.

"I think some o' t' local 'osiers 'ave offered 'em a new deal," said Sampson. "There wor a meetin', last nait, burr only seven turned up. They'd lost all 'eart."

"Yer towd 'em what they'd get, din't yer?" asked Jerry.

"An 'undred guineas, a pound o' bread, a pound o' beef, an' a quart of ale fer ev'ry man?"

Sampson nodded.

"An' what did they say?"

Sampson hesitated.

"Well?"

The Bulwell delegate took a deep breath.

"They said yer must be mad, if yer thought they'd swallow that!"

"It's *them* as is mad!" growled Jerry. "Some on 'em'd believe owt t' 'osiers promised 'em!"

He slammed his fist hard onto the table, then lapsed into sullen silence, feverishly revising his plans in the light of this setback.

"Worr about them seven as turned up?" he demanded. "Can we rely on 'em?"

Sampson shrugged.

"Looks like there's just me, Jerry. I'll stay 'ere in Nottingham, an' meet yoh on t' Forest, Monday nait."

Jerry reached forward and laid a hand on Sampson's shoulder. Then, turning to Tom, he announced: "Men like 'Enry'll be t' backbone o' t' new republic."

Henry Sampson blushed and stood up.

"Monday, then," said Jerry, extending a hand to him.

"Aye."

Sampson shook hands and departed, leaving Jerry staring at the embers in the fireplace.

"D'yer reckon any more'll drop out?" asked Tom.

Jerry's gaze remained transfixed, and Tom repeated his question.

"'E'll be lucky if a dozen turn up!"

Both spun round at the sound of Ann's voice. She was staring at her husband with a mixture of pity and contempt. Sometimes, Tom felt, she treated him as if he were a child!

"I've towd yer," snarled Jerry, "there'll be thousands."

Ann pointed to two bundles that lay nestled at the side of the table.

"Goin' somewhere?"

"Yer know I am. Pentrich. I'm tekkin' Tom 'ere wi' me."

"'Course!" replied Ann, with no attempt to hide her sarcasm. "T' precious revolution couldn't start wi'out *yoh*, could it?"

"That's 'cos there's only a few on us knows what's goin' on. We reckon t' plans are already bein' leaked."

Tom felt a frisson of guilt, but Jerry wasn't looking in his direction.

"Call it off, then!" said Ann, with blunt practicality.

"We can't! It's too late to turn back, now! Remember — I'm doin' this for all on us!"

He embraced his wife, but she drew back, as if stung by an insect, and grabbed his coat.

"Worr've yer got there?"

"Nowt!" said Jerry, turning away, as she tried to put her hand inside his coat.

235

Tom had often heard his sister and aunt claim that women were the stronger and more persistent sex, and Ann Brandreth proved no exception to the rule. After a brief scuffle, she stepped back, brandishing a pistol, her face flushed with triumph and terror in equal measures.

"Gi's it back!"

Jerry roughly snatched the weapon from his wife's hand. Her façade of bravado rapidly cracked and she sank into a chair, tears pouring uncontrollably down her pale, worn cheeks.

Even Tom was unnerved by the sight of the pistol. Of course, he had known all along that the revolution would be bloody, but the full horror had only just registered in his mind.

"Worr about more petitions?" he suggested.

Jerry shook his head ruefully.

"Sir Francis Burdett, Sir Robert Wilson, Admiral Lord Cochrane." He counted off the names on his fingers. "All on 'em's spoke up for us — but where's it gorr us?"

Ann slowly lifted her tear-stained face to look at him.

"Oh, Jerry, what's 'appened to yer? Yer used to be so gentle. Yer were never a violent man."

He took her hands tenderly between his own.

"These are violent times, Ann."

"But to talk o' killin' t' King . . ." protested Ann.

"T' King's evil, 'cos 'e lets 'is subjects starve!"

"Burr 'e's still t' King, Jerry," said Ann, laying a hand on her husband's arm. "You're just a stockinger."

"'E's just a man, like me," replied Jerry. "'E eats, sleeps an' pisses, just like me. T' only diff'rence is, 'e wor born rich, an' I wor born poor."

Ann looked sadly at her husband, and wiped the tears from her face.

"Yer've changed, Jerry. You're not t' same man as I married."

Jerry put an arm round his wife's shoulder and gently drew her close to him.

"When we married, we 'ad ev'rythin' to look forrard to. We 'adn't got much, but we got by. We've got nowt, now. Believe me, Ann — if there wor a peaceful way o' gerrin' justice, I'd tek it. But look around yer. Thousands wi' no jobs, an', if yer've no job, it's either t' work'ouse or starve — an' no fam'ly o' mine's goin' in *that* 'ole!"

He slowly released her, crossed to the table, where there stood a stone jug of ale he had brought back from the Punch Bowl, the day before, and poured himself a generous measure.

"I've seen it 'appen to folk I've know fer years. I've watched 'em lose all 'ope o' wokkin' — seen 'em gi' away their most treasured possessions, so's they could buy a bit o' bread! Thank God, we've bin lucky. We've never bin *that* low. Then, one day, I thought: What's God doin' about it? Why's 'E lerrin' it go on?"

"Mr Cursham sez t' poor'll get justice in t' next world, not this 'un," cut in Tom.

"Who's Mr Cursham?" demanded Jerry.

"T' vicar o' St Peter's, in Mansfield."

"An' yoh agree wi' 'im?"

"'Course not!" answered Tom defiantly.

"We're all children o' God — a God o' justice — an' 'E put each on us on this earth for a purpose. There's only two ways yer can get justice in this world, lad — buy it or fait for it. An', so long as I've strength in my arm an' breath in my body, I'll fait fer t' raits of ev'ry poor, starvin' man, woman an' child in this land!"

"It's not t' only road," said Tom. "Worr about learnin'? Mr Jessop sez books . . ."

"Learnin'? Books?" echoed Jerry. "It an't gorr 'im far, 'as it? Tutor to t' brat of a rich parasite like Slack!"

"Slack made 'is fortune from nowt!"

Tom broke off. Why was he defending Slack, when the man had refused to speak out on *his* behalf?

"Slack made 'is fortune from exploitin' t' likes o' yoh an' me!" snapped Jerry. He was looking at Tom's livery. "An' yer can't wear *that* to go to Pentrich in. I've an owd coat, trousers an' a pair of owd boots yer can borrow. I wun't be seen dead wearin' that man's livery!"

"Burr it's norr 'is fault — or t' other 'osiers' — that there's no wokk now. An' 'e's 'elped our Ann an' Jonathan wi' food an' things."

Jerry's face had clouded.

"I thought yoh were be'ind t' Cause?" he said, a quiet menace creeping into his voice.

"I am."

"Then shurrup!"

"Leave t' lad be, Jerry," interjected Ann.

Before Jerry could reply, Timothy and Elizabeth raced in

238

and rushed up to their parents, hugging each in turn with a feverish passion, as though sensing this might be the last occasion the family would be together.

"Yoh were just in time," smiled Jerry, kissing them. "Me an' Tom's off, in a minute."

"'Ow long will yer be gone?" asked Ann.

"I'll be back wi'in a week — ridin' in a carriage-an'-pair!" boasted Jerry.

Ann gripped his sleeve tightly.

"It's not rait, Jerry! God'll punish yer fer this. I know 'E will!"

Timothy tugged at his mother's skirt.

"God wun't do that, would 'E, Mam?"

Jerry drew Ann to one side.

"Yer mun't talk like that, duck," he whispered. "Norr in front o' t' kids!" Turning to Timothy, he said: "No, lad, God wun't do that — not to someone who's carryin' out 'Is will. Now, look after yer Mam an' yer sister, while I'm gone."

Timothy's breast seemed to swell with pride at this great responsibility that had been laid upon him.

"Yes, Dad."

"Good lad! Rait, we're off, then."

"I thought yer weren't marchin' till Monday," said Ann.

"We're not; burr I've another meetin', tomorrer nait, in Pentrich, to mek t' final plans."

He kissed Ann, picked up his bundle, and moved towards the door, signalling to Tom to do the same.

As they turned down Barker Gate, in the direction of the city centre, Ann called out: "You're a bloody fool, Jerry Brandreth — burr I love yer!"

Jerry's even pace faltered for half a second, then he continued down the street without a backward glance.

"This is it, lad. T' White 'Oss."

Jerry pushed open the inn door and walked in, as a tall, thickset man with a bovine countenance emerged from the smoky interior.

"George Weightman!" shouted Jerry, adding, for Tom's benefit: "T' landlady's son."

Tom extended a hand, which George seized in a bear-like paw.

"Tom Stone."

"'E's a friend o' Brutus," explained Jerry.

George Weightman led the way up a flight of stone steps, opened the door to an upper room, and indicated two men sitting at a table in the far corner.

"Isaac!" shouted Jerry. "Tommy!"

The two men looked up and the younger one, a powerfully built fellow in his fifties, stood up to greet them.

"This is Isaac Ludlam, Tom," said Jerry. "'E's a stone quarrier an' a lay preacher; so, if 'e starts quotin' t' Bible at yer, yer'll know why!"

The other man was in his mid-sixties: short, with a yellowish, pockmarked face, and shoulder-length, white hair that had receded from his brow and temples.

240

"Tommy Bacon," announced Jerry. "Another stockinger fallen on 'ard times."

Bacon acknowledged Tom's presence with a curt nod, whilst Isaac Ludlam offered him a warm, firm handshake.

Jerry first told them of Tom's background, and his narrative was greeted with snorts of derision at the mention of Samuel Slack and murmurs of sympathy at the false accusations levelled against Tom.

Tom was touched. These men were total strangers, yet they instinctively believed in his innocence.

Jerry then relayed the events surrounding Oliver and the meeting at the Punch Bowl.

"You're tekkin' a risk, lerrin' 'im go to London like that," said Bacon guardedly.

Jerry grinned ruefully.

"Yoh'll never change, will yer, Tommy?"

"That's t' secret o' livin' to a ripe owd age — trust no bugger! Now, I reckon we should ay some sort o' proclamation — to set out our grievances an' encourage others to join us."

"Damn it! We'll ay no time to read papers!" said Isaac.

"Well, if yoh've gorra better idea . . ." muttered Bacon. "In just over forty-eight hours, we're due to gather on Nottingham Forest. It dun't gi' us long."

"Tomorrer," cut in Jerry, anxious to avoid dissention, "we go round Pentrich an' South Wingfield, an' we recruit ev'ry able-bodied man we find."

"Worr if they refuse to join us?" objected Bacon.

Jerry opened his coat and extracted the pistol.

241

"We blow their brains out!"

CHAPTER 25

Sunday, 8th June, 1817

"'Owd up a minute, Jerry! Me feet are killin' me!"

Tom leaned back against a dry stone wall, eased off his right shoe and examined the blister that had started to form beneath his big toe. The boots Jerry had lent him were at least a size too large, and the rough leather insole was chafing his foot.

"I wor bad enough, yest'dy, walkin' from Nottingham," he complained. "Now, this!"

"It's gorra be done, lad," replied Jerry. "It's paid off. We've just gorr another forty comin' from South Wingfield."

"They've *said* they're comin'," Tom pointed out. "But sayin' summat's one thing: doin' it's another."

Jerry took a sheet of paper from his pocket and shook it under Tom's nose.

"I know who's promised — so woe betide 'em if they fail!"

Tom replaced his shoe and took a few halting paces along the lane.

"It's no good!" he wailed. "I'll be in no fit state to march, tomorrer."

"If yer 'eart's in it, yer feet'll foller," answered Jerry, with a smile. "Come on. Only another couple o' miles, an' there'll be a pint o' Nan Weightman's ale waitin' fer us."

Tom followed gamely behind Jerry, only wishing he could share his leader's optimism. True, when pressed, men had declared their intention of marching, the following night; but Tom sensed the responses had been prompted by a sense of fear, rather than enthusiasm.

With every step, the blister sent a sharp stab of pain through his foot. What if it got worse? What if he had to have the limb amputated, could no longer work, and was forced to spend the rest of his life like poor Ned Hopkins, begging for what odd scraps of work he could get?

Thoughts of impoverishment led his mind back to Ann and Jonathan. He felt guilty abandoning them, especially when Caleb was beginning to show signs of turning the corner.

Then there was his Aunt Margaret. Had she heard about the accusation of theft and his escape? She was bound to have done: news of such crimes would spread round such a small town as Mansfield like wildfire. Old Caleb and Amos would turn in their graves at the shame and disgrace he had brought on the family name.

Well, things would change after the revolution — so Jerry said!

Tom limped into the upper room and lowered himself onto a chair.

"Tired, lad?"

Tom looked up, to see Isaac Ludlam in the seat he had occupied the night before, a large book spread out in his lap.

"Worr're yer readin'?" asked Tom.

"T' Bible. I've a sermon to prepare fer tonait."

"Sermon?"

"I'm a lay preacher at t' chapel," explained Isaac. "I'll be preachin' on t' parable o' t' labourers in t' vineyard."

Tom looked puzzled.

"T' vineyard owner agrees a fair wage wi' 'is men — an' sticks to it. 'Appen it might prick a few consciences!"

"So, you're gonna preach God's word tonait, then brek it tomorrer?" asked Tom.

This time, it was Isaac's turn to look bemused.

"'Thou shalt do no murder,'" quoted Tom.

Isaac reached inside his coat and produced a pistol similar to the one Tom had seen in Jerry's possession.

"Yoh ever 'andled one o' these?"

He had, just the once. His brother had let him hold his army pistol. He remembered the feel of its firm contours, the cool, smooth texture of the steel. Will had said that handling a firearm was like caressing a woman.

"Could yoh look a man in t' eye an' pull that trigger?"

"Aye," declared Tom, with an air of bravado.

"Then, tomorrer nait, yer'll be doin' t' Lord's wokk."

There was a bustle of noise from the stairs outside, then the door flew open and a group of about twenty men,

245

including Tommy Bacon, Henry Sampson and Jerry, entered the room.

"Ay yer 'eard what Jessop's done?" Jerry blurted out.

At the mention of his tutor's name, Tom's ears pricked up. Was he here? Or was it bad news? Had he betrayed the Cause?

However, it soon became obvious, from Jerry's next words, that he was referring to another Jessop altogether.

"'E's sacked 'aif-a-dozen men at Butterley Ironworks for 'owdin' republican views."

"Poor buggers!" muttered Isaac.

"It may be an ill wind for *them*, Isaac; burr it could blow *us* some good. We've already got two men from Butterley joined us."

He indicated two individuals behind him: one tall and stout, the other short and wiry.

"Anthony Martin an' Shirley Asbury," announced Jerry.

Tom extended a welcome to the two strangers, but Isaac was more circumspect.

"Who can vouch for 'em?"

"*I* can," replied Sampson.

There was the sound of more footsteps ascending the stairs and George Weightman joined them.

"Bloody 'ell!" exclaimed Isaac. "Yer managed to find yer way up 'ere all rait, then?"

The rest of the company dissolved into helpless laughter. Tom had the feeling, from the way George blushed, that he was a frequent butt of their humour.

"Me an' me Mam 'ave a business to run!" countered George defiantly. "She can't manage by 'ersen. Talkin' o' which — when do we get paid for all t' ale yoh lorr've supped, these past weeks?"

"Call it doin' yer bit fer t' Cause, George!" replied Jerry, releasing a further gust of laughter, which he at once stilled with a simple gesture. "Rait, shurrup, an' let's run through t' final plan agen."

George Weightman went off to fetch more ale, and the rest gathered round the table in the middle of the room, as Jerry spread out a map across it.

"Now, then," asked Jerry, "d'yer all know 'Unt's Barn, at South Wingfield?"

"On t' north side o' Garner Lane?" asked Isaac.

"That's rait. We all meet there at ten o'clock, tomorrer nait. Now, 'ow are we off fer weapons?"

"I've got forty pikes 'idden in Colborn Quarry," said Isaac.

"An' I've managed to gerr 'aif-a-dozen guns," added Bacon, "though one o' t' muskets dun't wokk."

"No matter," smiled Jerry. "When we leave 'Unt's Barn, we'll march south. There's a couple o' farms on t' way. We can pick up arms from there. When we get to Fritchley, we split into two groups. One'll go round by Colborn Quarry, pick up t' pikes, then go on to Wire Mill. T' other party'll call at t' big 'ouse in Wingfield Park."

"What? Owd Ma 'Epworth's place?" gasped Isaac, in disbelief. "Yer'll get nowt from 'er!"

"She's got men wokkin' for 'er," replied Jerry, "an' she's bound to keep at least one gun fer protection, in a lonely

247

spot like that, an' we need both."

At that moment, George Weightman returned with the ale, to be greeted by a chorus of raucous catcalls.

Jerry quenched his thirst, and then turned his attention back to the map.

"Now, t' two parties'll meet up again at Pentrich Lane End, then back 'ere."

George Weightman was about to leave, but Jerry caught him by the sleeve.

"George, tell yer Mam we'll need plenty o' bread, cheese an' ale fer t' march."

George shook himself free.

"We've already laid on free ale, nearly ev'ry nait fer t' last two months. We can't afford no more."

The two men squared up to each other. It reminded Tom of the cockfights he had witnessed behind the Cock Inn, in Mansfield, each combatant waiting for the other to make the first move.

In the end, it was George who backed off, retreating to the far corner of the room, muttering dark threats.

An uneasy atmosphere lingered, for several moments, after his departure.

Tommy Bacon scratched his jaw thoughtfully and broke his silence.

"It's not goin' to be easy, though, is it, Jerry? I mean, I thought t' feedin' o' t' 5,000 wor a miracle — but 30,000's a bit much!"

"There's plenty of inns between 'ere an' Nottingham," said Jerry, cutting in on the raucous laughter that had greeted Bacon's quip. "We'll commandeer beef, cheese, ale an' rum on t' road. Rait, now, after we've stocked up 'ere, we march on to t' Butterley Ironworks an' pick up more men. An' I'm countin' on yoh two to talk round any waverers there," he added, turning to Martin and Asbury.

"An' if they'll not come?" queried Asbury, with a nervous glance at his companion.

Jerry said nothing, but merely drew a finger across his throat.

"Any more questions?"

Martin and Asbury shook their heads.

"Good," said Jerry, in a soft voice that carried a hint of menace. "Now, from Butterley, we march on to Ripley, then Codnor, Langley Mill, Eastwood, Giltbrook, Kimberley, pickin' up more men on t' way — then on to Nottingham. I've marked t' inns where we'll stop off."

This last piece of information caused the others to crane forward even more eagerly.

"At this rate, we'll be pissed by t' time we get there!" cut in George Weightman.

Martin and Asbury had been huddled together in a whispered exchange, during the latter part of the conversation. The former now stepped forward and cleared his throat.

"Mister Asbury an' me are special constables," he announced, "an' we should warn yer, in t' King's name, that this is 'igh treason!"

The room fell silent, as Martin and Asbury suddenly found themselves the focus of some twenty pairs of eyes.

"Spies!" yelled Tom, springing to his feet, and instantly

249

regretting it, as the pain of his blister was reactivated.

The others closed in on the two special constables.

"Now, mind what yer say!" said Asbury, trying to assume an air of authority.

"We'll say as we please an' do as we please!" hissed Isaac, taking a pace towards him.

"Worr're we gonna do about 'em?" demanded Henry Sampson, turning to Jerry.

"We'll stuff 'em up t' chimney!"

Despite their loud protestations and constant invoking of the King's name, Martin and Asbury were seized and dragged towards the door.

"I've gorra length o' rope downstairs," volunteered George Weightman. "We can string 'em up!"

"No, lerrus go!" pleaded Asbury.

"We'll not say nowt!" promised Martin.

Jerry was in no mood for clemency. With a jerk of his head, he signalled for them to be dragged downstairs.

All left, save Tom and himself. They crossed to the window and looked out. The last traces of the day bathed the street outside in a soft, orange glow, as the crowd poured out of the main door, dragging the luckless specials behind them. Amid jeers, they were pointed in a general southeasterly direction, and required no further incentive to effect their escape with all possible speed.

"If they go to t' magistrates, we're done for!" said Tom.

Jerry laid a reassuring arm around his shoulder.

"They'll not go to t' magistrates, lad," he chuckled.

"They'll be shittin' theirsens, all t' way back to Butterley!"

They could already hear footsteps coming back up the stairs.

"Well, that's t' last we'll see from *them*, I reckon," announced Tommy Bacon confidently.

Isaac turned accusingly on Sampson.

"Yoh said yer could vouch fer 'em!"

"Well, 'ow wor *I* to know 'e'd sworn in a fresh bunch o' specials?" complained Sampson.

"Who's sworn 'em in?" asked Tom.

"Colonel Halton," explained Isaac. "T' local magistrate."

All the talk of magistrates sent a shiver through Tom's body.

"What's 'e like?" he asked.

"A bastard," replied Tommy Bacon bluntly. "There's four men in Derby Gaol now, waitin' to be 'anged on 'is account. Claims they set fire to 'is 'ayricks."

"Then, *I* say we go round to 'is 'ouse, smoke 'im out, then 'ang 'im," said George Weightman.

"No," advised Isaac. "It'd be wastin' time."

There were general murmurs of assent, during which Jerry climbed onto the table.

"Rait," he declared. "It's time to gerrup off our knees an' claim what's ourn. There may be only an 'andful on us 'ere in Pentrich, but, by this time tomorrer nait, there'll be thousands on us, marchin' on London fer truth, justice an' liberty — an' no one can stop us!"

Unbidden, the whole group launched passionately into

their anthem:

Ev'ry man 'is skill must try.
'E must turn out an' not deny.
No bloody soldier must 'e dread.
'E must turn out an' fight for
bread.
The time 'as come, you plainly see.
The Government opposed must be.

Not for the first time, Tom felt a prickling sensation at the base of his neck. On the last occasion he had heard this song, he had been a mute witness, noting down every word to pass on to his brother: now, he joined in with full fervour, his voice rising above the rest.

Tomorrow night, he, Tom Stone, would turn out and not deny! There could be no going back now!

CHAPTER 26

Monday, 9th June, 1817

"It's gonna piss it down!"

Tom spoke the words to no one in particular, as he stared at the slate-grey sky, then turned up the collar of his coat. He was surrounded by some thirty or forty men, huddled in small cliques, muttering discontentedly amongst themselves.

"It's 'aif-past nine," said Isaac. "'E's cuttin' it fine, John."

"I towd yer it wor all fancy words, din't I?" replied John Mackesswick, a tall, well-fleshed frame worker.

"'E'll be 'ere," replied Tom confidently. "'E promised."

His bold voice belied the anxiety he felt. Jerry had set off at dawn, ostensibly to travel to Crich, Fritchley and other outlying villages to drum up more recruits. Perhaps he had been arrested — or perhaps, as many like John Mackesswick whispered, he had never intended to return.

"Yer dun't think Jerry'll show, then?" asked Isaac.

"No," replied Mackesswick. "I say we gi' 'im five more minutes, then set off wi'out 'im."

"I'll not listen to yer lies!" cried Tom, squaring up boldly to the frame worker, who stood a good head taller than him.

"So, Brandreth's little pet dog's got teeth, eh?" chuckled Mackesswick. Then, in a soft, menacing whisper, he added: "Well, if yer dun't want 'em rammed down yer throat, lad, yer'd best mind yer manners!"

"Stop it, t' pair on yer!" barked Isaac, stepping between them. "There'll be faitin' enough before t' nait's out!"

Tom and Mackesswick each took a step backwards, but continued to glare at each other.

"I reckon John's rait, though," conceded Isaac. "We can only gi' Jerry another five minutes. 'E's supposed to be pickin' up owd Tommy Bacon, an' all."

"An' where's George Weightman, an' all?" demanded German Buxton, a doleful-looking man, who had been gazing at the inn door for signs of Weightman's appearance.

As if on cue, the door flew open, and Weightman appeared, followed by a short, squat woman in her fifties.

"Yer'll march to London, if I ay to kick yer arse ev'ry bloody step o' t' way!" yelled Nan Weightman, aiming a blow at that part of his anatomy.

The barracking that greeted George's humiliation was only halted by the arrival of Jerry, clearly out of breath.

"See!" cried Tom triumphantly. "I towd yer!"

"Why in't Tommy wi' yer?" demanded Buxton.

"'E's not comin'," replied Jerry, trying to avoid the man's gaze.

"Why not?" asked Isaac.

"'E's sick."

Was it Tom's imagination, or had Jerry hesitated a fraction before answering?

"What wi'?" asked Mackesswick. "Cowd feet?"

Again, there seemed to be a slight pause.

"There's a warrant out fer 'is arrest," said Jerry.

"There'll be warrants out fer *all* on us, after tonait," said Buxton gloomily.

"Aye, burr 'e's sixty-four," Isaac pointed out, "an' 'e's not . . ."

"When t' King's toppled, 'e'll expect 'is share o' t' spoils," objected Buxton. "We took an oath to share t' dangers. I say we go round to 'is 'ouse an' drag 'im out!"

"Yer'll not find 'im there, anyroad," said Jerry. "'E's 'idin' out at James Booth's 'ovel, on t' edge o' t' village."

"We're wastin' time," complained Isaac. "There's to be 30,000 on us meet in Nottingham. One more or less in't goin' to mek no difference."

"Isaac's rait," cut in Joseph Hunt, a short, rubicund farmer. "'E's not worth t' trouble."

"Where's Sampson?" asked Isaac, looking round.

"'E'll be meetin' us in Nottingham," replied Jerry.

"Is 'e bringin' anyone?"

"A few from 'Ucknall, 'e 'opes — but not Bulwell or Arnold."

"Why?" demanded German Buxton.

Jerry related the conversation he had had with Sampson,

on the Saturday morning.

"There *is* goin' to be 30,000 waitin' for us, in't there?" asked John Mackesswick sceptically.

"'Course," Jerry reassured him. His eye then lighted on George Weightman. "A pint apiece afore we go, George," he commanded.

"Yer'll bloody bankrupt us!" complained Weightman, but a glance at the antagonistic faces surrounding him persuaded him that further argument was pointless, and he ambled back inside.

Several minutes later, he re-emerged, followed by his mother and two young women, bearing tankards and jugs of ale that was soon distributed amongst the men.

When everyone had been served, Jerry raised his tankard aloft in a toast.

"To t' Republic — an' death to t' King!"

"To t' Republic — an' death to t' King!" echoed the others, and Tom felt the blood tingling in his veins, as they marched off, singing their battle-hymn at full volume.

"'Ow far 'ave we marched?" asked Tom. The blister was still causing him pain, and he was beginning to doubt if he would make it as far as Nottingham, let alone London. No, he *must* go on! He owed it to his family, especially young Caleb. He was determined to ensure that his nephew would grow up in a fairer, freer world.

"About a couple o' miles," replied George Weightman, with a grin.

To their left, a farmhouse was silhouetted against the last rays of the evening sun, and, up ahead, the party had veered off the narrow lane in its direction. A dim light, visible through the grimy, cracked panes, indicated that the building was occupied.

"Wait!"

Jerry's sharp command brought the marchers to an abrupt — and welcome — halt.

"George!"

Weightman moved forward to the front of the column.

"'Enry Tomlinson's a friend o' yourn, in't 'e?"

Weightman nodded.

"Rait, then. Yoh knock."

Weightman stepped forward and tapped on the door.

"Louder!" yelled Jerry. "'Ere!" He brushed Weightman aside and hammered violently with a stout stick he had picked up on the way.

"In God's name, who is it?" hissed a voice from inside.

"'Enry? It's me — George Weightman."

The door opened fractionally, revealing a small, balding man in his late forties.

"George, what d'yer . . ." Henry Tomlinson broke off sharply, as the faint glow from inside the house lit up the faces of the men behind Weightman. "God protect us! What's 'appenin'?"

"We need weapons fer t' revolution," cut in Jerry, making no effort to conceal his mounting impatience. "Gi' us yer gun!"

"I an't gorrit!" protested Tomlinson feebly. "I took it into Derby, yest'dy, to gerrit repaired."

Tom had often heard his father talk of people's knees knocking with fear. This was the first time he had actually witnessed the phenomenon.

"Liar!" snapped Jerry. "Search the 'ole 'ouse!"

The crowd behind him surged forward, as Tomlinson tried to force the door closed.

"No! Wait! I'll gerrit!"

The crowd backed off.

"That's berra!" said Jerry softly. "Shows a bit o' sense."

Tomlinson disappeared inside the house, returning shortly with a musket, which he thrust into Jerry's hand, as though it were red-hot.

"'Ere! Tek it an' go!"

"No," replied Jerry. "Yoh'll come wi' us."

"I can't."

Jerry held the musket in the air and prepared to smash the butt down on Tomlinson's bare, glistening pate.

"All rait!"

Tomlinson held up one hand to protect his skull, whilst raising the other in a gesture of surrender.

"Come on, then!" commanded Jerry. "We're be'ind schedule, as it is. Let's gerr on to Nottingham."

Turning, he launched once again into the revolutionary anthem, as he led his men back down the track to the country lane.

Tom noticed that Weightman and Tomlinson were still standing by the farmhouse door, and hung back to overhear their conversation.

"George, fer God's sake, 'elp me!" pleaded the little farmer.

"'Ow?"

"I can't come wi' yoh an leave me wife all alone 'ere."

Weightman pondered the dilemma.

"Look," he said eventually, "come wi' us so far. Then, when I gi' yer t' nod, drop out an' run back 'ere."

Tears streaming down his thin, bewhiskered cheeks, Tomlinson embraced the innkeeper's son.

"God bless yer, George Weightman! Yoh've bin a true friend to me, this nait!"

Tom decided he would need to keep a vigilant eye on George Weightman, over the next few hours!

"Where are we?"

Tom looked up at the outline of the big house.

"Mary 'Epworth's place," answered German Buxton.

Tom remembered the name from the previous evening. Jerry had been confident they would find men and guns here.

"Open up!" yelled Jerry, hammering the butt of his pistol against the heavy oak door.

"Hold your noise and clear off!" came a woman's voice from inside the house.

"Open it — in t' name o' t' Republic!"

The woman remained unabashed.

"Get away, and leave God-fearing folk to sleep!"

Jerry stepped back, and, for a moment, Tom thought he was about to abandon the quest. Instead, he summoned half a dozen of the burliest men in the assembly.

"Brek t' door down!"

The men searched for a suitable battering ram and finally located a large plank of wood. Gripping it tightly, they launched themselves forward, and the sound of splintering timber rent the night air. The end of the plank had split, but the door remained intact.

"Rait!" roared Jerry. "Smash a window!"

"No!" came the woman's voice. "Robert, let them in!"

Several moments later, Tom found himself in an ornate lounge, which made even Samuel Slack's house seem poorly furnished by comparison. In the middle of the room stood a handsome woman in her fifties, who surveyed the motley crew of men in front of her with disdain.

"What do you want?" she demanded.

"Men an' guns," replied Jerry.

"We an't got no guns."

The speaker was a raw, gangling youth, barely two years older than Tom.

"Liar!" said John Mackesswick. "I've seen yer out, shootin' rabbits!"

"'And it over!" demanded Jerry.

"No!" replied the youth defiantly.

The woman smiled at him.

"Give it them, Robert. Don't risk your life for a gun."

"We want yoh, an' all," said Jerry.

"Never!" declared Robert.

"Yer wanna be free, dun't yer?" asked Tom.

Robert turned to his mistress for guidance.

"Go, Robert. I won't stand in your way."

Robert thought hard.

"No! Stuff yer revolution!"

He turned, and marched towards the door at the back of the room.

"Stop!"

Jerry had drawn his pistol, and was taking aim at the retreating Robert.

"Jerry! Don't!"

Tom sprang forward and grabbed his arm, but the older man pushed him roughly away and fired.

Robert stopped in his tracks, his body jerked violently, then he crumpled to the floor and lay still.

Tom turned away and was sick.

CHAPTER 27

Monday, 9th June, 1817

"Murderer! You've killed him!"

It was Mary Hepworth who broke the silence.

"Shurrup, y' owd bitch!" snapped Jerry, "or yoh'll get t' same!"

He had turned his pistol upon the woman, but his hand was shaking uncontrollably.

"No, Jerry!" begged Tom, wiping the last traces of vomit from his lips as he stood up. "One murder's enough!"

"T' lad's rait, Jerry," said Isaac.

Jerry crossed to the inert body, its arms flung wide in an obscene parody of the Crucifixion, and poked it tentatively with his toe.

"We dun't know 'e *is* dead!" he said, without conviction.

Tom knelt down beside the servant.

"'E is!" he declared, his voice rising in panic. "Worr've we done?"

"Why did yoh ay to kill 'im?" demanded Isaac, drawing Jerry into a corner. "We coulda took 'im along on t' march."

"Better he's dead than join with scum like you!" said Mary Hepworth, turning her withering gaze on the rioters. "Is this what your wretched revolution's for — the right to kill servants and scare old women?"

Several of the men had the good grace to look ashamed.

"Shurrup!" yelled Jerry. The hand that held the pistol trembled wildly. With a sudden, violent movement, he raised the weapon as if to strike her.

"No, Jerry!" pleaded Tom. "She's rait! That's *not* worr it's about!"

"Shurrup!" repeated Jerry, turning on him. "Search the 'ouse an' find as many weapons as yer can!"

Tom felt the urge to be sick again. He gazed at Jerry with mounting shock and horror. The whole business was like a nightmare, running wildly out of control.

"Go!" repeated Jerry.

Tom rushed from the room. Once out of sight of Jerry, he hid behind the door and peered through the jamb, straining to catch the ensuing dialogue.

"We'll 'ang, fer sure, now!" said Isaac. Huge beads of sweat had formed on his brow and his naturally florid features had grown redder.

"Not yoh, an' all!" snapped Jerry.

Isaac did not answer. Instead, he turned to Mary Hepworth, and gazed pleadingly into her pale blue eyes.

"*I* 'ad nowt to do wi' it!" he whispered. "Nor t' lad as 'as just left. Yer'll tell 'em that, won't yer?"

Mary Hepworth stared back unflinchingly.

"You're *all* animals!"

"But t' lad an' me did nowt!"

Jerry grabbed Isaac roughly by the arm.

"If one 'angs, we *all* 'ang," he growled. "That's t' oath we swore!"

Sensing a fight was about to break out, Tom dashed back into the room.

"Couldn't find nowt," he lied.

"There *must* be a gun!" insisted Jerry.

"We've no time to argue," protested Isaac. "We've gorra gerr on to Butterley Ironworks."

A flash of lightning suddenly bathed the room in a blinding white light. After three seconds, an ominous roll of thunder followed.

"Shit!" snarled Jerry. "That's *all* we need!"

The night sky glowed a bright orange above Butterley Ironworks.

Tom was limping badly; yet, despite the pain in his foot and the events of the night, which had threatened to eat away at his resolve, he remained as determined as ever to complete the march.

A large stone building reared up in front of them: possibly a storage area, Tom guessed. A long pale face appeared at the upper window, peering out through the solid curtain of rain that had been falling for the past hour.

"Who's 'e?" asked Tom, pointing.

"George Goodwin," answered John Mackesswick. "'E's one o' t' owners."

"Open up, Goodwin!" commanded Jerry, yelling to be heard above another clap of thunder.

"What d'you want?" demanded Goodwin. "What's your object here?"

"We want yer men!"

"You shan't have them," replied the foundry owner. "You're too many already. Disperse. The Law will be too strong for you. You'll be hanged."

"'E's rait," whispered Isaac.

"Can't yer see?" hissed Jerry despairingly, through gritted teeth. "'E's tryin' to turn us agen each other."

And succeeding! thought Tom.

Isaac, however, shook off Jerry's restraining hand, rushed forward and stared up at Goodwin.

"I'm as bad as I can be. I must go on. I can't go back."

"Nonsense, Isaac Ludlam!" boomed Goodwin, through the pounding of the downpour. Despite the limited visibility, he clearly recognized Ludlam's voice.

Perhaps, Tom reflected, he had heard him preach in chapel.

"You're a man of God," continued Goodwin. "Remember the Scriptures: 'Love God: honour the King.' Repent and go home!"

"Lord 'ave mercy on us!" cried an unidentified voice from the back. "Save us, Mr Goodwin!"

"Come in, lads!" yelled the foundry owner. "You're safe here. Come and warm yourselves by the fire."

The double doors at ground level slowly creaked open on

unoiled hinges, and the light and heat from within at once hit them like a blow in the face. All were drenched and cold, and most were tempted.

Only a few succumbed, rushing forward to be embraced by the warmth within.

"Jerry! Stop 'em!" cried German Buxton.

"Lerrem go!" replied Jerry. "We've no need o' faint-'earts!"

"Sinners rushin' into t' flames of 'Ell!" Isaac yelled after their retreating backs, but there was no response, and the doors soon slammed behind them, cutting them off forever from their former comrades.

"Now what?" asked Buxton.

"We're wastin' time!" said Jerry. "We'll press on to Nottingham! March!"

His mind concentrating on young Caleb, Tom drew his sodden clothes about him and set off in blind obedience to his leader's call.

He looked round for a sight of Henry Tomlinson. Nothing! George Weightman must have tipped him the wink.

Somehow, he felt relieved.

"At last! An inn!"

Behind Tom, George Weightman heaved a deep sigh of relief.

"Where are we?" asked Tom.

"T' Junction Navigation Inn at Langley Mill," answered

Weightman, squinting at the faded inn sign.

"I'm famished!" came the voice of German Buxton.

"Me, an' all!" said John Mackesswick. "Where's this beef an' ale we were promised?"

"Yer'll gerrit from 'ere," said Jerry, striding up to the door and banging on it.

Well, reflected Tom, he was certainly hungry and thirsty. He noticed, though, that all the windows were tightly shuttered and that no trace of light from within pierced them.

Doubts were beginning to surface in the back of his mind. Would there *really* be thirty thousand men to meet them in Nottingham? How many would Jessop and Ned be bringing from Mansfield — assuming they ever set out? Jessop had been full of fine words, quoting from books; but *he* had no need to "turn out and fight for bread": he had a reasonably comfortable life in the Slack household, from which he could safely publish his pamphlets under the pseudonym of Brutus. Would he dare put all that at risk?

As they marched along, he could see, in the inky shadows of every hedgerow, the fixed, sightless eyes of Mary Hepworth's servant staring accusingly at him. In the Black's Head and the Punch Bowl, Jerry had made it all sound such a noble enterprise; but, with the youth's death, it now seemed dirty and squalid.

"What do we pay wi'?" asked another man, John Onion, whose short, squat figure reminded Tom of the vegetable whose name he bore.

"We don't," answered Jerry brusquely. "We tek what we want."

"That's stealin'!" Tom hissed in Isaac's ear.

The lay preacher was clearly wrestling with his own conscience. At length, he smiled at Tom and shrugged.

"It's either that, lad, or starve!"

Sounds from inside the inn were now audible.

"D'yer know what bloody time it is?" demanded a deep voice.

"Aye," answered Jerry. "Open up!"

"What d'yer want?"

"Liquor. Now. 'Urry up, or we'll smash t' door in!"

There was a pause, and a woman's voice was heard in urgent consultation with the man.

"All rait," said the innkeeper. "Wait a minute."

The door opened, and the soaked, shivering rebels thrust their way in.

"Joseph! Worr in t' name o' God . . ."

The innkeeper's wife stood on the stairs, holding aloft a lighted candle.

"Shurrup, woman!" snapped Jerry. "'Aif-a-pint of ale, an' bread an' cheese fer ev'ry man!"

"An' if we refuse?" queried the woman.

Jerry drew his pistol and cocked it.

"I'll blow yer brains out!"

No! prayed Tom. Not more bloodshed!

"Come on, luv," sighed the innkeeper. "We've no choice."

His wife set the candle down on the bar, and busied herself drawing off pots of ale, which were snatched up as fast as she could serve them.

"Aye, *we've* no choice, neither," said George Weightman, "but we've started now. There's no turnin' back. It's life or death."

"Jerry," suggested Tom, "I'll keep an eye on t' door — just in case anyone 'as second thoughts."

Jerry smiled at him — the first time he had looked relaxed, all evening.

"Good lad! Remember: t' Government o' this land's robbed t' people. We must fait or starve." He turned to two men whose faces were obscured from Tom's view by the shadows. "Yoh two! Gerrin t' back room an' see what yer can find!"

He found a spare pistol and handed it to Tom, who took up his station by the door.

"Tharr'll be 28 bob," announced the innkeeper, who had been doing rapid calculations with chalk and slate. The next moment, he found himself staring down the barrel of Jerry's pistol.

"Damn you!" snapped Jerry. "By t' time we come back, we'll mek things so's yer'll sell beer at threepence a quart!"

"If it in't paid now, it never will be," said the innkeeper, a deep frown creasing his forehead.

"The 'ell it won't! If we offered yer a Bank of England note, it'd be no use now."

The innkeeper took a deep breath and squared his shoulders.

"Pay up — or there's no food an' drink!"

As Jerry's finger hovered over the trigger of his pistol, there was a loud crash from the back room.

Instinctively, Tom fired off his pistol in the direction from which the sound had come.

There was a sharp cry, then pandemonium broke out.

"God preserve us!" yelled the innkeeper's wife. "What wor that?"

"I 'eard a noise an' . . ."

Even as Tom spoke, it sounded to him as though the words were coming from far away, outside his head.

John Onion had dashed into the back room at the sound of gunfire, and now returned.

"Charles Walters 'as bin 'it!"

Tom felt the room sway in front of him.

"Is 'e dead?" he managed to croak.

John Onion shook his head.

"Leg. Flesh wound."

The news should have brought Tom intense relief, but he still couldn't rid himself of the fear that the youth must be dead. Two deaths in one night!

"We'll ay to gerrim to a doctor," said Isaac. "Is there one near 'ere?"

"There's Mr Davenport, t' surgeon," said the innkeeper, stroking his unshaven jaw. "Lives about a mile down t' road."

"We're way be'ind time," said Jerry. "We've less than an hour to get to Nottingham. We'll ay to leave 'im."

"Yer can't leave 'im," protested the innkeeper's wife. "S'pose it's woss than yer thought? S'pose 'e dies?"

Isaac drew Jerry to one side.

"We can't afford to tek t' chance. We'd best get t' doctor."

Jerry clenched his jaw until the veins stood out on his temples.

"All rait," he conceded. "George, tek an 'oss from t' stables, an' go an' fetch t' doctor."

The innkeeper at once registered his objection to this, but drew back at the sight of Jerry's pistol.

"If *this* goes off, it'll not be an accident!" hissed Brandreth.

"Lerrim go, Joseph!" pleaded the innkeeper's wife.

"Twenty-eight bob's-worth of ale — an' now me 'oss!" cried her husband, rolling his eyes heavenwards.

Before the man could say any more, Jerry pushed him and his wife into a corner, his pistol still levelled at their heads.

"George, go — an' dun't be all nait about it!"

As the door slammed shut after George Weightman, an uneasy silence descended on those left behind.

Tom had raced through to the back room, where Charles Walters sat on a bench, his injured leg resting on a chair. His teeth were tightly clenched, and pain was etched across his thin, pale face, which seemed to have grown prematurely old. A makeshift tourniquet had been tied round his leg, and the tightness of this, as much as the actual wound, seemed to be the cause of his discomfort.

Isaac stood nearby, deep in conversation with the innkeeper's wife. Tom strained to overhear them.

"Yer look all in," said the woman.

"I am."

"Yer can 'ide in t' cellar till fost light, then mek yer way back 'ome."

In the flickering light of the lone candle, conflicting emotions passed across Isaac Ludlam's gnarled features. Several times, he opened his mouth as if to speak. At length, he regretfully shook his grizzled head.

"I can't," he whispered hoarsely. "I've gorra go on."

Unseen by her husband, the woman flashed him a sad, toothless smile.

"Well," said Jerry, "there's nowt we can do till George gets back. Landlord, more ale!"

The innkeeper laid a fleshy hand across his wife's broad shoulders.

"Come on, luv," he sighed wearily. "Seems we've got no choice."

His wife, however, was made of sterner stuff, and rounded on Jerry with a defiant gleam in her eyes.

"Yer'll not gerr away wi' it — an', when they catch up wi' yer, I 'ope they 'ang yer!"

CHAPTER 28

Tuesday, 10th June, 1817

The next hour dragged by as if it had been ten, until George Weightman ushered in the surgeon, Davenport, a young man who seemed totally unfazed by the sight of forty armed men occupying a public house in the early hours of the morning.

He made straight for the back room, where Charles Walters, thanks to copious draughts of free brandy, was now in a semi-comatose state, so that he did not feel the surgeon's sharp instruments probing at his bloodstained right calf.

"Flesh wound," pronounced Davenport, straightening up. "Bullet went clean through. I'll dress it, but he'll have to stay here for the night."

The surgeon looked at the innkeeper and his wife, who nodded their assent.

Tom felt a wave of relief surge over him. The lad was going to be all right!

"'E can't!" cut in Jerry. "We've to march on Nottingham. We're late, as it is."

A humourless smile flickered at the corners of

Davenport's mouth.

"He's not marching anywhere on that leg!"

Jerry was about to draw his pistol, but Isaac gripped his arm firmly.

"No more killin', Jerry!"

"Worr if 'e sends fer t' Militia?" demanded Jerry.

"I'll say nothing to anyone," vowed the surgeon. "I'll dress his wound, then go straight home. If *you* choose to march on to Nottingham, there's nothing I can do to dissuade you, but leave *him* here," he added, pointing to Walters.

The innkeeper seemed about to say something, but his wife held a finger to her lips.

"All rait," conceded Jerry, pushing the pistol back inside his coat.

"Is it still rainin'?" asked John Onion.

Davenport nodded.

"We'd best be off, then."

"Worr about my 28 bob?" demanded the landlord.

John Mackesswick took a sixpence from his pocket and tossed it onto the bar.

"Tek that, an' be thankful!"

The innkeeper pocketed the money, whilst the rioters gathered together their belongings and prepared to leave.

"They'll 'ave set off fer London wi'out us," grumbled German Buxton, gazing mournfully at the torrential downpour.

"If t' weather an't purrem off!" answered Onion.

Tom felt a hand on his shoulder.

"Dun't lerr it worry yer. Accidents 'appen."

"It means we're a man short, though."

"What's one man among 30,000?" said Isaac. "Purr it out yer mind. When you're dinin' off o' t' Prince o' Wales' silver plate, tomorrer nait, yer'll think all this 'as just bin a bad dream!"

"Tek 'eart, lads!" cried Jerry, above the noise of the pelting rain. 'We're nearly at Kimberley. Nottingham's six or seven miles, at t' most."

"Seven miles!" groaned Tom, turning to Edward Moore a tall, thin shoemaker, a few years his senior. "It might as well be an 'undred!"

"Look!" cried Moore. "Over there! An inn!"

"God be praised!" sighed Tom. "Warmth an' shelter!"

"We'll brek ranks at t' next turnin'," said Moore. "It's dark. No one'll see us."

"But Jerry said . . ."

"Dun't worry, lad. There's more than us 'as t' same idea."

"Burr it'd be betrayin' 'im — an' t' Cause."

"It's ev'ry man for 'issen, now, lad."

"But t' oath we swore . . ."

"We're not t' only 'uns as 'ave broken promises," Moore pointed out. "Worr about t' free beef an' ale we were promised? It wor only 'cos o' listenin' to me Dad as I come."

"Worr about Charles Walters?" said Tom.

"'E'll be all rait," smiled Moore. "T' doctor said it wor nobburra scratch."

"Burr it wor me as shot 'im!" protested Tom. "I shot a brother-in-arms!"

"It wor an accident," said Moore. "Nobody blames yer."

But still the guilt would not go away. Tom pointed a shaking finger at Jerry's retreating back.

"'E does. 'E's bin lookin' at me, all strange, like, since we left Langley Mill. It's as if 'e feels I've lerrim down."

"Y' owe 'im nowt," declared Edward Moore.

George Weightman appeared behind them.

"Are yoh two in t' same mind, then?"

Tom looked puzzled.

"Mekkin' a run fer it," said Weightman.

"Aye, an' I reckon we're not t' only 'uns!" grunted Edward Moore.

"I reckon we've *all* 'ad it," sighed Weightman, "so get ready to run when I tell yer."

Before any of them could make a move, Isaac Ludlam, at the head of the column, yelled: "Look! Over there!"

The men stared into the darkness ahead. Above the noise of the pelting rain, a horse neighed.

"My God!" gasped Jerry. "Soldiers!"

"Now!" cried Edward Moore tapping Tom on the shoulder.

At the sound of Moore's voice, Jerry wheeled round

sharply.

"No! Stand yer ground, lads, an' lerrem come!"

In the distance, came a faint voice shouting, "Charge!" This was swiftly followed by the pounding of horses' hooves: first, a trot; increasing to a canter; finally, at full gallop.

"It's too late, Jerry!" wailed Isaac.

Tom looked towards the open fields to his left. Flight was his only option, and he could see from the faces of others that they had formed the same conclusion. He ran until he thought his lungs would burst, never daring to chance a swift look over his shoulder, even though he could hear the sounds of fighting on the main road behind him.

The field sloped upwards, and at the top were thick woods, which would provide a refuge until the danger had passed. Another ten yards, and he would be safe — unless God chose to intervene and punish him for his role in the night's escapade!

Whether God deliberately raise up the ground, or whether the tussock had been there since the Creation, Tom didn't know. All he *did* know, was that, one moment, he was racing at full tilt towards the comforting embrace of the forest; the next, he lay on the sodden grass, winded and dazed, with a violent pain throbbing through his left ankle.

Running footsteps were coming through the grass behind him. He tried to turn his body, but this only increased his agony.

The footsteps stopped.

"Yoh!" bellowed a voice above him. "Gerrup!"

"I can't!" winced Tom.

A leather boot crashed into his ribcage, in an effort to encourage him to adopt a vertical posture.

He had managed to drag himself up into a kneeling position, when a hand gripped him by the collar and hauled him to his feet.

He heard the ominous click of a pistol hammer being drawn back.

"That's berra!" chuckled the soldier. "I never shoot a man when 'e's down!"

Tom froze. That voice! It couldn't be!

He slowly turned his head, and found himself staring into the familiar features of his brother William!

It was difficult to tell who was the more shocked!

"Worr, in t' name o' God . . ?" Will was the first to recover his voice. "Worr're *yoh* doin' 'ere?"

"I ran away," stammered Tom.

"So I 'eard," cut in Will. "Wanted fer theft — pinchin' a watch off owd 'All, t' lawyer."

"I din't!" protested Tom. "Honest! It's all lies! It wor Richard!"

"They *all* say that!" snarled Will. "Anyroad, this is far woss than stealin' a pocket watch. Yer could 'ang fer this!"

"But yoh," said Tom. "Worr're *yoh* doin' 'ere?"

"Drafted in as reinforcements."

"Burr 'ow did yer know we'd be 'ere?"

Will shook his head pityingly.

"We've known fer months!" He broke off and laughed. "Dun't forget, lad — it wor *yoh* as gi'd us most o' t' details, at a bob a time!"

Tom felt sick. He had become so carried away by the rhetoric of revolution that he had forgotten his earlier role as a spy. The whole enterprise had been doomed from the start!

More footsteps sounded behind them. Perhaps rescue was at hand! However, before his hopes had time to rise, he found himself confronted by a figure in a scarlet uniform weighed down with acres of gold braid.

"Well done, corporal," said the stranger, in cultured tones. "That's most of 'em rounded up!"

"Where's Brandreth, captain?" asked Will.

"Escaped!" replied the captain grimly.

Tom didn't know whether to feel elation or anger. On the one hand, he was glad Jerry was safe; yet they had all sworn an oath to give their very lives for the Cause. Hadn't they? The memories of the last few days seemed so vague, now.

"Never mind," said the captain. "We might get some information out of this one."

Tom looked at his brother, and the irony of the captain's statement was not lost on either man.

"Well, lad," prompted the captain. "What have you got to say for yourself? It seems your gallant leader's deserted you!"

Tom's mouth had filled with saliva. In one final gesture of defiance, he spat it into the captain's face. Then, a sharp pain shot through his skull as the butt of Will's pistol smashed into the back of his head. Nausea flooding through his whole frame, he sank to the floor, and stared up, through unfocused eyes, at the officer's leering face.

"Take him off to Derby Goal with the rest of them! Perhaps a night or two there'll help change his mind!"

It was the last thing he remembered, as unconsciousness swept over him.

Even when he opened his eyes, the world still looked black, and when he ventured a deep breath, he almost choked. Where was he? A cesspit?

Then, he remembered the captain's words, just before he had passed out: Derby Gaol. Samuel Slack and Robert Hall would have been delighted at the news: a liar and a thief brought to justice! It was ironic that he had first joined the rebels in order to avoid going to prison!

His eyes gradually became accustomed to the gloom, and he was able to take in his surroundings. A faint evening glow filtered in through a high, barred window, and, by its light, he was able to see that he was in a room some ten feet square, which contained, in addition to himself, five huddled figures, whose features he slowly recognized: George Weightman, John Mackesswick, John Onion, German Buxton and Edward Moore. Six men crammed in a cell scarcely large enough for two! The others must be elsewhere.

He knew, though, that there would be one notable absentee: Jeremiah Brandreth! The captain had mentioned that Jerry had escaped. Perhaps it had been Jerry who had betrayed them to the authorities!

No! That had been his own doing — selling secrets to his

280

brother at a shilling a time! And he had then tried to escape; so he could hardly blame Jerry for doing the same!

Yes, he could! Jerry was the leader: he should have set the supreme example to his men!

Tom looked down, as he felt something rough and furry brush against his hand. A rat!

However, at that moment, his mind was occupied with thoughts of *other* vermin!

CHAPTER 29

Wednesday, 23rd July, 1817

Six weeks they had festered in that hellhole, and still no word of Jerry!

And he was not the only notable member of the party who had made good his escape near Kimberley: Tom had since learnt that a warrant was also out for the arrest of Isaac Ludlam.

The only sound was the drone of John Mackesswick's voice intoning the battle-hymn, except that it not longer sounded like a gloriously triumphant call to arms, but a funeral dirge:

> *Ev'ry man 'is skill must try.*
> *'E must turn out an' not deny.*

"Shurrup, will yer, Mackesswick!" groaned Tom.

"What's wrong wi' it?" demanded Mackesswick. "Yoh were proud enough to sing it, once!"

"Once!" agreed Tom. "Afore I found out worra treacherous bastard 'e wor!"

Mackesswick looked at him closely.

"Jerry?"

"Aye, an' Isaac Ludlam!"

"Who've *they* betrayed?"

"Me!"

"They were no traitors!"

"They turned us in to t' Militia!"

Mackesswick shook his head pityingly. His once fleshy face was now gaunt and drawn.

"Jerry an' Isaac turned us in? Yoh've bin in this cesspit too long, lad! T' damp in t' walls 'as addled yer brains!"

"Neither on 'em stayed to 'elp us at Kimberley," Tom pointed out. "P'r'aps both on 'em's in America, by now."

"America!" sighed John Onion wistfully. "Now, *they* know about revolutions! P'r'aps Jerry an' Isaac's goin' there for 'elp. Aye, that's it! They're gonna gerr 'elp, so that, next time, they'll not mek t' same mistakes!"

"Aye, an' left us 'ere to rot!" grunted Tom. "I reckon it's *yoh* what's 'ad 'is brains addled! There won't *be* a next time — fer none on us!"

"Not fer me, that's fer sure," sighed Mackesswick resignedly. "By this time next month, I'll be dancin' t' Tyburn jig. But there's still yoh, an' others like yer."

"Me?" said Tom. "No, *I'll* 'ang, same as t' rest on yer."

"'Ow owd are yer?" asked Buxton.

"Sixteen."

"Yoh'll not swing, then."

"I've known a good many my age 'ang," replied Tom, with a rueful shake of the head, "an' for lesser crimes than treason."

"T' jury'll tek pity on yer," said Weightman.

"I dun't want pity!" snapped Tom. "I'm a man. I'll die like a man. I've nowt to live for, anyroad."

"Yoh've plenty to live for!" countered Weightman. "Wi' any luck, we might get sent to Botany Bay. A few years there, an' we'll be free to mek new lives fer oursens. It's all sunshine an' fresh air, over there, they say. Berra than livin' in a stinkin' 'ovel 'ere an' dyin' o' cholera."

"Berra than America — where *they* are now?" asked Tom.

"They may've saved their own skins," conceded Mackesswick, "but they never betrayed us."

"Who *did*, then?"

"There's Oliver, fer one," said Buxton. "Owd Tommy never trusted 'im."

"'E wor in London, that nait," said Tom. "'E couldn't 'ave tipped off t' Militia in Kimberley."

"Who do *yoh* reckon it wor, then?" asked Weightman.

"Worr about yersen?"

"Yoh reckon I . . ."

George Weightman was about to launch himself at Tom — a difficult feat in the cramped conditions — when German Buxton intervened.

"Wait, George! Let t' lad ay 'is say."

"Yoh were never at any o' t' meetings, were you?" Tom pointed out. "Allus reckoned yoh 'ad to 'elp yer Mam. She even threatened to kick yer arse all t' way to London!"

The rest giggled like young girls at the memory of this.

"Then, I saw yer tip t' wink to 'Enry Tomlinson — an' it took yer t' best part of an hour to fetch t' doctor to Charles Walters. Time to ride to Kimberley an' alert t' Militia. Then, yer towd *me* to run away. Why? 'Cos yer knew they were comin'?"

Weightman let out a harsh, dry laugh.

"John wor rait. T' damp '*as* got to yer brains! Aye, I let 'Enry Tomlinson go 'ome. 'E's norra rebel — not like us. 'E's just 'appy tendin' 'is farm. Even Jerry's threats wunta changed 'is mind. Aye, I 'ad my doubts — burr I worr proved rait, worn't I? T' glorious revolution! There were only us daft buggers turned out, that nait!"

"But worr about the thousands who were supposed to march on London?" asked Tom, thinking especially of Henry Jessop and Ned.

Weightman shook his head.

"There were never goin' to be thousands! It wor a trick by t' Government to lure us out there."

"While we're at it," said Tom, determined not to be diverted. "Worr about owd Tommy Bacon?"

"Never!" said George Weightman. "'E's 64!"

"Aye," said Tom accusingly, "an' 'e's yer uncle, an' all! Yoh *would* stand up fer 'im!"

"No, lad," cut in Mackesswick. "George is rait. 'E'd never 'ave made it. My money's on Martin an' Asbury. I reckon they'd more bottom than we gi'd 'em credit for, an' legged it straight to t' magistrates."

A silence fell, and talk of betrayal sent Tom's mind racing back to Mansfield, and the image of Susannah — beautiful, curvaceous, perfidious Susannah! Had she only told the truth, his name would have been cleared, he would never have needed to run away, and he would not be lying here, awaiting trial for treason! Somehow, though, the memory of that Saturday afternoon, when their bodies had united, wiped out the pain of her treachery. He would have given anything to lie between those comforting thighs once more!

"'Appen yoh were rait all along, lad," sighed Weightman, at length. "'Appen it wor your darling Jerry betrayed us an' took ship to America. But, wherever 'e is, 'e must be laughin' at us!"

George Weightman's conclusions could not have been further from the truth, as the next half hour was to prove. The sullen silence that had descended upon the occupants of the cell was broken by the sound of a key turning in the lock.

"I've brung a friend to join yer!" announced a gruff voice, propelling a human form through the doorway.

The face was pale and haggard, the beard dirty and unkempt, but, when the figure whispered, "Evenin', lads," the voice was unmistakeable.

"Jerry!" gasped Tom.

"What's left on 'im!" replied Jerry, forcing a grin.

"Worr 'appened?" asked Mackesswick.

"It's a long story," sighed Jerry.

"Well," chuckled Onion, "it's norr as if we an't got time to 'ear it!"

The rest joined in the laughter, and, for the first time for weeks, some of the old camaraderie returned. To Tom, it seemed they had spent the whole period of their incarceration bickering and fighting, exchanging accusations of treachery. Now, suddenly, they were relaxed.

"Where did they find yer?" asked Tom, relieved to see the familiar features. All his doubts had now evaporated.

"No," said Mackesswick. "Start at t' beginnin'. Worr 'appened after t' Militia arrived?"

"We ran off," whispered Jerry, shame and humiliation etched across his face. "Me an' 'Enry Sampson."

"Worr about Isaac?"

"'E ran, an' all," said Jerry.

"Where to?" asked Onion.

"Uttoxeter. T' gaoler towd me news on 'im 'ad come through, this very hour. 'E wor took, this mornin'. 'E'll be 'ere wi' us, tomorrer."

Well, thought Tom, that was two suspected traitors eliminated. Had either Jerry or Isaac been in league with the authorities, they would have arranged full pardons and free passage out of the country.

It was a hot day, made even hotter by the overcrowded conditions inside the cell, but Jerry was shivering.

"Worr 'appened to Sampson?" asked Weightman.

For several moments, Jerry made no movement. Then, his whole body was racked by a violent convulsion, and Mackesswick threw an arm round him to save him from falling.

"Gaoler!" yelled Onion.

A grim, unshaven face appeared at their window.

"What?"

"Water! This man's ill!"

The gaoler seemed to hesitate, as though weighing up whether this was some sort of trick, but a look at Jerry told him the man was genuinely ill.

Whilst they waited for the water, Mackesswick took off his threadbare coat and draped it round Jerry's shoulders.

"Yer were sayin' about Sampson?" prompted Tom.

"It wor 'im as betrayed me."

The words were faint, but crystal clear.

Before they could pump him with further questions, the gaoler arrived with the water, which Jerry gratefully gulped down.

Once the gaoler was safely out of earshot, Onion, his voice rising in disbelief, asked: "D'yer really mean it? Sampson — a traitor?"

Jerry nodded.

"No wonder t' Arnold an' Bulwell men never turned out! 'E gi'd me some cock-an'-bull story about t' 'osiers offerin' new terms! 'E'd warned 'em not to turn out, 'cos 'e knew t' Militia 'ud be waitin'! Burr I'm gerrin' a'ead o' missen. After we left Kimberley, I 'id in Sampson's 'ouse in Bulwell for a few days. After that, I made my way down to Bristol, an' tried stowin' away on a ship for America."

Tom and Weightman exchanged looks.

"T' buggers caught me an' turned me off," continued Jerry, trying to force a laugh, which became a rasping cough.

"Where did yer go then?" asked Tom.

288

"Back to Bulwell. I'd 'eard there wor a packet due to sail from Cardiff, this comin' Friday, burr I'd no money. I thought Sampson'd gi' me some. Instead, I got back yest'dy, an' found t' Militia waitin' fer me!"

"Did 'e say why?" asked Onion.

"Money. Said 'e 'ad six kids to feed — an' t' Government were offerin' two guineas a week to spy on t' meetings."

Tom felt sick again. Two guineas a week! He had done the same for a shilling! Yet, however great or small the reward, the guilt of betrayal weighed just as heavily on his conscience. What would he not have given to be able to turn back the clock!

"That's not t' wost on it," whispered Jerry. "Just afore they took me away, 'e showed me a newspaper. Sir Francis Burdett's disowned us in Parliament — sez we're just misguided!"

"What d'yer expect from someone wi' a 'Sir' in front of 'is name?" snorted Mackesswick.

A slow realisation was creeping over the inhabitants of the cell: without the backing of their "supporters" in Parliament, their lives were doomed for certain!

CHAPTER 30

Saturday, 16th August, 1817

How slowly the wheels of Justice turned! On 26th July, 46 men had finally been indicted for their part in the uprising on 9th June, including, in his absence, Thomas Bacon. Eventually, it was announced that charges against eleven of them were to be dropped. For one brief moment, Tom had hoped that his own name had been included on that list. After all, several of his companions had assured him that he would be treated leniently on account of his youth. Perhaps it was his wounding of Charles Walters, in the Junction Navigation Inn, that had persuaded the authorities to proceed against him; or perhaps he was to be charged, not in connection with the uprising, but with the theft of Robert Hall's watch. Will had known all about it; maybe the authorities also did.

The remaining 35 defendants had been remanded to Derby Gaol, and dates for their trials had been set for mid-to-late October. Jerry, Isaac, George Weightman and a man named William Turner were to stand trial separately from the rest. All had entered pleas of "Not Guilty", on the advice of the lawyers appointed for their defence, but few of them had any illusions of being acquitted.

There had been one or two other changes. On the day following his arrival, Jerry had been moved to another cell, to make room for Isaac Ludlam, who had been conveyed from Uttoxeter, following his arrest. His welcome had been as warm as that afforded to Jerry, even though his presence made the cramped cell even less habitable.

On that stifling Saturday in August, spirits were at their lowest ebb. The previous day, four men, who had been held in custody since May, had finally been executed for their part in burning down the hayricks of Colonel Halton, the magistrate.

Tom was as downhearted as any of them. Some eight weeks to his trial, and then what? The gallows, transportation, or — dare he hope? — freedom. So much remained undone. The sight of his companions' faces covered with scars and sores reminded him of the bruised and battered features of Aunt Margaret. He still had a score to settle with Ben! Then, there was Susannah, for whom his lust was now as strong as his hatred. He still could not believe she had lied of her own volition. Perhaps Richard had some secret hold over her. The more he brooded on the episode of the stolen watch, the more sharply a possible scenario became etched on his brain. Supposing Richard had discovered Susannah had been unfaithful, that Saturday afternoon, and had threatened to tell her father, unless she lied about knowledge of his debts. Yes, that would make perfect sense. It comforted him to see her in the role of unwilling cat's-paw rather than scheming liar.

He was aroused from his reverie by the sound of the key turning in the lock.

"There you are, old man!" chuckled the gaoler. "Better late than never!"

Seven pairs of eyes focused on the figure in the doorway, who bravely supported his frail, stooping frame with a

291

stout oak stick.

"Tommy!" cried Isaac. "Tommy Bacon!"

"Uncle!" gasped George Weightman, in disbelief, as he clasped the yellowing, gnarled hands.

Bacon's eyes lighted on Isaac Ludlam, and he forced a wan smile.

"Well, Isaac, I'm back!"

"Yoh look awful!"

"Who wun't," chuckled Bacon, "on a diet o' fresh air?"

"When did yer last eat?" asked Weightman.

"Three days back."

Weightman began to search feverishly through the pockets of his coat.

"I think I've still got some bread left."

After a few moments, he triumphantly held aloft a small crust, which Bacon gratefully seized.

"It's a bit stale," apologized his nephew, but the old man seemed oblivious to the fact, as he chewed ravenously.

"Good?" enquired Weightman.

"Fine," smiled Bacon. "Mind yoh, rait now, I'd eat owt!"

"'Ow far did yer get?" asked Onion.

"Huntingdonshire," replied Bacon, through a mouthful of bread. "St Ives. When they come for me, I laid out two o' t' buggers wi' my stick!"

He brandished the weapon for all to see, and there was general laughter.

All this while, Tom had sat mutely in the corner. Now,

Isaac dug him in the ribs.

"In't yer gonna say 'ello, lad?"

Tom grunted.

"That's no way to greet an owd friend!" remonstrated Isaac.

"Friend?" echoed Tom. "Where wor 'e whilst t' rest on us were marchin' round in t' pissin' rain?"

"I couldn't come," pleaded Bacon. "There wor a warrant out for me."

"It's no good blamin' Tommy," said Isaac. "It's traitors like that rat Sampson as landed us in 'ere."

"What's that?" asked Bacon.

Isaac relayed to him the story of Jerry's capture.

"Where is 'e?" asked Bacon.

"In a cell round t' other side," replied his nephew.

"I bet Sampson made a packet," said Bacon.

"We 'eard since as 'ow 'e made 200 guineas," said Mackesswick.

Bacon let out a long, low whistle.

"Oliver, an' all," he added. "I wor rait about 'im, worn't I? But nobody'd listen — norr even Jerry. We'd no chance. T' Government knew ev'ry move afore we made it."

Tom shuddered involuntarily.

"To be honest," continued Bacon, "it wor that as much as t' warrant as put me off comin' wi' yer. Jerry thought it wor cowardice — no doubt some o' *yoh* did, an' all — but what's t' point o' purrin' yer life at risk in a fait yer can't win?"

"Worr 'appened to yer dream o' t' Republic?" demanded Tom.

"It'll not come in *my* lifetime, lad — nor in yourn," said Bacon, with a bitter grin. "In fact, these last few weeks, I've done some 'ard thinkin' — an' I reckon it'll *never* come."

"Never?" repeated Isaac. "But worr about t' lad 'ere — an' t' thousands out there like 'im? 'E'll escape t' gallows and maybe — 'cos of 'is age — Van Diemen's Land, an' all. *They'll* carry on faitin' fer t' same dreams as us."

"T' world's changin', Isaac. We can't stop it." Bacon looked at Tom with a mixture of bemusement and sadness. "Look at 'im, Isaac. Does 'e look like a faiter, now? You're rait. 'E'll go free, an' 'e'll reckon it's taught 'im a valuable lesson — that there's two sorts o' people in this world: t' exploiters an' t' exploited. An' I reckon 'e'll see which side 'is future's safest wi'!"

Tom felt a burning in his cheeks, and it was not the result of the hot weather.

"Are yoh sayin' I'll desert t' Cause?"

"Put a decent suit o' clothes on a man's back and an' 'andful o' guineas in 'is pocket, an' 'e'll soon forget 'is dreams o' justice an' equality."

"Do yoh think I'd betray ev'rythin' I believe in, just fer a suit o' fine clothes?"

Tom's whole body was now shaking violently: not because Thomas Bacon had accused him of betraying his principles, but because he knew those accusations were true. He remembered well the pride had felt at first putting on the livery Samuel Slack had provided for him — and he remembered the pleasure he had derived from spending each shilling he had earned from Will.

Thomas Bacon's rheumy eyes stared at him for several moments, and he felt as though they could penetrate through his flimsy clothing and see into his very soul.

"We'll see, lad," said Bacon quietly. "We'll see."

CHAPTER 31

Saturday, 25th October, 1817

After 137 days' incarceration, the fateful day had finally arrived for Tom!

For some, though, the waiting was already over. On the Wednesday of the previous week, Jerry had finally gone on trial. It had lasted just three days. At five minutes past ten on the morning of Saturday, 18th October, the jury had retired. It was out for a mere 25 minutes, returning with the inevitable verdict of "Guilty".

Jerry had still been able to laugh at his situation, when he relayed the details of his trial to the others. By skilful cross-examination, his lawyer, John Cross, had made many of the witnesses look foolish. He recalled particularly the gales of laughter that had greeted the evidence of the special constables, Martin and Asbury.

The judge — no less a personage than Sir Richard Richards, Chief Baron of England — had shown little mercy. One thing he had said, in particular, had burned itself on Jerry's brain: "A crime is no less a crime because the man who commits it is poor."

Tom's memory had stirred at those words: his father had often said the same thing to him.

William Turner had gone into the dock, on the following Monday, to be followed, on succeeding days, by Isaac Ludlam and George Weightman. All were duly convicted.

Weightman had been the unluckiest. It had subsequently emerged that one of the jury, a Mr John Endsor, of Parwich, had been unconvinced of his guilt, and it was only as a result of pressure from his fellow-jurors that he was persuaded to alter his opinion.

Now, it was the turn of the remaining 31 defendants. Most seemed resigned to their inevitable fates. Even Tom had given up hope of freedom.

Old Tommy Bacon, though, remained obdurate.

"The trials aren't valid," he kept insisting. "T' Law sez a man 'as a right to be tried by a jury of 'is peers. Those men aren't yer peers. They're not stockingers and labourers. They're landowners: the ones who'd 'ave 'ad most to lose under t' New Order."

No one took much notice of him now, though. However pure and honourable the Cause, the judge had already ruled that it did not justify their breaking the Law.

"Thomas Stone!"

Tom was dimly aware of his name being called; although, since he was unused to being addressed as "Thomas", the summons did not register initially. He glanced up, as the burly figure of the gaoler advanced towards him and hauled him to his feet.

The gaoler continued to read out the list of names: "John Mackesswick, John Onion, Edward Moore."

Each stepped forward as his name was called, and was ushered out of the door.

Within moments, they were in the open air. It was the first time he had been out of his cell in nearly a week, and, although the day was overcast, the light still hurt his eyes.

They were taken across courtyards, through corridors, from one building to another, until his head began to grow dizzy trying to get his bearings. On the way, they met up with other prisoners whom Tom vaguely recognized, and, at length, they were assembled in a hallway.

A dozen of them, including Tom, were manacled together and set on one side.

The rest, including Jerry, Isaac, Weightman and William Turner, were manacled separately.

They found themselves herded through a set of double doors into the courtroom, where they were all packed, like cattle, into the tiny dock.

Below them, the main body of the court was filled with bewigged figures in black. In front, raised in magnificent isolation above throng, was an empty, throne-like chair that would duly be occupied by Sir Richard Richards, Chief Baron of England.

Around the other three sides of the courtroom ran the public galleries, which were packed with men and women of every rank and station in life. Many, Tom knew, had come to gloat at their downfall: others clearly felt some sympathy for this forlorn group of undernourished wretches.

Just below the Chief Baron's dais sat another bewigged figure: the Clerk of the Court, who stood up and commanded: "All rise!"

Everyone obeyed, eyes fixed on the dais, as a tall, gaunt figure entered, its grim face framed by a shoulder-length wig.

The whole Court bowed to the Chief Baron who returned the courtesy with a slight inclination of the head before sitting down.

In a clear, resonant voice, the Clerk read out the names of Jeremiah Brandreth, Isaac Ludlam, George Weightman, William Turner and the nineteen prisoners who were manacled with them, and each acknowledged his presence.

As the Clerk sat down, the defence lawyer rose to his feet.

"M'lud, the defendants Brandreth, Ludlam, Weightman and Turner have already been tried and convicted of treason. The other nineteen defendants have now formally changed their pleas to 'Guilty'."

The Chief Baron cast his eye over the defendants, finally focusing on Jerry.

"Jeremiah Brandreth, you stand convicted of high treason. What have you to say, why sentence of death should not be passed upon you, according to the Law?"

"I ask for mercy," replied Jerry, "if mercy can be extended to me. Let me address you in the words of Our Saviour: 'If it be possible, let this cup pass from me; but not *my* will, but Your Lordship's, be done.'"

Tom felt a shiver of disgust. Where were the heroically defiant speeches he had heard in the Black's Head and White Horse?

At a signal from Sir Richard Richards, the Clerk of the Court picked up a black tricorn hat, and placed it, somewhat precariously, atop the Chief Baron's wig.

Sir Richard Richards cleared his throat.

"Your insurrection, thank God, did not last long; but, whilst it continued, it was marked with violence, and with the murder of an innocent man, who did not offer the least provocation. That conduct has shown the ferocity of your heart. Your object was to wade through the blood of your countrymen, to extinguish the law and constitution of the country, and to substitute, for the liberty of your fellow subjects, anarchy and the most complete ruin. God be praised! Your purpose failed."

He looked down at the sheet of paper in front of him and, in a flat, impersonal voice, read out the names of each defendant in the dock.

"It is now my solemn duty to pass sentence upon you. It is the sentence of this court that you be taken to the gaol, from which you must be drawn on a hurdle to the place of execution, and there be hanged by the neck until you are dead. Your heads must then be severed from your bodies, which are to be divided into four quarters, and to be at His Majesty's disposal. May God have mercy upon your souls!"

Tom felt sick. All condemned! He had thought that at least Tommy Bacon would have been spared, on account of his age.

But no, there was to be no mercy. Even now, they were being led away.

Why, though, had he, and the eleven to whom he was chained, not also been condemned? What worse fate could befall them?

Even as these thoughts ran through his mind, he heard his own name being called and duly answered.

And so the list went on.

As the Clerk finally sat down, one of the figures in the body of the Court rose slowly to his feet. This, Tom had been warned, was the Attorney-General.

"M'lud," he intoned gravely, "the Crown has decided that all charges against these twelve defendants shall be dropped."

Whether it was the sheer relief, lack of food, or a combination of both, Tom felt his head swimming, and the figures of the lawyers began to spin round madly in front of his unfocused eyes. He felt himself falling, until a pair of powerful hands gripped his arm to steady him.

All attention was now on the Chief Baron.

"Take warning by what you have just seen!" he thundered. "Thank God you have been spared. Endeavour to live sober and religious lives, and strive day and night to reform yourselves, so that you may become a credit to society. Go home, thank God, and sin no more!"

Free!

He still couldn't believe it, even when the guards began to remove the manacles from his wrists.

Strangely, his first thought was not for himself, but for Jerry, Isaac and the rest. He especially worried about Tommy Bacon, cantankerous and stubborn to the last; yet surely, at 64, too old to go to the gallows. Tom could picture him, though, standing alongside Jerry, as the hangman prepared to place the hood over his head, cursing the King's name to the last.

He vowed he would go back and visit them. First, though, he felt deep inside his pockets. He remembered having had some money on him, at the time of his arrest.

He counted out the coins. Tenpence-halfpenny! Enough

to buy a pint of ale and his first decent meal for four and a half months!

"Yoh!" cried the gaoler, his face lighting up in a smile of recognition. "In a bloody 'urry to get back inside, in't yer?"

"I'm visitin'," answered Tom cheerfully. Now he had eaten, he felt ready to face the world once more.

"Who?"

"Jerry Brandreth."

"The Nottingham Captain 'issen!" chuckled the gaoler, revealing large, yellow teeth. "This way, then!"

He led the way to a small compound at the rear of the gaol, where prisoners were occasionally allowed to take exercise under the keen scrutiny of the armed guards.

Jerry strolled by the far wall, smoking his pipe, but his gait had lost its piratical swagger. He barely registered the presence of either the gaoler or Tom, when they approached him.

"Jerry!"

Brandreth slowly turned at the sound of the familiar voice and a smile lit up his face.

"Tom!"

There was an awkward hiatus.

"They let yer off, then?" said Jerry.

"Aye," sighed Tom.

"Yer might sound 'appy about it!" remonstrated Jerry.

"Why?"

Jerry gaped at him in disbelief.

"'Cos you're goin' free!"

Tom nodded.

"Owd Tommy said I would. 'E said t' judge'd reckon yoh all led me astray."

"Good owd Tommy!" smiled Jerry. "'E dun't deserve to 'ang — norr at '*is* age! I reckon t' death sentence is just a gesture, fer most on 'em — to please t' landowners an' t' rest. Me an' Will Turner an' Isaac'll 'ang, but t' rest'll be transported."

"P'r'aps *yoh'll* gerroff, an' all," said Tom optimistically.

Jerry dismissed the idea with a shake of his head.

"I led t' rebellion an' I shot Mary 'Epworth's servant."

"That wor an accident, worn't it," said Tom, "like me shootin' Charles Walters?"

Jerry took the pipe from his mouth and turned his head away.

"Yoh *meant* to kill 'im?" cried Tom.

"If I 'adn't, 'e'd've run off an' alerted t' Militia. We din't know then as that rat Sampson 'ad already tipped 'em off."

"But yer killed 'im fer t' Cause, din't yer?"

"I killed 'im 'cos I panicked," Jerry burst out, his face twisted with pain and remorse, "like I did when I ran away at Kimberley."

"But yoh were off to America to gerr 'elp to start a new revolution."

"Who towd yer that?" replied Jerry, with a harsh laugh. "'Appen someone who still thinks that, one day, we'll 'build a new Jerusalem/In England's green and pleasant land'!"

Tom found it odd hearing Jerry quote the poem which Jessop had made him read.

"Why not?" he retorted. "Even if yoh an' t' rest go to t' gallows, it dun't mean *others'll* not carry on t' dream."

"Who?" snapped Jerry. "Yoh?"

"Aye!" declared Tom proudly. "Tommy Bacon reckons, fost chance I get, I'll turn gentleman an' forget all about t' Republic."

"'E may be owd, burr 'e's no fool, in't Tommy," said Jerry, with a gentle smile. "Remember what t' judge towd yer — to lerrit be a lesson to yer."

"Do *yoh* think I'll forget t' Cause?" demanded Tom, stung by his leader's attitude.

Jerry laid a hand on his arm and motioned him to sit beside him.

"I think yer should, lad."

Tom shook his head violently. Had his long incarceration caused his senses to play tricks? Had he heard Jerry aright? Forget the Cause? Go back to Slack, clear his name, and then resume where he had left off?

"I know why you're doin' this," he said, with a sudden understanding. "It's gaol fever, in't it?"

"No, lad. Common sense."

"But yoh said . . ."

Jerry turned his head away and sighed.

"I said a lorra things, Tom. I've 'ad time to think — to compose missen an' mek me peace wi' God. It's time to mek me peace wi' yoh, an' all."

Tom continued to stare at him. What had happened to all the old rhetoric about Justice and Equality?

"I've done yoh a terrible wrong, lad," said Jerry. "I filled yer 'ead wi' dreams what nearly led yer to t' rope's end."

Tears were pouring down the gaunt cheeks into the tangle of unkempt beard.

Tom got to his feet, his whole frame shaking.

"Yoh 'ave done me a great wrong," he snarled, "burr it worn't that. Yoh gi'd me dreams, yeah — but then yer smashed 'em! *That's* worr I can't forgive yer for!"

Tom spun on his heels and stormed off to find the gaoler. He couldn't bear to be there a moment longer.

As he crossed the courtyard, he heard Jerry's voice calling after him for what he knew would be the last time.

"Tom! Worr've I done! God forgive me!"

CHAPTER 32

Sunday, 9th November, 1817

The stagecoach lurched into the Swan Yard, its wheel hubs scraping against the stonework.

As it came to a halt, Tom climbed down from his seat on the top and stretched his legs. Then, having ensured that the coachman's attention was diverted elsewhere, he relieved himself behind the vehicle.

It was strange to reflect that his recent escapade had begun on this selfsame coach, back in June. The only difference was that, this time, he was travelling as a *bona fide*, fare-paying passenger.

He had been free now for a fortnight, taking odd jobs at inns and stables around Derby to earn a few shillings to keep body and soul together. It was ironic, really. All this had started because he had wanted to escape from the drudgery of being an ostler; yet it was still the only work he knew.

That was not the only reason he had stayed in Derby. He had still not been able to forgive himself for walking out on Jerry, that day, even though he could still not understand the strange transformation that appeared to have affected him. In Nottingham and Pentrich, he had been a visionary, burning with zeal to eradicate the

306

injustices and inequalities that were eating away at the heart and soul of the country like maggots. God, he had said, wanted him to destroy the Monarchy and build a new, free society. Why, then, did God now want the man to repent for carrying out His orders? It didn't make sense. Didn't God know His own mind?

Tom had felt drawn to the execution, along with the ghouls who normally gathered for these public spectacles, but not, he reassured himself, from the same motives. Almost to the end, he had still been convinced that Jerry's show of piety and repentance had been an act for the benefit of the authorities. Come the hour, he had believed, Jerry would disdain the last rites offered by the parson and pour forth one final torrent of invective against this corrupt Government.

Come the hour, however, he had stood as meekly as the proverbial lamb, whilst the noose was slipped over his head. Isaac Ludlam and William Turner had likewise offered no resistance, as the hangman had launched them into eternity.

Even as the bodies had remained swinging, the executioner clinging to their legs like some demented bell-ringer, Tom had prayed for a miracle. If Jesus Christ could raise Lazarus from the dead, why could he not do the same for Jeremiah Brandreth?

All was not bad news, though. Jerry had been right about one thing: the death sentences on the other prisoners had been commuted. George Weightman, Thomas Bacon, John Mackesswick and John Onion were all transported for life, whilst Edward Moore was sentenced to twelve months' imprisonment.

And he, Tom Stone, was free. As they had approached

the outskirts of Mansfield, he had been reminded of the fate that might have befallen him. At the crossroads, at the top of Nottingham Road, stood a gibbet, from which hung a skeleton dressed in the remains of a coat and breeches. It was of a simple-minded young man, Robin Down, who, some twenty years before had been hanged for murder. When his lawyer had pleaded for clemency, on the grounds that Robin was not in full possession of his faculties, the judge had offered the lad two coins: one silver, one gold. Robin, poor wretch, had chosen the gold one, proving, the judge declared, that he was in his right wits.

Tom was desperate for a drink, but where could he go? Certainly not the Old Eclipse or the Black's Head: he was too well known in both. The Swan, on the other hand, would be the perfect cover for someone wishing to remain anonymous.

Elbowing his way through the packed, smoke-filled bar, he was relieved to see that most of the customers were coach travellers stopping for refreshment, rather than local regulars. He reached the bar, and, lowering his voice to a hoarse growl, ordered a pint of ale.

As he waited for the landlord to draw it, he looked over towards a neighbouring table, where a large, florid-faced gentleman and his tall, angular companion sat with a copy of the *Nottingham Courant* spread out on the table in front of them. From their black attire and the gleaming white stocks at their necks, Tom guessed they were clergymen.

"I see they hanged 'em, then?" commented the florid man.

"Who?" asked his companion, who seemed more interested in a red-haired girl of about fourteen, who was serving meals to the occupants of the next table.

"Those fools from Pentrich," said the florid man, wiping foam from his thick, sensuous lips. "Let's hope it puts others off."

The tall, angular man dragged his gaze away from the serving girl and grunted.

"It seems hard," he sighed. "They were only fighting for what they believed in."

"Shame on you, John!" chuckled the other. "You're beginning to sound dangerously like a Nonconformist!"

His companion smiled.

"It's for God to judge them, Henry, not us," he replied gently, his eye now focused on something on the wall just behind Tom.

Tom turned to see what was fascinating the cleric, and his eye came to rest on a yellowing notice pasted on the wall above the bar, whose wording struck him like a knife through the heart:

REWARD!!
On the 5th of June, 1817, THOMAS STONE, servant to MR SAMUEL SLACK, of West Gate, Mansfield, absconded from this town, having stolen a gentleman's pocket watch, the property of MR ROBERT HALL, Attorney-at-Law, of Church Street, Mansfield.
A reward of TEN GUINEAS is offered for information leading to the arrest of the said THOMAS STONE.

Branded a thief for the whole world to see!

Luckily for him, the two clergymen were strangers to the town, and he breathed a deep sigh of relief when they turned their attentions elsewhere. Nevertheless, he involuntarily turned up the collar of his coat and was about to drink his ale in a single draught, when he paused. Not a wise move: it would only draw attention to himself.

Besides, he had seen something — or, rather, someone — else: Cousin Richard. He was surprised. It was half-past ten on a Sunday morning. At this time, Richard was usually seated beside old Hall in his pew in the parish church, listening to the spiritual exhortations of the Reverend Thomas Cursham.

Tom tried to shrink even deeper inside his upturned coat collar. If, as he suspected, Richard was still in dire financial straits, the prospect of ten guineas easily earned would be too tempting to resist.

The reason for Richard's presence soon became apparent, when he was joined by a raven-haired young woman of about eighteen. Words passed between them, money changed hands, and they disappeared together up a flight of stairs at the rear of the room.

Tom took a long, slow drink of ale, as he weighed up the situation. Was Richard's engagement to Susannah now over, or was this to form the pattern of their married life together: mutual infidelity behind a public veneer of respectability?

Richard would not conclude his "business" for some while, but Tom felt the time was ripe to leave and make for the sanctuary of Bark Court.

"Will towd us yoh'd bin 'anged!"

310

Aunt Margaret's face still registered disbelief.

"Some on us were lerroff," said Tom. "Come 'ere!"

He held her close, in a tender embrace, so that she could feel the solid reality of his existence.

His aunt plied him with a little food and a generous measure of gin from Ben's secret stock, and assured him that Ben would be at the stables until at least sunset, if not later.

"T' less I see on 'im, t' better," Margaret confided, pointing to the fading scars and bruises round her face. "'E even threatened to tek me down to t' market an' sell me, burr 'e reckoned no one in their rait mind'd buy me!"

Tom remembered seeing such auctions by husbands of unwanted wives, carried out as if a cow, pig or horse, not a human being, was on offer. They were cruel, but acknowledged as necessary. The rich might be able to afford the luxury of a legal divorce, but, for the poor, such sales were often the only way to end domestic misery.

For the next half hour, Tom regaled his aunt with all that had happened to him since the night he had stowed away on the Nottingham stagecoach.

"Yer faither'd turn in 'is grave," his aunt said, at the conclusion of his narrative. "'Ardly ever went to church, burr 'e wor allus a God-fearin' man."

"T' main thing is, I'm back safe," said Tom.

"But yer could still be 'anged fer stealin' that watch," Margaret pointed out.

"I never stole no watch!" insisted Tom. "Surely *yoh* don't think I did it?"

"It dun't matter worr *I* think. Slack thinks yer did it.

311

That's all as matters."

"Burr I din't," repeated Tom, getting up. "Anyroad, I've gorra be goin'."

"Where?"

"Mitre Court. See Ann an' . . ."

Margaret caught hold of his sleeve.

"They're not there no more."

"Where *are* they, then?"

Margaret made several attempts to answer, but could not force out the words.

"Where are they?" demanded Tom, seizing his aunt by her frail shoulders and shaking her as though she were a rag doll.

She finally made herself utter the words: "T' work'ouse."

It was now Tom's turn to struggle for words.

"Why? 'Ow?"

He sat down again, and Margaret laid a hand on his arm.

"Slack stopped gi'in' Jonathan wokk," she said. "Said it wor only 'cos o' yoh an' 'is daughter pleadin' wi' 'im as 'e'd gi'd 'im special treatment, in t' fost place. Said 'e din't see why 'e should go on showin' favours to t' fam'ly of a thief! T' bailiffs come round, t' end of August, an' took all their stuff."

"They're still alive, then?"

Margaret let out a sharp laugh.

"If yer can *call* it livin'! They split 'em up there. Men live one side, women t' other, but t' Master lets 'em see each other fer an hour a day."

Tom felt the anger boiling inside him. Conditions sounded worse than those he'd endured in Derby Gaol! At least he had spent his incarceration amongst friends, not strangers!

"Worr about young Caleb?" demanded Tom.

Tears welled up in his aunt's faded brown eyes and flowed freely down the bruised cheeks.

"'E *is* still alive, in't 'e?" asked Tom.

"Two weeks after yoh left, 'e died," said Margaret. "They were so poor, we 'ad to gi' 'em t' eight-an'-sixpence fer t' coffin an' t' funeral! After that, it seemed as if neither on 'em 'ad owt to live for. Jonathan 'ad no knittin'. Once or twice, 'e sent messages to George Hicks — see if 'e could ay a word wi' Miss Rachel an' gerr 'im a bit o' wokk on t' side — burr 'e wun't. Too scared o' Slack!"

"Worr about Ann?"

"It 'it 'er woss," sighed Margaret. "'Er mind's gone. She'll not believe 'e's dead. She carries round this bundle, made from an owd shawl, an' treats it as if it wor Caleb! Talks to it, all day!"

Tom could stand it no longer. He sprang to his feet.

"Where're yer goin'?" asked his aunt.

"I've gorra gerrem out o' there!"

"'Ow?" asked his aunt plaintively.

"I've gorra prove I din't pinch that watch. I've gorra catch the *real* thief!"

"Burr it could be anybody."

313

"No," said Tom quietly. "I know who it wor —
Richard!"

Margaret went pale and turned away.

"Our Richard wun't steal owt!" she gabbled.

Was she hiding something from him? Tom explained
about the gambling debts.

"Besides," he added, "'e lives in 'All's 'ouse. 'E'd know
where all t' valuables were kept. An' I saw 'im goin' into
t' pawnbrokers, that Sat'day."

It was a faint chance, of course, but it was just a
possibility that John Gresham could help him clear his
name. He vowed he would go there, in the morning. His
first priority, though, was to find accommodation for the
night.

"Can I stay 'ere?" he begged his aunt.

Margaret considered the suggestion.

"Well, there's t' attic, I s'pose."

"But worr if Ben . . ?"

"'E'll not go up there. By t' time 'e gets in, tonait, 'e'll
be too pissed to do owt but fall into bed an' snore 'is fat
'ead off!"

Tom put his arms round Margaret and kissed her gently
on the cheek.

By ten o'clock, when Ben finally rolled through the door,
reeking of stale gin, Tom was asleep; but his dreams were
haunted with visions of Ann, Jonathan and Caleb.

Poor Caleb! He had never stood a chance of survival!
Why should God allow wretches like Richard to roam at
liberty, letting others take the blame for their actions,

whilst not lifting a finger to save one innocent child?

Let the Reverend Cursham explain *that* away!

CHAPTER 33

Monday, 10th November, 1817

"So, the bad penny's turned up, at last!"

Tom slowly opened his eyes and gradually focused on the familiar features of Samuel Slack, who was bent over his attic bed, his lips parted in a sickly grin. His gaze then travelled to the door, where Ben was leaning against the frame, jingling a handful of coins.

"It wor all my fault, Tom!" came the voice of Margaret. "'E worn't as pissed as I thought. 'E saw yer cup an' plate, an' . . ."

She saw Tom looking at her face, and her hand instinctively flew to the fresh bruise that had appeared on her right cheek.

"'E made me tell 'im, an' . . ."

"It's all rait," said Tom soothingly. That was *another* hiding he owed Ben, but he would wait. For the moment, he had more pressing business.

"You're comin' wi' me an' Mr 'All to see t' magistrate," said Slack, and, for the first time, Tom noticed the dumpy figure of the lawyer behind the hosier's right shoulder.

"I'm innocent!" Tom protested. How many times had he said that? Still no one listened to him!

"Why did you run away, then?" demanded Hall.

"'Cos I knew I wun't gerra fair trial," replied Tom. "None on yer 'ud listen! It wor Richard!" insisted Tom. "Why dun't yer believe me?"

"'Thou shalt not bear false witness against thy neighbour.' Exodus: Chapter 20, Verse 16," intoned Slack, but Tom was in no mood for pious injunctions.

"I saw 'im come out o' Gresham's, t' pawnbroker's," said Tom. "We can go round to 'is shop, fost. *'E'll* tell yer it worn't me!"

"You've just spent five months in Derby Gaol for your part in this insurrection, I believe," said Hall stiffly.

"Aye," answered Tom, without a trace of remorse.

"And are we to give credence to the words of a traitor?"

"I'm norra traitor — an' I'm norra liar, neither!" replied Tom vehemently.

"So, you're still standing by this ridiculous story that Richard first approached Susannah, then stole and pawned my watch to pay off gambling debts?" asked Hall.

"Aye!"

"But Susannah has already denied any such approach."

The sound of a loud sob from the far side of the room caused them all to look. Aunt Margaret stood, her hands covering her face, rocking to and fro. As she lowered her hands, they could see tears coursing down the thin, creased cheeks.

"What's the matter, woman?" barked Hall.

"Tom," said Margaret, ignoring the little lawyer. "D'yer remember that day yer come round an' found me lyin' in

317

bed?"

"The day *'e'd* bin beatin' yer?" shouted Tom, stabbing his finger viciously in the direction of his uncle.

"I lied to yer, Tom. It worn't Ben — well, norr *all* on it."

"What d'yer mean?"

"That bit about Ben seein' me in t' Black's 'Ead Yard wor rait — an' 'e gi'd me a black eye for it — but that wor all."

By now, even Ben was no longer grinning.

"Worr about t' other bruises? Yoh towd me yer'd fell down t' stairs!"

"I lied," answered Margaret simply.

"'Ow *did* yer gerrem, then?" demanded Tom.

"It wor Richard."

The response was barely audible, and Hall had to ask her to repeat it.

"It wor Richard. 'E come round an' said 'e wor in desperate trouble — said 'e owed money."

"How much?" asked Hall. "Did he say?"

"About 30 guineas, I think — though where the 'ell 'e thought *I* could get 30 guineas from, God knows!"

Slack let out a sharp snort at this show of blasphemy.

"Go on," prompted Hall.

"'E said I should strip down the 'ouse an' sell ev'ry stick o' furniture. When I said no, 'e . . .."

She broke off, her body once more racked with sobs.

"D'yer see?" said Tom. "Twenty fer Jacob Smalley, an'

ten 'e owed George Tully. Remember 'ow they nearly come to blows outside t' church, that Sunday?"

"And you expect us to believe this?" asked the little lawyer, ignoring Tom's interruption.

"D'yer think a mother teks pride in admittin' 'er son's a bully an' p'r'aps a thief? Do yer?" cried Margaret, her face red with shame.

By now, even Hall's rosy-apple cheeks had lost their colour.

"I see. This puts a somewhat different complexion on the matter."

"D'yer believe me, now?" asked Tom.

The lawyer had taken out a large linen handkerchief and was mopping his glistening bald pate.

"I'm a fair man — as is Mr Slack. I still feel we should take the case before the magistrate, but I'm willing to humour you, for the moment, over the matter of the pawnbroker."

"Gentleman's pocket watch!"

John Gresham peered at the poster that Hall handed to him, then tossed back his thick mane of grey hair and roared with laughter.

"You may know all about the Law, Mr Hall, but you know precious little about *this* business. Do you know how many gentlemen pawn their pocket watches, each week?"

Hall puffed out his chest, as though about to answer, but said nothing.

"What date did you say?" asked Gresham.

"T' 31st o' May," cut in Tom. "It wor a Sat'day — an' I wor stood over there." He pointed through the window in the direction of John Coutts' shop. "I saw 'im come in 'ere, an' . . ."

"Never mind that, for the moment!" snapped Hall. "We haven't yet established that the watch was, in fact, pawned here; although I'm aware that businesses such as this are used by members of the criminal fraternity for disposing of stolen property."

"I hope that last remark wasn't directed at *me!*" said Gresham, casting a withering look in the lawyer's direction. "I'd not hesitate to sue for defamation of character, if it was!"

"Not in the least!" replied Hall, exposing his ivory dentures in an apologetic smile. "I was merely making a general observation."

"Good," replied the pawnbroker, with a loud grunt of satisfaction. "Now, what date did you say?"

"T' 31st o' May," answered Tom.

Gresham took down a thick ledger from the shelf behind him and began to thumb through the pages.

"The 31st of May," he said, at last, stabbing the relevant page with a long, bony finger. "There were five gentlemen's pocket watches brought in, that day: four have been redeemed."

"The one that's not been redeemed," said Hall, an optimistic gleam lighting up his pale blue eyes. "Who brought it in?"

The pawnbroker shrugged.

"I never keep a note of names. It's a matter of protecting

my customers, you understand. It can be embarrassing for some, coming in here."

"I'm sure," replied the lawyer. "May we see the watch, then? Perhaps I'll be able to identify it."

There was an anxious wait of some three minutes, whilst John Gresham disappeared into the back room and rummaged through shelves full of boxes. He finally emerged, carrying a gentleman's pocket watch.

"Thank you," said Hall, holding out his hand.

Gresham snatched the watch out of his reach.

"How would you be able to identify it as yours? Are their any distinguishing marks or inscriptions on it?"

"Open the back," said Hall. "You'll find an inscription, which reads: 'Thomas Marston, 1737.' He was my maternal grandfather. He bequeathed it to my mother, who, in turn, left it to me."

The pawnbroker carefully scrutinized the watch through a jeweller's eyeglass.

"Well?" snapped Hall impatiently.

Satisfied, Gresham closed the back of the watch before handing it to the little lawyer, and then peered at the ledger once more.

"Yes, I *do* remember this one, now. He became quite aggressive, I seem to recall. He wanted 30 guineas for it! I beat him down to 20!"

"See?" cried Tom triumphantly. "'E used that to pay off Smalley, burr it still left 'im owin' ten guineas to George Tully!"

"Quiet!" growled Slack, grabbing Tom by the shoulder;

but Tom saw a worried expression appear in his former master's pale blue eyes.

"Twenty! It's worth many times more than that!" Hall was spluttering.

"To a watchmaker, perhaps," said Gresham, with a slightly condescending smile, "and, as a family heirloom, it's no doubt priceless. I, though, have to make a valuation purely on its metal content."

"Never mind that! Do you remember the person who brought it in?"

Both Hall and Slack were now directing accusatory stares at Tom, who was staring fixedly at the floor. Even though he knew he was innocent, he still could not face his tormentors.

"Is *this* the wretch?" demanded the lawyer, his gaze now directed at Gresham, even though his finger pointed at Tom.

Tom's mouth had gone dry, as he looked pleadingly at the pawnbroker.

"He's your servant, isn't he?" Gresham asked Slack.

"Was," corrected the hosier.

"I thought I recognized him. Well, it certainly wasn't him."

"Are you certain?"

"My eyes mayn't be as strong as they used to be, Mr Hall, but I can still tell the difference between a strapping young lad with dark hair and a taller man with hair the colour of ripened corn."

Richard! The description fitted perfectly!

"Tom! Yer dun't know 'ow glad I am to see yer agen!"

Hannah Green flung her arms round Tom and hugged him to her capacious bosom.

"It's good to see yoh, an' all, 'Annah!" smiled Tom, planting a kiss on her left cheek, in the middle of the strawberry birthmark.

"*I* knew yoh 'adn't pinched no watch!" said Hannah loyally, and she cast a withering look at Slack and Hall, who at least had the good grace to look ashamed.

"And I, too, knew you were innocent," said another voice, and Rachel stepped towards him, her plain, ruddy features illuminated and transformed by a beaming smile of welcome.

"All the same," said Hall, "we still don't know definitely that Richard's guilty."

"But Gresham's description . . ."

"It could have fitted any number of men," answered Hall, who was still smarting over Gresham's insistence that he should pay a redemption fee of 20 guineas to recover his own stolen property!

"But 'ow many on 'em woulda know'd yoh kept yer watch in that desk?" demanded Tom, who was still annoyed that, despite the fact that his innocence had now been established beyond all doubt, the little lawyer had still not fully apologized to him.

"We can discuss all this later," said Slack, ushering them into the dining room. "We must eat, fost. 'Ow long is it since yer tasted mutton, Tom?"

Tom shrugged, as his former master poured him a glass of dry sherry.

Tom took the glass, mumbling grateful thanks, and the rest of the company watched in amazement, as the pale amber liquid disappeared down his throat in a single draught. They had now been joined by Mrs Slack and Susannah, who looked as radiant as ever in a dark brown dress.

Tom looked at her, but she studiously avoided his gaze.

"Are we all 'ere?" asked Slack.

"Where's Mr Jessop?" interposed Tom. More to the point, he thought to himself, where had he been on the night of June the 9th?

"Teachin' in Woodhouse, t' last I 'eard," said Slack. "I dismissed 'im fer 'elpin' yoh gerr away."

No! Tom felt a pang of guilt. He must see Ned, as soon as possible, and find out what had happened to his mentor. I can't let him starve on *my* account! he thought.

"Any road," continued Slack. "I worn't satisfied wi' t' way young Joseph wor progressin'. Jessop worn't learnin' 'im rait."

Tom managed to stifle a smile, as he remembered Jessop's description of young Joseph's academic abilities.

"I've gorra new man in — Stephens," said Slack. "Yer can start yer lessons an' yer owd job agen, as from tomorrer — that is, if you're stayin'."

He looked to both his wife and Hall for moral support, but neither showed any inclination to help him out. Indeed, the little lawyer was glowering at Tom, as though he considered that educating him was a waste of time, and that such as he should be content to remain in the gutter, where they belonged!

Despite all that had happened, he still can't bring himself to believe that Richard's guilty! thought Tom.

"We've done yer a great wrong, Tom," continued the hosier, rather hesitantly. "The Lord's Prayer instructs us to forgive those that trespass against us. Can *yoh* ever forgive us, Tom?"

Tom thought back over the events of the past five months. It would have been tempting to tell Slack exactly what he could do with his offer. He could almost hear the voice of Jerry Brandreth urging him to do it.

Certainly, that's what Jonathan would have done — starved rather than accept a farthing's-worth of charity. And look where it had got him! No, the fact was that he needed to earn some money. If he saved diligently, perhaps he could soon earn enough to pay off Ann and Jonathan's debts and free them from the ignominy of the workhouse.

"Yes, sir."

The hosier held out his hand and Tom clasped it in a firm handshake.

"I only wish there wor summat I could do by way o' compensation," sighed Slack.

"There is."

All eyes looked towards the far corner of the room, as Rachel stepped forward.

"I understand your sister and her husband were taken to the workhouse, Tom."

"Yes, miss."

325

"I also heard that their young son had died."

"Caleb. Yes, miss."

"I'm sorry, Tom."

"It worn't *your* fault, miss."

"The poor should be discouraged from having children, if they can't afford them!" muttered Hall darkly.

Rachel silenced him with a withering glare before turning her attention back to Tom.

"I know it won't bring the child back to life," she said, "but what if Father were to pay off their debts?"

"What did yoh say, Rachel?" gasped Slack.

"You can afford it. Go round there, this afternoon, and pay off every penny they owe. It's the least you owe Tom!"

CHAPTER 34

Monday, 10th November, 1817

"Dear God, what a place!"

Robert Hall grimaced, as he took in his surroundings. They stood in the men's quarters of the parish workhouse: row upon row of spartan wooden cots, which now accommodated their occupants during their periods of earthly sleep, and would later serve for their eternal one.

The parish workhouse stood on Nottingham Road: a grim stone building evidently designed to discourage the poor and destitute from crossing its threshold; although few of them came there voluntarily. It was also at a convenient distance from the town centre; so "respectable" citizens could happily forget its existence.

For the moment, the room was empty: the inmates were in other parts of the buildings, busy with their various tasks.

"Be thankful *you'll* not end your days here, Mr Hall," boomed a voice behind them, and they turned to see the tall, well-rounded figure of the Workhouse Master.

Hall and Slack each shook hands with him, whilst tom remained in the background.

"I understand you've come to see Jonathan Parker and

his wife," said the Master.

Hall nodded.

"And who's this?" asked the Master, pointing to Tom.

"Ann's brother," replied Tom.

The Master shook his head gravely.

"When did you last see her?"

"Five month back," replied Tom. "I've bin — er — I've bin away."

"You'll notice a change in her," said the Master, a note of sympathy creeping into his voice.

"Me a'nt said so."

"A sad case! Very sad!" mutter the Master, ushering them out of the men's quarters into his office.

"Look," interrupted Slack, who clearly wished to conclude the errand as speedily as possible, "'ow much do they owe?"

The Master consulted a thick ledger on his desk.

"Five pounds, eighteen shillings, and fourpence three-farthings."

Just under six pounds! So small a sum had brought them to this!

Slack had taken out a purse and was already engaged in counting out the sum mentioned.

The office door opened, and Ann and Jonathan shuffled in. Jonathan hung back in the doorway, his hands crossed in front of him, his head bowed.

It was fortunate that Aunt Margaret had forewarned Tom

of his sister's condition; yet nothing could have prepared him for his first sight of that wretched figure. She carried the rolled-up shawl, just as his aunt had described, but her dress was unbuttoned, and she held the bundle to her naked, shrunken breast.

Tom gasped in horror. She was trying to suckle it!

"Ann!"

She raised her head and turned it towards him. The brown eyes looked straight through him.

"Ann! It's me! Tom! Yer brother!"

"She'll not know yer, Tom," said Jonathan. "When they lerrus see each other, she dun't know *me*, 'aif o' t' time."

Tom reached forward to touch the bundle.

Ann leapt backwards, as though stung.

"Dun't touch 'im! Leave 'im alone!"

Her long, thin fingers stroked the "baby's" head.

"Yer Mam'll not lerrem tek yer!" she shrieked.

"'E's a fine, 'andsome lad!" said Slack, craning forward to look at the bundle. "'E'll grow up to be a credit to 'is Mam."

"'E's goin' to be a soldier," said Ann proudly, "like 'is Uncle Will."

Slack turned to look at Tom, his eyes full of pity — and perhaps, thought Tom, a twinge of guilt, too.

"I never knew it 'ad 'it 'er so bad," whispered Slack, unable to look at Ann any longer.

"Worr're *yoh* doin' 'ere?" asked Jonathan eventually.

"I've come to pay off yer debts," replied the hosier, trying to sound brisk and businesslike once more.

"Why?"

"I owe it to Tom fer doubtin' 'is honesty. I s'pose I owe it to yoh, an' all, in a way — though George Hicks wor quite wi'in 'is rights to tek t' wokk off on yer, if 'e din't think yoh were up to it."

Tom was disgusted. Even now, he was trying to push some of the blame onto Jonathan! Wasn't it to prevent the likes of Ann and Jonathan rotting in the workhouse that he, Jerry and the rest had set out from Pentrich, that night?

A pale, gaunt man, his head shaven, had entered the office and begun to sweep the floor with a worn besom. There was something vaguely familiar about him, but Tom could not have said what. The man stopped sweeping and looked at the Workhouse Master.

"Don't mind us. Carry on," said the Master, and then made a gesture to the others indicating that the newcomer was not in full possession of his senses.

"Margaret towd us yoh were s'posed to 'ave stole a watch, or summat," said Jonathan.

"*My* watch!" cut in Hall.

"Aye," said Tom, pointing to the little lawyer. "'E said I stole it, burr 'e gorrit back from Gresham, t' pawnbroker, an' *'e* said it worn't me as pawned it."

"*I* coulda towd yer that," said Jonathan, addressing Hall. "Our Ann allus brought 'im up honest." Tears began to stream down his face at the mention of his wife's name.

"I know who *did* pinch it," Tom went on, "burr 'e'll not believe me!"

The lawyer gazed at Tom's pointing finger and let out a sharp laugh.

"Nonsense, boy! My clerk, Richard Miller, would never steal from anybody!"

"Oh, 'e's a thief, all rait!"

Everyone looked round, wondering where the new voice had come from. Their eyes fell on the shaven-headed man with the besom.

"What do you mean?" growled Hall. "Who are you?"

"Jack Miller," said the stranger. "Richard's long-lost bastard 'aif-brother!"

Jack Miller sat, hands folded in his lap, looking at his audience, like an actor judging the effect of a dramatic pause. He turned now to Tom.

"Yer'll not remember yer A'nt Mary, will yer?"

Tom shook his head.

"She wor yer Uncle Ben's fost wife. A couple o' months afore they married, a young woman called Bessie Andrews turned up, wi' me in 'er belly, claimin' Ben wor t' faither."

"And was he?" asked Hall.

"Oh, aye," chuckled Jack, his lips parting to reveal blackened teeth. "Could never resist t' chance to get 'tween a woman's legs, couldn't Ben! Proud on it, so A'nt Mary said."

Jack's eyes misted over.

"She wor an angel, wor that woman! Went on wi' t' weddin', took me in, an' brung me up as if I wor 'er own!"

331

Tom marvelled at how this emaciated wretch, who had obviously suffered so much, could still manage to laugh!

"When I wor two, Mam — I allus thought on 'er as me Mam — died. It din't tek Ben long to find someone else! To be fair to Margaret, though, she wor as good to me as Mary 'ad bin. Two years later, they 'ad Richard — on t' rait side o' t' blanket, fer once! Ben doted on 'im. Dearest little Richard couldn't do nowt wrong!"

"Get to the point!" yapped Hall irritably. "You said earlier that Richard was a thief. From what he'd told me — not that he mentioned you often — *you* were the thief!"

"No, sir. I wor t' one as wor punished! It all started ten year ago. I wor sixteen an' wokkin' wi' me Dad in t' Owd Eclipse stables: Richard wor fourteen an' still at school. One nait, a traveller left 'is 'oss at t' stables an' went into t' Eclipse fer a meal an' a drink."

Hall was already growing impatient, drumming a rapid tattoo on the table.

"Anyroad," continued Jack, "'e suddenly remembered 'e'd left some valuables in 'is saddle-bags; so 'e goes back to t' stables. As 'e gets to t' door, 'e bumps into Richard, who sez, 'Ayup, mester, 'e's pinched summat o' yourn!' When t' man shines 'is lantern inside t' stable, there's me wi' t' valuables in me 'and!"

Again, Jack paused for effect.

"Wor 'e din't know, wor that *I'd* seen Richard tekkin' 'em out o' t' saddle-bags. There wor a fait, an' I took 'em off 'im. I wor just purrin' 'em back."

Jack looked pleadingly at his listeners.

"Well, who were they goin' to believe: golden-'aired, angel-faced Richard or Jack the bastard?"

It was all coming back to Tom, now. He had been six, at the time, but he still remembered the effect it had had on everyone: Margaret had wept constantly; Ben had got blind drunk; and Old Amos and Caleb had called down all the curses of the Almighty onto Jack's wretched head. Henceforth, it was decreed that the name of Jack Miller was never to be spoken in the Stone household again.

"Worr 'appened to yer, then?" asked Slack.

"Transported to Botany Bay for seven years! Left to rot!"

"It's been the making of many men," cut in Hall. "Given the chance to start a new life."

"I coulda stayed there, burr I wanted revenge. I *still* want it — for both on us, now," said Jack, putting a hand on Tom's arm.

"We 'eard yoh'd died out there," said Tom.

"That's worr I *wanted* folk to think! I got back in England, three year back, determined to come 'ome an' prove 'im a thief an' a liar."

"Yoh've bin in this place three year?" asked Tom incredulously.

Jack shook his head.

"I din't get straight back. I stopped off in London. I tried to find a proper job, burr all I could get were bits o' labourin' – norr earnin' enough to feed a sparer! I gorrin wi' a bad crowd an' ended up in gaol – as a *real* thief, this time. T' shame on it! Mary musta turned in 'er grave! After all she'd brung me up to believe in!"

He stood, turned round and pulled up his shirt at the back.

"Good God!" cried Tom, staring at the criss-cross pattern

333

of faded scars.

"That's 'ow it's bin till May," said Jack. "Whipped in ev'ry parish 'tween London an' 'ere as a vagrant! Finally, I managed to prove to 'em 'ere that I wor from Mansfield, t' parish agreed to tek me, an' this is where I've bin ever since."

"A burden upon honest citizens!" Hall muttered under his breath.

"T' Crown & Anchor!" gasped Tom suddenly.

The others looked at him — all except Ann, who continued to stare at her bundle, talking to it continuously in a muted voice.

"It wor yoh as bumped into Richard, outside t' Crown & Anchor, that day 'e pawned t' watch. I knew there wor summat familiar about yer! Aye," said Tom, "yoh followed 'im."

"I can move round like a shadow," grinned Jack, "'cos nobody teks no notice on me. To them, I'm just 'that madman from t' work'ouse'. That's when I 'eard 'e wor in debt! I've known Gorge Tully, long since. I went to see 'im, that afternoon, an' 'e towd me all about it!"

"An' yoh were outside t' church, t' next day, when Richard nearly 'ad that fait wi' George Tully!"

Jack nodded.

This could be it! thought Tom. The vital proof he needed. He leaned forward anxiously.

"'E din't say where Richard got t' money to pay off Smalley, did 'e?"

Jack shook his head.

334

"No," he sighed, "burr 'e *did* say 'e'd a fair idea it worn't come by honest!"

There was silence, followed by a grunt from Hall.

"This is pure speculation!" thundered the lawyer, who had risen, put on his hat, and was preparing to leave.

Slack stood up and held his arm. His brow was deeply creased in a puzzled frown.

"'Appen so, burr I think, for 'is an' Tom's sake, we should look into it."

CHAPTER 35

Monday, 10th November, 1817

Tom felt frustrated: their further investigations had so far revealed nothing.

Their first port of call had been Kelham Neale's butcher's shop, in Market Place, to find George Tully.

"'E's took t' day off," replied the butcher, with an airy wave to indicate that he was not hiding the man in some secret corner of his premises. "Gone to visit a sick uncle in Skegby."

George Ellis had proved equally unhelpful.

"Jacob? I sent 'im to Bulwell an' Nottingham, to settle some accounts I owe."

Tom inwardly questioned the wisdom of entrusting such a shifty creature with so responsible an errand.

To take his mind off Richard's crime — for he was now, more than ever, convinced of his guilt — Tom decided to refresh his brain with a pint of George Cadman's ale. He also needed to speak to Ned Hopkins. Where was Jessop, and what had happened to the pair of them on the night of June the 9th?

He reached the door of the Old Eclipse, and was about to open it, when his attention was arrested by the sound of a familiar gruff baritone voice:

> *And it's o'er the hills and o'er the*
> *main, To Flanders, Portugal and*
> *Spain.*
> *King George commands and we*
> *obey;*
> *Over the hills and far away.*

Tom pushed open the door, as a smattering of applause greeted Ned's rendition. There were few people inside, as Tom made his way to the bar.

"Pint," he announced.

"Tom!" said Cadman, his jaw dropping open. "I never thought to see *yoh* agen! Yer wanna be careful!"

He pointed to a faded copy of the "Reward" notice.

"It's all rait," replied Tom, and explained how the visit to John Gresham had finally established his innocence, if not Richard's guilt.

"On the 'ouse, then," smiled Cadman, placing the foaming tankard in front of him. "Good 'ealth!"

Tom returned the toast and drank deeply. Then, he looked round for Ned, who had finished circulating amongst the sparse crowd and was now seated in the far corner, counting out his meagre takings.

The former farrier glanced up from his task, and his face turned pale, as if he had seen a ghost.

"Tom?" he gasped, half-rising.

"Stay there," smiled Tom, walking over to join him. "'Ow much 'ave yer made?"

"Tenpence."

"'Ere," said Tom, digging deep into his pocket and finding two pennies, which he pressed into Ned's hand.

"Thanks," said Ned, with an effort, forcing a weak smile.

"You're welcome. So, 'ow's things?"

He had decided to approach the subject obliquely.

"Gerrin' by," replied Ned with a shrug of his massive shoulders. "Could be berra — burr it could be a damn sight woss, I s'pose. I 'eard about Ann an' Jonathan — an' t' poor mite."

"Well, at least *some* good's come out on it," said Tom. "Slack's paid off their debts an' they're out o' t' work'ouse."

"If it worn't fer George, that's where *I'd* be!" confided Ned, with a rueful jerk of his thumb in the direction of the bar.

An embarrassed silence followed, during which Tom's gaze wandered round the room. Eight people in! He wondered how George Cadman managed to stay in business. Back in May, he had talked of having to reduce staff in order to survive. Perhaps Tom's departure had helped. He would always need good ostlers, like Ben, and his kind heart would never let him turn away a loyal soul like Ned. It was a puzzle, nonetheless.

"Worr 'appened, then?" asked Tom, eventually.

Ned shifted uneasily in his seat.

"'Appened?"

"T' revolution," prompted Tom. "June t' 9th."

Ned did not answer immediately. Instead, he drained his tankard and crossed to the bar for a refill. When he returned, he took another long drink and wiped his lips on the back of his sleeve.

"We 'ad a meetin' in t' Black's 'Ead, on t' Sunday nait — if yer can call me an' 'Enry Jessop a meetin'!"

"Just t' two on yer?" asked Tom incredulously.

"Aye," nodded Ned. "Slack'd kicked 'im out fer 'elpin' yoh gerr away."

"I know."

"So, 'e wor stayin' wi' me. Anyroad, when we found out there wor only goin' to be two on us, I thought 'Enry'd call it off. I mean, whoever 'eard of a two-man revolution?"

"'Enry once towd me it only took *one* man wi' an idea — so long as t' idea wor big enough," said Tom.

"That's worr 'e towd *me*, an' all," said Ned. "Said Jerry 'ad promised there'd be 30,000 on t' Forest to meet us."

Tom remembered the sheet of figures Jerry had produced in the Black's Head. Men from Sheffield, Wakefield, Leeds — the list had seemed endless.

"So, 'Enry wor all fer goin'?" asked Tom, anxious to get his facts straight.

"Aye."

"So, what stopped yer?"

"About nine o'clock, that delegate from 'Ucknall turned up. What's 'is name?"

"Sampson!"

"Sampson," repeated Ned. "I 'eard tell it wor *'im* as betrayed Jerry to t' Militia."

"T' bastard!" snarled Tom, nodding in confirmation.

"'Im an' that William Oliver," said Ned. "They reckon the 'ole country wor packed wi' Government spies!"

Tom felt a sharp pang of conscience.

"Aye, 'appen so," he mumbled.

"Well, Sampson towd us it wor all off."

"What?"

"'E said 'e'd 'ad word from all over t' North an' t' Midlands as nobody wor goin' to turn up in Nottingham, on t' Monday nait."

"'E went round to Jerry's 'ouse in Nottingham, on t' Sat'day mornin', to tell 'im t' 'Ucknall an' Bulwell men worn't comin', burr 'e said nowt about t' North an' t' Midlands. If it's true they weren't turnin' out, then 'e let Jerry go off to Pentrich, knowin' Nottingham wor goin' to be deserted."

"Aye," said Ned. "An' if 'e'd already alerted t' Militia which route they'd be tekkin' from Pentrich . . ."

"Seems the 'ole thing wor doomed from t' start! T' Republic'll never 'appen now!" sighed Tom.

"Jessop thinks it will," said Ned, "burr 'e reckons it's all t' fault o' t' workers theirsens. 'E sez, next time, it'll be men like *'im* — men as wokk wi' their brains, not their 'ands — as'll bring it about!"

"An' do *yoh* still believe in t' Republic?" asked Tom.

Ned clasped a large, hairy hand over Tom's mouth.

"It's still not safe to talk about it, round 'ere," he hissed. Then, softly, he added: "No."

"Where's 'Enry, now?" asked Tom.

"Woodhouse, I 'eard. Teachin' in a school. I've not seen 'im for months — not since August."

The two drank in silence, for several moments.

"Did yoh — did yoh see Jerry, when they — when they 'anged 'im?" faltered Ned, at length.

Tom nodded.

"'Ow wor 'e?" asked Ned. "Swearin'? Still callin' fer t' King's 'ead?"

"Aye," smiled Tom, laying a hand on the ex-farrier's shoulder. "'E made a brave end."

Well, it wasn't for *him* to trample on Ned's dreams!

"Yer can't lerrem put 'er in there, Tom! She's all I've got left, now!"

Jonathan looked pathetically at Tom, and wiped a tear from his pallid cheek.

"Mebbe it's fer t' best," Tom managed to say, despite the lump in his throat.

"Leave 'er in t' asylum, fer t' gentry to come an' gawp at?" cried Jonathan.

Tom had no answer. They were now back in the cottage in Mitre Court, and he cast a glance over to the far corner of the room, where Ann rocked backwards and forwards, her dress still open, trying to "feed" the bundle clasped to her withered breast. He immediately jerked his head away. It was too painful to watch.

He unwrapped the parcel of food Hannah had thoughtfully provided and offered some to Jonathan.

341

"Not fer me. Thank Mr Slack fer t' food, though — an' fer bailin' us out. It wor rait kind on 'im."

"Yer've got to eat!"

"I'm all rait," insisted Jonathan.

"Worr about Ann?"

"She'll norr eat owt. I've tried prayin'," said Jonathan, "beggin' God to restore 'er wits."

"Prayin' not do no good," barked Tom. "'Er wits are past mendin'. I'm surprised yer waste yer time wi' that Chapel. If there'd bin a God who cared, 'E wunta let Caleb die or Ann go mad. If there'd bin a God who believed in Justice, King George an' t' Prince Regent 'ud be dead, not Jerry Brandreth. If there'd bin a God, Jack wunta suffered, an' Richard woulda got worr 'e deserved. An' if there'd bin a God . . ."

His head slumped forward, and he wept bitterly, pounding the table in anger and frustration until his fists bled.

Jonathan slowly put his arms round Tom's broad shoulders, and pulled him close, their bodies locked in shared grief.

"I married 'er fer better or woss, Tom," whispered Jonathan. "It's *me* as should look after 'er. An', at the Day o' Judgment, she'll be made 'ole agen, an' we'll be reunited wi' Caleb in everlastin' bliss. T' Bible promises us that. 'For God so loved the world, that He gave His only begotten Son, that whosoever believeth in Him should not perish, but have everlasting life.' St John: Chapter 3, Verse 16."

Tom groaned. Would *nothing* convince his brother-in-law that his faith was futile?

CHAPTER 36

Tuesday, 11th November, 1817

"Go away, Tom! You can't come in here!"

Susannah wrapped the robe around her lithe, naked body and turned her back on him.

"I've gorra talk to yer!"

Susannah glanced back over her shoulder.

"Give me five minutes."

She closed the bedroom door, and Tom paced nervously up and down the landing, mentally rehearsing his interrogation. Slack was away on business, and his wife and Rachel had gone into town, leaving Susannah alone. It was probably the only opportunity he would get.

After what seemed an eternity, a voice from behind the door announced: "You can come in, now."

Tom stepped over the threshold, opened his mouth to speak, and stopped. She was seated on the edge of the bed, in a lilac silk dress, looking more beautiful than ever: even more beautiful that that Saturday, when they had lain together on that selfsame bed and . . . No! He must put all such distractions from his mind! There were painful questions to which he *must* have answers!

"Whilst you're here, you can button up my dress," she said, getting up and turning her back towards him.

Momentarily forgetting the purpose of his errand, Tom meekly obeyed, remembering how, on that Saturday, he had taken such pleasure in unbuttoning it!

The task completed, she sat down on the bed once more.

"Well?"

The lips parted in that familiar, seductive smile, showing the white, slightly irregular teeth. He mustn't let it affect him!

"Why did you lie?" he asked bluntly.

The smile swiftly faded.

"What did you expect me to do?"

Tom's jaw shot open. It certainly wasn't the answer he'd anticipated. He'd expected *some* expression of remorse!

"You heard what my father said: if it was true about Richard's gaming debts, he was going to call off the marriage. I panicked."

"So, yoh lied, an' yoh'd 've lerrem 'ang me, just to save yer precious marriage to Richard!"

Susannah said nothing.

"Yoh could see yersen losin' all that money 'e wor due to inherit from 'All, couldn't yer?"

"I was confused!" said Susannah pathetically. "The idea of Richard being a thief — why, it's preposterous!"

"Is it? I wor outside that door, that Wednesday nait. I 'eard 'im tell yoh 'e wor in trouble an' ask yer to pawn yer jewels."

Susannah blushed.

"Yes, he did."

"Yet, on t' Sat'day, yoh towd me yoh 'adn't gi'd 'im nowt to pawn."

"I didn't."

"Burr 'e got twenty guineas to pay off Smalley from *somewhere*, that Sat'day mornin'."

"And you think it was through stealing Robert Hall's watch?"

"Where *else* could 'e 'a' gorrit? I saw 'im, wi' me own eyes, comin' out o' Gresham's pawnshop. If it worn't your jewels 'e popped, it wor 'All's watch. Apart from 'All an' me, there'd bin no one else go near 'All's room for days afore t' watch went missin'. Gresham's description o' t' man who pawned it din't fit me or 'All — burr it *does* fit Richard!"

Susannah clapped her hands over her ears and turned away, her whole body rigid.

"I won't hear any more!"

"An' I've got *more* proof!" continued Tom, and proceeded to outline all that Margaret and Jack had told him, the previous day.

She neither moved nor spoke.

"Now will yer believe me?" cried Tom, gripping her firmly by the shoulders and swinging her round.

Tears cascading down the smooth, porcelain cheeks, she threw her arms round Tom's neck and buried her face in his shoulder. He longed to run his fingers through the chestnut ringlets, undo the buttons he had so recently

345

fastened, kiss the smooth, swanlike neck, and caress the firmly-moulded breasts.

He remembered the long, lonely nights in Derby Gaol, when his thoughts had been preoccupied with her. Sometimes, he had dreamed of enjoying the delights of her soft, warm body between silken sheets: at others, of exacting a thousand and one revenges on her if ever he were to get free and return to Mansfield.

Despite all she had said and done to protect Richard and his promised inheritance, despite the callous indifference with which she had so nearly condemned him to the rope's end, there still lurked within his heart some grain of pity for her, if only she would admit how she had wronged him.

He cupped his hand under her chin and raised her head.

"Do yer believe me?" he repeated softly.

"Yes. I *knew* he'd done it."

"Yer knew? Then, why din't yer tell t' truth to 'All an' yer faither?"

Susannah turned her head aside.

"Because he threatened to beat me, if I didn't lie for him," she managed to whisper.

"An' yoh'd marry a man who threatens to beat yer?" asked Tom incredulously.

She looked at him hopefully.

"He'll change, once we're married."

Yes, mused Tom, and no doubt Aunt Margaret had thought the same, when she married Ben!

With a sudden cry, Susannah threw herself back on the bed, her arms flung wide.

"Tom! Hit me! Beat me black and blue! I don't care! I deserve anything you choose to do to me!"

Tom looked down at her and shook his head. No, he didn't believe a word of it: it was only play-acting, designed to wring sympathy from him. Perhaps he would be able to forgive her, one day — but not yet.

He walked out, slamming the door behind him.

Tom interrupted his stroll down West Gate to pause by the duck pond and watch the antics of the birds. How long was it since he had had the leisure to enjoy such innocent delights?

He stood, for several seconds, taking in his surroundings. Behind him was the imposing Cromwell House, home of the Reverend Samuel Catlow's Literary and Commercial Seminary, the seat of learning that appeared so sadly to have failed Master Joseph Slack! To left and right, either side of the duck pond, were trees and shrubbery, adding an idyllic, rustic charm to the scene. Then, across the water, he saw Duck Lane and the festering hovels of Bark Court and Mitre Court. So small a space separated wealth and poverty!

He turned, to continue his journey into the centre of town, when his attention was arrested by a tall, fair-haired figure in a bottle-green coat approaching. Cousin Richard!

"Good Lord! You!"

Richard stopped in his tracks, his right hand tightening over the silver knob of the stick he carried. His face, however, betrayed no emotion.

"Thought yer'd never see me agen, din't yer?" asked Tom.

Richard made no reply.

"Thought I'd rotted in Derby Gaol wi' t' other rebels — or gone to t' gallows for that watch *yoh* took!"

The colour drained from Richard's face, except for two spots high on his prominent cheekbones.

"What if I did? You'll never prove it!"

"I saw yer comin' out o' Gresham's pawnshop."

Richard smiled, but there was no hint of warmth in the gesture.

"Hall's told me all this," he sneered, "but, as he says, the evidence is purely circumstantial."

"An' Gresham described yer."

"Gresham's description could've fitted any number of people!" answered Richard airily. "It proves nothing. Besides, what motive could I have for stealing a watch?"

"To pay off what yoh owed Smalley an' Tully."

"Get out of my way!"

Richard took a pace forward, but Tom barred his way.

"There's another score to settle, fost!"

Richard looked puzzled.

"A'nt Margaret," said Tom. "I s'pose yer'll deny it wor yoh as beat 'er, 'cos she wun't gi' yer no money?"

"Stupid woman!" snarled Richard. "I knew she kept money in the house. She used to hide it from *him*!"

"But to beat yer own mother!"

"Serves her right. She should've handed it over, when I asked her!"

Tom found it unbelievable that any man could speak so disparagingly of the woman who had brought him into the world.

"Then, yer tried gerrin' Susannah to pawn 'er jewels."

"She specifically denied that in front of her father and Hall," replied Richard calmly. "You were there."

"Well, she's towd 'er faither that wor all lies," fibbed Tom, "an' she's willin' to go to court an' say so!"

Richard uttered a short gasp before swiftly recovering his composure.

"Susannah would always lie for me!"

"Only 'cos yoh threatened to beat 'er!"

"She'd have done it, anyway. She knows she's got too much to lose, if it should ever come out that I stole the watch."

"So, yer *did* steal it!" yelped Tom triumphantly.

Richard froze, realizing what he had just let slip. In a second, though, he was his arrogant self once more.

"Of course," he admitted, with a casual shrug. Then, waving his stick at the passing throng, who were far too absorbed in their own affairs to take notice of other people's quarrels, he said: "It would be your word against mine, though, and I should deny it in court, or in front of Slack and Hall. Now, as I've nothing further to say to you, would you kindly step aside? I've a wedding to arrange!"

As he brushed roughly past, Tom caught his sleeve.

"Yoh ain't goin' nowhere," barked Tom. "Yoh'll go to 'All an' tell 'im t' truth, if I ay to thrash it out on yer!"

Richard wrenched himself free and lashed out with the

stick, catching Tom a painful blow on the right shoulder. Then, he set off in the direction of Slack's house.

He had gone barely four paces, when he felt a hand on his arm. He swung round, to receive the full force of Tom's right fist on his nose, and staggered backwards, raising a hand to staunch the imminent flow of blood. For several moments, he stared in disbelief at the patch of red on his palm.

"You'll pay for that!" he cried, launching himself at Tom with another wild swing.

This time, though, Tom was prepared. He ducked low beneath the stick, so that his eyeline was now level with his cousin's midriff. Then, he charged forward and felt his head make contact with the soft smoothness of the brown velvet waistcoat.

From above his head came the sound of retching and gasping. The next moment, Richard crumpled to the ground, the stick flying from his hand, and Tom's momentum carried him forward, so that he landed on top of his cousin, driving the last ounce of air from his lungs.

Many years ago, both his father and Old Amos had taught him the rudiments of the pugilist's craft. He had even been taken to prizefights, where local champions, such as the three Charlton brothers, took on all-comers with their bare fists. Apart from the brush with Smalley, outside the Old Eclipse, and a few schoolboy scraps, he had rarely had much cause to put his acquired skills into practice: few people, noting his thickset, muscular frame, bothered to pick a quarrel with Tom Stone.

Richard, he knew, had had no such lessons, having eschewed such tuition in favour of his academic studies. On the other hand, Richard was now a desperate man. He had confessed his guilt to Tom, and, though he would doubtless deny it all, he could not risk the chance that Slack and Hall might by now believe Tom's word before his.

So, indeed, it proved. Richard might never have seen a bare-knuckle contest, but he was wise to all fighters' low tricks: gouging, biting, scratching and kicking. His strong white teeth were already sunk into Tom's right hand, in an effort to immobilize it, whilst the fingers of his own right hand clawed desperately at Tom's face.

Richard gradually manoeuvred himself into a position where he could draw his right leg up under Tom's body. Then, with a supreme effort, he straightened the limb, and Tom found himself catapulted into the air, to land, with a sickening thud, on his still-throbbing right shoulder.

By this time, the passers-by had forgotten their own self-absorption, and were taking a keen interest in the spectacle before them. Some had even begun to take bets on the outcome of the brawl.

Blood still running down his face from the marks made by Richard's nails, Tom dragged himself into an upright posture, to see that Richard had retrieved his stick and was now halfway to his feet. Both were out of breath.

Tom was the first to recover complete command of his senses, hurling his muscular body towards his cousin. Richard had barely recovered his balance, when he caught the full weight of Tom's left fist just below his right ear. Tottering backwards, he caught his leg in one of the chains slung between posts, which formed a barrier round the duck pond. For a moment, he stood, arms waving in all directions. Then, he keeled over into the pond, scattering its feathered inhabitants.

As the waves subsided, only a small circle of bubbles betrayed Richard's presence beneath the water. Then, without warning, he surfaced.

"Help! I can't swim!"

Do you think I'd fall for an old trick like that? thought Tom derisively, as he turned away, wiping blood from his face on the back of his sleeve.

"Tom! Help!"

He was thrashing wildly now, and even Tom could see that the panic-stricken look on his face was no act. He couldn't let him drown. Not only would it be wrong, but, if Richard died, his confession died with him, and he would never stand trial. He *must* rescue him!

Throwing off his coat, Tom took a deep breath and plunged into the water.

The pond was not as deep as he had anticipated; though deep enough for a man to drown in. Tom stood up, the water reaching to his waist, and grasped his cousin firmly underneath the armpits. Lifting Richard's head clear of the water — despite the temptation to submerge it — he then began to haul his burden to the side of the pond, where eager hands were waiting to pull them to safety.

The two combatants lay, side by side, gasping for air.

"It's him!"

Tom looked up to see the tall, grey-maned figure of John Gresham, accompanied by Robert Hall.

"What are you talking about?" snapped the little lawyer.

The pawnbroker was pointing, with a trembling finger, at the sodden form of Richard Miller.

"Hall, *that's* the man who pawned your pocket-watch!"

CHAPTER 37

Tuesday, 11th November, 1817

Robert Hall gazed down upon his articled clerk in thunderstruck disbelief.

"How could I have been so blind?"

The pawnbroker placed a consoling hand on Hall's shoulder.

"Perhaps we've *both* been blind," he sighed. "After you came in the shop, yesterday, I must confess I never gave the matter another thought. As I told you, young men are pawning pocket-watches all the time. I'd probably have forgotten the matter altogether; but, this morning, he came in again with a sapphire ring. I don't normally enquire *too* closely into the provenance of items brought in, but there was something suspicious about this — I can sometimes sense when an item doesn't belong to the person who brings it in. Then, as I looked at him more closely, I not only recognized him as one of my 'regulars', but also as the man who'd pawned *your* watch, back in May. So, I came straight round to your office."

Hall was only half-listening. Richard was now recovering his senses, and the little lawyer was staring at him, his cheeks glowing redder by the minute."

"Get up!"

With a strength born of fury, Hall bent down, gripped Richard by his dripping collar and hauled him into a kneeling position.

"What *else* have you taken, besides the watch!" he yelled, shaking the wretched figure.

Unseen by Gresham and Hall, Tom jabbed his knuckles hard into Richard's kidneys.

"Tell 'em what yer towd me!"

"There's no need for that," said Hall. "We've got all the evidence we need to go before a magistrate. In the meantime, I suggest we get the pair of you round to Slack's house and out of those wet clothes!"

"Good idea," concurred Gresham. "I'll go back to my shop, pick up one or two items and join you there in about half an hour."

Tom breathed a deep sigh of relief. He was finally about to be vindicated!

"I — er — that is . . ."

For a man accustomed to public speaking, Robert Hall was remarkably inarticulate. To cover his confusion, he took out his tortoiseshell snuffbox and helped himself to a generous pinch.

Hannah, meanwhile, was busying herself with hot claret, bitter oranges, sugar and spices, concocting a large, warming bowl of bishop.

Candles and a roaring fire bathed the room in a warm, comforting, golden glow; but the atmosphere in the room was far from warm and comforting.

Samuel Slack paced the room, clenching and unclenching his fists. From time to time, he would turn on Richard, as though about to speak. Then, words would fail him, and he would continue his anguished perambulations.

Richard and Tom had removed their sodden garments and were now wrapped in blankets, glaring at each other from either side of a newly-stoked fire. Their outer extremities were gradually getting warmer, but only a fortifying cup or two of bishop would completely dispel the chill that seemed to have penetrated the very marrow of their bones.

Tom decided that November was not the ideal month for diving, fully clothed, into the duck pond — especially to save such a miserable wretch as the man who now faced him. His face still felt sore where his adversary's nails had torn at it; but, from a casual glance in the mirror, he had reassured himself that his wounds were only superficial.

Richard, he was gratified to note, had fared much worse! An ugly, purple bruise had appeared on his right cheek, and the slender, aquiline nose, which he regarded as his most attractive feature, was now grotesquely swollen. It was, reflected Tom, some repayment for the savage beating the brute had inflicted on Aunt Margaret!

Susannah sat in the far corner, her face buried in a large linen handkerchief. For whom, Tom wondered, was she weeping: Richard or herself? Perhaps the tears were genuine, this time, her remorse heartfelt.

Behind Susannah, her mother stood, ineffectually patting her shoulder and muttering words of comfort.

"Er, um, Tom."

Robert Hall had by now recovered his voice, but clearly found it difficult to address this social underling by his baptismal name.

"Tom, I owe you an apology."

That had cost even greater effort!

Tom made a gesture that could have been a nonchalant shrug of acceptance or merely an involuntary shiver resulting from the chill.

"I only trust you can forgive me — forgive all of us!" said Hall, holding out his hand.

"'Ere y' are, Tom!" cried Hannah, thrusting a cup of bishop into his hand. "Gerrit down yer! It'll do yer good!" Then, turning to the lawyer, she added: "Let t' poor lad gerr 'is breath back!"

Hall's mouth assumed a frozen smile that even the hottest cup of bishop would have failed to melt, and, as he watched Tom gulp down the steaming ruby fluid, he took another pinch of snuff.

With grim reluctance, the cook-housekeeper then thrust a cup into Richard's hands, causing some of the contents to splash into his lap.

Richard let out a howl of pain and clasped his hand to the scalded area.

"Good!" crowed Hannah, adding: "An' may the Good Lord choke yer wi' it!"

"Hannah!" admonished Sarah Slack, through tightly-clenched jaws. Her "Waterloo" teeth were still clearly troubling her.

"Sorry, ma'am," said Hannah, with a demure smile, before flashing a triumphant gloat at Richard. Then,

357

satisfied that everyone had been served, she marched out of the room.

"Rait," began Slack brusquely, turning to Gresham, "yoh say Richard wor t' man as pawned Mr 'All's watch, back in May?"

"And several other items," confirmed the pawnbroker, pointing to a box and a thick ledger that lay on the table in the centre of the room. He began to remove articles from the box, in the manner of a conjuror, and he was clearly enjoying his role as the centre of attention.

His audience watched in silence, transfixed.

"Item One: a gold locket, containing a lock of blonde hair," announced Gresham holding up the object. "Pawned on Wednesday, the 2nd of July, for five guineas."

"My mother's!" gasped Hall. "It was a betrothal present from my father!"

"Prove it!" yelled Richard.

"There should be an inscription inside: 'James & Anne, 1751,'" said the little lawyer.

Gresham examined the locket intently through his jeweller's eyeglass.

"That tallies," he declared, at length.

"What else did you take?" demanded Hall, advancing savagely upon his clerk.

Richard remained mute, as Gresham detailed four subsequent items, pawned between July and October, each of which Hall duly identified by some mark or inscription.

"How could I have been so blind and stupid?" cried the lawyer. "Why steal, when you stood to inherit everything after my death?"

A change suddenly came over Richard's battered features. He was like a child, pathetic and helpless.

"I was desperate!" he pleaded. "I knew neither you nor Mr Slack approved of gambling. If either of you had found out, I'd have had no job and no prospect of marrying Susannah! Becoming your articled clerk was a step up out of the mire of poverty, and marriage would have *kept* me out!"

"What was it?" demanded Hall. "Cards? Dice?"

"Cards," replied Richard, in a hoarse whisper. "It all started in the back room of the White Hart, one Friday night in early April. Jacob Smalley was there, George Tully, and a couple of others. I only joined them, initially, to make up the numbers. That first night, I came away a guinea down. So, the following week, I went back, determined to recoup my losses."

"And lost even more, I suppose?" replied Hall acidly.

Richard nodded.

"Another five."

"So, you went back, time and time again, and continued to lose more, on each occasion!"

"A fool an' 'is money are soon parted!" grunted Slack, who had so far held his rising temper in check. "Yoh knew Mr 'All an' me wun't bail yer out; so yer stole 'is pocket-watch! Then, wi' Tom branded as t' thief an' out o' t' road, yer carried on stealin' an' lyin', knowin' as Mr 'All wun't even think to check! An', as fer *yoh* . . !" he yelled, turning on his daughter.

"No, Samuel," interceded his wife. "She only did worr

any woman woulda done fer t' man she wor betrothed to."

"Betrothed!" bellowed Slack. "Yer can forget that, me girl! I'll norr 'ave *my* daughter gerrin' married to a thief — a man who'd norr only send 'is cousin to t' gallows, burr even lerr 'is own 'aif-brother be transported fer a crime 'e committed!"

Richard looked stunned.

"I don't know what you're talking about!"

"Jack towd us 'issen," cut in Tom softly. "Yest'dy."

"Jack's dead, long since!" scoffed Richard.

Tom shook his head.

"'E's in t' work'ouse. 'E towd us all about yoh stealin' them valuables from that traveller's saddle-bags, then sayin' as 'e'd done it."

"You'll be lucky to escape the gallows for this!" snapped Hall, thrusting his round, ruddy face close to Richard's.

Slack began pacing up and down, once more.

"I'm norr 'appy about tekkin' 'im in front o' t' magistrate. If word ever gets out, think o' t' disgrace it'll bring on *us*, as well as 'im!"

"What do you expect *me* to do about it?" asked Hall. "Forget it? I'm a servant of the Law. I can't just turn a blind eye to this!"

Slack drew the little lawyer aside.

"I've gorr an idea. I'll gi' 'im twenty guineas . . ."

"Twenty guineas!" yelped Hall. "Have you taken leave of your senses?"

Slack held up a placatory hand.

"Let me finish. I'll gi' 'im twenty guineas, if 'e promises to be out o' Mansfield by sunset tomorrer. Tharr'll be enough to start 'im on a new life somewhere." He turned to Richard. "You're not to try an' contact Susannah by letter, an' if y' ever set foot in this town again, I'll see you're brung before t' magistrate an' charged. What d'yer say?"

Richard puckered his brow, as the room fell silent, every eye focused on him.

"Twenty, you say?"

"An' yer never set foot in Mansfield agen!"

"Agreed."

There was a sharp cry from Susannah in the corner of the room, but her father deliberately ignored her.

"Rait! By t' time yer've finished that drink, yer clothes should be dry. Get changed, then gerr out o' my 'ouse!"

Richard gulped down the bishop and got to his feet.

"Suppose we said thirty?"

The veins on Slack's neck expanded so far that Tom feared he would split his collar.

"Be bloody thankful you're gerrin' twenty! Now, out!"

Gripping Richard's blanket tightly, Slack almost frogmarched him out of the room.

Susannah sat crumpled in her chair, like a marionette whose strings had been severed, and Tom suddenly forgot all the wrongs she had done him, and longed only to hold and caress her.

That night, he slept well and dreamt of Susannah: dreams that would have driven the Reverend Cursham into a state of apoplexy!

CHAPTER 38

Wednesday, 12th November, 1817

Tom woke up to the enticing smell of freshly baked mutton pie and the sight of Hannah with a tray, which she set down on the bed in front of him.

"Mr Slack's orders," she said. "An' there's a tankard o' porter to wash it down. 'E said to make sure yoh ate it all up!"

"I wun't leave a single crumb!" chuckled Tom, cutting through the crust. "Yoh mek t' best mutton pies in Mansfield. Yer should set up yer own pie shop!"

"Gerrit down yer afore it gets cowd!" replied Hannah, giggling with embarrassment. She sat down on the edge of the bed.

For several minutes, Tom ate and drank in silence under the cook-housekeeper's watchful eye.

"'Ow's Miss Susannah, this mornin'?" he asked, at length.

"In bed."

"She took it bad over Richard."

"She'll gerr over it. I warned yer she wor trouble, din't I?" said Hannah, softening the reproof with a gentle smile.

"If she'd towd t' truth, in t' fost place, yoh'd never 'ave 'ad to leave — an' that cousin o' yourn 'ud've gorr 'is just deserts a damn sight sooner!"

"'E wor ambitious," said Tom, through a mouthful of pie. "Mr Slack allus reckoned there wor nowt wrong wi' ambition."

"There's ambitious an' ambitious," replied Hannah gravely. "'E wor a rait young gentleman, when 'e fost come courtin' Miss Susannah. Burr I watched t' change in 'im, over t' months — 'ow 'e treated folk as if they were beneath 'im, even though 'e only come from Bark Court. Oh, beggin' yer pardon!" she gasped, suddenly remembering Tom's own recent address.

"You're rait," said Tom. "Even if *I* became a gentleman, like 'e wor, I'd never look down on folk like that."

"I know yer'd not!" smiled Hannah, leaning forward and kissing him on the temple. "Now, gerrit ate an' get dressed, 'cos Mr Slack wants to see yer in 'is study."

"What for?" asked Tom.

"I dunno," replied Hannah. "I just tek t' messages."

She remained sitting on the edge of the bed, smiling indulgently, as Tom devoured the food with a hearty appetite. She reached out and ran her finger the length of one of his scratches. Her hands, normally wrist-deep in dough, were surprisingly soft and gentle. What a contrast to her rough handling, that first Friday morning, in the kitchen! Then, she leaned forward and kissed the wound!

Tears welled up in Tom's eyes. His mind went back to childhood cuts and grazes, and he remembered how Ann had "kissed them better". Poor Ann, lost to him forever: locked away in her private world of grief and madness!

By now, he had finished his meal, and Hannah took the tray from him. Then, he lay back on his pillow, satisfied.

Hannah's hand slipped beneath the coverlet.

This time, he did not resist.

Some twenty minutes later, Tom was dressed and on his way to Slack's study. Hannah had only done to him what Susannah had done, that first Saturday; yet it had all felt somehow so different. This time, he hadn't felt as if he was being used. Hannah loved him — *really* loved him! Through the slow caress of her fingers, he had felt the warmth of her heart.

He remembered all the kindness she had shown Ann and Jonathan, and how she had shared his grief and tears over the death of young Caleb. She had been right about one thing: if he ever became a gentleman, he would never look down on her. She would always hold a special place in his heart.

Passing the back door, he paused and looked out into the yard. In the middle, stood the piebald, now healthier than when Tom had last seen him; but it was the skeletal, shaven-headed figure grooming him who caught Tom's attention. Jack!

"Ah! There y' are, Tom!" boomed Slack's voice from behind him.

"What's 'e doin' 'ere?" asked Tom, pointing to his cousin.

"I wor goin' to tell yer. I've gi'd 'im your owd job."

Tom looked blank.

"Burr I thought . . ."

Slack's face cracked open in an expansive grin.

"I've summat berra lined up fer yoh, Tom — *much* berra. Come on up to t' study."

At a table in the middle of the study sat young Joseph, sucking the end of a quill and staring out into space.

Behind him stood a tall, earnest, dark-haired man in his early twenties. From the expression on his face, it was as clear that he was having as little success with Joseph as Jessop had.

"Stephens," barked Slack, "this is Tom."

"Frederick Stephens," announced the young man, extending a hand. "My new pupil, I believe?"

"Well, er . . ."

"Yoh'll be ayin' lessons wi' Mr Stephens full-time, from now on," said Slack.

"I've been looking at some of your work," said Stephens. "I was impressed — most impressed."

"Aye," said Slack, "Jessop wor a bloody fool, burr 'e knew a good scholar when 'e saw one: I'll gi' 'im that."

Tom felt a warm glow of pride.

Young Joseph merely sniggered, earning a malevolent glare from his father.

"Full-time," repeated Tom slowly. "Why?"

"Come downstairs an' I'll explain."

Once they were ensconced in Slack's private room, the hosier poured out two generous glasses of sherry and handed one to Tom.

"Try that, lad!" beamed Slack. "Fresh consignment from

Spain."

Tom took a sip. It was bone dry. Like drinkin' 'oss piss! he thought; though he was too diplomatic to say so. Instead, he asked: "Where's Richard?"

"Went, last nait," replied Slack, "an' bloody good riddance! Burr it's norr 'im I want to talk about: it's yoh. There's a lorr 'appened to yer, there's last six months, an't it?"

Tom nodded.

"An' ay yer learnt yer lesson from it?"

Tom looked blank.

"All this republican nonsense," said Slack. "I'd never've thought a bright young lad like yoh 'ud've swallowed all that stuff about equality. If yoh *'ave* come to yer senses, there's a bright future for yer."

"Where?" asked Tom.

Slack drained his glass, crossed to the window and gazed out across the top of West Gate at the passing throng of humanity.

"Factories," he said, at length, turning back. "That's where t' future lies — yourn an' mine. The day o' the framework knitter in 'is tiny cottage is over, Tom. That's where yer friend Brandreth went wrong. 'E wor a dreamer, livin' in t' past. Steam power — that's t' future. Machines as can do ten men's wokk. An' all t' Luddites in world'll norr 'owd *that* back."

"But worr about Jonathan?"

"I'll see 'im rait, dun't yoh worry. Is 'e still set on not purrin' yer sister in an asylum?"

366

"Aye," said Tom. "'E sez 'e'll norr ay folk gawpin' at 'er."

Slack tugged thoughtfully at the lobe of his left ear.

"Meks sense. I'll gi' 'im a job, so's 'e can support t' pair on 'em."

"'E dun't want charity! 'Ow much wor 'is debts?"

"Five pounds, eighteen shillings and fourpence three-farthings," came back the answer, without a second's thought.

"'E'll pay back ev'ry penny."

Slack smiled.

"I dun't want 'is money. That wor done as a favour fer yoh fer wrongly brandin' yer a thief. Burr I want one thing understood: if I gi' 'im this job, 'e's got to prove 'issen."

"'E will," promised Tom. "But where do *I* come into all this?"

"I'll be gi'in' *yoh* a job in t' factory, an' all. Norr on t' machines — yer've too much brains fer that. In t' office, doin' t' books."

"Burr I know nowt about 'osiery!" protested Tom.

"Yoh'll learn," replied Slack confidently. "I wun't be doin' this if I din't think yer were up to it. Yer'll be under George Hicks, fost off; burr I reckon, wi'in five years, yer'll be ready to tek over runnin' yer own factory. That's why I want yer to concentrate on yer lessons. It'll tek till t' middle o' next year to set up t' fost factory. By then, yer'll know enough to get started. From then on, it'll be up to yoh."

"Where?" asked Tom.

"Nowt's finalized yet. Derbyshire, most probably. Yer'll not mind movin' away, will yer?"

"No — but worr about Ann an' Jonathan? Middle o' next year, yer said. Worr're they goin' to do till then?"

Slack refilled his glass and smiled.

"I'll find 'im summat. I've friends as could gi' 'im wokk till then, even if *I* can't. Not 'osiery — an' not well paid — burr enough fer 'em to get by." He paused and smiled. "You're fond on 'em, in't yer?"

"Aye."

"That's good; but dun't get *too* soft-'earted. Sentiment an' business don't mix."

"When me Mam died, Ann took over. I can't bear to see 'er like she is now."

"I know; but nowt can bring back Caleb," sighed Slack sympathetically, "or yer sister's mind. Like I said, yer've gorra look to t' future now."

Tom sighed. It was true: he couldn't turn back the clock. Caleb was dead, and, to judge from her recent appearance, Ann would not be long following him into the next world.

"When do I start me lessons, then?" asked Tom.

"This afternoon."

"Can I go round to Mitre Court, then, fost, an' see Jonathan, an' tell 'im t' news about t' factory?"

Slack ran his fingers through his sparse, greying hair.

"All rait — but tell 'im not to spread it around. I don't want too many folk knowin'' me business."

Uttering murmurs of gratitude, Tom took his leave. In the

hallway, he encountered Susannah and Rachel.

Susannah had now recovered some of her former composure, but her lips seemed to have lost their sensuous curve and the smile she gave him was cold and distant. Her occasional sniffs and the redness around her eyes betokened a night of weeping. All the warmth she had displayed, that Saturday afternoon, had evaporated, and for the first time, Tom understood what the Reverend Cursham had meant about the difference between love and lust.

What a contrast with Rachel, who greeted him with a warm "Good morning" and a gentle smile. Indeed, he could almost have fancied that she blushed! She would make George Hicks a far better wife than he deserved.

Marriage, however, did not figure in Tom's immediate plans. He thought of Hannah, with her gentle heart masked by her blemished face, and knew that, when the time came, he would know better than to choose on the basis of outward appearance.

Meanwhile, he must tell Jonathan the good news.

"Derbyshire, yer said?"

Jonathan stared down at the floor, knotting and unknotting his fingers, as he slowly assimilated what Tom had just told him.

"'Appen a change of air'll do 'er some good," he ventured.

Tom looked across to the corner, where his sister rocked to and fro, still clutching the shawl to her breast. There seemed to be little change from the last time he had seen her. It was as though she had lost all interest in living. She certainly recognized neither her husband nor her brother.

"'Appen so," replied Tom trying to sound optimistic. Then, fearing to raise his brother-in-law's hopes too high, he decided to change the subject. "George Hicks is goin' to teach me all about t' 'osiery trade."

"Oh, *I* can tell yer all about t' 'osiery trade!" replied Jonathan bitterly, jerking his head in the direction of the attic, where the long-neglected knitting frame still lodged.

"'Ow are yer fer money?" enquired Tom.

"All rait. Slack paid off t' debts an' gi'd us another two guineas. Tharr'll see us through fer a bit."

"'Ere," said Tom, reaching into his pocket. "Tek this."

"Another guinea!" gasped Jonathan, gazing at the coin in his brother-in-law's hand.

"'All gi'd it me, last nait," said Tom, smiling grimly at the memory. "It wor 'is way o' mekin' up fer wrongly accusin' me. It'll do *yoh* more good than me."

"Thanks."

With trembling fingers, Jonathan took the coin and put it on the table.

"Owt else yer need?" asked Tom.

Jonathan shook his head.

For several minutes, the two men sat looking at Ann, neither knowing what to say.

"Ay yer towd Ben an' Margaret, yet?" asked Jonathan, at length.

"No."

He wasn't looking forward to telling them. In fact, he felt guilty. Ben would scoff, of course, but he could cope with that. What worried him was that, if he took up Slack's offer, Margaret would be left alone at the mercy of Ben's unpredictable moods.

He thought, too, of the fiercely independent framework knitters, their frames now lying idle. How would they adapt to factory life, their every working minute regulated and supervised?

He knew what Slack would say: that he should think of himself first. Perhaps he was right. The world was his oyster now. He would be a fool to turn down such a chance.

Yet, there was a strangely empty feeling, deep inside him. He remembered the warning of Tommy Bacon: that he would one day forget the fight for justice and equality.

For all the materialistic advantages that awaited him, he knew that a part of him had died on the gallows with Jeremiah Brandreth.